To Sandy,
Thanks for getting
a book. I hope you
enjoy it. Happy!!
Love You,
May 2024

The Carrington Affairs

Susan Gooch

Copyright © [2024] by [Susan Gooch]

All rights reserved.

No portion of this book may be reproduced in any form without written permission from the publisher or author, except as permitted by U.S. copyright law.

To Those I Love

Prologue

Searcy, Arkansas
July 12, 2012

The moment the black SUV pulled up to the gates of the Carrington estate, reporters rushed forward with microphones in hand and cameras rolling.

"Senator Carrington, is it true? Are you and Mrs. Carrington separated?"

"Are you getting divorced?"

"How do you know Poppy Thompson, and what is the nature of your relationship with her?"

"Are you still on the shortlist for a possible cabinet position?"

Questions flew at the car's passengers from every direction. It should have been impossible to hear one over the other. But it wasn't. Each one was a rock pinging off the side of the car.

Joules had warned them about the media circus camped outside their home for the last few hours. Honestly, neither was shocked at the reporters waiting to devour them. In truth, it had been a long time coming. If they were surprised by anything, it was how long it had taken them to sniff out the story. To help control the situation, Joules had arranged for two security guards to do crowd control. At the moment, it did not feel very controlled. Bennett and Taylor stared straight ahead. Their lack of response did nothing to deter the horde of journalists who continued their verbal assault. Rapidly firing questions at the couple, the various news crews jockeyed for the best camera angle. Each knew they were sitting on the juiciest political scandal in years.

The two security guards finally forced the crowd back just enough for Bennett to pull through the gates and drive up the winding drive to the house. Bennett and Taylor did not say a word until they were inside the garage with the large wooden door closed firmly behind them.

Taylor could already see the sound bites in her head that would soon be playing on every news channel in the country. Dishing dirt on Arkansas's political golden couple would sell well. She supposed she should be grateful the questions weren't worse. They certainly could have been. Right now, the reporters just had a whiff of a scandal. Little did they know, the truth was even more shocking than any of them yet suspected. It was all going to come out. At best, they had a day, two at the most, before everybody knew all the gritty, dirty details of their crumbling lives.

Bennett looked over at Taylor and with his voice full of anguish and shame, he said, "I'm so sorry. I never meant for any of this to happen. The last thing I ever wanted to do was hurt you." Nodding her head in agreement, Taylor, feeling overwhelmed and stunned, answered, "I know. Me either." There had been a time when she would have blamed all of this on him. Him and his dirty little secrets. But, that was before she had her own secrets. They were both responsible for the dumpster fire their lives had become. Giving him a look of utter despair, she asked, "What in the hell are we going to do now?"

Shaking his head, Bennett said, "I have no idea." For a man who always had an answer for everything, this time he had nothing.

Taylor sighed deeply and said, "Me either, but one thing I do know, it will get a lot worse before it gets better."

24 Hours Later
Searcy Municipal Airport
Searcy, Arkansas

Bennett Carrington sat inside a hangar at the airport in Searcy watching his wife Taylor fly away with her fiance Greer and thinking about how his life had basically imploded in the last 48 hours. Sitting inside the borrowed 3 Series BMW, he realized his life had become a shit show.

In February, he had the world on a string. As the junior senator from Arkansas, his approval ratings were through the roof. A happily married man with a reputation for being an outstanding family man, he was a leading contender for the vice-presidential spot on Larry Anderson's presidential campaign. He and his beautiful wife Taylor were excited to begin trying again for a child. The doctors had given them every hope they would be successful this time. He had life by the tail, and he knew it.

What a difference five months could make. During that time, he had seen his marriage crumble, destroyed his political career and reputation, and lost the love of his life to gossip and innuendo. As he sat alone in the car, Bennett realized he had truly hit rock bottom. Making up his mind to start reclaiming his life, he fired up the car's engine and roared off with one goal in mind, putting his life back together again, one piece at a time.

Part One - One Big Happy Family

Carrington House
Searcy, Arkansas
November 20, 2023

Slicing through the water, Bennett maintained complete control as he swam. He had to keep moving forward, making slow and steady progress. He set a pace, and he followed it with military precision and was so close to reaching the goal. As he neared the end of the pool and prepared to make the turn, Poppy was there. She was naked. Singing her siren song, she called to him as she always did. All of Bennett's focus, plans, hard work, all of it was forgotten. Instead of completing his laps, he began to tread water. Suddenly, Poppy was touching him everywhere. Instantly, he was swallowed by a vortex of lust and passion. He was drowning in her. Knowing he must do something, or he was going to die, Bennett clawed his way to the surface and drew a deep breath.

Instantly he jerked awake and realized he was not in a pool but rather in his bed. Poppy was waking him up in the best way possible. He could feel her soft curls draping across his stomach. Laying back and enjoying his wife's early morning gift, Bennett gave himself entirely over to the moment, his dream forgotten.

A short while later, with her mission accomplished, Poppy sat up, reached over and clicked on the bedside lamp. Bennett threw his arm over his eyes as soft light filled the room.

After a moment, he glanced at his phone. "You realize you woke me up when I still had ten minutes to sleep, right? If I did that to you, you would kill me."

Poppy pulled a tee shirt over her head and replied, "The rules for me are not the rules for you. I would have thought you would have figured that out by now." Planting her hands on her slim hips, she gave him a look and added, "And are you complaining?"

"Hell no! Wake my ass up every day early that way. I am just shocked you were awake. Sleep is sacred to you."

"True," she said."but this is a big day. Closing arguments day! All your hard work for the last two years wrapped up in one summation. I knew you would have put me off if I waited until your alarm sounded. The minute your eyes opened, you would be focused on all you had to accomplish today. I wanted to start your day off right regardless of whatever happens later. Now, I am going to run downstairs to make you breakfast. Do you want bacon or sausage?"

Reaching out to grab her arm as she headed towards the door, Bennett said, "I am not hungry. Skip the food and join me in the shower. We can continue this good start."

Laughing, Poppy said, "Oh, how cute. Look who thinks he is still in his twenties. Another time, stud. Go take a hot shower. I will have breakfast ready when you come down."

After she left, Bennett turned off his alarm and forced himself out of his warm bed and into the shower. Poppy had been right. He would not have been able to enjoy his wife's gift so much if his alarm had sounded. His mind would not have been in it.

Less than thirty minutes later, Bennett strolled into the kitchen. True to her word, Poppy had fried him some bacon and made homemade pancake rolls that she put into a baggie for him to take. A sizeable insulated metal cup full of hot coffee also stood ready. Sliding up to her, Bennett slipped his arms around her and took her in a deep embrace. Roaming his hands down her back and over her body, he held her close. Poppy was just before groaning with pleasure when a sleepy voice from the other side of the bar interrupted them.

"Gross, Daddy! Why do you always want to put your tongue down mommy's throat? Ain't you ever heard of germs?"

Their six-year-old daughter Lola's voice startled both Poppy and Bennett. Bennett was grateful that the kitchen bar hid most of what had been happening from his child's eyes.

Giving his precious daughter a look, Bennett asked, "First of all, we don't say 'ain't,' and second of all, what are you doing out of bed, Sweet Pea? It's way too early for you to be up. You don't even have school today."

Without missing a beat, Lola replied, "I smelled bacon and pancakes. Is it ready? I am starving."

Bennett and Poppy both laughed. Lola could smell bacon frying in the next county since she was three.

Poppy moved towards the cabinet to get a plate for Lola's breakfast as Bennett leaned in for a quick kiss goodbye. "To be continued," he said as he moved away.

"Promises. Promises," Poppy replied before grabbing the baggy of food and coffee and handing them to him. As Bennett walked towards the back door, he kissed Lola on the head and said, "Be a good girl for Mommy today. Love you."

Poppy and Lola returned the sentiment, assuming it was meant for them. Once he was gone, Lola gave her mom a very serious look and said, "Now about those pancakes…"

Nine Hours Later
Federal Court
Little Rock, Arkansas

The jury had only been out for about two hours when Bennett Carrington was given the word that a verdict had been reached. It had been a long morning with both he and the defense giving their closing arguments. As closings went, it had gone as well as he could have hoped. He had hit all the high points of the case and had stuck to the plan he had rehearsed for the last week with his co-counsel. Bennett had just finished scarfing down a package of crackers and a soda when he had gotten the text to return to the courtroom.

He and the others involved in the case quickly returned to the courtroom to await the results. Nervous energy buzzed through the room. A case that had taken over two years to prosecute and had required a venue change to ensure the defendants got a fair trial had only taken a few hours to decide. Such a quick verdict usually signaled good news for the prosecution. However, as a special prosecutor, Bennett knew that juries could be unpredictable. He had felt confident in the case he presented and expected a guilty verdict. But, not one jury member would make eye contact with him as they filed in. Suddenly, he felt a moment of trepidation. He knew the case could go either way. Sending up a quick prayer to the law gods for a bit of help, Bennett remained standing with the others in the room until the judge took his seat on the bench.

Once everyone settled, the judge, the Honorable Harold Neal Henderson, looked directly at the tall African-American woman who had been selected as the jury forewoman and asked, "Forewoman, have you reached a verdict?"

Looking straight at the judge, she nodded, "We have your honor."

The judge asked, "And was this decision unanimous?"

Without missing a beat, she replied, "It was." There was not a hint of doubt or hesitancy in her voice.

Bennett tried to weigh if that was a good or bad sign. He hated uncertainty. He never asked questions he did not know the answer to. At that moment, he had no idea what was about to happen. He knew what should happen. But justice was sometimes blind, deaf, and dumb. He hoped this would not be one of those times.

Shrugging as if to accept the unlikeliness of such a complicated verdict being decided so quickly, the judge turned to the four men seated at the defense table and asked them to rise along with their respective attorneys. As they did so, the judge said, "Madame forewoman, please pass the verdict to the bailiff."

Once the judge had the verdict, he skimmed it quickly and read it briefly and without emotion. "In the matter of the state of Arkansas vs. Theodore Allen, Lyles Logan, Andrew Westersmith, and David West, the jury finds the defendants guilty on count one of fraud. On count two, the jury finds the defendants guilty of money laundering. In regards to the third count, the jury finds the defendants guilty of possession of illegal substances with intent to sell. The defendants will be remanded into custody and will remain so until their sentencing hearing tomorrow at 9:00."

A collective gasp reverberated through the courtroom. Giving the room a stern look as he banged his gavel, the judge returned the room to absolute silence. With a final hit of his gavel, Judge Henderson added, "At this time, court is adjourned."

Suddenly, the previously silent courtroom erupted with everyone talking at once. Some were clapping; others crying. Bennett felt himself expel the large breath he did not even realize he was holding. All around him, his colleagues began to congratulate him. They were calling him a hero for helping to put away the four most senior members of a crime syndicate that had run an illegal drug ring from Fort Smith to West Memphis with ties to police and government officials. He could not believe it was over. He had won. The case he had dedicated the better part of two years developing and prosecuting was finally finished. The late nights, the weekend hours spent away from his family building his case, and all the ballgames, dance recitals, and missed family dinners had been worth it.

All he could think about was getting home and sharing the good news with his girls, Poppy, Lizzy and Lola. They had supported him through the whole ordeal and only complained a little when he failed to attend yet another event over the last two years. Since it was the week of Thanksgiving, school was out. They would be at home. He could hardly wait to get home to share the fantastic news. Thinking of Poppy, his mind immediately wandered back to earlier that morning and the awesome start to his day she had given him. Quickening his pace, he quickly collected his files. But, like many other times in his life, God just laughed when Bennett Carrington started making plans.

Every few steps out of the courthouse, he was waylaid by someone wanting to congratulate him on a job well done. Reporters from every newscast tried to interview him. With the sentencing phase of the trial set for the next day, Bennett did not want to jinx anything by saying too much publicly about the case.

Two Hours Later...

Bennett had just cleared the Jacksonville bottleneck when his phone began buzzing. He immediately declined the unknown number assuming it was probably a news reporter with questions about the case. It was the third time that number had rung since he left the courthouse. The next call that came through was from his secretary. Using the hands-free options, he clicked accept.

"Great work today, boss. Score one for the good guys," his secretary Tammi said excitedly. Her slow, Southern drawl was as strong at sixty as it had been as a young girl growing up in rural Mississippi.

"Thank you. I appreciate that," Bennett replied quickly. "Of course, it was a team effort, and we all worked really hard for today's results."

"That is true, but no one worked harder or more passionately than you. You were the heart and soul of this case," she stated matter of factly. "You are the man of the hour. Enjoy it. You've earned it."

Uncomfortable with praise, Bennett tried to shift the conversation. "I don't know about all of that. But thank you. Any calls from the press? I have had several calls from random numbers since I left Little Rock."

"Yeah, we have had several requests for interviews. I have put them off until after tomorrow's sentencing. I can set something up then if you want. Maybe an on-air interview at the television stations unless you would rather do it at your office. Let me know."

"I will think about it and get back to you," Bennett replied, almost unable to believe the case was almost over.

"Okay, sounds good. You also have several messages from Jameson Williams."

"Jameson Williams?" Bennett barked out the man's name in surprise and disbelief. "What did that old fart want?"

"I have no idea," replied Tammi, "But he has called several times and left multiple messages. He wants you to call him. Do you have his number?"

"Somewhere, maybe?" said Bennett.

It had been more than ten years since he had talked to Williams. Once upon a time, they often spoke about fundraising and how Bennett's political career could best serve the will of the people of Arkansas, if not Williams himself.

But that was before Bennett's life had radically changed. Over ten years had passed since his life and the lives of those he loved had been turned upside down.

Thinking of Williams, Bennett assumed the man must have heard about the case and wanted to congratulate him on the win. Williams had been a loyal supporter years ago. He had not been happy when Bennett had decided to walk away from a life he had spent years building. In the end, though, Williams had let him know that while he would have preferred a different outcome, he understood and supported his decision.

"Send me his number, please. I will call him," stated Bennett, deciding he had just enough time left on his way home for a quick call.

"Will do, boss. Let me know about the press for tomorrow," replied Tammi. Bennett could hear her clicking something into her phone as they talked.

"I will. I am going straight home and spending the rest of the day with my girls."

"Good for you. You deserve it." With that, Tammi rang off, and the number for Jameson Williams popped up on his phone. Surprise, surprise. It was the number he had been declining for the last hour.

It only took a second for Bennett to get Williams' office on the line and ask to be connected to him. Bennett had only been on hold for a few seconds when he heard the loud, gruff voice of Jameson Williams booming over his car stereo.

Talking a mile a minute and expecting everyone to keep up, Williams yelped, "Congratulations, Bennett, my boy! You really slayed the dragon today. That is all anyone is talking about at the Capitol. Good for you. I always knew you would be back. Just didn't think it would take this long."

As uncomfortable as receiving compliments from Williams, as he had been from Tammi, Bennett tried the same defusing tactic again, "Well, thank you, sir, but it was all in a day's work. And my team did an incredible job helping me pull it all together."

"Don't give me that shit," screeched Williams. "I know you, remember. I know how much of yourself you threw into winning this case. And boy, it is going to pay off big for you this time."

"Well, not sure about all of that, sir. Just happy justice was served," replied Bennett, unsure where the conversation was going.

Crackling, William responded, "Yeah, yeah, yeah. I hear you. You never were any good at taking a compliment. Humble sells better than cocky shit, so it is all good."

It might have been more than a decade since he and Williams had spoken, but it was becoming clear the more things changed, the more they stayed the same. Williams was the same old blunt ass he always was.

Choosing his words carefully, Bennett said, "Not looking to sell anything other than the truth these days, but as I said, I am glad justice was served. It was a long time coming."

At that moment, Bennett heard the noise level on the other end of the line significantly increase. William said, "Sorry, it is getting loud in here. Look, I can't really talk right now. I am in the middle of a major strategy meeting. We took a break for me to take this call, but the natives are getting restless. I called because I have something really important to run past you. How about we meet for breakfast at The Community Bakery at 7:00 AM in the morning?"

Thinking of all he needed to get done and be at the courthouse by 8:30, Bennett incredulously repeated, "7:00?"

He meant it sarcastically as if to say there was no way he could make that work. But, Williams, being Williams, did not pick up on it.

Instead, he heard it as a confirmation of the time and replied, "Yes, see you then." Before Bennett could correct him, the line went dead.

"Well shit," said Bennett, hitting the steering wheel. Now, he was committed to a meeting he did not want or had the time for. And all for a meeting that he was unsure what it was about.

Chapter 2

The Community Bakery
Little Rock, Arkansas
November 21, 2023

The next morning, Bennett pulled into The Community Bakery. As always, he was early. He hated being late. But, Jameson still beat him there. His 1979 gray Braum Cadillac was parked out front in all its glory. Williams had driven the car for as long as Bennett had known him. It was as much of an institution as the old man himself. He stood no more than 5 '7" and was as wide as he was tall. Yet, he could fill a room better than men twice his size.

Walking in, Bennett spotted Williams immediately. He was sitting in his favorite booth towards the back with a good view of the front door and the bathroom. That way, the old dog could monitor all the patrons' comings and goings. Local politicians and business people frequently met at the diner for an early breakfast. More deals had been done here than any golf course or legislative offices in the Capitol. It paid to know who was here and why, which is why Williams made sure he ate breakfast here every day that he could.

Williams waved him over. The heavyset man, in his eighties, made no move to get up but did extend his hand in a firm handshake as Bennett approached his booth.

"Good morning, young man. It sure is good to see you. It feels like a month of Sundays since I last saw you. Good work yesterday. I was happy to hear you are doing so well for yourself."

Nodding, Bennett said, "Thank you, sir. Yes, it has been a while."

They quickly exchanged pleasantries, and in true Williams fashion, he got right to the point and said, "I guess you are wondering why I asked you here today."

Nodding, Bennett said, "Well, yes, I must admit I am a bit curious. I assume it has something to do with the case."

"You're right. Mighty good work was accomplished with that win. There's been a lot of buzz around the state about you."

Shocked, Bennett felt taken back, "Why? All I did was my job."

"Yes, you did, and you did it with style, grace and flair. Three things all good politicians need to succeed."

"Politicians? I am no politician. Not anymore. I am out of that game," Bennett responded vehemently. "Or have you forgotten what happened that ended my political career?"

Bennett had been the up-and-coming politician in the country once upon a time. Years before, the sky had been the limit for him, but all that changed overnight. In many ways, he and his family were still dealing with the fallout from it all.

"No, I have not forgotten, but most voters have. The world is a different place after that damn pandemic and two divorced presidents with more dirty laundry than a boys' college dormitory. Add in a government insurrection with a ping-pong economy, and it is a whole new ballgame. After your big win against a major drug trafficking organization made front-page news, the powers that be think you are just the next man in line for the Governor's mansion. What do you say? Are you ready to throw your hat in the ring and give this another go?"

Leaning in close to Bennett so that only he could hear him, Jameson whispered, "You can't tell anyone this, but our current governor is about to be appointed to a high level cabinet position by the new president. When that happens, we are going to have a special election in late 2025 for the governorship. You are our man."

The governor's race? It was the last thing that Bennett expected Williams to say.

Not once since he had resigned from the Senate almost a decade ago had he even contemplated running for office again. Yes, he had been appointed special prosecutor by the current governor.

"I can see by your face that I have surprised you. If you are worried about what happened in the past with the press, we have a plan for that. You still have those all-American good looks. If rumors are to be believed, you have a stable family life and enjoy a close relationship with your ex-wife. You still have what it takes to win. The only real question is whether or not you are ready to return to the arena. You got any fight left in you, boy?"

Bennett put his hands up, making the slow down motion."Whoa. Slow your roll there, Jameson. First of all, who is we? And secondly, what do you mean, you already have a plan for the press?"

He shook his head and added, "Have you forgotten the skeletons in my closet? Because I promise you, reporters have not. They will drag my family back through all of that again the second any one of them gets a whiff if I even consider another crack at running for office."

Jameson chuckled, "Calm down, boy. You are wound tighter than a kid's wind-up toy. It's 2023 for heaven's sake. Social media changed everything. It is a double-edged sword. As much as it can kill a career, it can resurrect one. The public's willingness to overlook past indiscretions has increased. Voters today are more concerned with electing someone who will grow the economy and provide leadership that focuses on issues they are concerned about, not who someone slept with twenty years ago.

"And yes, your past will have to be addressed, but the party leaders feel we can get in front of that issue. What used to be a major issue now barely raises any alarms. With the 24-hour-a-day news cycle, stories come and go quickly. The public has a short memory. We spin your story as a love story. Arkansans love a good comeback story. And a pretty boy like you who messed up and then did better will sell like an ice cream on a hot day in August. The public is going to lick it right up. The fact you have two gorgeous, accomplished women who managed to rise above everything that happened and found a way to become one big happy family will make you all candidates for Family of the Year. More importantly, we need you Bennett. The state of Arkansas needs you."

Bennett knew it was madness even to consider the offer, but something inside him stirred at the thought. While his heart leaped at the mention of a comeback, his head kept him from readily agreeing.

"I just don't know Jameson. I can't even consider it without talking to Poppy, Ben, and Taylor. There's a lot of moving parts to this. I am not going to lie. I am intrigued. But I need a couple of days to think about it. I will talk to my family and let you know."

With that, Bennett stood and extended his hand again, "I hate to do this, but I need to run. I have to be in court shortly."

Taking his hand and giving it a firm shake, Williams replied, "Sounds good. Just know that if you agree to it, we'll get together and find someone to do a full article on you and your family. Tell the whole story from your perspective. We'll run it in one of the glossy lifestyle magazines in the state. We will have complete spin control. Nothing will be shared that you are uncomfortable with."

Bennett almost snorted at that. He was utterly uncomfortable sharing any of it and figured that went double for Poppy and Taylor. Who knew how Ben would feel?

Nodding, Jameson, sensing that Bennett was open to the idea, added, "We can do this. We can tell your story in such a way as to take away the shock value and make it a non-story. This is your chance, son, to go back to doing what you were born to do."

Once upon a time, Bennett had been so sure he knew what that was. Now, who knew? He did know that he had to get a move on. Being late for court would not help his case or any future campaigns, so with a nod, Bennett said, "Thank you for thinking of me. I will be in touch."

With that, Bennett walked out of the cafe and headed to court with his mind buzzing with a million thoughts, not one of them about the case he was headed to finish.

15 Hours Later...

After a long day in court, which saw all four defendants assigned long prison sentences for the myriad of crimes they had committed, followed by an afternoon and evening of interviews, Bennett drove home exhausted but excited. He had been featured on all the major news outlets around the state. He had watched a few sound bites on his phone. There had been a short interview on the courthouse steps followed by two in-depth interviews done in studios at the two larger stations in Little Rock. One done by Melissa Jones and the other by Pat Patterson.

Tammi had texted him that the story had been picked up and was running on several national news broadcasts. Jameson had sent him a text congratulating him again and reminding him not to let all the great publicity go to waste. Bennett was surprised that Williams could text. He could not exactly envision a man who had campaigned for Reagan being able to access modern communication technology so well.

The prosecutor in him would typically have been replaying the events of the day from court over in his head, but today, his mind was singularly focused on the governorship. He would have liked to have said that he had moved past his old desires to lead and be a part of the movers and shakers politically, but he hadn't.

He truly believed he could make a difference for the people of Arkansas, and dammit, he wanted an opportunity to try. However, the reasons he left politics before were as valid today as they had been more than a decade earlier. His family. He had resigned to protect those he loved. Could he risk exposing them to the negative publicity that sharing their story could generate?

He was brave enough to admit that getting back into politics excited him. In the end though, he had to honor those who, if he ran, could be hurt. He decided to tell Poppy, Ben, and Taylor about the opportunity. If any of the three did not want the story told, he would not run. Period. They had to come first.

It was after eleven when Bennett walked into a silent, empty kitchen. He knew that he had to feel Poppy out about sharing their story as soon as possible. However, Bennett could not deny he was relieved not to have to talk about it right away. After eating cold leftovers, he quietly slipped into bed next to her. Bennett wrapped himself around her and fell asleep, pondering the possibility of a future he never dreamed he might ever have again.

Chapter 3

Carrington House
Searcy, Arkansas
November 22, 2023

Bennett spent the day looking for the right time to approach Poppy about running. However, an opportunity did not present itself between shopping and preparing for the next day's Thanksgiving dinner. The moment he was looking for came once the girls went upstairs to watch a movie. He insisted that Poppy go upstairs and take a hot bath while he cleaned the kitchen, which was a major disaster. With order restored downstairs, Bennett poured Poppy a large glass of Sauvignon Blanc and headed to her.

Sticking his head in the bathroom door, Bennett quietly asked, "Permission to enter?"

Laying back, relaxing in her over-sized tub, Poppy replied, "Only if you have wine."

"Always, my love," replied Bennett as he walked into the bath and handed her the glass.

Taking a long sip, Poppy let out a sigh and said, "Thank you. I needed that." Dropping to his knees next to the tub, he began to massage her feet. Instantly, she began to moan her approval. The only thing Poppy liked more than a foot rub was a foot rub while soaking in a tub full of bubbles. The more he rubbed, the more she moaned.

"Oh my God. That is so good," she groaned as he continued to increase the pressure on her instep.

"Anything for you," he replied.

After several more glorious minutes, Poppy gave him a very sexy look, and said, "So, should I let some water out so you can join me in this big old tub you insisted we needed?"

Bennett continued to work magic with his hands and said, "Nah, that's okay; I'm good just seeing how much you are enjoying this."

Poppy's eyes widened, and she pulled her feet out of his hands. She sat up in the tub so quickly it caused water to slosh over the side. Spearing Bennett with a look, she said, "Okay, out with it. What have you done?"

Feigning shock, Bennett replied, "What? Can't I just give my wife a foot massage for no reason?"

"A foot massage. Yes. It is all of the other things you have been doing in the last hour that make this suspect. First, you volunteer to clear a hell of a mess in the kitchen when you have never, not once in ten years, willingly cleaned anything. Then you show up with wine and a killer foot massage. Next, you forgo an offer of water sex in order to continue to give me a killer, never-ending foot massage. No, something is up. I hate it when you do this. Whatever it is, just tell me."

Bennett raised his hands in a gesture that showed he surrendered and said, "I haven't done anything. At least not yet."

When Poppy responded with only a raised eyebrow and pursed lips, he added, "But, there is something I need to talk to you about."

"Oh Lord, please don't say you have already been asked to take on another special case to prosecute. We just got you back. You promised you wouldn't." Poppy hated the whinny sound she heard in her voice, but the last two years had taken a toll on all of them.

He patted her leg and reassured her, "No, nothing like that. But I have been approached about a new opportunity, and I want to see what you think about it."

"New opportunity? What kind of opportunity? And by whom?" asked Poppy. After almost ten years of marriage to Bennett, Poppy had learned that new opportunities often meant more time away from the family.

He had just been a small-town lawyer in private practice for the first six years of their marriage. Over the years, she realized he needed more excitement and challenge than the job offered. But she longed for the simplicity of those days when he made it home for dinner every night and was all in on their little family. Even then, though, she sensed something was missing in his life. He had had such a successful, illustrious public career before her.

Many times over the years, she had felt guilty about all he had given up for them, especially during election season. She knew he missed many of the aspects of his old life.

She had to remember that whatever this new opportunity was, he obviously was more than a little interested in it or he would not be so secretive. She had to try and support it if at all possible.

Realizing the water had gone cold, and the conversation was about to heat up, Poppy stood and handed Bennett her wine glass. She grabbed a towel and said, "Let's continue this in bed."

Fifteen minutes later, Poppy was lotioned, dressed in her most comfy pajamas, and sufficiently plied with alcohol to discuss "new opportunities." Bennett paced around the room like a caged animal who could not find a comfortable place to land.

Poppy was nestled on her side of the bed. Taking a final sip of Dutch courage, she said, "Okay, I am ready. Tell me all about this new opportunity."

Bennett looked at her with a deeply serious look as if he were searching for where to begin. Running both hands through his dirty blond hair, he swallowed hard and said, "I have been approached about running for governor."

Incredulously, Poppy looked at him and asked, "Governor? Like for the state of Arkansas?"

Holding her gaze, he nodded. "Yes, governor, like for the state of Arkansas."

Bennett held her gaze and tried to gauge her feelings over what he had just said.

For a moment, Poppy said nothing. Then, she asked, "But how? Why? You can't run for office. You left all that behind years ago. You know what will happen if you do. The press will be all over us. It will be just like it was ten years ago."

"I want you to know that I will only do this if you are totally on board with it," he rushed to reassure her. "You and the children come first." Pacing back and forth around the front of the bed, he talked as fast as he was walking. Poppy could literally see how nervous he was even discussing this with her. Stopping and looking directly at her, he added, "Of course, I need Benjamin and Taylor's permission as well. This is their story, too. But, again, I won't do it if any of you are uncomfortable with it."

Uncomfortable with it? Of course, they would all be uncomfortable with it, Poppy immediately thought. But that was not what she said. Instead, she asked, "I don't understand. You win a big case, and suddenly, all the reasons you walked away from politics are gone?"

"Not gone, just different," he responded. He was so focused and passionate that she could almost imagine him as he had once been on the Senate floor, arguing for a cause he was passionate about. Only this time, she was his audience and what he was championing was his long-dead career that she had helped kill. He continued to make his case, saying, "The world is a different place now than it was ten years ago. We have all survived a pandemic," he added, using much of the same rhetoric Jameson had used earlier to pique his interest.

The longer he talked, the more the words poured out of his mouth. Once he got going, it was as if he had to get it all out. "Williams says that the last two presidential races have changed what voters want in a leader. They are less concerned about their private life and more about their policies and leadership abilities. I still have strong name recognition in the state, and winning the case has certainly helped. If we tell our story honestly, I think the people of Arkansas will see that our love is a story of survival and perseverance. If they can understand why we made the decisions we did, then I believe we can make the whole thing a non-issue."

The more he talked, the louder the buzz in her head became. All she could think about was seeing her face plastered all over the news with the tagline, "*Poppy Thompson-Senator's Mistress and Baby Mama.*"

She could not go through that again. Most of what Bennett was saying was not registering. He kept droning on about spinning the story and controlling how much was shared. She was too much in her head to really listen. All she knew as he rattled on about how he would not do anything she was uncomfortable with and how the decision was up to her. She knew she was never going to be okay with it. The one thing she knew for sure was that as much as she did not want Bennett to run for governor, that was how much he wanted to.

After thirty minutes of going in circles, Poppy realized that the wine had kicked in, and her brain had become too fuzzy to discuss it further.

Yawning, she said, "I get that this is something you want. I don't know if I can go through this again." Wanting to bring the conversation to a quick end, she added, "Let me sleep on it. We'll talk more tomorrow. I love you." Giving him a quick kiss goodnight, she snuggled under her covers and closed her eyes.

Bennett gave her a quick kiss on the forehead and said, "I meant what I said. I won't do this if you, Ben, or Taylor say no. I will never hurt any of you again." With that, he turned off the light before heading to the bathroom for a quick shower before bed.

Chapter 4

Gulf Shores, Alabama
November 22, 2023

"Rosie!" yelled Greer for the third time as his ten-year-old daughter came down the stairs with her earbuds blasting. Seeing her dad, she broke into a large, metal grin. The bond between them was incredible. For a man who thought having a family had passed him by, Greer thanked his lucky stars every day for her. Because of a few stupid mistakes made by some very careless people, himself included, he got to be her dad. As she met him on the stairs, she reached over to graze his cheek with a soft kiss.

Yanking the nearest earbud out, he said," Turn that down. I will be paying for hearing aids next. Mom's about ready. I put your suitcase and duffle in the trunk."

Motioning to her jacket and pillow, he asked, "Is that all you want up front?"

Holding up the items in her hands, she said, "I am good. Mom's got snacks, right?"

Laughing, Greer nodded. "Of course. Already put them in the car." Before Rosie, he had no clue how much kids ate. She was always hungry and was a complete beanpole. They could not fill her up. "You sure you don't want me to grab Mr. Rabbit?"

"You wish. You know I have not slept with Mr. Rabbit since I was eight," replied Rosie.

"I know. I keep forgetting you are practically grown." She was correct; he did wish she was still little. She was growing up so fast. Looking closer as she continued down the stairs, he nearly had a heart attack, "Are you wearing lipstick?" Little pieces of pink littered the silvery braces of her top teeth. She looks slightly ridiculous and entirely too old all at once. His first instinct was to order her to come back and wash all of it off her face. However, she raced down the stairs before he could stop her.

She slowed down long enough to yell back, "Mom said I could do it since we were driving all day. I wanted to show Aunt Joules."

Yelling "Taylor!" at the top of his lungs, Greer went in search of his wife as Rosie slipped outside. He stomped into the kitchen, where his wife was finishing filling a cooler with drinks.

"You will not believe what your daughter has on!" He was bellowing. He tended to do that when he was stressed or frustrated.

Not reacting to Greer's sudden outburst, Taylor calmly replied without even looking up, "She had on leggings and a sweatshirt the last time I saw her."

"Not her clothes! Makeup! Hot pink lipstick! It is everywhere!" he barked. "She said you said she could put that shit on."

Zipping up the cooler and handing it to him, Taylor replied, "I did. It is fine. She wanted to show Joules the new trick she learned on YouTube. What's the big deal? We are just going to ride in the car most of the day and then eat with Joules for dinner. Chill."

"Chill? Chill?" he repeated. "You want me to chill? I don't like it. She is growing up too fast."

Taylor patted his shoulder and said, "I know. But, give her this. What does it hurt?"

Accepting defeat, he replied, "I guess you are right, but tell her to get it off her teeth." Then, with a growl, he added, "I still don't like it."

"Yeah, me either. But that's life." Gesturing to the cooler he was holding, she said, "Put that in the car, and we are ready."

Following her out of the kitchen, he said, "Speaking of things I don't like, explain why we have to drive eight hours to Arkansas to have Thanksgiving with your ex-husband and his family?"

Pinning him with a don't start with me look, she pursed her lips and said, "You know why. Bennett and Poppy aren't just my ex-husband and his new family. Besides, you only have to see them one day by going there. I could have invited them for the weekend if you preferred."

Giving her a look of horror, he replied honestly, "Oh God no! One day is enough. Plus, it will let me check in on Aunt Edna."

Walking out ahead of him, Taylor got in the car and sarcastically grumbled, "Yeah, Aunt Edna!" She had forgotten about promising to spend the night at her house. Time spent with Edna Stone was always trying for her.

Rosie removed an earpiece from the backseat and asked, "What did you say, Mom?"

"Oh, nothing," Taylor replied, "Just thinking about how nice it will be to see your Aunt Edna again."

"Oh yeah. Okay." Rosie replied, giving her mother a substantial pink-encrusted grin before losing total interest in the conversation. She was munching on dried fruit snacks and singing along to the song in her ears.

Oh my! Greer was right, Taylor thought; that was a lot of lipstick. Oh well thought Taylor, the way her child was munching it would be eaten off by Mobile.

Four hours into the trip, they pulled into a gas station to fill up and use the bathroom. As they piled back into the car, Taylor noticed that Rosie had already put her earbuds back in and was absorbed in her book. Reaching over to Greer's side of the car, she took a moment to give him a sexy smile. "Thank you. I know it is not how you would like to spend the holiday. I appreciate you doing this for me and Rosie."

Greer flashed her his seriously devilish smile and gave her a wink as he pulled her in close. Nibbling on her neck he growled, "Woman, don't you know I would go to hell and back for you? Just didn't expect hell to be in the middle of Arkansas."

Laughing as much from how his whiskers tickled her, as his words humored her, she replied, "Oh well, think on the bright side. At least it is November and not August."

"That's the truth. But, even without the 100 degrees and 100% humidity, it still qualifies as the throne of darkness, complete with its own devil," he quipped.

"Oh, play nice," Taylor whispered. "Searcy is not that bad, and Bennett is actually a really good guy. You know that. And besides,..."

"Blah blah, blah," he cut her off. "Why don't you use that beautiful mouth for something better like kissing me than talking about him?" With that, Greer captured her lips in a full-on tongue-snogging to keep her from singing her ex-husband's praises.

The kiss extended longer than was appropriate in front of their daughter, and Rosie did not let them forget it even though her parents had momentarily forgotten her.

"Yuck. Stop that. It's gross!" Rosie yelled from the backseat, effectively ending the kiss and getting the trip rolling again.

They got to Little Rock a little after six. Joules was there to meet them, and they ate dinner at her little cottage in the Heights. Around ten, Greer and Rosie said goodnight and took themselves off to bed. Joules and Taylor stayed up until almost two in the morning talking. At times like this, Taylor wondered how she could have moved seven hours away from her. But whenever she asked herself that question, she immediately knew the answer was Greer.

He had claimed that he would go to hell and back for her. Well, she would walk through the fires of hell for him and very nearly had.

Chapter 5

Bill and Hillary Clinton National Airport
Little Rock, Arkansas
November 23, 2023

Thanksgiving Day dawned early and was more hectic than the day before. Bennett and Poppy's oldest child and only son, Benjamin, was coming home for the holiday. His flight was due to arrive at Little Rock National at 8:30. Poppy decided that everyone should go to meet him. Not only because they were all greatly missing Ben, but he was bringing home what he termed "a friend." Said friend just happened to be female. All they knew about her was that she was a drop-dead gorgeous Hispanic girl from Napa named Ella. They had learned those tidbits when he had casually announced that she would be coming with him for Thanksgiving the week before. This was the first time he had brought anyone home to meet the family. No one knew quite what to make of that.

They knew Ben had dated several girls over the last five years, but nothing seemed serious. Something significant must have happened to change that. Neither one had felt right asking Ben too many questions. He was a great kid with a strong head on his shoulders. Both knew he would share what was happening between him and Ella when he was ready. Ben was finishing his master's degree in Political Science. The plan was for him to finish in the spring, return home, and start law school at the University of Arkansas Little Rock in the fall. What impact, if any, this Ella person might have on that plan was a primary unspoken concern for both Bennett and Poppy. Both knew that if he fell in love with a girl in California, it might mean he would stay there and never return to Arkansas. Neither one was ready even to contemplate such a scenario. They had both missed him so much.

Ben and Ella had spent the last five days skiing in Colorado. They met up with some of Ben's college friends who had moved to Denver after graduation. The biggest clue that something had changed, besides bringing her home for the holiday, was when Ben told Bennett that they would be staying in their own condo for privacy in Denver. The need for privacy was a red flag. In the past, all of his friends had all bunked in together. The last few days, Poppy had been in a real snit trying to decide if she should make up the guest room for Ella or just assume the girl would be sleeping in Ben's room. While Poppy considered herself hip and cool, something about allowing her son to sleep in the same bed as his "friend" with his younger sisters down the hall had convinced her she probably wasn't. After all, Lizzy and Lola were only seven and six. Bennett had convinced her that she was overreacting and to go with the flow by letting the kids choose their accommodations. In the end, that was what she had done. The guest room was made up, but if they decided to be together, she would do her best to let it go.

They arrived at the airport with just a few minutes to spare. Even though she had promised to discuss the run for governor more in the morning, Poppy was glad that Bennett had yet to bring it up. Every time he looked at her, Poppy could tell he wanted to. She could literally see the words dancing on the front of his tongue, just dying to rush out. So far, Bennett had managed to restrain himself from pushing her for an answer, and she had worked to pretend they would never have to discuss the whole awful business again. As they walked towards baggage claim, Poppy knew what she had to do. Grabbing Bennett's arm, she whispered, "I have thought about what you asked last night. I have decided to go along with whatever Taylor and Ben say. But please promise me you won't bring it up until after dinner tonight. If they are good with it, so am I."

The smile that broke out over Bennett's face told her everything she needed to know. Grabbing her and pulling her in for a deep kiss of gratitude, Bennett used his lips to let Poppy know how much her answer meant to him. The kiss also told her that Bennett wanted this badly. He wanted to be governor. God help her; she prayed that her son or Taylor would have the strength to tell Bennett no because there was no way she could.

Bennett hugged his wife, saying, "With that settled, let's go get Ben and find out the deal with him and this mystery woman. Remember, go easy on the questions. We don't want to scare her off."

Giving him a look, Poppy said, "I make no promises."

Ben and Ella were already at the luggage carousel when the family caught up to them. The first thing that struck Bennett and Poppy was how young Ella was. Like barely legal young. Her age gave them pause, and they exchanged a concerned look but said nothing. Instead, they engulfed Ben in a family hug and made so much noise, shrieking and laughing, that the other passengers all turned to see what the commotion was. Ella stood off to the side and said nothing until

Ben extricated himself, walked over, and, putting an arm around her shoulders, said, "Mom, Dad, meet Ella."

Immediately, Poppy swooped in, gave Ella a hug, and said, "I am Poppy. It is so nice to meet you. Welcome to Arkansas."

Right behind her, Bennett gave Ella an abbreviated pat-hug and echoed his wife's sentiments. "Yes, welcome. I am Bennett, Ben's old man. We are happy to have you."

Lizzy and Lola then swarmed Ella and gave her side hugs while commenting on how beautiful she was and how gorgeous her long dark hair was which fell like a curtain of black silk.

While the women began to get acquainted, Bennett and Ben moved to the luggage carousel to collect their belongings. Bennett had expected them to have a ton of luggage since they would have their snow equipment and suitcases. However, Ben had arranged to ship their snow gear home before leaving Denver. All they had were their individual bags. They quickly located their suitcases, loaded the car, and headed home.

The car ride home was a noisy affair with Lizzy and Lola asking questions a mile a minute. Bennett repeatedly asked them to calm down and give Ella and Ben a break, but both young people just laughed and took it all in stride, claiming it was fine. They realized the girls were excited to see the big brother they both adored. They also seemed to have fallen entirely under Ella's spell as well. Bennett had no trouble seeing what his son saw in the beautiful young woman. She was gorgeous. But talking with her, Bennett realized she was also intelligent, witty, and confident in her own skin, especially for one so young. At the first opportunity, he planned to find out just how young she actually was. It took a lot of moxie to spend a holiday with people you barely knew. A bonus of the girls' non-stop questioning, it kept Poppy from having to ask a bunch of intrusive questions. The girls were basically asking what Poppy wanted to know anyway, but it came off much better from them. Poppy seemed to understand this, and so she sat back and just listened.

So far, they had gleaned that Ella's family owned a diner in Napa and that she had worked there since graduating high school. No mention of college or training had yet been mentioned. Bennett could tell that Poppy was dying to ask what year she had graduated from high school but was managing to hold it back. Lola finally asked the right question and got the answer they were all wondering about.

She said for the tenth time, "You are so pretty." And then she added, "You remind me of Savannah, our babysitter, but I think she is older than you." As a younger sister by fourteen months, age was a big deal for Lola. She had spent her whole life trying to catch up to her big sister. Without missing a beat, she added, "She is in junior high school. Is junior high school what you go to next after high school?"

Everyone in the car laughed, and when Lola did not understand why, Poppy said, "Sweetie, junior high comes before high school, not after."

"Oh," replied Lola. "Well, you still look younger than her. She is 14. Just how old are you?"

Bennett immediately jumped in and said, "Lola, it is not nice to ask a lady her age."

To which Lola responds, "Hum, Ella's not a lady. She is Ben's friend."

Ella and everyone laughed at Lola's words and said," It's fine. I don't mind answering." Looking right at Lola, Ella said, "I am nineteen. I graduated from high school at 16 in 2020."

"16!" replied Lizzy. "You must be a genius. Do you go to college like Ben? He's a genius, too."

"No, he is not," interjected Ben before adding, "but you are right, Ella actually is. I think that is enough questions Little Turds," which brought the non-stop interrogation of Ella to a halt. Little Turds was Ben's nickname for the two little sisters he never knew he wanted until he got them.

As he listened, Bennett could see Poppy's mind spinning. Thank goodness no one else could read her face the way he could, or the merry mood in the car might not have been so cheery.

An Hour Later
Searcy, Arkansas
November 23, 2023

The minute they returned to town, they headed to the Chit, Chat, and Chew Cafe. On the drive from Little Rock, Ella had asked if they could have breakfast there as Ben had mentioned it often. She had heard so much about it she was dying to try it. The C4, as it was known, was open on Thanksgiving morning until noon for breakfast and pick-up orders for those who preferred a catered homemade Thanksgiving dinner. It was the best place in town for a big, country breakfast. As usual, the food was excellent, and the service was superior. Poppy was dying to ask Ella how the C4 compared to her parent's diner back home. Any time anyone tried to ask her a question, Ben would smoothly change the subject. Poppy was beginning to worry he was hiding something. She had no idea what, but experience had taught her that secrets in this family always ended badly. She hoped she was wrong.

Several people dropped by their table to congratulate Bennett on his win. As always, Bennett thanked them even though he was very uncomfortable taking compliments. More than one person commented on how they wished he was still their Senator and what a great job he had done for the state. Some went so far as to say that his leaving office had been a real shame.

Every time someone would stop to chat, the table conversation would halt. After a brief chat, the person would move on and the family would go back to visiting. When Poppy apologized for so many interruptions, Ella surprised her by commenting that it was nice that everyone in the town seemed to know them. The only insight she gave to her background was when she commented that for a tourist town, Napa was much the same way when it came to the locals. Ben had already warned Ella it would be this way.

Having moved to Searcy at eleven after having lived in New York City all his life, he had to get used to the small-town ways. He did over time, but he still missed living in a large city where everyone was a stranger. That was one of the reasons he applied to colleges far from home. That and the fact that Jack and Jorge lived nearby.

In a place like Searcy, no one ever really lets you forget that you were the love child of the artist who left town and returned to destroy a perfect marriage and a promising political career. Sure, over time, things improved. His parents had worked hard to help him understand that just because people believed something did not make it true. He never talked to his parents about it, but he had felt the stares and heard the whispers, especially in the early days. He had learned the hard way that life in a small southern town was not all sweet tea and pecan pie.

While everyone seemed to acknowledge the people who came and went, only Bennett seemed to notice how much quieter Poppy got with each one. The sparkle that had been in her eyes from the moment she spied Ben at the airport dimmed a little with each visit. Bennett hoped that did not mean that she was changing her mind about his running. He knew that if she were, he would stand by his word and not run. No matter how much he might want a second chance at a political career, it would not be worth Poppy's happiness. She was his everything.

But, damn, he knew that walking away again would be even harder than it had been the first time.

The family finished up their meal and spent a few hours taking Ella around the town showing her the different sites. They took her by the historic courthouse and the quaint shops downtown. Next they stopped off at the Black House, where several of Poppy's paintings were on display. They also showed her various landmark churches and the local college.

Ella asked about all of the lights she saw everywhere. Ben explained that the town and university go all out at Christmas with millions of lights and holiday scenes that had been set up at all the parks and town square. He promised to bring her back after dark so she could see them lit up later that night and take a carriage ride around the court square.

They ended their trip with a visit to Art Alley. Several large murals were painted all around downtown. The largest collections of works were in an alley off a side street just one block down from the court square. They spent time looking at the various murals done by local artists. Poppy explained that the work was constantly changing. She had two murals that she had done. One was of two little girls running through the waves at a beach. Ella immediately recognized the girls as Lizzy and Lola at about three and four. The other was of Bennett standing in front of a podium. He appeared to be giving some kind of speech. His face was so taut and stressed that it was almost impossible to recognize him. Ella knew that Ben's mom often painted from photographs. She could not help but wonder what speech had inspired the mural. In it, he looked very different from the easy going, carefree man she had spent the morning getting to know.

The family got back to the house around three. Ella was clearly impressed with the house as they drove up the winding drive. Ben had tried to prepare her, but the house was out of character for the boy she had come to love. Large and imposing, it looked like a French chateau dropped in the middle of a small southern town. Ben could sense Ella becoming overwhelmed. She knew that Ben came from money, but seeing the house he grew up in was a shock to her system.

Walking into the house, Ella whispered to Ben, "You should have told me your parents lived in a mansion. I was not prepared for all of this," she said, gesturing to the huge house and lawn.

Giving her a reassuring hug and a kiss on the forehead, he quietly whispered in her ear, "I know it is a lot. But believe it or not, it is much better than when I first saw it. Mom and Dad did a total gut after the first year they were married. It was so stuffy with tons of antiques and very traditional. It felt more like a museum than a home. But Mom fixed that. It is much more homey now. Besides, it is just a house at the end of the day. The part that makes it a home is the people who live in it, and they are going to love you because I do."

His comforting words reassured Ella. The house did feel totally different inside. The chateau demeanor of the exterior was nowhere to be found inside. It was decorated in bright colors with tons of art covering the walls and comfortable couches and chairs everywhere. The inside was night and day compared to the outside. Ella could not help but think the house was like Ben. He was a rich kid whose dad was a former senator. He was gorgeous and brilliant. He could have been the biggest, most arrogant asshole in the world, but he wasn't. He was one of the kindest, most thoughtful people she had ever met. She knew about his early life and that Ben had not known Bennett was his dad until he was eleven. She could only imagine how going through all that at such a young age could have warped him. It hadn't. Instead, it seemed to help form him into the man she had fallen deeply in love with.

As they walked in, the awkwardness of addressing where everyone would sleep was avoided when Ben casually took Ella's bag and said, "I will just put these in our room."

Bennett gave Poppy a look and shrugged as if to say, "Well, that answers that question."

Poppy just gave him a weak smile and shrugged back. She had not rebounded from all of the people who had talked to them at the restaurant earlier in the day. All morning, she had gone through the motions and said all the right things.

Bennett could tell she was backpedaling. He had promised not to bring the governor's race up again until they were together. He knew Taylor, Greer, and Rosie would be there for dinner by six. He hoped they would have some time to talk after dinner. Poppy reminded him he had two turkeys he needed to deep fry. So Bennett spent the next several hours setting everything up while Poppy, Ella, and the girls set the table and got to know each other.

Out on the patio, Bennett was tempted to broach the subject with Ben while they were alone. But Poppy had asked him not to, and so he didn't. Ben was his son, but sometimes, because she had raised their son alone for so many years, it felt like Ben belonged more to her than to him. He had worked hard to close that distance in their relationship, but some things were beyond repair. So, he held his tongue and hoped that an opportunity presented itself after dinner when they could all talk. However, like any parent would, Bennett did allow himself to broach the subject of Ella.

Very casually, Bennett said, "Ella seems like a very nice girl. Beautiful but a bit young."

Ben laughed and said, "I wondered how long it would take you to ask that. She is nineteen, but she is an old soul, in case you missed it, and brilliant. Besides, age is just a number."

"No, I did not miss that. She is obviously extremely bright. How did you two meet?"

Taking a long swig of his water, Ben said, "We met at her family's diner. Remember how I went with a few buddies to Napa over fall break? Our cottage was across the street from their place. We ate there several times. I met her then, and we have sort of been together ever since."

Giving his son a strange look, Bennett asked, "What do you mean, you have sort of been together?"

"I mean, we have been texting and talking, and a few weeks ago, we decided to give this thing a real shot. She has moved into my place in Malibu. We are considering marriage."

With an incredulous look, Bennett asked, "You are living together? Marriage? What about school? What is she doing about a job? Have you thought about this? It feels very sudden." The questions and concern came pouring out of Bennett. He couldn't help it. He hated prying into his son's private business, but this was much more than expected.

Holding up one hand to stifle his father's flow of questions, Ben said, "I know you have concerns. But, you are going to have to trust me on this. I know what I am doing. I am still in school and on track to graduate in the spring. Ella is looking for a job, but that is really not our number one priority right now. We have a lot of details to work out, and when we do, you and Mom will be the first to know. Until then, I need to know you have my back and trust that I have got this."

"I do trust you, but slow down. You are both so young, especially her. What is the rush? Date each other. Get to know each other. A few months is hardly enough time to be talking about marriage. You don't want to rush into something that you will both regret."

Ben held up his hand and said, "Dad…" but Bennett was on a roll and kept saying how young they were and how they had all the time in the world to settle down.

Ben tried three times to get a word in before he blurted out, "Dad, Ella is pregnant."

Bennett's head snapped back in shock. "Pregnant? Is it yours?"

"Would we be having this conversation if it weren't?" The look Ben gave him told Bennett that there was no doubt about the child's parentage.

"Okay, well, it is 2023. No one has to get married just because of a baby. You have lots of options."

"That is just it, Dad. I don't need a lot of options. I know what it is like to grow up not knowing your father. I won't do that to my child."

While Ben had not said that to hurt Bennett, it still stung. Sadly, it was also the truth.

"Can you honestly look me in the eye and tell me that if you had known about me, you would not have married mom twenty-three years ago?"

"No, son, I cannot. You're right. I would have done exactly what you are doing."

"Thank you for that. I don't have all the answers, but I am doing my best here."

Bennett was taken aback by the adult look of strength in his son's eyes.

He had yet to get all the answers he wanted. Hell, who was he kidding? He had a thousand more questions, but he could tell Ben had shared just about all he planned to at that moment. He knew he should not push, but he could not help himself. He had to ask one last question. "What about law school? Are you still planning on coming back to Little Rock and starting in the fall?"

With a weak nod, Ben said, "At the moment, that is still the plan. I am not making any promises. If there is one thing I have learned in my twenty three years, it is that life can change on a dime. That has certainly been the case in the last few weeks. I promise that you and mom will be the first to know if those plans change."

Nodding, Bennett thought his son was more right than he ever imagined. Enveloping his son in a hug, he said, "I am proud of you, Ben. I trust you to do what is best for you and your child. Just know that your mom and I are here if you need us. Always."

Hugging his father back, Ben nodded. The two men stood tightly embraced for a second longer before breaking apart.

Stepping back, Bennett looked down as his watch buzzed. It was a text from Williams.

Have you made a decision yet? We really need to strike while the iron is hot. If your family is on board, I can have a reporter there tomorrow morning to begin the process. Please get back to me as soon as you can.

Bennett read the text, felt the old familiar stress, and fought back a wave of panic mixed with excitement. He texted back a quick note.

Understand. I am working on it. Will hopefully know something later tonight. I will text when I have a final answer.

He read his response and then added,

Am very interested but have to make sure everyone here is on board with it. Will talk soon.

Once he hit send, he began putting together a plan to bring it all up later in the evening. And as he did so, he once again reminded himself that he had to be good with whatever they said. If they said no, it was a no. He just hoped that enough water was under the bridge, and they were ready to let old fears go and move forward.

Carrington House
Searcy, Arkansas
November 23, 2023

Taylor, Greer, and Rosie arrived at the Carrington's right at six the next evening. After spending most of the morning with Joules, the family headed to Searcy to spend the afternoon with Aunt Edna.

A powerhouse of a woman her whole life, Edna had all but run Searcy's society for the better part of the last fifty years. In the last few years, she had been forced to cut back her activities. She made a painful move to sell her large home and moved into a smaller, more practical one. Buying in The Dominion, a subdivision across the street from the Searcy Country Club, she was able to drive her golf cart over for lunch most days with the other widowed women who regularly met there.

This year, the widows decided to have Thanksgiving lunch at the club and invited Taylor, Greer, and Rosie to join them. It was a wonderful meal and allowed them to visit in relative calm. Taylor found time spent with Aunt Edna challenging. Taylor's mom had never liked her. There had been bad blood between her mom and Edna and her daughter, Anita, dating back to her mom's high school days. Whenever Edna was around, Taylor's mom would always say that Edna thought she was in charge of the universe. As a child, Taylor had not understood what she meant. As an adult, she totally got it. Beyond that, Taylor never completely got over the fact that it was at Edna's insistence Poppy had returned to Searcy with a love child in tow. An event that led to the demise of her first marriage.

However, it was not fair to lay the blame for her divorce at Edna's feet. She knew her marriage was doomed long before Edna Stone brought Poppy back to town. She also had to acknowledge that her life was a million times better than it would have been if things had turned out differently. But, being with Edna was a bit like having to eat something that previously had made you very sick. Even if the thing you ate was not what made you sick, just the thought of it turned your stomach. That was what Edna was to her. It was crazy because, in some ways, she held Edna more accountable for her divorce than the woman her husband had cheated on her with. Also, being back in the club, which held way too many bad memories, left Taylor feeling vulnerable and fragile. These were two emotions she did not endure easily.

After the luncheon, the family followed Edna on her golf cart, which Rosie insisted on driving, to her house. Taylor and Greer planned to stay with Edna that night and then drive back home Friday. It was only one night. She could do it. Taylor knew that her feelings for Edna were not warranted, and she worked hard to ensure her expressions and actions never gave away her true feelings. Hiding her emotions was something that Taylor was a pro at, even if she had not had to use that particular skill for over a decade.

The evening called for a second Thanksgiving dinner at Poppy's and Bennett's home. All three of them were stuffed but knew they had to go and try to eat something. As they entered the gate code and made the long, winding drive up to the house, Taylor realized she would never get over the strange feeling of having to ring the doorbell and be a guest in a house she had lived in for almost a decade. While the house looked virtually the same on the outside, inside was a different story. Nothing was the same as it had been when she lived there. Gone were all the stuffy antiques and Persian rugs. In their place were comfortable couches and bright colors. It was really a family home. It was a strong metaphor for how each of them had changed and become more comfortable in their own skin once they found their forever homes with the ones they desperately loved.

Though she tried to hide it, Greer immediately sensed Taylor's anxiety as they approached the front door. Rosie, who in the past had raced to the front eager to see Lizzy and Lola, held back. It was as if she, too, could feel her mother's tension.

Laying a soft hand on her back for comfort, Greer groaned into her ear, "It is okay. It is just one meal. We can leave whenever you want."

Taking comfort in his words, Taylor plastered a smile on her face, and all three walked to the door together. They had barely rung the bell when Lizzy and Lola came running, excited to see Rosie.

Hugs and kisses were handed out, and before Taylor realized it, she had been ushered into what had once been her kitchen. Though, honestly, it in no way resembled the formal home she remembered. Everyone seemed to be talking at once. It was obvious that the girls really missed each other, and they escaped to the playroom. Greer, Bennett, and Ben shook hands and headed outside to supervise the turkeys frying. Bennett offered Greer a beer on their way out the back door while she and Poppy seated themselves at the kitchen island. Poppy introduced Ella as she offered both ladies a large glass of white wine. Taylor grabbed it like a passenger on the Titanic reaching for a life preserver. Ella declined the drink, preferring to stick with water. They spent the next hour getting to know Ella and learning about her life in Napa. It was all small talk and smiles, which was fine with both Poppy and Taylor. Both women were more than impressed with Ella, who seemed very together for someone so young. In addition to helping run her family's diner, she also took classes online and worked at a local winery on weekends and holidays. It was very apparent that Ben had not been exaggerating when he said she was brilliant, accomplished, and ambitious. By letting Ella drive the conversion, Poppy and Taylor found an easy peace that did not always permeate their conversations. Ella offered a buffer that helped keep everything light and easy. Taylor decided she very much liked Ella and could see what Ben saw in her.

To anyone who did not know the backstory, it seemed like every other family holiday - nice, sweet, and routine. It was anything but. Taylor wondered how much Ben had shared with Ella about his family and its unusual dynamic. Over time, they all managed to develop a family bond that spoke to the power of forgiveness. The adults had forged enough of a relationship over the years that the girls did not feel any of the awkwardness that the adults worked so hard to overcome. After all, families come in many packages, and this one comes wrapped in a lot of hurt, anger, and pain. Over time, those things fade, but the memory of how it felt in those hurtful moments could, and did, still linger in the recesses of the subconscious.

For Taylor and Bennett, it was not so hard. They had been family all of their lives. They had faced unbelievable tragedy together. They shared a bond that even divorce could not break. It was so strong that it also forced the people who loved them to put aside their hurt feelings and embrace the others out of affection. That was how this motley crew of wives, husbands, ex-wives, ex-husbands, and lovers had become a makeshift family. A family with buried secrets that had refused to stay hidden. So, for all those reasons, each year, for one meal, they all sat down for a big, family Thanksgiving. More than that would have been too hard. But anyone can get through one meal a year. And, it gave the girls all something they would otherwise not have had, cousins of a sort. So, for their girls, they all made the sacrifice.

After a glass of wine, Taylor began to relax. Greer's beer chilled him, and he was actually laughing and conversing with Bennett without it feeling forced. With everyone working together, dinner went on the table promptly at 7:30. It was a noisy affair with lots of joking and storytelling. It was almost 9:00 pm when Poppy began serving pecan pie with ice cream. As everyone was finishing up their dessert and proclaiming they were never eating again, the doorbell rang.

It was Maryanna, the Carrington's long-time housekeeper. Bennett and Poppy did not have a live-in maid as they had turned the maid's apartment into Poppy's studio. However, Maryanna had been helping Poppy since before Lizzy was born. She knew Poppy would have an awful mess to clean up. So, after celebrating with her family, she came by to help clean up the kitchen. Normally, Poppy would have refused, but for once, she was grateful for the help.

After dinner, the girls decided it was time to put on their pajamas and watch the parade that they recorded earlier that morning. It had already been decided that Rosie would spend the night there as Edna's house only had one guest room. The girls rarely got an opportunity to spend time with each other. Before racing up the stairs, all three launched a campaign to convince Ben and Ella to join them. Neither Ben nor Ella were overly interested, but the girls wore them down.

Just as Ben and Ella were about to head upstairs behind the girls, Bennett stood and asked, "Ben, would you and Ella mind hanging back for just a moment? I have something I need to talk to you and the others about."

Poppy immediately shook her head, "Bennett, I am not sure this is the best time." She instantly knew what he was going to discuss and was desperate to put it off as Ben and Ella resumed their seats at the table.

Walking over to Poppy, Bennett took her hands and kissed her forehead to reassure her. Then he calmly said in an almost pleading voice, "I am under the gun here. Jameson wants an answer tonight. I want to do this in person. Please understand." Bowing her head, Poppy resigned herself to the fact that her reprieve was over.

Both Taylor and Greer exchanged a look of bewilderment. They were having trouble following what was happening. It appeared that they had stepped into a family drama that did not involve them.

Wanting to get out of a sticky situation in which he felt they did not belong, Greer stood and said, "It looks like you have some family issues to discuss. We'll kiss Rosie good night and get out of your hair."

Rising to accompany him, Taylor added, "Thank you both for a wonderful dinner. It was nice to visit and catch up and…"

Whatever she was about to say next was cut off by Bennett saying, "No, this involves you as well. Please sit back down. I need to tell you something, and I am sorry for the timing. I hope it does not ruin what has been a really nice visit."

"Oh, that sounds ominous," replied Greer.

"It is," replied Poppy before she could stop herself. Poppy and Greer exchanged a look while Bennett shot her a look of frustration. Poppy shrugged but did not respond.

Taking a deep breath and then blowing it out as he began formulating his words, Bennett blurted out, "You know how I won that big case." Of course, they did.

Greer and Taylor had both congratulated him on it earlier in the day. "Well, the publicity from that case has garnered some interest."

"Interest? What kind of interest?" asked Greer, struggling to see how Bennett's case had anything to do with them.

"Interest from Jameson Williams." He said this, looking directly at Taylor. If anyone in the room would get that, it would be her.

"Jameson Williams, as in the political fat cat committee chairman, Jameson Williams?" Taylor asked.

Bennett nodded.

"Why is he interested in you? I mean, you are not a politician anymore." Looking at him, it clicked. She knew that look. The look he only got when he was about to start a new campaign. "Oh no, you are not thinking about running again, are you? I thought all of that was behind you. Behind all of us." The look of fear on Taylor's face was almost enough to make him back out before he even told her everything. Almost, but not entirely.

"I did. I have, but with the win and the changes in the world, Jameson thinks I could make a run for the governorship and win."

"Who the hell is Jameson? And why the hell are we even discussing this?" Greer bellowed. "We are all not going through that again. Once was enough for a lifetime."

"I thought so, too, until a few days ago. But after talking to Jameson, I think I have a real shot at this thing," replied Bennett.

"But how? The minute you announce, reporters will be all over it again," replied Taylor. A decade as a politician's wife had taught her all she needed to know about the media and how the game was played.

"Jameson has a plan for that," replied Bennett. Very quickly and succinctly, he recounted to them basically what he had explained to Poppy the night before. He detailed how they would control the narrative by doing a story for a local glossy magazine. It would be a story of family, love and acceptance."

He rattled on for almost ten minutes, and no one said anything. He closed by telling them that Poppy had already agreed. So, it was ultimately up to Ben and Taylor. He again promised that he would not pursue the opportunity if they said no. By the time Bennett finished, everyone at the table sat expressionless and bewildered. None of them ever expected this issue to come roaring back to life. To have it done so quickly and so unexpectedly was almost too much to take in.

"Well," said Bennett, running his hands through his hair frustratedly, "somebody say something."

Ben was the first to speak. Getting up and going over to his father, he hugged him and said, "Dad, there is not a better man in the whole state better suited to be the next governor. If Mom is good with it, I am good with it. Ella and I totally support you. Right, Ella?" Ben asked, turning towards his girlfriend.

Nodding, Ella enthusiastically responded, "Yes, of course. I support whatever Ben feels comfortable with." Honestly, Ella was not so sure she completely understood all the ramifications of Ben's dad making a run for office or how Ben and her issues might play into that. But Ben had her back from the day she showed up at his apartment, overcome with morning sickness and fear. From the get go he had supported her, so if this was something he was good with, so was she.

The look of relief and joy that covered Bennett's face was palatable.

Looking over at Taylor, he said, "That just leaves you. Can you do this? I know it will require you to share things you would rather forget. If you say no, I won't do it."

Without missing a beat, Greer said, "That's easy. The answer is no."

Everyone turned and stared at him.

"What? There is no way I am letting you and Rosie go through all of that again just so this pretty boy Ken doll can have another shot at ruling the world," replied Greer, looking directly at Taylor.

"Greer!" snapped Taylor. "Apologize right now." It was the first time in a decade that Greer had referred to Bennett as a pretty boy Ken doll. It went down now, about as well as it had back then.

"Pretty boy Ken doll? Really, we are back to that?" quipped Bennett, giving Greer a sneer. "With all due respect, this is not your decision. It is Taylor's. This is her story. I want to hear what she has to say."

Without missing a beat, Greer replied, "Trust me. Her answer is no. And as for me calling you a pretty boy, that is what you are when you start pulling crap like this that only benefits you and puts the people I love most in the world at risk. Only a self-absorbed, petty asshole would do that. Wasn't going through that once enough?" asked Greer. Then, looking over to Taylor, he said, "Let's give Rosie a goodnight kiss and get out of here before I say or do something that you will really regret."

Sighing deeply, Taylor nodded. Reaching to touch his arm, she said, "Fine, we will go, but please calm down. We will talk about this in the car."

Shaking his head, Greer responded, "Already talked about it. Discussion is closed." With that, he stood up and headed out of the room. He only paused long enough to turn back and address the others in the room independently. "Poppy, dinner was wonderful. Thank you for a delicious meal. Ben, it was great to see you again. Good luck this last semester. Ella, it was nice to meet you." Looking directly at Bennett, he added coolly, "Hear me clearly, there is no way that I am going to let Taylor do this. Not now. Not ever." Then he left the room, yelling for Rosie.

Shaking her head from equal parts embarrassment from how rudely Greer acted and shock that this situation was back at the forefront of her life, Taylor said, "I am sorry. He does not handle surprises well. And he is very protective of Rosie and me. Let me talk to him. I will text you if anything changes." With that, Taylor got up, hugged everyone, thanked them for the dinner, and left to say goodnight to Rosie.

On the ride to Edna's, both Greer and Taylor were very quiet. Greer spent the short ride back to Edna's gripping the steering wheel with a death grip. Taylor quietly stared out the window, desperately trying to think of a way to restart the conversation without a huge ordeal or ending up in a massive fight.

Just as they were about to turn into Edna's subdivision, Taylor reached over, stroked Greer's arm, and said, "Can we drive around town for a few minutes? I want to show you something."

Giving her a quizzical look, Greer asked, "What are you up to?"

Reaching over and snuggling him, she replied, "Nothing. I missed the lights around town and want to show them to you. Can we head towards downtown? It has been a long time since I have seen them."

Never able to tell her no, Greer bypassed the turn into his aunt's house and steered the car toward the center of town. They stopped off at Stu's Brew to get a couple of hot chocolates. The Joyful food truck was there as well. Even though they were full, they picked up several delicious macaroons as a gift for Aunt Edna for hosting them. Then they resumed their ride around town to look at the lights.

Once at Berryhill Park, they drove in companionable silence, enjoying the lights. From there, they rode to Spring Park and drove around the downtown court square with several large light displays. They finished their tour with a drive through the local university campus. The light displays all across the town had the effect on Greer that Taylor was hoping for. Gone was the grumpy, angry man earlier. In his place was a calmer, more relaxed man.

As they headed back to Edna's house, Taylor quietly said, "You know that I am going to do that interview. Right? After all, I owe him. Bennett has done so much for me over the years, and I need to do this for him."

Instantly, Greer's ire returned, "No, you are not. You don't owe him a damn thing."

Calmly, Taylor said, "Yes, I do. Thanks to him, we had a chance. If he had not done what he did ten years ago, our lives and Rosie's would have been much more difficult. He gave up everything for Poppy, Ben and us. And, truthfully, he was the least at fault of all of us."

"Least guilty?" Greer roared as he pulled the car into Edna's drive. "Have you forgotten his little escapade at the art show that started all this?"

Unbuckling her seat belt, Taylor reached over and wrapped her arms around Greer. "No, of course not. But should a person be forever held responsible for five minutes of carelessness in a lifetime of goodness?"

Pulling her closer, Greer asked incredulously, "How can you be okay with opening this Pandora's box from the past? And this time, all of the crap will come out. Everything about you, me, Poppy, plus all their history. How can any of that do anyone any good?"

"Honestly, I think some of those secrets have been held for way too long. It is long past time for the truth to come to light. Besides, I am not embarrassed by our story or how we came together. All the people I care about already know it all anyway. By sharing the story this way, we can take some of the mystique out of it. If that helps Bennett get his life back, it is worth it. All he has ever done is put others first. This is a chance for us to open a door to the past. Air out the truth and truly put it all behind us."

Turning her face so he could look deeply into her eyes, he earnestly asked, "Are you sure this is something you want to do?"

Taylor replied, "Yes, I know in my heart the time is right to address it publicly and then move on."

He closed his eyes and shook his head, resigning himself to the fact that, once again, he could not deny her anything she wanted. "Fine," he said, "if this is what you want to do, I support you." Then, he opened his eyes and added, "But at any moment, you change your mind, I have no problem ending the interview and calling a halt to all of it."

Reaching to give him a sweet kiss, she replied, "Of course you wouldn't, my knight in shining armor."

Accepting the inevitable, he asked a final question, "So when are you planning on doing this interview? We are supposed to go home tomorrow."

"I will text Bennett that if he can arrange the interview for tomorrow, I will do it in person. Otherwise, it will have to be done over Zoom. If he can arrange it, you could take the girls to that movie Lizzy and Lola talked about tomorrow at the Rialto. It should not take too long, maybe a couple of hours. You like to get on the road early, but in the worst-case scenario, we could be headed home by three. If we have to stop and spend the night on the way home, so be it."

Giving her a quick kiss and nodding his agreement, Greer said, "Okay, sounds like a plan. Text pretty boy and see what he says." Then, releasing Taylor, he unbuckled and reached for the door, saying, "Let's go in before Edna comes out to see if we are making out in the car."

"As if," replied Taylor. "We are going to do that in her frilly floral guest room in one of her tiny twin beds!"

"Well, in that case, Mrs. Stone, get a move on. Floral decor never sounded so sexy."

Once inside, Greer took a quick shower while Taylor texted Bennett and asked if he could arrange the interview for the next morning by eleven while the girls were at the movie. He immediately texted back he could and thanked her profusely.

Even though Bennett had no idea how Taylor had persuaded Greer to let her do the interview, he was very grateful she had. He immediately texted Jameson, who said the reporter would be at the house by eleven the next day. Everything was coming together so quickly. Almost as quickly as it had all fallen apart ten years before.

Part Two - How It Fell Apart

Carrington House
Searcy, Arkansas
November 24, 2023

The following day, all three girls were excited when they found out that Rosie was staying for the day. That meant she would get to go to the movies with them. No one mentioned to the girls that a reporter was expected. Instead, Poppy, Greer, Ben, and Ella loaded up in two cars and took the girls for breakfast before the movie. After breakfast, Ben and Greer took the girls to the Rialto to see the movie. After the show, they walked over to the Soda Jerk and got them ice cream.

While they did that, Poppy took Ella on a whirlwind tour of the town. Bennett had sworn her to secrecy before telling her about the baby. The thought of her son and his family staying in California terrified her. It was going to be really hard to Mimi from a thousand miles away. Family was the most important thing. She was making it her mission to get them back to Arkansas as soon as possible. She hoped that by showing Ella what Searcy had to offer with adorable shops like doorframes, The Boutique, Sassy Stitch, Stotts, Dale's, Bliss, and more, Poppy might help her fall in love with the city. She even bought her a cute tea towel with "Searcy Has My Heart" on it as a gift. She was unashamedly selling Searcy because she truly believed that the old Searcy motto was right. It truly was where thousands live but millions wished they could.

At the Carrington house, Bennett and Taylor waited for the reporter to show up. At first, being in their old home felt weird with just the two of them. They had not been there alone since the night before Bennett resigned years earlier. Neither knew exactly what to say. They stuck to superficial conversation, but the awkwardness was there.

Just before eleven, Harvey Cox, a freelance reporter from Little Rock known for his work with national online political magazines, local news, and lifestyle publications, arrived. Tall and lanky, he was in mid-forties with shaggy dark hair and black glasses. He brought scones from Wild Sweet William's to help break the ice. He had heard about the amazing bakery and gotten into town early to try it.

After introductions, Harvey offered them a scone. Bennett took one, but Taylor was too nervous to eat. Bennett offered them something to drink. Both asked for water. After providing that, Bennett ushered them into his office and then excused himself so they could get down to business.

Harvey Cox's first impression of Taylor was one of surprise at how young and beautiful she still looked ten years after the last publicity photo of her had been published. If anything, she was even more stunning than she was then. A new marriage and motherhood agreed with her.

Opening his laptop, Harvey looked at Taylor and said, "I have been doing a lot of research, and I have a strong understanding of you and Bennett's background until he announced he was resigning as senator. What I, and frankly no one else, seem to know is what led up to that moment. What can you tell me about what caused you two to break up and what led to the end of Carrington's political career?

Chewing nervously on her bottom lip, Taylor took a deep breath and let it out. She silently prayed that she was making the right decision in publicly sharing the whole sordid story. Wishing she'd asked for liquid courage, she took a deep breath and said, "Well, I guess we should start at the beginning of the end."

Searcy Country Club
Searcy, Arkansas
March 2012

Pulling her white Mercedes into the Searcy Country Club, Taylor Carrington looked down at the buzzing cell phone in the console and ignored it. She could not stem the flare of irritation that rippled through her as she saw Bennett's name flash on the screen. How many calls did this make? Three? Four? She made no move to answer the phone this time, any more than she had last night or earlier this morning. Instead, she just let it go directly to voicemail.

Bennett would be quite ticked off at her by now. He had left several messages, but she had yet to listen to any of them. It was childish and petty not to answer. Bennett was being Bennett, the responsible, good husband he was. But, as rude as it was, Taylor was just not up to another surface conversation between two polite people talking about absolutely nothing.

In a classic Bennett move, he had Joules start calling her when she did not answer. She has ignored those calls and texts as well, except for letting Joules know she was okay and asking that they all stop texting her. She will be in touch soon.

It was not that Taylor had not expected the calls. She had. As had been his habit since he had brought her back from Scotland as a lost twenty-two-year-old over a decade before, Bennett always checked on Taylor at least once every day, even before they married. After their wedding, he continued the tradition whenever they were apart overnight. A common occurrence once Bennett won his first US Senate seat almost ten years earlier. Since then, he spent nearly six months a year in Washington while Taylor often remained in Searcy.

In the early days, Taylor, who was still teaching then, had looked forward to those calls. Back then, she used the calls as a way to try and connect with Bennett. She had seen them as a bridge that would allow them to stay connected while apart. Somewhere along the way, that changed.

The calls now felt forced and scripted. Each call followed the same sequence. It would begin with Bennett apologizing for calling too late. Then he would explain that he only had a few moments to talk as he had a late meeting with one group or another. This would be followed by the perfunctory questions about her day. These end-of-day calls had become a boring dance that had lost its rhythm.

Some nights, Taylor fantasized about telling Bennett some wild tale to see if he was even listening. She never did for fear that no matter how she answered the question about her day, he would still say, "Great, I am glad you had a good day," before telling her he loved her and wishing her a good night. Instead, she played her part in this charade, and the calls continued in their expected fashion. He'd call, and she would tell him everything was fine, even when it was not. She never said that she was sad, lonely, or bored though she often was. She was unable to share almost anything with the one person whom she should have been able to share everything.

As the phone continued ringing, Taylor realized at that moment, being sad, lonely, and bored pretty much summed up life for the last several years. But as she always did when such emotions threatened to overtake her, Taylor quickly pushed them down. Now was not the time to start thinking about that. If she had learned anything over the last decade, it was that life keeps moving no matter what happens to you. You had to keep moving with it. So, she had become a master of hiding her true feelings. She put on a happy face each morning and forged ahead. What else could she do? She had done it with her family. She had done it with her babies, and she was doing it with her marriage. Right now, life was not about her.

Bennett had a campaign to win. He was counting on her to help him do that. She owed him so much. Maybe when the campaign was over, they would have the time to talk, really talk. To reconnect. To fix the unspoken, broken parts of their marriage. But not today. Today required her to play the part she had perfected over years as the caring, supportive wife of the junior senator from Arkansas.

With her emotions checked, Taylor took a final peek in the rear view mirror to ensure her makeup was flawless. Confident that she had effectively masked her internal turmoil, Taylor reached for the doorknob just as she heard the familiar ping on her phone alerting her she had a voicemail. Ignoring it, she threw her phone into her purse. What could missing one more call hurt? They would still be waiting on her when her afternoon event was over.

Slipping out of her car, Taylor made the short walk across the parking lot to the entrance to the local country club that she had been a member of her whole life. She had grown up within the walls of the stone and marble building. It never ceased to amaze her that such a beautiful club was located in her small Arkansas town. Many times over the last ten years, as the wife of Bennett Carrington, she had had the opportunity to attend events across Arkansas and other states. She had been in some of the swankiest, most exclusive, private clubs across the country. Yes, most were bigger, cost more, and had more amenities, but not one was more special to her. It was her personal history with the place that endeared it to her. Many of her cherished memories had taken place there.

It was the one place in the world she still felt close to her family. In the Founders' Bar, there were pictures featuring her father and brother. The numerous photos had been taken after each had won various tournaments over the years. Each summer, her father's golf shoes and bag were still placed on the first tee box on the first day of the club championship, along with the other past winners who were no longer living. Her brother Tatum achieved a similar level of success in tennis as their father had in golf. He had been ranked in the top five in high school and played tennis for the University of Arkansas. The end of the summer tennis tournament still carried his name as a lasting tribute to his contribution to the club's tennis program. Making a promise to swing by the bar later to see her families' photos, Taylor walked into the club feeling lighter and more hopeful than she had in weeks. All thoughts of Bennett and his annoying calls were forgotten.

The event that Taylor was attending today was very important to her. For the past seven years, Taylor has acted as the events chairperson for the Annual Art Preview

Luncheon. This year, she had dropped out of it, per doctor's orders. She had been told she had to reduce stress as she recuperated from a procedure she had almost six months earlier. Even though she was not organizing the event, Taylor was excited to attend and lend her support. The luncheon was a preliminary event to raise interest in the annual Hospital Gala Extravaganza held at the club in a little over a week's time. The Ladies Auxiliary Corp of Searcy sponsored both events to raise funds for the White County Hospital and the free after-hours clinic the group supported financially. Walking in, Taylor could feel the buzz of nervous energy flowing around her. She knew too well how stressful these events could be and was grateful to attend as a guest. For the first time in years, she was looking forward to it.

Most years, artists from across the state were invited to showcase their work, with a portion of the proceeds from the sale going to the hospital memorial fund. This year, only one artist, Poppy Thompson, was featured. Poppy was a White County native but now lived in New York City.

Taylor's and Poppy's paths crossed many years ago as Poppy's grandmother had been Mr. Carrington's maid. Family dinners at their home were common given that her father and Bennett's were law partners. Taylor had not seen her since she left for Scotland just before her last semester of college. Taylor remembered that Poppy and her grandmother had lived in the apartment over the Carrington's garage. She never knew where the girl's parents were and why Poppy did not live with them. Taylor did not remember much about her other than she had not been very friendly. In fact, Poppy had been downright rude to Taylor on the few occasions they met. She was never sure what she had done to make the girl dislike her so much. But, honestly, it had never bothered her. Poppy was a few years younger, and the two had not run in the same circles.

Taylor wondered briefly how difficult it must have been for Poppy being surrounded by the luxury of the Carrington mansion but never really belonging. Taylor would like to think that back then, she and her friends were not bratty snobs who looked down on people who had less than they did, but she could not quite convince herself that was the case. A little nagging flame of guilt flared in her chest, but Taylor ignored it. Whatever had happened in the past, she hoped it stayed there. Taylor made a mental promise to be extra kind to the artist and make her feel welcomed and accepted by her hometown today as she should have been years ago.

With that thought in mind, Taylor walked into the club's large reception area and saw an impressive banner announcing an exhibit entitled *Growing Up New York*. Taylor felt excited about meeting the artist and seeing her work. From what Taylor had heard, it was causing a stir in the art world. All around her, Taylor could see beautiful ladies of various ages making final preparations for the luncheon.

Scanning the room, Taylor immediately noticed a group of older ladies huddled in one corner. Having chaired this event for years, Taylor knew something was off. In the middle of the group, holding court, was Edna Stone. She was surrounded by her entourage in an intense discussion. Taylor had never been more glad to not be in charge of something in her entire life.

Taylor was more than a little intimidated by Edna Stone. She had grown up hearing stories about her, specifically about Edna's daughter, Anita, and her own mother, Janice. They had been fierce rivals in high school. Both were smart, beautiful, accomplished young women who competed in everything. One year, one would be named class princess, and the next year, the other would. This back and forth fight to be the class queen bee created a lot of hurt and resentment over the years. As her mother told it, Janice was expected to be the homecoming queen her senior year. However, a week before the team voted, the Stone's gave a large endowment for new uniforms and a new scoreboard to the football team. Anita was named Homecoming Queen and later Prom Queen. Taylor's mother never got over losing out. She accused the Stone family of buying the two events. Lots of angry words were spoken. Anita married and moved away, but Edna remained in town. Taylor's mom had to socialize with her at everything. It was always awkward, and she imparted those feelings to Taylor. Thinking about the group, Taylor knew that whatever was wrong, it was not good.

While the little drama with Edna was playing out across the room, Taylor scanned the room and realized that she knew almost everyone there. Several friends and acquaintances such as her good friends Marla Henard, Tonya Stringer, and Jackie Allison, and many others who could always be counted on to help with community fundraisers, hugged her and offered support and good wishes on Bennett being named a possible vice-presidential candidate in the upcoming election. After all, it had been a foregone conclusion that it was his legacy to be the next president from Arkansas. He'd been groomed for the role his whole life.

While nothing was set in stone, the media had been offering his name as a strong contender for several weeks. The truth was, Bennett was being vetted for the position. Of course, Taylor did not acknowledge that. She simply thanked everyone for their support and kind words. She made small talk by asking about their families and catching up with old friends she had not seen in ages.

In just a matter of a few minutes, the room filled to overflowing. Taylor was pleased to see that the event was shaping up to be a success. Glancing around the ever-growing crowd, Taylor continued to wave and smile to friends and acquaintances. But it was Poppy, the artist, she did not see anywhere. This was surprising to Taylor. She personally knew one of Edna Stone's hard and fast rules regarding this event was that exhibiting artists had to attend the luncheon. Edna believed more art would sell if the artists were there to make the buyer feel good about the purchase. So, where was she? Taylor wondered if the missing artist was the reason for the tension coming from Edna and her crew. Looking at her watch, Taylor realized the event was about ten minutes behind schedule. Edna Stone was a stickler for following a schedule. If an event was supposed to begin at 11:30, by God, it would start at 11:30 on the nose. Taylor knew that if the luncheon was starting late, it was not good. Once again, she was thrilled she was just a guest and not in charge. Heaven help Johnna Wright, this year's chairwoman.

As the minutes ticked by, Taylor could not help but think more about Poppy. She wondered about the artist's work. She did not know much about it. Since she was not involved in this year's committee meetings, she only knew that Poppy was selected because Edna Stone had pushed for her. Evidently, Edna had a nephew who had an excellent eye for art, and he believed that Poppy was the next big thing in the art world. It did not hurt that the event's committee hoped that having a homegrown artist would increase interest in the event across the state, translating into more dollars for the hospital. Taylor could not argue with that logic. From the looks of the crowd, Taylor supposed the committee had been correct.

Determined to be one of the first to welcome Poppy back to Searcy, Taylor continued to scan the crowd for any sight of her. A waiter had just handed Taylor a glass of chardonnay when Johnna Wright broke free of the group of ladies whom Taylor had been watching and made a beeline for the podium at the front of the room.

Introducing herself as this year's chairperson, Johnna said, "I want to thank everyone for coming today. I am sorry to inform you that Ms. Poppy Thompson, our featured artist this year, has not yet arrived. As you can see, we are already about fifteen minutes late starting. Rather than continuing to wait for and delay the luncheon further, we have decided to proceed with the unveiling without her. I am sure she will join us as soon as she can. Please feel free to go ahead and peruse the art at your leisure. Her original pieces are on loan to us today from the Emerson Children's Museum. You may purchase signed prints of each and every one. Also, Mrs. Thompson has offered new original pieces for auction. Please make sure to look at those. We will be auctioning them off at the Gala. The luncheon will begin once she arrives."

So that was what the big pow-wow with the power queens had been about. Taking a healthy sip of her Chardonnay, Taylor breathed a sigh of relief that this was someone else's problem and felt a genuine smile graze her face. A simple, stress-free afternoon enjoying a nice lunch, some good art, and no drama sounded wonderful. She did feel some sympathy for poor Johnna, however. Edna was not an easy person to deal with when she was happy. Angered and irritated, she was downright awful.

Brushing off the thought, Taylor joined the crowd, moving into the room adjacent to the main hall, where the art was displayed. As she did so, she picked up a pamphlet about the exhibition and quickly scanned the information about the artist and art. The art had been placed on easels all around the large banquet hall. In total, there were thirty pieces. The collection, like the event, was entitled *Growing Up New York*. Each photo and painting showed a different landmark around New York City. Somewhere in each one, a small boy was featured. To avoid the crowd's crush, Taylor decided to view the exhibit in reverse. She moved to the end of the still vacant room and began her viewing.

Taylor had read on the event brochure that the exhibit featured photos and paintings of the artist's son, capturing the child as he grew from newborn until preadolescence. Walking backward through time with the photos, Taylor was enthralled. Some photos were black and white, and others were in color. It was interesting to compare the photographs to their corresponding paintings.

All the paintings were watercolors painted with vibrant jewel tones, allowing one to fully experience each scene, even the black and white photos. One could almost hear the city sounds in the background as the elements included were so vivid and detailed. The boy's flaming red hair was as much a statement in each painting as the landmarks in the background. Taylor had no idea how old the child was now, as the pictures had no dates posted. But, given the last time she had seen Poppy was just over twelve years ago, the first painting she viewed and the latest in the collection must have been pretty recent.

As she moved through the room, watching the child age backward, Taylor became absolutely captivated. With each new painting, she felt more and more connected to the work on a deep emotional level. She assumed it was because of her deep-seated desire to become a mother and her continued lack of success in that department.

Looking at the child, she could not help thinking that he looked exactly how she had always pictured her son looking, if she and Bennett had ever been fortunate enough to have a son minus the carrot-red hair. For some reason, that thought made Taylor chuckle to herself. Wandering around looking at the exhibit, Taylor wondered briefly who the boy's father was and why he was not featured in any of the pictures. She surmised that he probably was the one taking the touching photos. Taylor made a mental note to ask about the boy's father later.

She realized that she was enjoying herself for the first time in a really long time. She was unsure if it was the art, the wine, or the lack of responsibility, but she felt relaxed and happy. This foreign feeling was one she had not felt in a very long time. The light feeling lasted right up until the moment she made her way back to the first painting in the collection. That was when it all started to go wrong.

The crowd had moved on to the other paintings, leaving Taylor plenty of room to closely view the first painting in the exhibit. Taylor's gaze flicked back and forth from the photo and its corresponding colorful sister painting. Both showed Poppy holding her newborn son mere seconds after his birth. In the photo, the white, cheesy vernix covered the baby's face, and he was screaming with all of his might. His round little face was drawn, his eyes tightly cinched, and his mouth wide open with his tongue thrust out. Angry screams emoted from the silent photo. Inside her head, Taylor could hear the baby's piercing cries, furious at being removed from his mother's loving, warm womb seconds earlier. The anger and injustice of his situation played entirely across his face. And Poppy. Poppy was breathtaking. Clad in a blue and white hospital gown, clutching her son with a death grip, Poppy embodied every new mother, holding her child for the first time. Tears streamed down her face as her bright red hair wildly stuck out in every direction. In the painting, as with the photo, one could hear the child's screams coming through the silent canvas. Taylor was so moved by the emotion depicted that she could not stop herself from mourning her lost moments. She had been denied the joy of ever holding her own child. The photo struck a chord in Taylor's chest that almost caused her to unleash a sob.

She had spent most of the last eight years trying desperately to have a baby. She could conceive, but getting past eleven weeks gestation has so far been impossible. Having a baby to hold in her arms was her greatest desire. Five pregnancies and five miscarriages had left her with empty arms and a broken heart.

She had been doing everything she could to heal her body and get it ready to be able to carry a child to term since her last miscarriage. Six months ago, she had undergone an experimental procedure that the doctors felt would significantly increase her chances of carrying to term.

Last month, she and Bennett traveled to New York for her final appointment. The doctor had given her a clean bill of health and had been so encouraged by how well she had healed that she was prescribed another round of fertility drugs and encouraged to try again.

That was the day the Anderson campaign reached out and began vetting Bennett for the vice-presidential spot. Since then, they had had no time alone to have dinner, much less try for a baby. Nevertheless, Taylor continued to take the fertility drugs faithfully while holding on to one last hope of a baby.

Perhaps it was just the hormones raging through her, but Taylor barely managed to blink back tears and keep a firm grip on her emotions as a wave of grief and hopelessness threatened to carry her away. All of the happy, positive emotions from earlier in the day were washed away. In their place was a depressed heaviness that filled her heart. She could barely breathe and instantly knew she was just moments from breaking down.

Standing in the middle of the room, surrounded by women happily chatting about babies and children, was not the best place for her. She needed some fresh air to clear her mind. She needed an escape, and she needed it now.

In pure Taylor fashion, she swallowed past the lump in her throat and forged ahead. With only one thought in mind, she deliberately and methodically began making her way toward the door of the exhibit room. She had to get out of there immediately, or the carefully constructed public life she had crafted for herself was in danger of being destroyed.

Chapter 2

Office in Carrington House
Searcy, Arkansas
November 24, 2023

Harvey Cox took Taylor's hand and softly said, "I am so sorry for your losses. I had no idea how much you two were going through. On the outside, you looked like the perfect couple."

"Yes, we did, but as you know, looks can be deceiving," replied Taylor.

Harvey nodded and said, "You are right. From what you have told me so far, it sounds like seeing the paintings of the child affected you."

"Yes, at that point in my life, I had lost hope of ever being a mom. It was what I wanted most in the world, and yet it was the one thing I could not seem to make happen no matter how hard I tried," replied Taylor.

"That must have been hard, especially once you realized your husband had a child with another woman. To be clear, at this point in your story, you had no idea that Bennett or Poppy had ever had a relationship, much less a child?" asked Harvey.

Nodding, Taylor quietly replied, "Yes, it sounds ridiculous now saying out loud, but I had no idea. I realized I should have. We just never talked about his past. You have to remember that when Bennett and I got together, I was knee-deep in grief. I was doing all I could to get out of bed every day. Delving into Bennett's past love life was not high on my to-do list," replied Taylor.

"That makes sense," replied Harvey. "Tell me exactly when you realized they had been a couple and had a child and how that affected you."

Clearing her throat, Taylor said, "Truthfully, I did not handle it so well. I don't look back on those days as my finest moments."

"Take me back to that day and help me understand what happened."

"Well. Okay…"

Searcy Country Club
Searcy, Arkansas
March 2012

Taylor's heels clicked across the wooden floor of the country club in a rapid staccato rhythm. She was just about to make her escape when Edna Stone intercepted her. Sporting a look of significant irritation, Edna was accompanied by several other ladies looking similarly distressed.

"Taylor, could we borrow you for a moment, dear? We seem to have a problem you could help us with. We've seemed to have lost our artist," said Edna graciously. The words had been phrased as a polite request, but Taylor knew it was a demand. One that Taylor had no intention of honoring. Holding on by a thread, she blinked several times, looking from Edna to the other ladies, and answered honestly, "I am sorry. I don't know how I can help you. I have no idea where Mrs. Thompson might be, and I was just on my way to …" said Taylor as she turned to escape out the pool door. But, Edna was too quick for her.

Without allowing Taylor to complete her statement, Edna took Taylor by the arm and began steering her toward the small reading room at the other end of the room.

Taylor dragged a ragged breath into her lungs and prayed that whatever Edna was about to ask would not take long. In fact, Taylor planned to break free of Edna as quickly as possible. If not for her determination not to lose it right then in front of the entire room, Taylor would have refused the demand. But, saying no to Edna Stone in such a public place was not an option, so Taylor allowed herself to be pulled along. She could do this. She had faced worse things than Edna Stone. She would find a way to quietly leave without causing a stir.

By the time the entourage reached the library room, Taylor's long legs had allowed her to reach the door first. Turning back to the group, she opened the door and gestured for everyone to enter. As she did so, Taylor looked directly at Edna and said, "Look, I understand you are concerned because you seem to have lost your artist, but I have no idea how I can …" but whatever Taylor was going to say next disappeared. She stopped suddenly mid-sentence as her gaze drifted across the room and landed on a couple draped across a table. The sight that greeted her left her stunned and speechless.

On an antique table was a man and woman in a very compromising position. The man's back was to them, but the woman was lying on her back with her long red hair spread out over the table. Her floral dress was unbuttoned. Taylor could see the top of the woman's milky white breasts from the door. A man's head was buried in the woman's chest and could not be seen.

However, Taylor could plainly see the woman's face. Instantly, she recognized Poppy Thompson from the photos earlier. Taylor was captivated by the haze of lust and desire playing across the artist's face. The whole scene was something out of a Renaissance painting.

For a second, no one said a word. Then, Edna screeched, "Oh! My! Lord! Poppy? Is that you?"

At that point, the lady on the table turned her head with a jerk towards the door and tried to cover herself.

Taylor felt a wave of sympathy for the younger woman for having been caught in such an embarrassing position. Her only thought was to get herself and, hopefully, the other ladies, out of the room as quickly as possible. She had enough of her own issues to deal with, and obviously, so did Poppy and her companion. Taylor turned to the women surrounding her and said, "I think that Poppy and her ... friend need a moment." Gesturing to the couple, Taylor said, "Why don't we all give them a few mmm......" Taylor had planned on saying a few minutes but the words quickly died on her lips. Suddenly, everything in Taylor's world clicked into place for a split second. Then, her whole world went flying out of control as a jolt of realization hit Taylor like a punch to the throat. Her gaze stalled on the man's back and, specifically, on his suit. It was dark gray with a light check. Taylor recognized it instantly.

It was the same one she had custom-made for Bennett last month. When he had gotten caught up in something at work and had been several hours late meeting her, she had ended up shopping all day to fill the empty hours that he had promised they would spend together. She had gotten the all-clear from her doctor to start trying again for a baby that day in New York. The plan had been to spend the day making babies. Instead, she had spent it ordering him a custom-made suit that he would wear for his vice-presidential announcement. It was a gift from her to show that she always had his back and was in his corner as he had always been in hers. At that exact moment, Taylor recognized the suit and realized it was her husband, currently enraptured in Edna's missing artist's arms.

"Bennett!?!" Taylor cried out her husband's name in shock and horror.

Suddenly, Bennett Carrington, seemingly unaware of the ladies' presence before, whipped his head around towards the door. He had a horrified look on his face as he made eye contact with his wife and cried, "Taylor?"

The look of fear, shame, and guilt that flashed in her husband's eyes as his gaze met hers was permanently seared into Taylor's brain. If she lived to be a hundred, she would never forget it. A combination of guilt and shame that one only encounters when forced to accept you are not the person you thought you were, a true man-in-the-mirror moment. A moment most men avoid their whole life if possible. Taylor saw it all.

But that was not all Taylor saw. She saw something much more hurtful. She saw the child's eyes. The eyes that she had spent the better part of the last hour watching grow up. Somehow, she knew that boy was Bennett's son.

On the table, the woman, who had been futilely struggling to cover herself, finally pushed hard against Bennett's chest in a scramble to get off the table. In the commotion, Bennett lost his balance and caused both of them to fall to the floor in a sea of red hair.

Taylor stood with her mouth hanging open as if in a trance. For once, Edna Stone proved as steady as her name suggested as she calmly began ushering everyone out of the room, saying, "Lynne, Michelle, Jacquelyne, Marcia, I think we need to give them a few minutes."

Taking Taylor's arm and guiding her out of the room, Edna shut the door behind her and said, "Everyone follow me. Now!"

This time, Edna made no effort to conceal her demand as a polite request. Instantly, all of the ladies obediently followed her to the nearest exit, everyone but Taylor.

She did not even consider following. Instead, she jerked her arm free and, with her head high, looked Edna in the eye and said, "If you will excuse me, I am leaving now." Walking way more calmly than she actually felt, Taylor crossed the room and went right out the club's front door. The second her feet hit the parking lot pavement; she took off running as fast as her heels would allow.

If anyone called after her or tried to stop her, she never heard them. Her entire focus was on getting out of there and away from Bennett, away from paintings of a boy with his eyes, and away from Poppy and all of that red hair as quickly as possible. One hateful thought kept racing through her mind as she ran. Bennett had a son, and it wasn't hers.

Chapter 3

**Highways Between Searcy, Arkansas and Gulf Shores, Alabama
March 2012**

Once she made her escape, Taylor didn't slow down. She walked out of the club, jumped in her car and drove. Almost immediately, her phone began ringing. Bennett's name flashed on the screen. Unwilling and unable to deal with him, Taylor turned off the phone and floored it. She knew she couldn't go home. The house she had lived in with Bennett for the last eleven years was his family estate, the home he had first shared with Poppy Thompson long before he shared it with her. Was the child conceived there? The child was at least eleven, if not older. The thought was so disconcerting that she forced it out of her mind. It was just too much for her to handle at that moment. Instead, she drove with no end destination in mind other than to get as far away from Bennett as possible.

Truthfully, she had no business driving, but she could not think of any place she wanted to go except as far away from Searcy as she could get. After two hours of off-and-on sobbing, Taylor was emotionally drained. Without her even realizing it, she found herself crossing the Mississippi River Bridge into Memphis. She had been driving for over two hours and was running low on gas. Wiping the tears off, she realized it was time to decide where to go from here. Groaning, she realized she meant that both figuratively and metaphorically. Finding a quick mart a mile past the bridge, she pulled in.

After filling her tank, Taylor checked her phone. Bennett had called repeatedly, leaving several voice messages and text messages. She skipped right over those.

Joules had also called multiple times. Taylor listened to Joules' messages. Joules was the closest thing to a sister and real family Taylor had left. The two had been friends since the third grade. Later, they were roommates and sorority sisters at the University of Arkansas. They supported each other in good times and bad. Taylor had been there for Joules when her parents had divorced her senior year of high school, and Joules had been the one to help Taylor through her miscarriages.

Joules had been Taylor's maid of honor and had been an integral part of both of Bennett's campaigns.

A political science major in college, Joules worked hard to be the change she wanted to see in the world. Joules had graduated at the top of her class at Fayetteville and the Clinton School of Public Service. After graduation, she became a significant player in the political fishbowl of Little Rock, not as a politician herself, but as an influential and respected campaign manager. She had directed Bennett's two campaigns for the US Senate and was now his chief of staff.

Taylor was sure that by now, Joules would be in complete damage control, killing herself to figure out how to undo the damage Bennett had done. She also knew that even though she would be neck deep in spin mode, Joules's main concern would be her. So, Taylor picked up her phone and called Joules back.

Joules answered on the first ring. "Thank God. Where are you? I have been calling you non-stop."

Fresh tears filled Taylor's eyes the second she heard Joules' voice. Until this moment, she had been in this alone. Now she had someone to help her through it. Swallowing back a sob, she said, "I see you have heard about Bennett's little escapade at the club."

"Yeah," her friend huffed angrily. "If I weren't working my damndest to save his sorry ass, I would kill him with my bare hands!"

At that, Taylor snorted at the image of her tiny friend, who was not five feet soaking wet, taking down six-foot muscleman Bennett. Then, the laugh turned into a sob that Taylor could not stifle.

Anger turned to complete empathy as Joules said, "Oh, TJ, I am so sorry. Tell me where you are, and I'll have someone come and get you."

TJ stood for Taylor Jane. It was the nickname Taylor's brother Tatum had given Taylor when they were children. It was what Joules always called her.

Doing all she could to keep it together, Taylor croaked, "I know you would, but I am okay."

She was trying so hard to be strong, but she sounded fragile, even to her own ears. It was past time she took control of her life and stopped depending on others to the degree she had in the past.

"I will get through this. I knew we needed a change, but I didn't think it would be so public and involve so many other people. I mean Poppy Thompson, for heaven's sake. Who would have thought it?"

"Yeah, I know. I was shocked, too," Joules replied honestly.

"Did you remember her? I worried I had not been kind enough to her in the past. At least, I did, right up until I found her screwing my husband in the middle of the country club. Now, not so much. Judging by her son's age, they must have been at it for years," Taylor said.

After a pregnant pause, Joules said, "Yeah, I remember her. She is closer to my little brother's age. He just turned twenty-eight, so she's a few years younger than us."

Trying to steer the subject back to steady ground, Joules said, "Now, listen, I know you are upset, and your pride is hurt. But we need to get out in front of this thing. Where are you? I have a team ready to come and get you."

Taylor knew her friend was just doing her job. But, right now, she wanted her friend's comfort and empathy, not rationalism and handling. "More than my pride has been hurt!" Taylor snapped back. "How can you say that to me? The whole town just saw him with his pants down with that..that...whore."

Joules had never heard Taylor use such vulgar language. To her knowledge, Taylor did not even use swear words. Gasping at her friend's use of the slur, Joules said, "Okay, slow down and take a deep breath. I know you are hurting, but that is a bit rough. Maybe you don't have all the facts? From what I heard, it never got that far."

"Have all the facts? Really? As far as how far it got, I can assure you that had we walked in five minutes later, it would have been much worse." Taylor's voice rose to a piercing level. "And why are you defending her?" Of all the people in the world, Taylor needed Joules to take her side. Anything else would be a total betrayal of their friendship, but this was the day for flagrant betrayals.

"I'm not defending her. Everyone needs to calm down before anything else happens to make this situation worse."

"Calm down! Calm down?" Taylor was basically yelling. "Why don't you tell Bennett and that woman to calm down? They are the problem, not me!"

"I agree. And I have," replied Joules in a soft voice. "What do you think I have been doing for the last two hours? Damage control. Now listen, I think we have contained the story here. Edna Stone and her crew are sworn to secrecy. They want the art gala to be a success and are willing to help squash this situation to make that happen. I need you to tell me where you are and let me have someone come and get you."

The part of Taylor's rational and reasonable brain knew that Joules was right. But something monumental had shifted inside her today.

Her foundation had been rocked once again, much like it had been eleven years ago. Back then, she had lacked the courage and strength to stand on her own two feet and had allowed others to think for her. Not today. Even if it was the wrong decision, Taylor was determined to face this on her terms. Having made up her mind, Taylor shook her head and said, "Well, no, I don't think that is going to work for me. I need time to process this myself."

"What are you even talking about?" demanded Joules, losing patience. "Look, I know you are hurting. Let's get you home where I can help you."

"You want to help me?" Taylor snapped, "Find me a quiet place to hang low for a few days. I can be in Gulf Shores by midnight. Get me a place to stay at the beach. That would really help me."

Taylor had no idea she wanted to go to the beach until the words left her mouth. But once she had uttered them, she knew she was onto something. A few days of solitude, just her, the sand, the waves, and the sun, were exactly what she needed. It is time for her to think and decide about her future without someone trying to do the thinking for her.

"The beach? Gulf Shores? What are you even talking about? Have you lost your mind? You can't just disappear off to a beach? Bennett and I need you here. Do you hear me, TJ?" barked Joules.

Betrayal could go two ways, thought Taylor. Yes, it would be easier for Bennett and Joules if she ran home with her tail between her legs, let them figure out her life, and gave her the words to make it all okay for the public. But, after today, that ship had sailed. Without any real plan, Taylor said, "I can go to the beach, and I am. Figure it out, Joules. A safe place for me to hide out for a few days. That is all I am asking for. After today, I think Bennett at least owes me that much. Call me when you have it all worked out and not before."

With that, Taylor hit the end button, effectively hanging up on her friend, who was still demanding that Taylor come home on the other end. Turning her phone back off and tossing it in her purse, Taylor pulled out of the quick mart and headed for the beach. As she drove, Taylor cranked up her radio and drove. Every time the images from earlier today tried to overtake her mind, she forced them out by singing louder with the songs on the radio.

Taylor made it to Mobile as the sun was setting. Needing some water, she pulled into a fast food restaurant. Before heading back onto the interstate, she turned on her phone and was pleased to see a long text from Joules outlining the details of a private beach house she had secured and the directions to it.

Taylor was not surprised that Joules had done what she had asked in such a short amount of time. Fixing things was Joules' specialty. A force of nature, she had a knack for making the impossible possible.

As she was plugging in the address for the beach house in her phone, Taylor's phone rang. She picked up the first ring and heard Joules say, "Thank God. I have been so worried. Stop turning your phone off!"

"Stop trying to make me come home!" Taylor responded hotly.

"I have," Joules shot back, "You have the beach house you wanted. I am doing everything I can to help you, TJ. Work with me here. You can't keep disappearing and not staying in contact by phone."

"Fine, I will leave my phone on if you promise to make Bennett stop calling me. I need some time," said Taylor.

"Done," retorted Joules. "But TJ, you are going to have to talk to him eventually. I know he did a stupid thing, but you two need to talk. There is a lot you don't know yet, and it is not my place to tell you. I am not defending him, but he is going wild with worry. I know this sounds ridiculous, given the day's events, but he does love you in his own way. It may not be how you wanted or needed it, but he does love you. He has been out of his mind since you took off."

"Yeah, well, seeing my husband devouring another woman on top of a table in the middle of the country club is not my definition of love." Taylor could feel herself getting angry and upset all over again. Any sense of calm she had garnered on the drive vanished in a haze of hurt and humiliation. She didn't want to argue with Joules. She needed her too much as a friend to risk a huge fight. And, if Joules started defending Bennett, Taylor would totally lose it.

Trying to end the call on a positive note, Taylor said, "Look, I am okay. I am headed to the beach house. Is there anything I have to know tonight? If not, I will check in with you tomorrow. I love you, but I have got to get off here. I can't talk about this anymore right now."

"Just that the house you are staying at is Edna Stone's. Her nephew lives nearby, and his number is in the kitchen if you need anything."

"Edna Stone? Really? Will that woman not get out of my business? She is everywhere I turn today," Taylor snapped.

"Well, you need to be grateful to Edna. She has been a real help today. I don't know what we would have done without her. That woman makes me look like a teddy bear," replied Joules.

Mentally and emotionally exhausted by the day, Taylor did not have it in her to listen to Joules sing Edna Stone's praises. So she said, "Look, I have got to go. I will call you tomorrow. And Joules..."

"Yes?" Joules answered.

"Thanks for everything you did today. I know I don't sound like I mean that, but I do. It's just been a lot, and I need some time."

"I know. No matter what, you can always count on me," Joules responded. For the first time all day, Joules sounded like the friend she needed instead of the political handler Taylor was positive Joules had been most of the day.

Taylor knew she had to end the call quickly, so she said, "I love you. Talk tomorrow."

It took Taylor another two hours of driving to get to the beach house. Once she reached Gulf Shores, she rationally surmised that it would be best to stop at an all-night drug store and purchase some basic toiletries.

Planning only to get the essentials, she was quickly surprised by the store's massive amount of merchandise. Everything from groceries to wine, pajamas, and various articles of clothing. Obviously, she was not the first person to show up at the beach at midnight with nothing but the clothes on their back. Her list of needed items quickly grew from essentials to clothes, flip-flops, and a swimsuit. As she was heading for the checkout, she added two bottles of the best Chardonnay the store had to offer, screw top and all. After spending a small fortune at the all-night pharmacy, Taylor stuffed her purchases into her front seat and drove the remaining miles to her beach house.

She had to turn off the main road for the last half mile, which was super dark. Taylor worried that she might have a hard time finding the house in the dark. But she needn't have. The property had motion lights that activated as she pulled into the drive. The house lit up like a Christmas tree as she approached. She was relieved at not having to get out in a dark, strange place. She was also pleasantly pleased with the beautiful wooden cottage.

The code that Joules had sent worked on the first try. Stepping inside, she realized that the house was smaller than expected. Given that Edna Stone owned it, Taylor was half expecting an overdone mansion similar to what Edna lived in Searcy. This was a pleasant surprise. Making a quick trip through the small cottage, she saw it only had two bedrooms. Cozy and well decorated in hues of turquoise and white, a nautical theme filled the space.

Exhausted after spending hours driving and dealing with the train wreck that had become her life, Taylor searched for the bags with the wine. Having located them, Taylor twisted off the top of one of the bottles of wine and drank heartedly from the bottle. Several times. Deciding she had enough alcohol to be able to sleep soundly in a strange place, she went into the master bedroom where she stripped off the beige sheath she had been wearing all day. Letting it fall on the floor, she crawled into bed in her underwear. She contemplated washing her face and brushing her teeth before bed. Both seemed way more trouble than they were worth. Deciding she might need at least one last swig of wine before bed, Taylor put the bottle to her lips and gulped. Then, she put the top back on the bottle, set it on the nightstand and let sleep claim her.

Chapter 4

Carrington Office
Searcy, Arkansas
November 24, 2023

"Wow! You literally caught them red-handed in the club in front of half of Searcy? Man, I am impressed. Joules must be worth her weight in gold to have kept the story quiet so long. I know you said Edna killed it, but Joules has kept it dead all these years. That took some fancy footwork. I researched all of you before coming today. I did not find anything about that," said Harvey Cox, impressed at how well it was buried.

"I really didn't do any of that. I was too busy feeling sorry for myself and having a full-blown pity party to know or care what was happening," replied Taylor.

"Totally understandable after what you had been through. I am shocked you were able to drive to the beach all alone after that," said Harvey.

"I would have driven to the moon if it got me out of that town and away from all that had happened," said Taylor. "In some ways, it was the best thing that could have happened to me. It forced me to take a cold, hard look at my life and face some facts about myself. It also led me to Greer and gave me Rosie. My life would not be complete without them," said Taylor, smiling for the first time since the interview started.

"I am glad something positive came out of something so hurtful. I understand you spent over a week in Gulf Shores before returning to Searcy for the gala. Do I have that right?" asked Harvey.

"Yes, I spent the time soul searching. It is crazy to think it was only a little over a week. So much happened that week that ultimately changed my life forever," said Taylor.

Chewing on his pen, Harvey said, "Please tell me about that week and why it was so significant."

Stone Cottage
Gulf Shores, Alabama
March 2012

Taylor woke the next morning to waves crashing on the shore. For a moment, she just lay in the big fluffy bed, quietly listening to the sounds of the beach outside. Her first thought right before she opened her eyes was that the day before had just been a bad dream. But lying there, with her eyes almost swollen shut from crying the day before, she knew it was not.

Rolling over, she instantly reached for her cell phone. Checking it, she was surprised to see no new messages from Bennett. True to her word, Joules had corralled him. Of course, Taylor had no doubt that he was probably pretty busy dealing with the media circus that surely was swirling around him, not to mention dealing with a long-lost lover and a surprise son. Taylor tried and failed to keep the bitterness out of her heart as she thought of the boy. None of this was his fault, but this all burned on so many levels.

Joules had assured her that she had killed the story, but Taylor could not resist digging through the internet for any signs of life. Again, Taylor was shocked at how thoroughly Joules had once again pulled off a miracle.

The fact that their little debacle had taken place in a small town must have helped the situation. Small towns could be a hotbed of gossip, but they can also be a fortress of protection when one of their own was at risk. It appeared that Joules had been right. Edna had rallied her troops and was doing all they could to protect the POS, as Bennett's high school friends had dubbed him. It stood for Pride of Searcy, a nickname that Taylor had never liked until now. Thinking of Bennett as a POS in the more traditional sense was on point for how she felt about him today.

Even though she could not find anything online, Taylor knew she would feel better if she checked in with Joules. The phone rang five times with no answer. Taylor was about to hang up when she heard Joules answer it in a rush.

"Hello. TJ? Is everything okay?"

"Yeah, it's me. I just wanted to call and check in to see how bad it has gotten. I hope I didn't wake you." Taylor replied.

With a snort, Joules said, "You didn't wake me. I have been up since before six. I slept at the office. As you can imagine, things have been crazy here."

Joules was in total campaign manager mode now. She even sounded different than when she was being her best friend. This Joules was a no-nonsense, take-no-prisoner kind of person.

"Okay," Taylor demanded, "tell me the deal. I have already checked the internet and all the local stations. I can't find even a blip about yesterday. What is going on?"

Sounding exhausted but in control, Joules replied, "You're right. So far, it has been handled."

"How in the world did you manage that? I was expecting this awful mess to be on the front page and every news channel from here to Little Rock," replied Taylor.

"It's like I told you last night. Edna Stone killed it. I mean, she stomped it out. Yesterday, after everything happened, she summoned Bennett to her house for a big pow-wow. Evidently, Edna already met with all those old women who hang on her like curtains and ensured that no one leaked so much as a word. You know she rules them with an iron fist. All is quiet on this front. "

Giving a long sigh, Taylor said, "Well, thank you for all you have done and especially for getting Bennett to back off. I could not have handled dealing with him. So, tell me, where is my faithful, adoring husband, laying in the arms of his mistress, or is he out in the backyard playing catch with his new son?"

Joules did not immediately respond to Taylor's hateful questions. When she did, she quietly admonished, "TJ, don't do this. Don't let this turn you into someone you aren't. Don't let this warp your kind, gentle spirit. You have faced worse things than this. You will get through this."

Understanding her friend's anger and hurt, Joules continued, "I know you are hurt, but other people are hurting too. There is a lot going on here, more than I think you realize. You really need to talk to Bennett. He has agreed to give you a few days to clear your head and figure some things out. But the two of you will have to sit down and talk this out one way or another."

Huffing, Taylor snapped, "One way or another! What does that mean? Does that mean divorce? Does he want a divorce? Or worse, am I supposed to continue as his perfect little political wife and turn a blind eye as he continues his political career while still carrying on with his mistress and love child?"

The emotions and hurt kept rocketing to the surface, and Taylor seemed incapable of reigning herself in. She hardly recognized herself at that moment.

Once again, Joules tried to help Taylor calm down and see an irrational situation rationally. "Look, I am not the person you need to ask these questions. I think you need time to think and reflect. You are too close to the situation right now. You need a few days to sit with it, and then maybe you will be in a better head space to deal with this more reasonably and maturely. That is what the beach house is for."

Nodding, Taylor responded, "You are right. I know you are right. But, at the moment, I am having a tough time not nose-diving head-first into a pity party. Mature and reasonable or not."

"You've earned a massive pity party, so go ahead and have one. But don't drown in it. Sooner than later, you and Bennett will have to make some decisions. And, since we are on Bennett, there is something you should know. But first, promise me you aren't going to wig out on me. I need you to hear what I am telling you, so you will have several days to prepare yourself for it," Joules pleaded.

"Oh Lord, what is it? I can't take much more."

"You are not going to like this, but Bennett had to promise Edna that his little show at the club would not impact the gala."

"Wow, good for him!" Taylor snapped sarcastically. "What is he going to do to save the event? Buy all of the paintings? I mean, they are all of his child."

Then, holding back a sob, Taylor realized something that she had not before this moment. The missing father in all of the photos and paintings was Bennett. Intellectually, she realized it, but emotionally, she was processing what it all meant. Taylor quietly asked, "Oh my, do you think that is why she painted them? So he could know and share in the child's growing up? Or does he already have some other painting hidden away somewhere? Was he there the whole time? Is that why the father was never shown? Oh God, how long has this been going on? Were they both mocking me behind my back because I was just some stupid woman who blindly trusted her husband? They must think I'm the biggest fool ever." Taylor was full-out sobbing by the time she finished talking.

Joules immediately tried to comfort her friend, "No, stop that. It was never like that. I can't go into this with you. I have already told Bennett, and I am telling you. I am not getting into the middle of this any more than I already am. I will tell you this. It is not what you think. They have not been carrying on behind your back all of these years. Bennett did not even know he had a son until very recently. You know what a good and kind man he is. Bennett would never abandon someone he loved, especially not his child. If he could do that, you would have never married him, and I would have never worked so damn hard to get him elected or to keep him in office. That is all I am going to say on the subject."

"When you are ready to talk to Bennett, call him. He will tell you everything you need to know. Until then, what I want you to know is this. To kill the story, Bennett had to promise Edna Stone that you and he would both attend the gala as a couple."

Taylor flinched as if she had been slapped, "No! No! No! No way, I am not walking back into that club with him ever. I mean it, Joules. You need to make that clear."

Joules said, "Listen, you must calm down and think about this rationally. Edna is afraid the bad publicity from the story could reduce the amount of money the gala will raise. You know she will not let anything stand in the way of funds for that hospital. After the hospital gala, you two can quietly divorce."

"Divorce?" Taylor croaked. "Bennett told you he wants to divorce me? If so, that might be something he wants to discuss with me before he starts sharing it with Edna Stone!"

"That was a bad choice of words. I meant that you two need to get through the gala and decide what the future holds for both of you. I didn't mean to upset you even more," Joules began apologizing. "Oh, TJ, I am so sorry; I would never do anything to hurt you. You know that, right? Everything is just so crazy right now. I, I ..." Realizing she was unsure what to say next, Joules's words faltered.

Neither woman spoke for several seconds. Taylor had never heard Joules at a loss for words before. Well, good! Joules had just left her a little speechless, too. No decisions had been made yet. At least none she knew about.

The fact that Taylor herself had come to the conclusion that her marriage was over the day before seemed momentarily forgotten. It was one thing to be the person who wanted the divorce. It was something else to be the person being divorced.

Taylor wanted to be the one to walk away from Bennett. Not the other way around. It was probably silly and childish, but she didn't care. They would be getting a divorce when and if she said so. Not Bennett. He had lost that right yesterday in the middle of the Searcy Country Club. She prayed he had not discussed their marriage with Edna Stone. That would add insult to injury.

After several more minutes of awkward silence, Joules said, "TJ, say something. I am sorry. I am a complete jerk."

After a moment, Taylor said, "It's okay. I am not upset with you. But, it is all so overwhelming."

"I know it is. And, for what it is worth, I am doing all I can not to take Bennett out back and shoot him with my granddaddy's old hunting rifle. If I did not know him the way I do, I would have already done it. But there is more here that needs to be unpacked before shots start being fired."

Despite herself, Taylor half laughed, half sobbed. "Well, the thought of shooting Bennett does sound appealing, but you are right. Killing him is not the answer. At least not yet. I need time to think of a good alibi for both of us."

"So true," agreed Joules, "But seriously, now is the time to think about what you want and where you want your life to go from here. We both know neither you nor Bennett have been happy for a very long time. Maybe it is time to stop and do some hard soul-searching about your life. No matter what that is, I am here for you."

Before Taylor could respond, Joules added, "I have to go now. Another big pow-wow with the Anderson campaign is about to start."

"Anderson campaign? Does that mean Bennett is still planning on running? Is he crazy? This is all going to come out," said Taylor.

Not wanting to address her friend's questions and worried Taylor would ask her more questions she was not prepared to answer, Joules said, "Love you and talk soon." The line instantly went dead.

Taylor was stunned. How could her friend leave her hanging like that? Turning her phone on silent, Taylor threw herself back against her pillows and literally growled out loud.

Taylor had mixed emotions about the story not being released. It would give her a few days of peace. On the other hand, she knew she would worry every day until it was all out. And eventually, it would come out. At least they had some lead time to put a good spin on it. But no amount of spin was going to change the fact that Bennett cheated on her in public, and half the club saw it. Oh, Edna might be able to keep everyone from talking because of the gala. But, once they separated or divorced, Taylor was pretty sure every one of those old ladies would be talking.

At the moment, all she wanted to do was go back to bed and pull the covers over her head for at least two days. So, that was pretty much what happened.

She did, however, take a long hot shower first. It had been less than twenty-four hours since she had showered, but it felt like six days. Once clean, she pulled on one of her new pj sets and wandered into the kitchen for food. All she had was the leftover junk food from the late-night pharmacy run. Deciding she wasn't starving, she fixed herself a large drink and returned to bed.

She spent most of that day lying in bed, watching reruns of sappy romantic movies. She'd cried and laughed at the appropriate times even though her mind wasn't even on the movie. She was operating on autopilot. Her big effort of the day had just been breathing. Several times during the day, she would think about her life when a scene would spark some memory of her life with Bennett. Then she would truly lose her ability to breathe. Gasping for air and feeling overwhelmed, she would fight to calm herself down by telling herself everything would be okay. When those moments came, she would count to ten and focus solely on breathing. For the most part, it worked, and she survived the day. Though she tried to avoid it, she could not stop thinking about Bennett and the life they had built together over the last ten years. Had all of it been a sham? Had any of it really meant anything?

Taylor was as confused by her situation as she was overwhelmed by it. She had known her marriage had problems. No question. A wife in a great marriage doesn't avoid her husband's calls for days if everything is hunky dory. But, she honestly never saw either one cheating on the other. They had been friends since childhood.

She couldn't remember a time when Bennett hadn't been in her life. Her earliest memories included Bennett, Tatum and her. Remembering treasured moments left her weepy and sad, yet oddly comforted, as if Tatum was there with her, trying to help her through this. She had gone months without thinking of her brother, and today, he seemed to be a part of every memory her mind was determined for her to remember.

God, how she missed him. Her big brother, her protector. If he were here now, she had no doubt Bennett would be sporting a huge black eye and maybe a broken nose. Catching herself, she was shocked at how violent her thoughts had become so quickly. She avoided violence of any kind. It surprised her and showed her how hurt she really was that her mind went there so quickly.

Pushing all thoughts of black eyes and broken noses out of her mind, Taylor lay back on her pillows and let her mind wander back over the early years with Bennett and Tatum. More times than she cared to admit, it was actually Bennett who had come running to her rescue. Any time Taylor needed something done or fixed, Bennett was there for her. She had never questioned why until that moment. The three of them didn't hang out as much as the boys got older. Oh, Bennett was always still around, but he and Tatum were more in their own little worlds. They played sports and had girlfriends.

Taylor remembered them getting their first cars. To this day, this memory is still one of Taylor's favorites. She remembered watching Bennett and Tatum climbing into their shiny new Jeeps, laughing, and being excited. Tatum had been so alive. So full of joy. It was hard to believe it had been almost twenty years since that day. Oh how her life had changed since then.

Thinking about the Bennett of her childhood, compared to the Bennett she married, she realized the carefree, joyous boy in him had died right along with the death of his best friend. Or so she had thought at the time. Now, she wondered if something else might have so greatly affected him. Given his son's age, Bennett and Poppy must have been involved. Maybe it was because of her that Bennett was so sad and lost.

Certainly, for Taylor, the loss of so many people that she loved had cut her to the bone. Thinking about all she had lost, the tears began to flow freely again. As the day turned into night, Taylor realized that she had not made any big decisions about her life, but she had begun the process of taking her life apart one piece at a time. Hopefully, doing so would allow her to find a way to put it all back together again.

Taylor spent the rest of that day and the next holed up in the cottage. She had very little appetite, but given that she had already drunk her way through the two bottles of wine she bought, and two more she found in the wine cabinet beneath the wet bar, she decided she needed a little food with her wine, other than chips and chocolate. Still dressed in the pajamas from two days before, Taylor scavenged through the kitchen cabinets to find several menus for local restaurants that delivered. She ordered food at least once daily and forced herself to eat at least a few bites before diving head-first into yet another bottle of wine and a vat of self-pity.

Chapter 5

Stone Cottage
Gulf Shores, Alabama
March 2012

The morning of the third day, Taylor wandered onto the cottage deck. It was the first time she had been outside in days. She was still wearing the same, now smelly pjs from the first day. She had not bothered to shower since that first morning. She washed her face and brushed her teeth at least once daily. That counted as her big move. She spied a set of beach chairs, coupled with an umbrella, only a few feet down on the beach with the name EDNA STONE on the back of them. Instantly, she realized that the chairs must come with the cottage. Seeing them, the first inkling of interest in something other than lying in bed watching reruns of bad reality television appealed to her. Racing back inside, she quickly scraped her hair into a ponytail, donned the swimsuit she bought a few days before, slathered on as much sunscreen as she could, grabbed two bottles of water, her phone, one of Edna's large, fluffy towels, and her sunglasses and headed to the beach.

She was only seated for a few minutes when a very muscled young man ran up and introduced himself. He was the beach chair man of the day. He used air quotes as he said "Chair Man" and chuckled as if he had said the most amusing thing in the world. He had seen her coming from the cottage and just needed to confirm she was a guest of Mrs. Stone. Once that was done, he explained that he was there to adjust her umbrella as needed and then provided her with a number to the restaurant in the next-door hotel. Mrs. Stone has a standing agreement that food and drinks were to be served as needed by calling the number.

Wow, thought Taylor, that would have been good information to have had the last two days. She could have gotten the wine without the pretense of food. But even as she thought it, she knew that the little bit of food she had eaten the last two days was all that was standing between her and a full-blown, all-out drunk. As it was, she had been sporting a pretty good headache since she got to the beach, some from crying, mostly from the wine. Speaking of which, her current headache would best be addressed by a little hair of the dog. She quickly dialed the number the guy had given her and ordered a large Sex on the Beach, complete with umbrellas and a large straw! She could not resist. The drink seemed the most appropriate given the week she had had. She also ordered some cheese fries and fruit for good measure. Junk food was quickly becoming her spirit animal.

It was amazing how quickly the order arrived. Taylor had not thought to bring any money with her, and when the food and drinks arrived, she was momentarily taken back about what to do. She explained that she would have to run up to the house for her purse when the waiter said the bill and tip had already been paid as Mrs. Stone had a standing account. As appreciative as Taylor should have been of the convenience of being able to charge the food, it irked her that, once again, Edna Stone was all up in her business.

Forcing all thoughts of Edna out of her mind, Taylor focused on enjoying her sugary drink and very unhealthy lunch. She only managed a few bites of food, but she did finish off the drink. Neither did anything to improve her mood, but her headache did subside.

Laying back in her chair, Taylor closed her eyes and allowed her mind to drift back past the last few days to when she and Bennett were a new couple. Her mind immediately landed on a memory she had almost forgotten.

It was from the night of their rehearsal dinner. Even then, she knew things were not exactly right. She almost called the whole thing off. In fact, Bennett found her crying in the front room of the club and took her in his arms to comfort her. Her comforter and protector. That was what he had always been.

She had told him she was unsure they were doing the right thing. Taylor tried to call it off and Bennett refused to hear of it. He told her it was just nerves. They both needed a fresh start after all the hurt and pain they had been through the previous year. At the time, she had thought he was referring to her parents and Tatum's death.

Now, she realized that Poppy Thompson had played some part in that hurt. Obviously, she and Bennett had been a couple, though no one seemed to have known about it. Taylor briefly wondered if Tatum had known. Probably not.

She guessed they must have been together while she was in Scotland doing her student teaching. Something must have happened to split them up. Whatever it was, a baby was conceived. Taylor believed wholeheartedly that Bennett would never have married her if he had known about the child. He would have moved Heaven and Earth for his child. So what happened, she wondered? Whatever it was, it had to have been massive. That, coupled with the deaths of her parents and brother, had left Bennett broken. No wonder he was looking for a safe place to rebound, and she had provided one. At the time, she thought he was once again rescuing her. Now, she wondered if it had been the other way around. After promising they deserved it, Bennett convinced her to go ahead with the wedding. They married the next day in a small private ceremony at the First Presbyterian Church and then drove to Hot Springs for a short honeymoon.

The first two years were the best. Coming into her marriage as a virgin, Bennett was a kind and considerate lover. He never rushed her, and the whole business was all very slow and soft, if a bit messy. He never pushed her to be adventurous sexually, and she certainly never broached that topic, either.

Of course, she would hear other women talking about sex and think how lucky she was that Bennett never demanded more of her. Most of what she heard others talking about sounded slightly gross, unclean, and possibly painful. She supposed their sex life would be considered boring by many, but it seemed to work for them. Bennett seemed happy, especially when she realized, shy of their second anniversary, that she was pregnant.

It had been a magical, innocent time. She had never known anyone who had had a miscarriage, so it was not even on her radar. Instead, she was knee-deep in baby books, thinking about names and picking out colors for a new nursery when everything went south. Just shy of ten weeks, she began to spot. Her doctor did not seem overly concerned but did advise her to go on bed rest until it stopped. She did, and it seemed to help. Then, on the third day, she got up to use the bathroom, and all hell broke loose. She began bleeding profusely. She immediately called Bennett, who rushed her to the emergency room. But it was too late; they lost the baby. They mourned the loss of their child together just as they mourned the loss of Tatum, together.

They continued to try to grow their family. Babies were conceived, and babies were lost. Again, together they mourned.

Back then, Bennett would often make love to her so softly and slowly as if he might break her. Looking back, she admitted it was nice, but sometimes, she yearned for something more. What that was, she was not sure. Her sexual experience was minimal; maybe that was the problem. And then, suddenly, a crazy thought popped into her head. Maybe their sex problems had not been her issue but his. Maybe Bennett just did not know what to do to turn a woman on sexually. Perhaps he did not know how to fill that yearning she had felt so deeply within her. That thought died a quick death when the image of Poppy Thompson's face filled with passion and lust flooded her brain. Nope, Bennett knew precisely what to do. He just never did it to her.

Not liking the turn her thoughts were taking, Taylor turned her mind away from her lackluster sex life and focused on memories from the last few years of her marriage. Once Bennett decided to run for state office and later for US Senator, they became united. They were too busy trying to get him elected to lament the lack of connection that seemed missing in their marriage. Instead, they spent their energy on campaigns and trying to have children. It was during these years that Taylor lost three more babies. During these years, their marriage and sex life were very civil, pleasant, and kind. They never fought or argued. Each always tried to be very considerate of the other. Except for the miscarriages, it was all so devoid of drama that it often bordered on boring. It was as if they were two friends playing house. When she was ovulating, they scheduled sex. If she was not, sex was not even discussed. Sex became only a part of the baby-making aspect of their life.

Bennett slowly stopped giving her a goodnight kiss on the lips and replaced it with one on her forehead. She could not remember the last time they really kissed or even hugged each other. If they held hands or he gave her a peck on the lips, it was for the cameras. Privately, they rarely touched. They had become a public only couple. That thought made Taylor very sad.

Forcing herself to think back to the last time they had been intimate, she realized it had been almost eighteen months. She had been ovulating, and they had timed everything perfectly. Just as planned, the pregnancy stick turned blue two weeks later. She carried that baby longer than any other. She made it just four days shy of thirteen weeks when she lost it.

After that, her doctors referred her to a specialist in New York. She underwent a new experiential procedure that promised her a much greater chance of carrying to term. The specialist also encouraged her to begin fertility drugs, given her advanced age. Taylor had laughed at that until she explained that women over thirty lost fertility much more quickly, and by thirty-five, she would be considered a high-risk pregnancy.

Since baby-making was put on the shelf as she went through the whole process, there had been no reason to be intimate. Neither one seemed too bothered by the lack of sex. If Bennett had pursued it, she would have complied. If he had made an overture, she would have responded. But he never did. He was always too busy or too tired. She should have realized that meant they were on a dead-end path to nowhere.

It had been a month since she was given the all-clear to start trying for a baby again, but they were too busy trying to get Bennett named VP to worry about a baby. Now, it seemed she had undergone everything for nothing. She was destined to walk away from her marriage with no husband, child, job, position, or family. She was right back where she was ten years earlier.

Only now it was worse because the one person in the world she would have sworn would never hurt her, had ripped her world apart. Worse, he had done so in a very public and humiliating way. Never in her wildest dreams had she ever thought he would have an affair. She never envisioned something so horrible as finding her husband in the country club screwing another woman. To be fair, they weren't actually screwing, but Taylor was confident the only reason they weren't was because they had been interrupted.

One question kept coming back to her like a boomerang. How long had it been going on? How long had Bennett and Poppy been involved? She had so many questions about Poppy, Bennett, and the boy. And no answers. Bennett was the only person who could give her those answers, and she was not ready to deal with him yet.

There was one person who might know something. Over the last three days, she and Joules had only texted. The poor woman was working double time to save Bennett's career. By now, Joules would have gotten every sordid detail out of Bennett. Taylor wanted to know what she had learned. Grabbing her phone and dialing the number before she could change her mind, Taylor called Joules.

Joules answered on the first ring, "Hey, TJ, you okay?" It was the first time in days that Joules had sounded like her childhood friend and not her husband's campaign manager.

"Yeah, I am doing better. Nothing a little wine and Sex on the Beach can't fix."

"I hope you are referring to the drink and are not about to give me yet another scandal to deal with."

"You are so funny," replied Taylor, giving her friend a fake laugh. "I wish I knew someone to have sex on the beach with. I promise I will happily give you the biggest scandal ever. Alas, that is not the case. I am still the good little girl I have always been."

"Good. I have about all I can handle here as it is. So, what's up? You sound better. Is that ocean waves I hear in the background?"

"Yes, I am currently sprawled out in Edna Stone's personal beach cabana, eating her food, drinking her wine, and charging all of it to her."

"Well, not technically. We are being billed for any charges you make. But, yes, it is currently going under her name. That was to keep your name out of it. We are still trying to keep a lid on this, you know."

"Yeah, so how's that working for you?" Taylor was not sure she was interested in keeping it all quiet anymore. But Joules had worked hard to keep it all under wraps. It would have been wrong to blow it all by making a public mistake.

"Good. Things here have quieted down. Poppy has gone back to New York. She will be back for the gala per Edna. Bennett has hit the campaign trail. He is traveling with Anderson all week. You two need to talk when he calls. Make sure you answer this time."

Rolling her eyes, Taylor responded, "Yeah, yeah. I hear you. I will cross that bridge when I get there. Until then, I have a few questions and need you to answer them."

Joules immediately sounded alarmed, "Oh no! I am not getting in the middle of this. I mean it. You two have to talk. After you talk, I will help you process any or all of it. But, if you want answers, you must get them from him."

"Look, you are supposed to be my best friend. Stop being a damn campaign manager for one minute and talk to me as my friend!"

Joules startled. She had never heard Taylor curse before. Swallowing, she said, "Okay, ask away. I am not making any promises. But if I can answer, I will."

Taylor was quiet momentarily, and then she asked, "Have you met her?"

"I assume by her, you mean Poppy, and yes, I have."

Taylor wanted to ask what she was like but was afraid of the answer. If Joules said she was great, it would only hurt her more. If she said Poppy was awful, Joules would know she was lying. Because, if she were awful, Joules would have already told her that, and Bennett would not be with her.

Taylor was quiet for another second before asking, "Have you met the boy? Bennett's son? It is his son, isn't it?" Taylor was amazed at how hard it was for her to say those words out loud.

"Yes, I have, and again, it is not my place to tell you all of this. But since you have already figured it out, he is Bennett's son. Bennett just recently found out about him, but the boy doesn't know Bennett is his father. Now, that is all I am going to tell you. If there is anything else you want to know about the boy, you have to ask Bennett. Understood?"

"Can you tell me if you have talked to her?"

Joules groaned before sighing heavily and saying, "Okay, yes, I have talked to her. I know you are not going to like this, but she seems to care about Bennett very much."

Taylor exploded, which is precisely what Joules was afraid she would do. This was also just one of the many reasons she did not want to discuss Poppy with her. "She cares about him! And what? I don't? If I didn't care about him, this shit would be all over the news by now. Wow! That is great coming from the person who is supposed to be my best friend!" Suddenly, all the anger that Taylor had been building up since the day before erupted on Joules. It should have been directed at Bennett, but suddenly, it got directed at Joules instead.

"Now, hold on a minute. I am your best friend, but you are not being fair. I never said you didn't care about Bennett. If I thought for one minute that you were really in love with him, that your marriage was worth saving, I might feel differently. But, be honest here. Things have been bad for a long time. It's a lot longer than Poppy has been in the picture. You're both miserable and have been for years. I just want to see both of you happy."

A cry burst from Taylor's throat, and she swallowed it back. In a childlike voice, she said, "You are supposed to be on my side. I don't have anybody else. He has an army to protect him. All I have is you."

Joules softened her tone. "I am on your side. I am always on your side. I am your whole damn Calvary! But life is messy, and this is a hot one."

Taylor stewed on that for a moment. She wanted to ask many more questions, but so far, the answers left her with more longing and hurt than she could handle. Maybe she needed to drop it before she fell headlong into a major depression. After a moment, she said, "You're right. I am sorry. I am just so hurt and humiliated. That woman has taken my husband. I don't know; maybe he was never mine to take. The child is at least ten or eleven. This has been going on a very long time."

"TJ, leave the child out of this. It is not his fault. And we both know this has not been going on that long. It might have started back then, but it has just started back recently, like the day of the art luncheon. You know, none of this is Bennett's style. He wouldn't have married you if he had still been involved with Poppy ten years ago. What happened before then, or since, I can't say. Also, I want you to think about something. It takes two people to make a marriage work, and two people to allow it to fail. Bennett certainly has a lot to account for, but so do you, TJ. I love you with my whole heart, but you do. If you can't be honest with me, at least be honest with yourself about the part you have played in allowing your marriage to become what it is today."

It did not matter that Taylor had already come to realize what Joules was saying on her own. She was not in any frame of mind to agree. Instead, she said, "I don't think we need to talk about this right now. I am just too angry. And besides, how do you know that Bennett hasn't been lying to both of us for a long time? Maybe he is just a big fat liar. He has spent most of the last seven years in Washington learning from the best." Taylor sounded petty and rude. And she did not care. She had had all the truth bombs she wanted for the day.

"It's okay to be angry. Anger can be good. I like you angry much better than the emotionally checked-out woman you have been for the last year and a half. I know you can't see it now, but this could be a wonderful new start for you. Who knows, you might meet someone and fall in love?"

"And then what, get married and pop out a couple with kids? We both know that isn't going to happen," Taylor snapped. "Already tried that. It's a no go unless you have been so busy saving his royal ass to remember."

"Wow! You are just a major little potty mouth today. I have never heard you use so many curse words."

"I am a late bloomer, and besides, I learned from the best, talking to you every day for the last fifteen years, so back at you bitch," Taylor sassed back. Then, she added, "You know I am not really calling you a bitch, right?"

"Of course, crazy woman! And you have a point; I will take it as a point of pride that I have taught you well, Grasshopper. Now, to the part about meeting someone, settling down, and having a family. We don't actually know that is a no go. You told me the doctors were very optimistic about that last procedure. So, maybe this is your Do Over?"

"My what?" Taylor practically screeched. For a woman who had never screeched a day in her life, the sound was not pretty, but nothing about her felt attractive at the moment, so she did not care.

"Your Do Over. Your chance to start your life over with more maturity and a better understanding of who you are and what you want out of life. And, lucky you. You don't have a lot of baggage that a house full of children would have brought."

"Thank you so much for reminding me how lucky I am to have had all of those miscarriages. I would not want to be loaded down with a ton of extra baggage as I start my new life. And who said I wanted a new life anyway? I was doing just fine with the one I had."

Sighing loudly, Joules shot back, "Now, who's the big liar? We both know that was not true. And I didn't mean the baggage comment the way you took it. I am just trying to help here. You have been only half living for so long. I miss you. I miss my friend. Over the last few years, you have become closed off. You know what I am talking about. This is me, TJ. Be real with yourself if you can't yet be real with me. Take the next few days and spend some time thinking, really thinking, about your marriage and where you want to go from here. Bennett will be calling. When he does, I expect you two to talk like adults." Joules was trying to be patient, but Taylor was acting like a brat. A hurt brat, but a brat nevertheless.

After a moment, Taylor said, "Fine. Whatever."

"I will fly down early on the jet Saturday and bring you back for the gala. I hate to do this, but I have to go. We have another strategy session that is about to begin. Ever since Edna Stone took over, all we do is meet. She is a force to be reckoned with. I may have to take some lessons from her because she has all of us running around doing her bidding. We will talk soon. If you need anything, call. Oh, and TJ, I really do love you. Please don't be mad at me for being honest with you. I only want the best for you."

"I know you do. And I love you, too. I am not mad at you. I am just…" Taylor's words faltered, and her voice cracked. Holding back tears, she said, "I don't know what I am." After a few more seconds, she added, "You go and deal with the sharks. I'll be fine. Talk to you in a few days. Love you."

Joules said, "Love you too." Then she hung up.

Taylor sat staring at her phone for several minutes, lost in her thoughts.

In one swell swoop, her life had been turned upside down again. She did not know exactly what the next stage of her life would entail, but she was no longer a little, lost orphan girl of twenty-two. She was done with knights in shiny armor. She had depended on that fantasy once before, and look how that turned out. Nope, no more Prince Charming for her. Whatever came next, she would face it on her own.

Chapter 6

Stone Cottage
Gulf Shores, Alabama
March 2012

After hanging up with Joules, Taylor gave Edna's little magic food number another call. This time, she ordered a grown-up meal, salmon, asparagus, and a salad. She resisted the urge to order another ridiculously sugary, inappropriately named drink. Instead, she opted for the most expensive Chardonnay they had. The restaurant agreed to drop the food off at her cottage, so she packed up and headed back to shower.

She had just finished dressing in her last set of clean clothes when the doorbell rang. Taylor thanked the delivery boy and gave him a stupid, crazy tip. Now that she knew Bennett was footing the bill for her little hideout pity party, she wanted to spend as much money as possible. The more it cost him, the better.

This was the first real meal she had eaten in days, and luckily, she only drank two glasses of wine. A vast improvement over the last few days. She watched a sappy rom-com and then turned in early. She was emotionally exhausted and physically spent. She slept like a baby and woke the next day starving. Taylor contemplated calling Edna's magic number again but decided against it. Better to get herself together and start taking responsibility for feeding herself. Dressing quickly, she made a list of what food staples she would need for the rest of the week and headed back into town.

There, Taylor hit up a local grocer and stocked up on several healthy meal options. She still had several more days at the beach, so she bought enough food to see her through. The shopping center also had a sporting goods store next to it. As Taylor headed back to her car, loaded down with bags of food, she walked by the store window and spotted her favorite brand of running shoes. After putting her bags in the car, she went into the store and was pleasantly surprised to find not only a new pair of running shoes but also all of the running gear, sports bras, and socks she needed to run at the beach.

Back at the cottage, Taylor put away her purchases. She fixed herself a quick lunch and then found a spicy romance and read for a few hours. It was not the type of book Taylor typically read as it was quite explicit, bordering on smut. She knew that Joules would say she was being a prude. The more she read, the more shocked she became. She was unsure if she was more shocked that the book was in Edna Stone's cottage or what the characters were doing to each other. She wondered if Edna had read it. Taylor could not imagine the stuffy old lady reading such a racy book.

As she read, images of Bennett and Poppy began filtering through her mind. Slowly, their faces began to replace the images of the characters in the book. Seeing Bennett and Poppy doing all the various explicitly described acts suddenly made Taylor sick to her stomach. Throwing the book down, she went to her room and quickly put on her new running gear. She did some light stretching and then took off down the beach trying to outrun the sexual images of Poppy and her husband dancing through her head.

Usually, Taylor ran about four miles a day without any problems. But, not today. A quarter of a mile into her jog, she had to stop. She literally could not breathe. With her hands on her knees to support herself, she was gasping for air. Her chest hurt, and her heart was racing. She was sweating like she had just run a marathon.

Suddenly, there was a roaring in her ears. For a second, she was afraid she was going to faint. All around her, the ocean roared ashore, and the sun was softly setting. Yet, she was not aware of any of it. It took every bit of concentration she had just to put one foot in front of the other. The emotional upheaval of the last few days was physically affecting her ability to breathe.

After a few minutes of trying to catch her breath, Taylor put her hands on her hips and tried again. Only this time, she was walking. She could not believe that the one time in her life she needed to run, she couldn't. Suddenly, the pain in her chest hurt so bad that she clutched it. She could feel herself falling face-first into the sand but could do nothing to stop it. And then there was nothing but black.

Gulf Shores Regional Hospital
Gulf Shores, Alabama
March 2012

When Taylor came to, she was lying on a hospital bed. All around her, machines were beeping, and lights were flashing. She was still wearing running shorts and shoes, but her tee shirt was gone. Her bright pink sports bra was still in place, but it was pulled so far down that her breasts were fully exposed. The wires attached to her chest were connected to one of the machines that was beeping loudly. She tried to sit up, but a sharp pain cut across her chest.

"Ouch, that hurts," she groaned, lying back on the bed, holding her chest.

"Easy there, sport." At that moment, the most beautiful man Taylor had ever seen stepped over and patted her arm.

"Where am I? How did I get here?" Taylor looked around the room, trying to remember what had happened as the pain in her chest began to subside.

"You are at Gulf Shores Regional Hospital. I am Doctor Stone, a heart specialist who happened to be on call when you were brought in. You passed out while running. The paramedics thought you were having a heart attack and brought you here. Do you remember going for a run or the ambulance ride? A couple of kids found you. Can you tell me what happened?" As he talked, he shined a small bright light into her eyes.

"I had just started running when all of a sudden, I couldn't breathe and had a sharp pain in my chest. That is the last thing I remember." She could hardly believe that she had been in an ambulance and didn't remember anything about it.

The gorgeous doctor smiled and said, "Well, an ambulance brought you in a few minutes ago. You were out cold. You gave us all a real scare until we were able to hook you up to the heart monitor to see if it was a heart attack or not."

"A heart attack?" Taylor croaked. This was all she needed. She was going to die in a little hospital in Alabama all alone.

Shaking his head and laughing lightly, the doctor replied, "No, you are not having a heart attack. Your EKG looks great. I think you might have gotten overheated or something. Is that possible? Did you get too hot while running?"

"No, I had just started running. I didn't go more than a quarter of a mile before I started having trouble breathing and having this pain in my chest. I usually run at least four miles almost daily with no problem."

Nodding, the doctor gave her a questioning look and asked, "Okay, any chance you could be pregnant?"

At that, Taylor all but snorted and said, "No chance. I am not pregnant. It's not possible."

The doctor responded by asking, "Are you sure? It won't take but a minute to check."

"Positive! No, I am not pregnant, and I wasn't overheated. What else could be causing me to have chest pains and shortness of breath?"

"Well," the doctor said, "it was probably just a panic attack. You are young and healthy. All of your vitals are good. The EKG was clean. Have you been under a lot of stress lately? Stress can cause them, and they can be very painful and make you think you are going into cardiac arrest."

Taylor's first thought was to say, "You have no idea." But, what she said instead was, "Actually, yes, I am. Do you think that is what caused it? Too much stress?" She was trying to sound calm and relaxed when she felt anything but.

Well, that was just great. Bennett's little affair turned out to be the gift that kept giving. First, it broke her heart and gave her a healthy dose of hurt and humiliation. Now, she was having painful panic attacks from all the stress. What is next?

On hearing she was not having a heart attack, Taylor was equal parts embarrassed and relieved. She certainly didn't want to have a heart attack, but it was beyond embarrassing to have been brought to the ER for a panic attack. Bennett and Joules were going to have a fit; so much for her keeping a low profile and not attracting attention.

Trying to sound in control, Taylor said, "I don't know what to say. I have never had a panic attack before. Is there anything I can do to keep it from happening again?"

Suddenly realizing she was not going to die, Taylor became very aware of her state of undress. Her breasts were displayed for all to see. She tried to pull the bra back up as much as possible, but the wires still left gaping holes.

Seeing her discomfort with the wires, the handsome doctor walked over and began to undo them. None of which did anything to reduce Taylor's stress level regarding her boobs hanging out. Having the hunky doctor's hands all over her chest, she was worried she might have another panic attack at any moment. It had been a long time since any man put his hands on her breasts. Just because he was a doctor didn't make it any less uncomfortable. The doctor was very professional; it was just Taylor's sense of modesty kicking in and stressing her out.

Speaking in a smooth and easy manner, the doctor said, "If you have been under a lot of stress lately, that is probably what is causing it. I have some patients that I need to see about, but before I go, I will leave you some scripts for anxiety and pain should you have another one." He continued to remove the leads and wires and straighten her clothes. "You will probably be quite sore for a few days. That is normal. Just take it easy."

Handing Taylor her tee shirt that had been removed earlier, he added, "Running is a great way to reduce stress. I think with the anti-anxiety meds, you will have yourself running again in no time. But, you might want to start by just walking at first, though, to see how you feel. If you are doing okay, I see no reason for you not to resume your normal running routine. I will get those prescriptions for you. If you have any questions, the nurse will be happy to answer them."

"No, I am good. I think I got it," said Taylor as she continued to struggle to get her modest C-cup boobs back into her suddenly very tiny sports bra.

"Good, the nurse will come back in and get some information from you since you didn't have any ID when you arrived. Good luck… um, I didn't get your name earlier," the doctor walked over to the door and stood.

Not wanting to use her real name, Taylor smiled and said, "TJ." It wasn't a lie. Tatum had always called her that and so did Joules.

Nodding, the gorgeous doctor said, "Good luck, TJ, and let us know if you need anything else," as he walked out the door.

Taylor quickly put the tee shirt back on. A nurse wearing a name tag that said Beth appeared almost instantly. The nurse explained that the doctor had been called away, but that he had communicated all the necessary information to another doctor on staff who was currently writing her prescriptions.

The nurse gave Taylor several forms to complete. Not wanting this incident to be fodder for the press, either now or later, Taylor decided to use only her maiden name and not to give her insurance information. She would pay for everything herself. She kept a credit card in her maiden name for when she wanted to fly under the radar. She promised to come by the next day and pay the bill in full. Hopefully, that would keep the press from being able to find her if the story broke. Once all the necessary forms were completed, the nurse took them and went to get Taylor's prescriptions. Within thirty minutes, Taylor was in the back of a taxi headed to the cottage.

Once she was home, she considered filling her prescriptions, but she decided to wait to see if she had another panic attack before doing so. She hated taking medicine of any kind. With that decision made, she fixed herself some dinner and spent the rest of the evening resting and watching reruns of seventy and eighties television shows.

She decided not to tell Bennett or Joules about her embarrassing adventure. It was bad enough to be rushed to the hospital with a panic attack, but she didn't need those two freaking out about it. She was definitely not up to listening to Bennett acting all concerned when he was the one who had started this whole mess in the first place. So, instead, she just took care of herself. And it felt good to know she was capable of doing that.

Chapter 7

Carrington Office
Searcy, Arkansas
November 24, 2023

"I hate to interrupt you, but are you saying that the first time you met Dr. Stone was not in Searcy but at a hospital? You were his patient?" Harvey Cox asked, shocked.

Taylor gave a long sigh and said, "Yes, but it is not what you think. I was only his patient that one time. Before you start asking too many questions, let me finish this part of the story. I promise it will all make sense."

Stone Cottage
Gulf Shores, Alabama
March 2012

The next day, Taylor did exactly as the doctor had ordered. She went for some low-stress walks on the beach and then spent time lounging in Edna's amazing beach chairs. As she did so, Taylor was forced to accept some pretty hard truths about herself.

She tried to take her marriage apart, piece by piece, and examine it for cracks. The one area that she kept coming back to was sex. Given her lack of experience and sex partners, she struggled to work out exactly where it all went wrong. After spending an entire afternoon contemplating it, she decided to reach out to the one person she completely trusted and who had enough sexual experience for both of them, Joules. Around ten o'clock, she rang her, hoping that by then, everyone would be out of the office, and Joules could talk privately.

Taylor expected her friend to be working late on the campaign or out on a date. Though dating for Joules was almost a joke. She only dated men for cover and the occasional distraction.

The truth was Joules had been seeing a married man on and off for the last decade. Taylor had no idea what Joules saw in the guy. He was much older and had been one of her policy professors. Taylor saw no future in the relationship, but given her recent relationship issues, who was she to throw stones?

Joules answered on the second ring. "Hey, what are you doing up so late? I thought you turned into a pumpkin at ten," Joules quipped as she answered, having already seen the call was from Taylor.

"The better question is, what are you doing? I'm not interrupting anything, am I? Are you still at the office or, heaven forbid, on a date?"

Chuckling, Joules responded, "No, I am actually home in bed. I am just lying here looking over some recent polls. What's up?"

"You're in bed? It's only ten. Are you sick?" Taylor was shocked. Joules was the original night owl. She never seemed to need much sleep. If she was home and in bed, that probably meant she wasn't alone. It suddenly occurred to Taylor that her friend might have someone there with her. If so, she didn't want to interrupt them.

"No, I am not sick, and before your overactive imagination goes into overdrive, I am alone. Dennis is not here. He is out of town. So, what's up?"

Taylor could hear how defensive her friend got whenever Dennis Harrison's name came up. Joules knew how Taylor felt about adultery. Given the events of the last few days, her prejudices against it were at an all-time high. However, she needed Joules to help her understand some things about her marriage, and if that meant talking about Dennis to do it, so be it.

"Um, well, I have been thinking and wanted to run some things by you. You know, to get your perspective on them."

Taylor was being vague. It was obvious that Joules didn't understand what she meant because she said, "Okay, what kind of things?"

Taylor paused for a moment and then said, "Sex things."

"Whoa!" her friend laughed out loud. "Let me get this right: you want to talk about sex things. Who are you and what have you done with my friend? You know Taylor Carrington, the girl who once told me it was not ladylike to talk about intimate details of sex."

"Point taken, I am being serious. I have been thinking about the first year Bennett and I were married."

"Yeah, and?" Joules replied, trying to figure out where Taylor was going.

"Well, I was wondering, is sex really that big of a deal? I mean, would bad sex have been enough to drive Bennett to cheat?"

"What? What do you mean by bad sex?" Joules could not keep the surprise out of her voice. Taylor could tell that Joules was not very comfortable having this conversation. "You know, bad sex. I don't know how else to describe it."

Joules seemed to consider the questions for a moment, and then she said, "Well, to be honest, I think sex is like pizza. Good pizza, okay pizza, or bad pizza, I am pretty much always up for pizza, and while some pizza is definitely better than others, I never turn down pizza. I think almost all men would agree with me when it comes to both sex and pizza."

"Okay, how about I describe it another way. Sex, good or bad, as a chore. Would that be enough to drive a man to cheat?"

"You mean you think sex is a chore?"

"Well, not always, but yeah, sometimes. Don't you? Or maybe not," fibbed Taylor, starting to feel very self-conscious. Maybe she was the only person who ever saw sex as being more trouble than it was worth.

"No, I don't. Of course, given my choice of partners, I don't get to have sex as often as I would like. But no, it is never a chore. Is that how you have felt about sex with Bennett the last few months?"

Taylor could tell Joules was uncomfortable talking about sex and Bennett, and she could hardly blame her. After all, he was her boss! Clearing her throat, she answered honestly, "Well, no, not the last few months. We haven't had sex in a long time."

"How long is a long time? What are we talking? A month, two, six?"

"Since the last miscarriage." Taylor was speaking so quietly that Joules could barely hear her.

"That was eighteen months ago. Are you telling me you two haven't been together since then?" Joules' voice was rising and was full of shock.

"No, but.."

Whatever Taylor was going to say was cut off by Joules saying, "Well, listen up, sister, that's your problem right there. If you're not sleeping with your husband, someone else is." Joules wanted to draw the words back in as soon as they were out of her mouth.

"Um, obviously. That is what started all this mess!" Taylor snapped at her friend. She knew Joules wasn't trying to be mean, yet her words hurt. For a woman known for her political savvy, she was doing a spectacularly lousy job choosing her words.

"Look, I am sorry I said that. It was insensitive. I don't know what you want me to say."

"I don't want you to say anything. I am just trying to figure out if sex is really that important, and I guess it is. It just never has been to me. I suppose I am just not a very sexual person. But I am beginning to think that the bad sex is what destroyed my marriage."

"First of all, sex did not destroy your marriage. Not talking to each other did that. And from where I am standing, you both are partly to blame. As for the other, Taylor, you are a beautiful, sexy woman who is just as sexual as the next. You have just never found the person that tripped your trigger. When you do, sex will make sense. I promise."

"Maybe I am just fated to be alone? I don't know if I even believe in fate. Do you?" asked Taylor.

"I believe we make our own fate. If you want to find the person who trips your trigger, you will have to look for him. Things don't just happen. If you put yourself out there, there is a good chance you will find someone," replied Joules.

Listening and nodding, Taylor said, "Maybe. We'll see." Then she got very quiet once more and asked, "Do you think Poppy is that person for Bennett?"

Joules didn't answer right away, and when she did, she said with a sigh, "Yes. I do."

"And Dennis, he is that person for you?"

"Sometimes." Joules' one-word answer left a dead spot in the conversation. Taylor waited for her to elaborate, but she didn't.

Taylor could tell that Joules was uncomfortable talking about this, but she couldn't let the conversation drop before she had some answers. For the first time, she felt she was finally asking the right questions. She just had to keep searching.

After a moment, Taylor asked, "Have there been others who did that for you? Tripped your trigger, so to speak?"

Joules was quiet for a minute more, and then, in a very small voice, she said, "Yes, a long time ago. There was someone I loved very much, and just being in the same room with him made my heart race. He touched every part of me with just one look."

"Who? When? You never told me about him." Taylor was stunned. She had no idea who Joules was talking about.

"It was when you were in Scotland, student teaching."

"Well, where is he now? Why aren't you with him instead of Dennis?"

Sighing heavily, Joules said, "For lots of reasons. None of which I am willing to get into at the moment. That is a conversation for another time. What Dennis and I have works for us. It's not for everybody, but he gives me what I need for now. And he is a very good man. You would know that if you ever tried to get to know him.

"There is a lot about his marriage that you know nothing about. He and his wife have an open marriage. I have told you this many times. His wife was the one who pushed for an open relationship. He was against it at first. It was only after she had been with several other men that he even considered going outside the marriage."

"Well, given that he was your professor when you two first started seeing each other, combined with the fact that he was and is still married, means that I have no intention of ever getting to know him better. Not ever." Taylor knew she sounded judgmental, but at the end of the day, adultery was wrong. Joules had tried to justify her relationship with Dennis for years, but to Taylor, it was wrong. Period.

Sighing loudly, Joules decided to cut her losses and end this conversation before either one said something they would regret. Taylor had been through a lot the last few days. It was best to end the conversation on somewhat of a good note. Fake yawning loudly, Joules said, "Listen, Sweetie, I am sorry. I don't know if I have helped you find any answers, but I am exhausted. This has been a killer week.

I have got to get off and snag some z's. Do you mind if we talk more about this another time?"

Taylor was not fooled by her friend's fake yawn. She knew Joules never went to bed before midnight. The woman was half vampire. But Taylor could feel the friction that always popped up when Dennis' name came up.

Not wanting her friend to be upset with her, Taylor said, "Sure. Thanks for talking to me. Get some sleep. I'll talk to you in the morning. And, Joules, I love you."

Joules said, "I love you too. Now, get some rest and stop overthinking every little aspect of your life. Things will work out. They always do. I will talk to you tomorrow." With that, Joules rang off.

Once she hung up, Taylor realized she had even more questions. Who was the mystery man that broke her friend's heart in graduate school? Is that what drove Joules into the arms of a married man? If so, could she be more forgiving of that? Taylor didn't know.

After she and Joules hung up, Taylor crawled into bed and lay for hours thinking about everything Joules had said and trying to figure out who the mystery man in Joules's life had been.

Chapter 8

Stone Cottage
Gulf Shores, Alabama
March 2012

The next morning, Joules sent Taylor a text letting her know the story was still contained, but it was taking a little curve. Taylor had missed two key campaign events, and people were beginning to wonder where she was. Joules told the press a story about Senator Carrington's wife being overly stressed and needing time to relax. Every reporter in Little Rock was asking if Taylor was again expecting and on bed rest. Even though there was not an ounce of truth to the story, Joules, who was great at tearing the hell out of the truth, kept her answers so vague that the reporters believed what they wanted. They collectively decided Taylor was expecting a baby. While all of them wanted to be the ones to break the story of a new heir, no one wanted to do anything that might cause the couple to lose another child. So, for once, they got a pass. Joules wanted to give her a heads-up so she would not freak out if she saw something about it. While it did give Taylor pause, it also gave her some much needed time on her own to figure this fiasco out.

To that end, Taylor spent the day under the big umbrella in Edna Stone's beach chairs. Sipping on a large thermos of water as she watched the waves roll ashore, she did some hardcore soul-searching, forcing her to get honest with herself about her life.

Instead of focusing on her marriage, she tried to focus on her life, the good and the bad. Joules had been right. She had been miserable for a very long time. She needed to figure out why and formulate a plan that would allow her to become the woman she wanted to be. The rest of her life was up to her, and no one knew better than Taylor how precious life really was.

It was time to start living, stop just existing, and make the most of the rest of her life. She just needed to figure out what made her tick and what she wanted without worrying about expectations or giving into fear. That was easier said than done when you have been taken care of your whole life. Where did she even start?

She was determined to become an independent woman, but it was proving more challenging than anticipated. Old habits die hard. She admitted to herself that one of the reasons she had ended up with Bennett in the first place was because it had been the easy thing to do. After the accident, she continued her life as before, with Bennett taking the place of her parents. That was a pretty ugly pill for a grown woman to swallow. She owned up to the fact that, in many ways, she had never emotionally grown up or had to fend for herself.

Before she could do that, she needed to go back to the beginning to fully understand when and where her life and marriage began to unravel. She had to force herself to return to the day that changed her life forever. The day an eighteen-wheeler had crossed the center line, and in an instant, her parents and Tatum were killed. One minute, she had a family and a home. The next, she had lost it all. In one fell swoop, she lost everyone she had loved in this world. Her grandparents had all died when she was a child, and her parents had both been only children.

Bennett flew to Scotland and broke the news to her. Taylor did not believe that she could have made it through those first few awful days if it had not been for him. He helped her pack and ensured she got home in one piece. Once home, he had helped her make all the funeral arrangements. For weeks afterward, he helped her deal with several financial and business decisions that she had been in no condition to make.

She had become very depressed and started sleeping a lot. She spent days in bed, sleeping, watching television, waiting to die, wanting to die. She had been adrift with no direction and no will to find one. She might still have been in that bed to this day if Bennett hadn't forced her out of it. He'd arranged for her to have an interview with the local elementary school principal, and then he made her go to it.

Looking back, Taylor knew she could not have made a good first impression. Overall, she had been a mess. She certainly would not have hired her to teach anyone anything. But Bennett had worked his magic. She got the job. Thanks to him, she found herself in a second-grade classroom, teaching twenty-two eager, hungry minds. That had been exactly what she needed to get up every day. Bennett and those kids had saved her.

From there, Taylor and Bennett meandered from close friends into dating and then into a marriage of convenience more than passion. It had just seemed natural that they should end up together. Certainly, everyone expected them to. It made for great copy. Searcy's golden couple finding each other after a horrible tragedy. While they had never shared a great passion, it was easy and as comfortable as an old pair of jeans you can't bring yourself to throw out.

They knew early on that something in their marriage was not quite right. But they never talked about it. Instead, they began building a life together, hoping that whatever was missing would fix itself over time. And for a while, it seemed to work. Bennett's law practice flourished, and then he won his bid for the state senate. They had decided Taylor would teach until they had a baby. Only the baby never came.

Though a long shot, Bennett embarked on his first United States Senate race when he sensed the state was ready for change. He won by a landslide. He got an apartment in Georgetown. Taylor decorated it, and at first, she spent quite a bit of time in DC, having resigned from her teaching position to be able to join him.

In eighteen months since her last miscarriage, their marriage had deteriorated into a political merger of two polite people who cared about each other, living and passing each other like cars on the street. Taylor had moved back to Arkansas and had not joined Bennett in DC. The only time they had spent together had been on the campaign trail.

When they were alone, they both worked hard to keep the conversation light and focused on neutral topics. They had not had an honest, serious discussion about their marriage or the lack of intimacy in it.

Taylor's little trip down memory lane forced her to face the fact that, as much as she wanted to hate Bennett for humiliating her, she couldn't. Too many times over the last eleven years, he had been there for her. Truthfully, over the days of deep soul searching, she realized it was one thing to love someone, but it was something else to be in love. She was not sure she had ever been in love with anyone. She did know that she loved Bennett enough not to stand in his way if he was in love with Poppy. By the look of things, he was. She knew she would step away from her marriage even though doing so was going to cost her greatly.

For Taylor, this was where it started to get sticky. By stepping back from her marriage, she realized she was the big loser in all this, even though she had done nothing wrong. Her image, job, and life were tied up in her marriage. She would have never admitted to anyone, not even Joules, but she had to be honest with herself. She was more sad about walking away from being a senator's wife than she was losing her husband. Sadly, it seemed she was more in love with being Mrs. Bennett Carrington, the senator's wife, then with Bennett himself.

Wow! That was an awful big truth pill to swallow. She was going to miss it, the job, the campaigning, the hosting, the whole shebang. She was good at it. She enjoyed it. She had been born to do it. What did that say about her? No wonder Bennett had an affair!

And as bad as that was, the next part was even worse. She realized she was resentful that she was the only one whose life was about to change. Bennett would get the love of his life, and the son he always wanted. Poppy was going to get to take her place, and they were going to get to live happily ever after in Taylor's house, no less. It had been in Bennett's family for forty years. She was going to be left all alone, with no home, no status, no position, no significant other, no children, and little to no hope of ever having any. That was the worst part.

It was just not fair. Bennett had cheated on her. Poppy had a secret love child hidden for years, yet they would get the life she had spent the last ten years building. It all made her so mad. As anger roared through her, she realized, for the first time in almost a week, she was not crying.

In fact, her tears had cried themselves out. They had left in their wake an angry, shallow woman. Whoever said a woman scorned, and all that, was right. At that moment, she would have liked to throat punch Bennett. For a woman totally against violence, that was the second time in a week she had fantasized about it. This whole thing was jacking with her head. Deciding to go for another run to clear her head, Taylor packed up and headed back to the cottage.

She threw on her running clothes and took off at a clip. She ran as fast as she could, trying to outrun the demons that had been dogging her all week. She ran for almost six miles. Soaked to the skin in sweat and with her muscles screaming for a break, she walked the last two miles back to the cottage. The run, while exhausting, had done the trick. She had worked off her anger and felt more in control of her emotions than she had in weeks. Best of all, she had no issue with breathing or any hint of a panic attack. Heading into the shower, she realized it had taken the better part of the two days to work through the issues and a blowout run to reach a place where she felt she was ready to talk to Bennett. She hoped she could do so calmly. Her week in hiding was coming to a close, and she needed to start making inroads with a plan for the future.

She decided she would not let others guide her through life anymore. She was also not going to live in fear or by other people's expectations. She was going to be bold and daring and try, with everything in her, to discover her passionate side, though she secretly worried that she might not have one. She might be as cold and unfeeling as her memories had told her she was. However, she promised herself that if she were ever given the opportunity to experience the kind of passion she had seen on Poppy's face, she would take it.

Thinking of Poppy, Taylor promised herself that from that day forward, she would do something each day that scared her and was unexpected. She was so afraid of disappointing people that she never had the courage to stand up and demand the life she wanted. She became a spectator in her own life. But, from now on, she vowed that would never happen again. She was taking control of her life beginning right then.

One on the heels of that thought, she admitted to herself that she missed teaching. There was no greater high in the world than having a hand in helping a child learn. She missed seeing the light bulb go off when a child finally comprehended a new concept or grasped a new skill. She hadn't realized how much she had missed it until she stopped and reflected on her teaching days.

Perhaps it was time she considered going back to work. Thanks to her trust fund, she was set financially. Bennett, to his credit, had grown her investments substantially, and if she had never worked another day in her life, it would be okay. But she missed the sense of accomplishment she got from working.

While it was true there were a few aspects of the teaching profession she had not missed, the overall experience had been amazing. Returning to the classroom would be a good place to start rebuilding her life. But before she could do that, she needed to talk with Bennett. It was time to face her past and start working on the future as an independent woman. Time to grow the hell up!

Chapter 9

Carrington Office
Searcy, Arkansas
November 24, 2023

Taylor, who had been talking for a while now, suddenly stopped and looked at Harvey Cox. He looked like a man who had just been hit by a Mack truck. Realizing he might need a break, Taylor, the perfect hostess, said, "I know this is a lot. Do you need a break to take it all in?"

Chucking softly to himself, Harvey replied, "No, I was just thinking that you have suffered so much in your life. And, yet, you are not bitter or angry. Loss can do that to a person. Even now, as you are recounting all of this to me, you are more worried about how it is affecting me than you. I am sure that it can't be easy talking about this. It was a really rough time in your life."

"It was," replied Taylor. "At the time, I was just realizing that I needed to grow up and stop being a little girl. I think part of me stopped maturing when my parents died. It took another tragedy to force me to stand on my own two feet and figure out what I wanted out of life."

"I don't know why, but I always thought Bennett was the one who wanted the divorce. It sounds like you had decided to end the marriage long before he did in the spring of that year. What caused that change?" asked Harvey.

Nodding her head in agreement, Taylor said, "Yes, you are right. That was what any reasonable person would have done. Only when you are in the middle of something like this can you find yourself calm and rational one minute and then stark, raving crazy the next. That's what happened here. I am not proud of what happened next, but I would not change it for the world."

"That sounds interesting. I can't wait to hear the next part," replied Harvey, with his pen ready to begin making notes.

"Well, get ready; it is a doozy."

Stone Cottage
Gulf Shores, Alabama
March 2012

After her shower, Taylor called Bennett on his cell.

"Taylor, is this you? Are you okay? What's wrong?" Bennett sounded worried, but his voice had an edge that Taylor had never heard before. He was sort of whispering. It was as if he was doing something he thought he shouldn't.

"Yes, it's me. I am fine. Nothing is wrong, but I thought we could talk for a minute if that's okay?"

"I only have a second, but not on the mobile phones. Are you at Edna's?"

Taylor replied, "Yes, but...,"

Bennett cut her off, "Good, I will ring you right back on the landline. Your absence has created too much interest. You never know when a reporter will hack the cell lines and hear everything we say."

"Umm, okay, but..." Why was talking to her husband always so complicated?

"Just hang up, and I will call you right back." He was starting to sound irritated, like she was the one who was not making any sense.

"Wait," she snapped, "do you even know the number?" Taylor didn't even know the number. She and Joules had been talking by cell all week. She knew there was a house phone but didn't know the number.

"Yes, I will call you in a sec."

"Okay, bye." Taylor hung up. The house phone rang almost instantly, "Okay, it's me. Is this better?" Taylor tried to be polite, but all this cloak-and-dagger stuff seemed a little over the top for Bennett.

"Yes, I don't want you to call me on my cell unless it is an emergency. Your absence has been noticed, and I want to avoid any nosy reporters intercepting our calls. There is no telling what they might discover if they did."

"Do you really think things could get that out of hand? And how did you get this number anyway?" From Taylor's voice, it was clear she thought Bennett was overreacting.

"Joules gave it to me the night she arranged the cottage. Also, as for how this mess might go, it could blow wide open at any time if the press knew what they were looking for and where to find it. I don't want to help them in any way. So please do me a favor and don't talk about this with anyone, even Joules, unless you are both on a landline. They are the safest. Okay, onto other matters, why did you call?"

Typical Bennett, he was all business. In the days since the "incident," his tone had gone from that of contrite and begging in voicemail messages to that of the annoyed politician whose wife was bothering him at work. Taylor thought about calling him on the carpet about his change in attitude but decided against it. This was supposed to be a friendly call.

Instead, she said, "Hey, maybe we should postpone talking to another time. I only called because Joules said you wanted to talk, but we can talk later." The last thing she wanted was a full-blown emotional conversation in which she came off as crazy.

"No, I am glad you called. We have much to discuss, but I want to do it in person. Which reminds me, Joules is flying down first thing in the morning to bring you back for the gala. I assume you already have a gown. It is imperative we look like the perfect couple. I know that is a lot to ask, but I am asking. Let's get through tomorrow night, and you and I can hash this whole thing out. Can you do that?"

"Sounds like you have it all figured out." She was working to keep the bitterness out of her voice.

"I have. I would come to get you myself so we could talk on the plane. But I can't get away right now. There is too much going on now with the campaign and other things."

Taylor noticed that he faltered when he said, "Other things." She assumed he meant Poppy and their son, but she had no intention of asking.

Instead, she said, "What about after the gala? Do you have that all planned out, too? Are we just going to continue to be the perfect couple until the election? And what does little Miss Poppy have to say about all that?"

"First of all, leave Poppy out of this. It has nothing to do with her." Bennett had an edge to his voice that Taylor had never heard.

"I'd say it has everything to do with her," snapped Taylor, not even trying to mask the bitterness.

"Taylor, I love you, but I am warning you. Don't even think about saying anything about her. I mean it. It would be best to keep all this under wraps until after the election and confirmation hearing in January, but I am not sure that is feasible."

"And then what? We divorce, and I go off and pretend none of this ever happened. I disappear into a black hole?" Anger punctuated her words.

On the beach, she had been so much more objective and reasonable. On the phone, she lost all objectivity. All the hurt, sadness, and embarrassment of being cheated on came roaring back to life. The calm, reasonable woman on the beach was nowhere to be seen. Back in her place was the scorned woman out for her pound of flesh.

"It won't be like that. You know that. I will always take care of you. You will never want for anything."

"I don't want you to take care of me. Do you seriously think that is why I am upset? I'll let you know that I can take care of myself. That is something I should have been doing all along." Taylor could hear the hysteria in her voice rising. The need to tell him to go screw himself was growing by the minute. Until that moment, she had never even so much as thought that phrase, much less had to muzzle herself from uttering it.

"Okay, fine, whatever. But I think the real reason you are upset is that your pride has been hurt. I get it. What I did was unforgivable. If I could go back and change how this all came about, I would, but I can't. There are more people involved now than just you and me."

"You think this is about my pride being hurt?" Forgetting that some of what he was saying was true, she said, "You are so wrong!"

"No, I don't think so. That is exactly what this is about. If you would stop being emotional for five minutes, you would see that. Things have changed. I have a responsibility to them. They need me."

"You have responsibilities to them? They need you? What about me? What about my needs?" Taylor was practically yelling. She couldn't remember ever yelling at Bennett the entire time they had been married. Now she was screaming so loudly that he had to pull the phone away from his ear. She was so angry and had no way to stem the tide of emotions threatening to overtake her at any moment.

Sighing deeply, Bennett said defeated, "Taylor, you never truly loved me like a woman should love and want a man. It was nice and comfortable, and we were great on paper. But really, we never fit. You never needed me in that way. Be honest, what have you ever needed me for besides being there for you when you lost your family? Nothing, that's what."

"That's not true," Taylor cried. "I did need you. I needed you when I lost the babies. I need you more than you will ever know."

Bennett was quiet for several seconds and then very quietly said, "You had a funny way of showing it."

"What is that supposed to mean?" Taylor demanded.

"It means you were always better off alone. I felt like an intruder in my own marriage. Things just seemed to run better when I was gone. When I was there, it was as if I was just another burden you had to endure. Another person you had to entertain." Bennett sounded so defeated and sad.

Never mind that Taylor had already reached the same conclusion earlier; now, she denied it. "That's ridiculous." At this point, Taylor was too angry to be honest with herself. Her anger felt good, and she allowed her emotional state to fuel her comments. "I assume she needs you."

"If you are talking about Poppy, then yes. She does." Bennett said. By this point, Taylor had built up a head full of steam, and she yelled, "Okay, Mr. Know It All, tell me this. If you couldn't tell whether or not I needed you, how can you be so sure that Poppy does?" Taylor thought she had lobbed the winning shot in this hateful game of destroying each other, but she was caught unaware.

Bennett was quiet for several seconds, then said, "Because I see it in her eyes when she looks at me."

Whatever Taylor had been expecting Bennett to say, it wasn't that. His words so took her back, she asked in a small voice, "How does she look at you?"

Without missing a beat, he replied, "Like I am the moon, the sun, and the stars all mixed together."

Taylor could hear the smile in his voice as he spoke. Refusing to back down, she said, "Oh, so since I didn't worship you like a god, that means I did not need you? What a bunch of crap. It was all I could do to listen to this." At that moment, she hoped her words hurt him as much as his words cut her.

Sighing deeply, Bennett tried to take the level of intensity of the conversation down. Calmly he said, "No, it is more than that. In her eyes, I see how much she loves me, desires me, and needs me. You never looked at me that way. Not once. I don't think you ever felt about me the way she does. If you did, you never acted like it. Your interest in sex is almost non-existent. Look, I am not saying all this to hurt you. You are one of my oldest and dearest friends. I want to tell you everything, but not over the phone. The story is too big and too personal. When we talk, I think you will understand why all this happened. I love you, Taylor. I always will. I am just not in love with you any more than you are in love with me. It is time to move on."

"You love me? Oldest and dearest friend?" Taylor screeched. Giving over to her rage, she yelled, "Well, with friends like you, I won't need any enemies." She knew it was a cheap shot but was too far into the sea of anger to care. "As far as hurting me, it is too late for that. I am hurt, and you will have to forgive me if I refuse to spend one more minute talking about how much your mistress needs you. Maybe you just never desired me the way you do her. Have you ever thought about that? You married me when you were so obviously in love with her. Why the hell did you not fight harder for her? Why did you settle for me when you only wanted her? This is on you, Bennett! And one more thing, I don't want your love because I sure as hell don't love you at this moment." With that, Taylor slammed the phone down.

Crying hysterically, Taylor collapsed in a flood of tears for several minutes. When she cried herself out, she felt anger replacing hurt. A plan for revenge began to take shape in the back of her mind. Some of her more enlightening and evolved epiphanies from the beach had started to permeate her rage-filled brain, while sadly, some others about being non-emotional still lay forgotten in the back of her mind.

She would become an independent woman that men desired. She would take chances and do the unexpected. With those pledges firmly back in her mind, she looked up various local boutiques and selected one. She drove into town and picked out the sexiest dress she could find. It was deep purple and hugged all of her curves. Low-cut and sexier than anything she had ever owned, Taylor quickly bought it. On the way back to the cottage, she passed a lingerie shop and popped in. Before she lost her nerve, she purchased the shearest lace bra and thong set she had ever seen.

Donning the lingerie and dress was akin to putting on armor for a soldier. Knowing she wore them made her bolder and prepared her for the night ahead. Her hair was brushed to a high sheen and twisted in a sexy chignon. Lastly, she slipped on her heels and painted her lips with a thin coat of cherry red lipstick. The one item that she did not put on was her wedding rings. She had taken them off the first night she had gotten to the beach and had not put them back on since. Glancing at them, she knew her days of wearing them were over. There had been a time when she felt almost naked without them. Now, she could barely stand to look at them. Dismissing the rings and the fear she could feel gurgling in her gut, she took a last look at herself in the bathroom mirror and saw a woman ready to do battle with her own life.

Chapter 10

River Rat Bar and Grill
Gulf Shores, Alabama
March 2012

Once in the car, Taylor had to remind herself that if Bennett and Joules could run around having affairs and then talk about it like it was no big deal, so could she. After all, she was the one who always played by the rules, and yet they acted like she was the one with the issues. Well, she would show them tonight.

She was going to experience all the desire and passion that Bennett and Joules were so hyped up about. They weren't the only ones with needs. Taylor promised herself the only regret she would have about tonight would be if she came home the same boring, sexless woman Bennett and Joules seemed to think she was.

The anger, hurt, and rage that Taylor had worked up during her phone call earlier carried her all the way into town with the single purpose of finding a man, seducing him, and proving everyone wrong. It was almost ten o'clock when she finally made her way down the main strip and weighed her choices. All the bars looked extremely busy. It was unlikely anyone would recognize her, but she was suddenly rethinking her plan to be bold and daring.

She didn't want to be spotted and ruin everything but she refused to give up.

She was just about to return to the cottage when she remembered the rundown shack of a bar at the end of that boat dock she ran past every day. It was doubtful anyone would know her there. With her mind made up, Taylor quickly drove to the boat dock. It was not where she would have expected to find herself on a hunt for a man, but that is what made it so perfect. She was doing the unexpected.

The River Rat Boat Dock Bar and Grill was little more than a shack with blinking neon lights. From the look of the place, she was sure no respectable person would ever be seen there, making it the perfect place for Taylor to lose herself for the night.

As she approached the entrance, she could hear the muffled sounds of country music wafting from the building. Opening the door and stepping inside, her eyes and ears were assaulted by blaring music and a dark, smoky cloud that seemed to rush out and cover her, blinding her for a second.

It took a moment for her eyes to adjust. Once they did, she saw the overall theme of the place was shabby cowboy. She felt like she had been dropped into an alternate universe because she had never been to any place like this before. Peanut shells covered the floor. A long bar dominated one wall. Booths lined the other walls, and various tables were scattered around. Everything was covered in a disgusting 1970's orange vinyl.

The lights were low, but there was enough light to see a dance floor in the middle of the room. Several couples were dancing to an upbeat, popular country song from a jukebox in the corner. It was seedy and in much need of a makeover. And honestly, Taylor loved everything about it. There was an ease to the place that called to her and terrified her at the same time.

Feeling intimidated and unsure of herself, she stood by the door for a moment more, gathering her courage. One thing was sure: her mother would roll over in her grave if she knew where she was and what she was about to do. Momma would take one look at this place and say, "There is nothing here but trouble." Well, that was just fine by Taylor. Trouble was exactly what she was looking for, so she had come to the right place.

Feigning a confidence she definitely did not feel, Taylor threw her shoulders back, smiled a smile she didn't actually feel, and began to walk across the bar as if it was the most natural thing in the world. Surely, at least one man here would find her desirable. She just had to find him.

The minute Taylor entered the River Rat Bar and Grill, the atmosphere completely changed. Almost everyone in the bar instantly became aware of her. The music kept playing, but otherwise, everything else seemed to stop. Even the dancers appeared to turn and look at her as she crossed the floor. Of course, Taylor was unaware of any of this or the man sitting at the bar nursing a long-necked Miller Lite.

Before Taylor walked in, Dr. Greer Stone had been sitting at the bar thinking that River Rat wasn't his kind of place anymore. In his younger days, it was just the kind of redneck, honky-tonk he'd been right at home in. In fact, it was exactly like several bars he had worked in during college and medical school to support himself. Thankfully, those days were long gone.

Now, most of his time was spent at the hospital. What little free time he did manage to squeeze out for himself tended to be filled with classier pursuits like wine tasting and art galleries. However, occasionally, on nights like tonight, when he needed the company of others, he found himself slumming at the Rat. Coming here gave him a feeling of home without the poverty or bad memories. So, while he was by no means a regular, he had been to the Rat several times and knew almost everybody there.

Greer had been polishing off his second beer when the pretty lady walked in the door. Her presence captivated everyone's attention including his. Greer readily admitted the woman was a looker. Her beauty alone made her stand out, but it was more than that. Her demeanor was too sophisticated and cultured to be at home in such a seedy place. She was clearly out of her element. Surprisingly, something about her looked very familiar. He just couldn't place her.

Watching her take a seat at the bar, Greer could see good taste and wealth rolling off her in waves. Every inch of her screamed class and money. She was the perfect package of poise and grace, complete with a strand of pearls around her neck and the gold Rolex on her wrist. He instinctively checked to see if she wore wedding rings. Seeing none, he could not suppress a groan of pleasure. This woman looked as good as an orange push-up on a hot summer's day, and he would bet his most expensive bottle of wine that she tasted just as sweet.

The mystery lady reminded Greer of Christine. Thinking of her and their failed marriage was always a downer. It would have been so much easier if Christine had been a first-class bitch like most of his friends' ex-wives and ex-girlfriends. He could have put her into the hate zone and moved on, but she wasn't. She was a lovely woman whose heart he had trampled because his priorities had been screwed up. He had valued success and money over her. Well, he had lost her to his best friend, and it had been his fault entirely.

Crap, he was not going on another guilt trip. He could handle a lot but not guilt. He didn't do guilty. Guilt was dirty, wet towels after a nice hot shower. Neither did anybody any good. So, instead, he checked himself and pushed all thoughts of his failed marriage right out of his mind. Instead, he just sat quietly drinking and tried to focus all his energies on watching the pretty lady now sitting down from him at the bar.

Once seated at the bar, Taylor watched as the very muscled young bartender approached her. The guy leaned against the bar and flashed her a sexy grin before asking with open curiosity, "Are you lost? Do you need some help?"

That was not the question Taylor was expecting. She assumed he was coming over to take her drink order. She supposed she should not have been surprised that he thought she looked lost. Given that she was now seated in this bar, dressed the way she was, with the intent of picking up a man, she was pretty worried that she had lost her mind. But she didn't say anything about that. Instead, what she said was, "No. I am right where I want to be." As she began to look around the bar, Taylor didn't add but thought, of course that was about an hour ago when I was really mad. Now, I am not so sure.

Greer was seated close enough to hear everything being said but far enough away to go unnoticed. Watching her, Greer could think of nothing a beautiful, sophisticated lady like that would want in a place like this.

Dewey, the bartender, seemed to share Greer's opinion because he just shook his head and said, "Um. Okay, well, you want a drink? Some wine, maybe?"

Taylor considered the bartender's question carefully. In truth, she hadn't planned on even drinking tonight; however, now that she was here, a little Dutch courage sounded like a great idea. Perhaps a glass of white wine was just what she needed to see her plan through. Then, remembering her promise earlier to do the unexpected, she rejected the idea of ordering wine. Instead, she racked her brain for a drink that was chic and daring. If she was going to do this, she should do it right. Suddenly, Taylor remembered what her father and brother used to order, so she said, "McCallan 15, with a big rock."

Greer expected the classy woman to order a very dry chardonnay. Given his knowledge of wine, it was just the type of drink he pictured her ordering. You could have knocked him over with a feather when she hesitated and then ordered the aged whiskey.

The young bartender was as shocked as he was by her order because the guy chuckled and said, "Sorry ma'am, but we don't carry that. How about a little Southern Comfort instead?"

"Southern Comfort?" Taylor mulled that over for a second. The irony was too sweet to be missed. With a small laugh, she said, "That sounds perfect. A little Southern Comfort is just what I need."

The young bartender flashed Taylor another cheesy grin and said, "Yes, ma'am! Southern Comfort coming right up." Then, he wandered off to fill her order.

Greer was stumped but enthralled. Southern Comfort? Really? He had no idea what the lady's game was. Was she a bored country club princess? Whatever her story was, she was a fish out of water in the Rat.

After a few minutes, the young bartender returned with the drink and placed it in front of Taylor, saying, "Here you go." He treated her to another one of his sexy grins, complete with a wink, and said, "You let me know if you NEED anything else."

The bartender's blatant flirting caught Taylor off guard. It had been so long since anyone had flirted with her that she had almost missed it. But how the guy had drawn out the word "need" undoubtedly got her attention. While it had been flattering, it had also been unnerving. The bartender was twenty-two, tops. Taylor suddenly realized there were limits to what she was willing to do. Robbing the cradle was not one of them.

Sitting down from her, listening to every word, Greer almost snorted when the young bartender had drawn out the word "need" for extra emphasis. He had waited, expecting the pretty lady to put the kid in his place. Instead, she smiled at the guy, patted his bulging muscles, and said, "Oh, aren't you sweet. I am way too old for you. I appreciate it, though, but no, I'm good. Thanks."

That was it. No sharp reprimand? No sharp retort? Greer was stunned. He had no doubt that Christine would have crucified the guy on the spot.

Greer's next thought came in the form of a question. If the kid was too young for her, would he be too old? She didn't look a day over twenty-five, but she carried herself much older. And, since he knew the kid behind the bar was not that much younger, Greer figured she had to be at least in her early thirties.

He, himself, was holding onto his thirties by a string. He couldn't believe he would be forty by the end of the year. He was single, with no kids and no prospects. This was not how he had expected his life to go. He assumed by now that he would be married with at least two or three kids. His inability to recognize the things in life that mattered the most had cost him dearly. He promised himself that if he ever got a chance to have that life again, he would grab a hold and never let it go.

Since Christine, the closest he had come to a real relationship had been one-night stands with very pretty, very flexible, and very shallow women. Perhaps he should feel guilty about that, but he didn't. All the women he had spent time with knew the score. They had used him as much as he had used them.

Glancing at the gorgeous woman down from him, Greer wondered if she would be willing to be the next contestant on Who Wants to Play Doctor in My Bed Tonight. He doubted it. She looked way too classy for that, even with her low-cut dress, killer heels, and smoking-hot red lipstick.

While Greer was contemplating his odds of hooking up with her, Taylor was thinking about her ill-advised plan to hook up with a stranger at all. The longer she sat at the bar, the more she realized that she was totally out of her league here with her little plan. When she left the cottage earlier in the evening, determined to seduce the first good-looking guy she found, she hadn't expected it to be a young rebel without a clue bartender, who was barely legal. No, she wanted a much different type of man.

If she were being honest, she didn't have any particular man in mind. And she had no idea what to do next. She supposed she should wait for one of the many men in the bar to walk up and offer her a drink. However, most of the ones she had seen were not really her type. Call her an elitist snob, but teeth and clean hair were going to be a must.

If she had her way, a gorgeous man between thirty and forty would walk up and sweep her off her feet. He would carry her home and make mad, passionate love to her until she cried. Of course, in her fantasy, she could never quite figure out how one went about asking about past health history and if any STDs might be involved. She never had to have such a conversation but imagined it would put a damper on the passion.

Feeling her bravo leaking away, she considered giving up and returning to the cottage. But to do so was akin to admitting that she was the frigid, sexless woman that Bennett and Joules thought she was. Just thinking those thoughts reignited the fire that fueled her harebrained trip to this sketchy bar in the first place. Determined for them not to be right about her and vowing for things to be different, Taylor picked up the glass the bartender had set in front of her, raised it to her lips, and defiantly tossed back the amber liquid.

Fire immediately rained down the back of her throat and into her chest. For a moment or two, Taylor could not breathe. Coughing and sputtering, she had to hold onto the bar rail to steady herself. Whatever she was expecting, this was not it. Slowly, the fire seemed to burn out and was replaced by fuzzy warmth that spread through her entire body.

Wow! That nearly killed me, she thought. How do people drink this? Doing this unexpected business is way more difficult than she expected. She wanted to do something different, but she didn't want to die doing it. All of these thoughts were crashing through her head. Slowly, the alcohol began to work its magic, and her body began to relax. After a second, she called out, "One more please."

Taylor threw the second drink back with slightly more finesse than the first. This time, she didn't have a coughing fit or nearly fall out on the floor. No, the amber liquid went down a lot smoother.

It took a few minutes, but finally, Greer remembered how he knew her. He recognized her as the pretty mystery lady who had been his patient the week before. She was the one who had come in with a panic attack. As he watched her unnoticed, Greer contemplated whether or not trying to pick her up would be a conflict of interest. Ultimately, he comforted himself with the knowledge that she wasn't a patient anymore—so, no harm, no foul. After all, he was a heart doctor, and her heart was fine. The only reason he had even seen her was that he just happened to be in the ER trying to talk the very lovely nurse named Beth into dinner and drinks when she had been brought in, presenting elements of a heart attack. As head of the cardiac department, he attended her because he was there and could. But, no heart problems, no need for a heart doctor. So, there was no conflict of interest in him getting to know little Miss Panic Attack better.

Looking his fill of her, Greer thought, man alive, didn't she clean up nicely. The last time he had seen her, her hair had been a mess, and she had been wearing a bright pink sports bra and running shorts. Once he had deduced that she was not having a heart attack, she had almost given him one with that bright pink bra.

He was a doctor, a very good and professional doctor. But he was still a man. He was diligent around beautiful women like this one to ensure the lines of professionalism were never crossed. As long as a beautiful woman was his patient, he never saw them as any more than that. It was all business and body parts, science and medicine. But once that barrier was removed, it was like scales fell from his eyes.

He remembered it had happened that way with her. When she first came into the ER, he was totally focused on treating her and saw her only as a patient in need. That all changed once he realized she was just having a panic attack. She was worrying with the leads and wires for the EKG, and his eyes had been drawn to her chest. In a rush to put the leads on, the nurse had just pulled the bra down low in the front, and her boobs were hanging out. They were not large breasts, but they were beautiful. He'd known right then that he had to get out of there and hand her off to another doctor.

That had been days ago, and he honestly had not thought of her since. Now, after seeing her here tonight, she was the only thing on his mind. He scooted back a little behind the guy next to him and put his head down so he could continue to watch her without her realizing it.

Three stools down, Taylor decided she had enough liquid courage to make her move. She did a quick three-sixty of the room. At first she did not see anyone that in any way interested her. She was about to give up, cry to her uncle, and head back to the cottage when she spotted her prey.

The second Taylor laid eyes on Greer, she literally felt a jolt of desire run through her. His head was down, so she could not see his face. However, everything else about him was amazing. He wore a black tee shirt that fit tightly across his shoulders, jeans, and scruffy cowboy boots. Taylor fixated on the boots for a few seconds. She had always had a thing for cowboys in books and movies. Slowly, she let her eyes sweep up his body. She was trying to figure out how to approach him when he raised his head, and their eyes connected. For several seconds, they just stared at each other. Neither one said a word.

Taylor didn't know if it was the alcohol working its magic, but the lightning bolt of lust she felt looking at the gorgeous cowboy blew her away. He was her fantasy man come to life. But really, who could blame her? He was absolutely delicious from the top of his dark hair down to his well-worn rugged boots. He was by far the sexiest, best-looking man she had ever seen, a real-life Marlboro Man just for her.

Greer had to give the lady credit. When he caught her staring a hole through him, she had not so much as blinked. Instead, she devoured him with her eyes. It had been a long time since anyone had looked at him the way she was now. He felt the first licks of lust kick start in his belly and then move lower. He saw a hunger in her eyes that surprised him and turned him inside out. His jeans began to get tighter by the minute.

Now that he knew who she was, Greer became concerned. He had just witnessed her slamming back whiskey. He seriously hoped she was not still taking the pain meds he had prescribed. Alcohol and pain meds were a terrible combination. Still watching her eyes closely, he knew the second that she recognized him.

Grinning at her like a Cheshire cat, he said, "Are you stalking me? Because if you are, you won't need to fall out with another panic attack to get my attention this time."

"Oh. My Word." That was all she said. She just sat there with her mouth hanging open in shock. After a second, she closed her mouth, cleared her throat, and said, "You are the doctor from the emergency room, right?"

She had been so mesmerized by his Hollywood hunk looks that she had not recognized him as the sexy ER doc from earlier in the week. Once she did, her confidence faltered. She knew no one in this town, yet she had picked the one bar where the one person in town who knew her was. What were the odds? She had almost backed off her plan to seduce him.

Putting out his hand, he said, "Greer. Please, call me Greer."

"Greer, well, um. No! I am absolutely not stalking you. No stalking here." She seemed awkward and unsure of herself. He found that to be at odds with the sexiness with which she had walked in.

Seeing how flustered she was amused and confused him at the same time. Giving her a huge grin that showed all his perfectly formed white teeth, he cooed, "Darn, I was hoping you were. There is nothing better than being stalked by a beautiful lady. Unless it is being caught by one."

Taylor blushed and swallowed deeply before saying, "Um, thank you. And thank you for your help the other day. I was so embarrassed. Nothing like that has ever happened to me."

"Oh, you have nothing to be embarrassed about. I was just glad it wasn't anything more serious," he thought, especially since if it were, I would not be here now talking to her.

Then he said, "Stress can raise havoc with your body. You just can't let it get to you. And, as your doctor, that one time, and hopefully, that one time only, I must say that mixing prescription drugs and alcohol is a terrible idea."

Gesturing to the empty glass on the bar, he added, "I trust that you are not doing that because if you are, I am going to insist you switch to water immediately. Plus, I am about to give you a long lecture about the danger to your liver and body and ….."

"No, no, no! I didn't." Taylor rushed to interrupt him, mortified that he thought she looked like the kind of person who would do that. Of course, she had no idea what that kind of person looked like, but she knew it was not her.

Fumbling and falling over her words, she explained, "I never even filled the prescriptions you gave me. I just took it easy and followed the doctor's orders. I promise. I'm good." She laughed and said, "I am even running again. So, it's fine. I'm all fine." Giving him a shy smile, she waited for him to say something.

Eyeing her for a second, Greer assessed whether or not she was being honest with him. He hadn't spent too many years around hospitals seeing people hooked on all kinds of drugs not to learn a thing or two about their habits and appearance. He could tell just by looking at her that she was telling the truth. Even with two shots of bad whiskey, her eyes were still clear.

Letting his eyes take all of her in, he felt desire kick hard in his lower gut again. She was true perfection. Everything about her was the picture of health and vitality, from her shiny brown hair to her sun-kissed skin. Not to mention her body! It blew his mind. If he didn't already know she was a runner, her body would have told him. She was long and lean.

Assured that she was straight with him about the pain meds, he gave her another heart-stopping grin and said, "Well, I am certainly glad you are feeling better, TJ. It is TJ, right?" While he was still talking, Greer scooted down three stools to sit next to her.

"How sweet. You remembered my name." Taylor was shocked this was happening. One minute, she was wishing her dream guy would show up and start talking to her, and here he was. The doctor was as fabulous as she had first thought. She could not believe he remembered her name.

With a wicked grin, Greer responded, "Well, that's because I am a sweet kind of guy."

Nodding, Taylor let her eyes sweep over him before giving him a sexy smile as she purred, "I can see that. I may have to start calling you Dr. Sweetness."

At that, Greer threw his head back and laughed as he roared, "Dr. Sweetness, my ass!"

They laughed at that and then just sat for a moment, looking at each other. Greer could feel the hum of physical attraction between them growing stronger and more intense by the second. Every part of her as a woman was calling out to him as a man. The smile on his face grew even bigger. He suddenly let himself hope that if he played his cards right, he might get to play doctor with lovely Miss TJ before the night was over.

After a few minutes of just eating each other up with their eyes, Greer, *Dr. Delicious*, as Taylor had begun thinking of him in her head, suggested they get a table. Pointing to the last booth in the back, he said, "How about we continue this over there?"

"Sounds like a plan, cowboy." Taylor was trying hard to sound flirty and sexy which felt strange and out of character but also empowering. She loved seeing the effect her words and actions were having on Greer. Looking at the way his eyes twinkled and danced when he looked at her made her feel desired and sexy. These were two uncommon feelings that she was very much enjoying feeling.

Laughing, he replied, "Oh, it's cowboy now. Well, at least that is better than Dr. Sweetness." Motioning her towards the booth, he added, "While you grab that booth, I'll get us another drink."

Walking across the bar to the back booth, Taylor snickered to herself, wondering what he would say if she called him Dr. Delicious. She would just bet he would hate that one for sure.

A few minutes later, Greer joined Taylor at the back booth with a beer for him and another whisky for her. She practically grabbed the drink out of Greer's hand and slammed it back in the same manner as the previous two. This whiskey was quite strong, and once again, she began to cough and sputter.

Greer reached across the table and patted her on the back, trying to help her catch her breath. Giving her a measuring look, he said, "You aren't much of a whiskey drinker, are you?"

Shaking her head, Taylor choked out, "What was your first clue? But, I am trying to expand my horizons." She hoped that sounded sexy and worldly.

He gave her another measuring look and asked, "Is that why you ordered whiskey? To expand your horizons?" If that was what this was all about, it was starting to make sense. Greer knew this woman had never been in a bar like the Rat. She was a mystery but one he would thoroughly enjoy solving.

Taylor shook her head and said, "No, I ordered that because I didn't want to be stereotypical and order my standard white wine. I wanted to be bold and daring, but I don't know any drinks that fit that description. Then, I remembered that my father and brother drank McCallan, so I ordered it. But, next time, I think I will stick with the wine."

"What, no more Southern Comfort?" He could not believe he had this incredibly beautiful woman's attention and was wasting time talking about whisky. He must be losing his touch.

She laughed at this gentle teasing. And, as easy as you please, he took the hand that had been on her back and moved it to her face. Caressing her cheek with the back of his hand, he asked, "How about I order us a nice bottle of wine? They have one or two decent wines here. Would that be okay?"

Taylor gave him a shy smile and nodded.

"Good, be right back." Then Greer went to the bar and returned shortly with a bottle of white wine and two glasses. Pouring them each a glass, he asked, "So, tell me all about yourself?"

Trying to appear mysterious and not revealing too much, Taylor replied, "Well, what do you want to know?"

Swallowing a quick sip, Greer replied, "Oh, you know. The normal things. Where are you from? What do you do? Things like that."

Knowing she had to be cagey in answering his questions, Taylor took a page out of Joules' book. She was as honest as possible but didn't always tell the whole truth.

Holding her wine glass up and twirling it around in her hand, she said, "I am staying nearby. I am a teacher."

"Really, what grade?" The interest in his eyes was evident.

"Well, I am not currently teaching, but I hope to be soon. I taught second grade for years. I love it. Children are like little sponges; they soak up so much. I love being a part of that."

A measure of truth could be found in all her responses. She had not told him where she was from, but she was staying nearby for at least one more day. She had been a teacher. She omitted the part about also being a housewife of a US Senator. Turning the tables on him, Taylor asked, "What about you? Are you from here?"

Greer settled back into the corner of the booth and said, "Not originally, but I have been here for several years now. As you know, I am on staff at GSRH but originally from Tennessee. My mom died when I was young. It was just my sister and my dad.

"I am so sorry. I lost my family in my twenties. It nearly destroyed me. I can't imagine losing a parent as a child. Are you close to your dad or sister?"

"Yeah, my sister, Alex, still thinks she is the boss of Dad and me. She makes sure we all come home for holidays and get-togethers several times a year. That offers me a sense of home that I would not otherwise have."

"It sounds wonderful." Taking another sip of her wine, Taylor thought about that. She wondered if that's what she had been missing, a sense of home and belonging. Now was not the time to explore that thought, so she pushed it out of her mind and said, "By the way, this wine is fabulous. I would not have expected them to have anything but boxed wine here."

Laughing, Greer nodded, "I can see why you would think that, but they carry a few decent wines. This one is a Californian wine. It is very crisp and light. I discovered it on my last trip to wine country. Are you a wine enthusiast?" Greer took a sip of his wine and waited for her to answer.

Taylor had been around expensive wines her whole life, but the truth was, she wasn't that big of a drinker and had never paid much attention to wines. At least not until this week. She had drunk more in the last few days than her whole life combined. But she had no intention of telling him that. Instead, she said. "I know what I like if that is what you mean."

Nodding, he said, "Well, that is a good place to start. Have you ever been to the wine country?

Taylor didn't want to outright lie. She had traveled extensively throughout Italy's wine country, but she had never been to Napa. So, she said, "No, I have never seen the wine country of California. Is it as beautiful as everyone says?"

"Yes, almost as beautiful as you." Taylor laughed at that. He might be laying it on thick, but her ego had been crushed. She would take all the compliments he wanted to bathe her in.

"Maybe I will take you to see it one day?"

Smiling, she said, "Maybe." In truth, Taylor thought the chances of that happening were highly unlikely.

For the next few minutes, they sat in silence, enjoying the wine and the music. Studying him as he slouched against the wall of the back booth, bobbing his head in time to the music, she realized that he was the embodiment of what Joules called "Sex on a Stick." Until that moment, she had never really understood what that meant. Now she did. He made her mouth water just looking at him.

They each finished their first glass of wine, and Greer refilled them and then asked, "So, have you ever been married? Or do you have any kids?"

Taylor had just taken a large sip of wine, and the question caught her completely off guard. She was so shocked that she literally spat the entire sip out of her mouth in a giant spray all over the table. Wine went everywhere. To say she was mortified would have been an understatement.

Grabbing napkins and wiping as fast as she could, Taylor tried to think of the best way to answer. After a second, she said, "Yes, once. It didn't go so well." She didn't elaborate, and thank goodness, Greer didn't ask her to. After a second, she added, "As for children, I always wanted them, but I couldn't have any."

Greer nodded and said, "Same goes for me. Divorce sucks. I would have loved to have had a couple of rugrats too. But it was not meant to be, so I totally get where you're coming from. My ex-Christine wanted kids from the time we got married, but I kept putting her off. I thought we had all the time in the world. I was more interested in being chief of surgery than daddy. I ate, drank, and slept my work. It was all I lived for, and now it is all I have left. I am not saying this to scare you off or anything. I am just working on being very honest and open. I am learning that life is too short to pretend to be something you are not. I was not the perfect husband, but I am trying to be a better person."

"Wow, that's pretty real. I would never have asked you this if you had not brought it up, but what ultimately happened? Did she get tired of you never coming home and just leave?"

"Something like that. Certainly, there were way too many nights I stayed at the hospital working when I could have been with her but wasn't. Often, when I was home, I was more focused on fishing or hunting with my buddies than being with her. I didn't value her or our marriage, and now I don't have either one. Long story short, she fell in love with someone else. It just so happens that he was my best friend. I couldn't blame her. He was and is a great guy. He was there for her when I wasn't. They are expecting their first baby any day now."

Taylor was quiet for a moment. So, he knew what it was like to be cheated on as well. Now, knowing how painful such an experience was, she was impressed with how calmly he was able to discuss it. She said softly, "That sounds rough. You don't sound the least bit bitter. Why is that?"

"I was for a long time, and then I just let it all go. The truth is I cheated first by not making her or marriage my number one priority. In doing so, I learned a life lesson about love. If you are lucky enough to find someone who loves you, you had better fight with all you have to keep them." Shaking his head for emphasis, he added, "I can promise you this, if I ever get the chance to have a loving wife and children again, I will not screw it up. I can be a doctor anywhere, but the love of a good woman is hard to find. But, enough about all that." Raising his glass, he added, "The past is the past. Let's toast to the future. Here's to new beginnings."

Taylor clinked glasses with him. She was awed by how open and honest he had been about what had happened in his marriage. She did not think she had ever met a man that evolved or together. She also felt very guilty about her inability to be honest about her own marriage.

As she took another sip of wine, she realized she had deliberately let him think she was divorced. Luckily, she had enough alcohol running through her veins by then that sustaining any level of guilt for more than a second was impossible. All thoughts of self-recrimination were thrown out the window the second Greer stood up and reached for her hand and said, "Dance with me."

Chapter 11

River Rat Bar and Grill
Gulf Shores, Alabama
March 2012

For the next hour, Greer and Taylor drank, danced, and talked. The more they drank, danced, and talked, the more comfortable Taylor became, and the thicker Greer's Southern accent became. The more he talked, the deeper she fell under his spell. Everything about her behavior was so out of character that it was like Taylor had become a different person. She held nothing back. She was simply enjoying the moment.

Almost all the songs they had danced to so far had been fast, up-tempo songs. Both Taylor and Greer were damp with sweat when a slow song about a love gone wrong came on the jukebox. As the sultry sounds of the song filled the room, Greer pulled Taylor close. She could feel his hot breath on her neck, and his hands burned everywhere he touched her. She knew he could feel the perspiration running down her back, but for the first time in her life, Taylor didn't care that she was sweaty and disheveled.

Instead, she allowed her entire body to relax into Greer's and let the music move her as her hips swayed seductively to the music. Her body was on fire with desire as she pressed herself against him. She had spent most of the night wondering if he was being as affected by her as she was by him. She was elated when she felt the proof that he was.

The longer they danced, the more sensual the movements became. If Taylor had been in the room watching them, she would have been appalled. She would have never believed she could be so blatantly sexual in public. She ought to have felt some measure of shame, but she felt none. All she felt was heat.

And then it hit her. She was in deep. In the sappy romance novel she secretly devoured earlier, the heroine fell madly in love with the hero at first sight. She had always thought that was ridiculous. No one fell in love at first sight. What she didn't know, until that moment, was that falling into lust at first sight was extremely possible. She was up to her eyeballs in lust.

She had come here tonight with a plan to seduce a man. But in the end, it was she who had been seduced. It felt wonderful to want someone as much as she wanted Greer. It felt even better, knowing he desired her as well. The question was, for all her bravado earlier in the evening, did she actually have the courage to do anything about it?

She was not sure if what was happening between them was that trigger thing Joules had been talking about or not, but this guy made her feel things she had never felt in her life. Turning her head slightly, Taylor could not resist putting her mouth at the base of Greer's neck and allowing her tongue to taste a few drops of sweat that rested there. The second her tongue touched his skin, she felt a shiver run through him.

Burying his face in her hair, Greer whispered, "Before you strike the match, darling, make sure you want the fire."

Pulling back just a fraction, Taylor looked up into Greer's eyes. The hunger and passion she saw simmering there almost made her knees buckle.

Gritting his teeth, Greer all but growled, "Stop staring at me like that, TJ, unless you mean it. It makes me want things I am not sure you are willing to give."

Taylor did not know how to respond. She wanted to ask him what he had seen in her eyes that he had wanted so badly when Bennett's earlier words floated through her mind. And suddenly she knew what he had seen, and it gave her courage to take the next step.

Placing her hands on each side of Greer's face, Taylor gently pulled his head towards her. Slowly, she melted her lips into his. Her tongue slipped into his mouth and caressed him. It was a long, slow, wet kiss, and when it was over, Taylor looked deeply into his eyes and said very determinedly, "I want what you want. And I want it now."

Her words were barely above a whisper. For a second, Taylor wondered if he had heard her because he did not respond. And then suddenly she knew he had because he became a man of action.

Not wanting to give her a chance to change her mind, Greer took her by the arm and practically dragged her off the dance floor and across the bar. Grabbing her purse from the back booth, Greer yelled, "Put it on my tab" to the bartender and they sprinted out the door.

Once outside, Greer was walking so fast that Taylor was having a hard time keeping up. She had no idea where they were going. She had expected him to go towards the parking lot, but he did not. Instead, he had turned and headed towards the area where several boats were docked.

"Where are we going?" Taylor asked.

"I live on a houseboat at the end of the dock. I don't like to drive and drink, so I always walk. It's not much further." The whole time he was talking and walking at breakneck speed.

Taylor was working double time to keep up with him. She was not a petite woman. At five-seven, she was above average for a woman, but his long legs made keeping up a problem. Add in the effects of the alcohol, and Taylor was basically a rag doll being pulled along behind him.

As they covered the short distance from the bar to the houseboat, Taylor replayed the events of the last several minutes in her head. She had to keep reminding herself mentally to breathe. All she could think about was being wrapped in Greer's arms again and kissing him until the fire he had started in her belly was extinguished.

They came to a steep set of stairs, and after several near slips on the steps, Taylor lost her footing and began to fall. Without missing a beat, Greer scooped her up. It was amazing how right she felt in his arms. She just snuggled into his embrace and held on with all her might.

With her in his arms, Greer sprinted down the short distance from the dock to where his houseboat was moored. Then, he carefully lifted her over the railing and sat her gingerly on the front porch of the boat. "Steady there, darling. You hold onto that rail until I can get on." Taylor was beyond words. She simply nodded her head and held on tight. She loved that when he called her darling, it came out darlin'.

In a split second, Greer bolted onto the boat, and Taylor was back in his arms. He opened a large sliding glass door and carried her into the front room. Once inside, he reached behind him to shut the door. The second the lock slid into place, he gently let her slide down the length of his body. His lips were everywhere, her face, neck, lips all at the same time. And she responded in kind. Like a ball of fire exploding in the night sky, their passion erupted in a fiery frenzy of kissing, touching, squeezing, and moaning. It was all so much and not enough at the same time.

As they made their way from the front door to his back bedroom, they left a trail of clothing that marked their path of lust. The pieces that could be removed quickly were left intact. Those that could not were ripped and left in tatters. By the time they made it to Greer's bedroom at the back of the boat, he was completely naked, and Taylor was down to her pearls and heels. Her last conscious thought as Greer pressed her down on his king-sized bed was that she still needed to take off her shoes and necklace. But just as she tried to sit up to do so, Greer pushed her back down on the bed and growled , "Leave them on." And she did.

Chapter 12

Carrington Office
Searcy, Arkansas
November 24, 2023

"Umm…" Harvey seemed to be struggling with the right question to ask. "What I um…" he tried again, "I don't know any other way to ask this than just to ask it. Did you break your wedding vows in a one-night stand with Greer Stone? I mean, that is just in such contrast to the goody two shoes image you always had."

"I hate to say so, but yes. I made a terrible decision that luckily worked out well for me, but one of the reasons I was hesitant to do this interview was knowing that my daughter, along with the rest of the world, would now know all my dirty little secrets," said Taylor. Her voice cracked as she spoke.

"Okay, let's get one thing straight. I do need you to be honest with me and tell me exactly what happened, but I am not like a newspaper reporter. I am a hired writer. The article I am writing is a marketing piece. I will not put anything in it that will embarrass anyone if I can help it. My job is to write an article that shows that love is complicated and messy in real life, but it is still just love. You, Greer, Poppy, and Bennett rose above all that happened back then and rebuilt your lives, richer and fuller than they were before from where I am standing. Even if Bennett were not running for governor, it would be a story worth telling." Harvey was so earnest as he spoke that, for the first time all day, Taylor was glad she had decided to do the interview.

"Thank you for saying that. Remember that when you start writing all the nitty, gritty details," replied Taylor.

"Promise," said Harvey. "Okay, let's get back to the grindstone. What happened next?"

Sighing deeply, she said, "All hell broke loose."

Greer Stone's Houseboat
Gulf Shores, Alabama
March 2012

"Bang! Clang! Bang! Clang!" Taylor clung to sleep as pain exploded in her head. She could feel herself rolling back and forth, from one side of the bed to the other. And with each roll, she heard a loud bang, followed by an even louder clang. How long this had been going on, she had no idea. She just wanted silence. Silence and sleep. She needed sleep. There was no pain in the blissful world of the silent unconscious.

"Ohhhh!" she moaned as the noise began again. Her head was going to split wide open. Each new sound felt like someone was hitting her head with a sledgehammer. Make it stop, she thought. Please, somebody, make it stop. But it didn't stop, and that was when she became conscious enough to know something was wrong because she had no idea where she was or where all that rolling and noise was coming from.

Lying perfectly still and holding her head with her hands, Taylor was able to stop her head from banging against whatever it had been hitting for a second, but the pain didn't go away. Slowly, she forced herself to allow consciousness to filter into her brain.

Refusing to open her eyes, she relied on her sense of touch to tell her where she was. Running her hands over the sheet covering her, she was able to deduce that she was not in her soft, lovely bed with the pristine white sheets made from 1200-count Egyptian cotton. Oh no! Most definitely not. These sheets were definitely not cotton. Opening her eyes a fraction, she saw herself swimming in a sea of black silk. Oh God! She was in a bed with black silk sheets. This was worse than she thought. Where in the world was she? For the life of her, she could not remember.

Closing her eyes tightly and trying to force her brain to work, Taylor tried to conjure up details from the night before. She remembered spending most of the day on the beach and doing some painful soul-searching. But that was where her mind went blank. Where was she? And how had she gotten here? She had no idea.

Her sense of touch wasn't giving her any answers either. So, she pulled up her big girl panties, metaphorically of course since she was not currently wearing any underwear, and forced her eyes open once again.

"Oh God!" She moaned again as the light attacked her from all directions. At that moment, she was sure she was going to die. She lay in the black silk sea and waited for the end. When she didn't die, she forced herself to open her eyes and focus.

From her vantage point in the bed, she could only see the most unusual pair of cowboy boots she had ever seen. They were directly above her. It took a moment for her to deduce precisely what was strange about them. They were being worn on the wrong feet. She wondered who in the world would wear cowboy boots on the wrong feet.

Before she could answer that question, a major dilemma presented itself. Nausea rose in her throat and threatened to spew everywhere. She was going to be sick, and it was not going to be pretty. She had to get out of bed and find a bathroom immediately. Moving faster than she believed possible, Taylor tried to hurl herself out of the bed. It was then she realized that she was the one wearing the boots on the wrong feet because when she tried to walk, she tumbled over the side of the bed in a heap of covers and boots. Time being of the essence, Taylor kicked her feet as hard as she could, and the boots went flying across the room. They came off quite easily as they were several sizes too big for her. With the boots gone, she pushed the cover to the floor and raced to find a bathroom. As she went, she realized that she was completely naked except for her mother's pearls. *This just keeps getting better and better,* she thought. Taylor spied the bathroom behind a half-open door in the corner and made a run for it. She just made it without a second to spare.

Lying on the small bathroom floor with her head draped across the toilet seat, Taylor realized she had hit rock bottom. Thank goodness Edna Stone and her crew weren't here to witness this.

That's when little flashes of the night before began to come to her, *the fight with Bennett, her decision to go to the River Rat, Greer, sweet, delicious Greer.* From there, she thought of all the wine she had drunk. *Yuck, all that wine.* Oh, no, thinking about the wine almost made her sick again.

Next, she remembered the dancing. She had loved dancing with Greer. Thinking about how bold and daring some of her dance moves were made her groan and cover her eyes. However, that paled in comparison to the next set of memories that washed through her mind.

With her eyes closed and her head still in her hands, she allowed scenes from the night before to replay themselves in her head. It would have been a triple xxx-rated movie for sure, given the array of trapeze tricks that had transpired once they had made it back to the boat.

Who am I? Taylor thought. What have I done? I have committed adultery and am now naked, puking my guts up in a strange man's houseboat. The anger that had sent her out the night before looking for revenge was gone. In its place was a boatload of guilt and self-recrimination.

Her shame was palatable. Each time she was sick, it was almost as if her body was as disgusted with her as she was with herself. All she could think about was finding her clothes and getting out of there as quickly as possible. She had no idea where Greer was. He wasn't in the bedroom or bathroom, and she didn't hear him moving around in the front of the boat. Taylor was praying she could escape without facing him as she had no idea what she would say to him if she did.

It took several minutes before she could move, but once she was sure she would not be sick again, Taylor reached out and grabbed a washcloth to clean herself up. The sight that greeted her in the mirror was not a pretty one. Remnants of last night's makeup could be seen in streaks and black marks smeared across her face. She lathered up the washcloth and washed her face as quickly as possible. Next, she finger brushed her nasty teeth and helped herself to a healthy portion of mouthwash sitting on the counter. Even with that, she worried she would never get the leftover liquor taste out of her mouth. She could still taste the after-effects of being sick. Spying some lotion on the counter, she squirted a dab into her hand and used it as moisturizer.

Her chignon from the night before had come loose. Her long dark hair hung tangled and matted in a half-up, half-down mess. Pulling the pins out, she tried finger-combing her locks into obedience. Realizing that was a joke, Taylor quickly platted it and used one of her pins to secure it at the base of her skull.

With all the most basic toiletries attended to, Taylor grabbed one of the decorative bath towels hanging outside the shower door. Wrapping it around her, she tiptoed back to the bedroom and began frantically searching for her clothes. Other than a ripped thong, all she could find in the bedroom were the ridiculously high heels she had worn the night before.

A naughty image of herself looking up at her heels as her legs dangled in the air above her almost had her running back to the bathroom. Promising herself that nothing like this would ever happen again, Taylor pushed all thoughts of the night before out of her head. She had to concentrate on getting dressed and getting out of there. She left the torn thong on the floor where it lay ripped to shreds but picked up the shoes and kept looking for her other clothes.

Quietly sneaking down the hall to the front room, Taylor followed a trail of clothing that told a sordid tale. Everywhere she looked, different pieces of clothing littered the room like pieces of evidence of her crime of adultery.

She noticed the decor she missed the night before. As Taylor was frantically searching the room for her missing pieces of clothing, she could not help but be impressed by the modern graceful lines of the chrome and black furnishings. Decorated in a minimalist style, the room appeared pristine and ordered, except for the clothing scattered around it. Several large and interesting pieces of art dotted the walls. Something about the pieces seemed familiar, but Taylor did not have the time to study them to figure out why. Instead, her attention was centered firmly on finding her dress, which she found draped across the corner of a couch.

Continuing her search, she saw that off to one corner was the boat's bridge, complete with the steering wheel, throttle, and a captain's chair. She had never ridden on a houseboat before. All the gadgets and buttons looked very complicated. There, she found her cream lace bra hanging from the ship's wheel. The one thing she did not see was Greer. Taylor was more than a little relieved to be alone on the boat. It gave the time she needed to dress quickly without having to talk.

Once she had dressed, Taylor toyed with putting the heels back on but decided she could walk faster barefoot. Any nagging guilt she had about sneaking out without saying goodbye or leaving a note was tramped down by reality. Taylor had no idea what she would have written in a note, so what would have been the point? It was best if she found her purse and got out before Greer returned from wherever he had gone. She spotted her purse on the bridge just as her cell phone started ringing. Grabbing it, she saw it was Joules.

"TJ? Where in the hell are you? Are you okay?" Joules sounded frantic.

Taylor had never heard Joules sound as stressed and worried as she did now. Whispering because her head was literally about to explode, Taylor replied, "I am fine. I am on a houseboat but am about to head back to my car now. How did you know I was not at the cottage?"

Sounding somewhat relieved but still irritated, her friend said, "Because I am standing outside of it. I have been ringing the doorbell and calling you for the last half hour. I almost called the police."

"Why are you here?" The events of the night before had left Taylor confused and on edge.

Sounding irritated, Joules said, "Remember, I am here in the jet to pick you up and take you home for the gala. But never mind that. Did you say a houseboat? What in the world are you doing on a houseboat at nine in the morning?"

Suddenly, Taylor remembered. The stupid gala was that night. She had to return to Searcy and face the music regarding her life, whether she was ready to or not. Taylor made her way up the long dock as she said, "It's a long story. Can we talk about it later?"

"Well, yeah, I guess," replied Joules. "Are you sure you are okay? Why are you whispering?"

"I am whispering because my head feels like it is in a vice," snapped Taylor, keeping her eyes peeled for any sight of Greer.

"Wait a minute. You are whispering because you are hung over. Aren't you? Did you even come home last night?" asked Joules. Taylor did not miss the accusatory tone in her friend's voice, but she did not respond to it.

After a second of silence, Joules practically yelled into the phone. "OMG, TJ, who are you with? What were you thinking? What if someone saw you?"

Joules continued to fire questions at Taylor, who made no effort to answer them. After several minutes of this, Taylor said, "Look, I can't talk anymore right now. I will be home in fifteen minutes. If you love me, please just shut up and have hot coffee and aspirin ready when I get there," and then she hung up on Joules for the second time in less than a week.

Throwing her phone in her purse, Taylor made her way up the stairs to the parking lot of the River Rat. As she did so, she could not keep her mind from remembering how Greer had swept her up into his strong arms here the night before. She honestly didn't remember everything that had happened in the night.

She was ashamed of herself for becoming the kind of woman who would cheat on her marriage vows. She acted foolishly and allowed her hurt pride to goad her into a situation she should never have been in. She was sorry she let it happen, but guilt and shame didn't kill you. They just made you more human. She could overcome them.

However another part of her, a deeper, more intimate part of her, was disappointed for a very different reason. She was sad because she knew the night before could never be repeated. Even though it had been wrong and shameful, it had also been glorious. She was thinking about how wonderful it had been. That sent a fresh bout of lust zinging through her body. Too bad, she thought, because she knew she could never see Greer again. She sadly accepted that Greer and the night they spent together would forever be a part of her past and had no place in her future. Getting in her car and driving away, Taylor promised herself that this would never happen again.

Chapter 13

Stone Cottage
Gulf Shores, Alabama
March 2012

By the time Taylor returned to the cottage, Joules had calmed down a little. At least she had the coffee ready and aspirin on the counter. "So, are you going to tell me what's going on or not?"

Taylor looked at Joules over her coffee cup and asked, "Is not really an option?"

Joules practically screamed, "No, of course not! I must know what is happening, or I can't protect you. Really TJ, after all we have done to keep this campaign afloat, how could you go off and pull something like this?"

Joules' words hit their mark, but Taylor's head still hurt too much to engage in a full-out discussion of the night before. She simply said, "First of all, I am not the one who put the stupid campaign at risk. Secondly, I could give two figs about that election. And lastly, what happened last night was a gross mistake that will never be repeated. No one saw me leaving, and there will be no repercussions from it. I will answer your questions the best I can, but we will never speak of it again after this conversation. Understood?" Taylor gave Joules a look that told her friend she meant business.

After a moment, Joules nodded and said, "Fair enough, but I do need to make sure of a few things before we drop it. Why were you on a houseboat, and how did you get there?"

Over the next few minutes, Taylor recounted as much of the evening as she could remember, leaving out the steamier details.

When she was done, Joules was stunned. After a second, she asked, "So, this guy, he used a condom, right?"

The look of shame and panic on Taylor's face was evident when she said softly, "I honestly don't know."

"How do you not know?" boomed Joules.

Covering her ears against the loudness, Taylor shrugged and said, "I was drunk. I told you. I don't remember everything. Just parts of it."

Joules shook her head and said, "Well, I hope they are the good parts, at least." At that, Taylor gave her a look. Unphased, Joules continued, "OK, we'll stop at the local hospital on the way out of town and get you tested. Hopefully, the guy doesn't have anything, but you can never be too sure."

Taylor yelped, "No, not here. I will do it on Monday. I promise."

"Where TJ? Someone might see you."

"I will drive to Memphis or Branson or something. I promise. I will figure it out. Right now, I just need to pack and get out of here. I want to go home."

And that was exactly what she wanted, to go home. However, over the last several days, she had stopped thinking of the house Bennett and she shared as 'home'. It was his home, his family home. She realized she no longer had a home and hadn't in over a decade. For the second time in her life, she was no longer sure where home was anymore.

Joules huffed and gave Taylor an exacerbated look, but in the end, she agreed. Over the next hour, Joules helped Taylor pack. After they packed the car, Taylor followed Joules, who was in a rental car, to the airport to meet Jamee, a staffer for Bennett. She had flown down that morning with Joules and was going to drive Taylor's car back. She waited at the airport to give them privacy. Once back at the airport, Taylor gave Jamee her keys, and she began the ten-hour trek back to Arkansas.

Once on board, as they waited for the pilots to finish going through their preflight checklists, Taylor looked at Joules and said, "I think we should keep what happened here between us. I don't want Bennett to know. He has had his little secrets, and now I have mine. Agreed?"

Joules just looked at Taylor for a second before nodding yes.

"Also, I have been thinking," Taylor said. "Obviously, I can't rejoin the campaign, but I don't want to sit around Searcy waiting and worrying that someone will find out about all of this. Rather, I would like to do something productive. I am ready to go back to teaching in the fall. Until then, I would love to find a volunteer position that would allow me to work with children while still being mostly incognito. Could you ask some of your Clinton School buddies and see if they know of a foundation or charitable organization that could use my help? I would really appreciate it."

Joules thought for a minute and then nodded, saying, "I'll make some calls. I'm sure I can find you something. Let me work on it."

At that moment, the pilots notified them they were ready for takeoff. The flight back to Arkansas took a little less than two hours. Taylor slept most of the way while Joules put some feelers out about possible options for Taylor to volunteer. They had just been cleared to land when Joules woke Taylor up.

"Hey, Sleepy Head, we're almost home. You need to wake up. I have a few instructions for tonight."

Taylor yawned and then listened as Joules laid out the plan for the evening. "I don't know if you know this, but Bennett has not been staying at the house. He has moved most of his things to the loft over his office. He will be by around six to pick you up for the gala. I know that you two need to talk. But I don't think he will try to have a major conversation tonight, so I think you are safe for now. Also, the Art Executive Committee Cocktail Party will be at six-thirty. The gala will begin at seven."

At the mention of cocktails, Taylor made a sour face. She was still feeling the effects of too much alcohol the night before to even think about a drink. Just the thought of it turned her stomach. "Well, I have no intention of imbibing any alcohol tonight or maybe ever again. Last night about did me in."

Giving her friend a sympathetic look, Joules said, "I hear you, but you have to attend the party. You don't have to drink, but you must be there. You don't have to do anything really but show up. As you know, normally, you would have been expected to introduce the featured artist and give a brief biographical sketch of her and her work. Given everything that has happened, Edna Stone has instructed Johnna Wright to do all that."

Taylor interrupted, "Won't that look suspicious?"

Giving Taylor a look, Joules said, "Well, would you have rather done it?"

Giving a rude snort, Taylor replied, "Are you kidding me? I do not want to do any of this."

"Exactly. Even if some people are surprised that tradition is broken and the past president doesn't act as the mistress of ceremonies, it is not that big of a deal. We will do our best to get through the night as it is without adding more drama. The less of a role you play, the better. So, if you are good with it, Johnna will take the lead."

"I am great with that. If I could get out of going, I would."

"Well, you can't. While we are on the subject of Johnna, I have been very impressed with her since all this happened. She has stepped up and done everything that needed to be done for tonight, and she has kept her mouth tightly shut. That first night, Edna called her to meet with us as the plan for tonight was devised. She was on point and seemed to really know her stuff."

"Yeah, she is great," replied Taylor.

Joules said, "I will have to make sure I thank her for everything she has done to keep everything under wraps and ensure the gala goes off without a hitch. Maybe a basket of expensive wine and cheese or tickets to a show and dinner in Little Rock."

The mention of expensive wines sent Taylor's mind directly to Greer. She knew he would know just what to send. Too bad she was never going to see him again to ask him. That thought made her sad, but it could not be helped. At that point, Taylor felt the plane touchdown. Taylor and Joules quickly deplaned and went to their respective homes to prepare for the night's event.

Chapter 14

Carrington House
Searcy, Arkansas
March 2012

At five-thirty, Taylor was dressed and ready for the gala. She hated to be late, and she didn't want Bennett coming in early and catching her undressed. A part of her felt like she was preparing for the fight of her life. Her hair, makeup, and gown were part of her armor. She needed the confidence that looking her best would give her to get through the night ahead.

When six o'clock came and went with no Bennett, Taylor became a little concerned and started calling his cell. She made three calls, and all went straight to voicemail. Finally, at six-twenty, Bennett called her.

Without bothering to say hello, Taylor answered and asked, "Where are you? We are going to be late."

"Hey, I know I am late, but something came up. Joules will be arriving any second to bring you to the club."

Irritated, Taylor sighed, "Really, Bennett? You are so pushing it. I am doing this for you."

Sounding more stressed and worried than Taylor could ever remember, Bennett said, "I know, but please don't ask me any questions. I have no right to request this, but could you trust me and just do as I ask? Just go with Joules to the club. I will meet you there as soon as I can. I am doing all I can."

After a second, Taylor sighed and said, "Fine. I'll meet you there, but you have a lot of explaining to do."

"I know I do. Thanks so much, Taylor. I owe you one." At that, Bennett clicked off.

A few moments later, she got a text from Joules letting her know she was in the drive. Trying to hurry, Taylor rushed outside and got into Joules' BMW.

Huffing Taylor said, "Can you believe this?"

"I know you are mad, but please, Taylor, cut Bennett some slack. He is under tremendous pressure right now."

Giving her friend an exasperated look, Taylor responded, "Well, guess what? He is not the only one. So, do you know why he is late?"

"No, I don't."

"If you did, would you tell me?"

Glancing at her friend quickly, Joules replied, "Honestly, I don't know. Things keep getting more complicated by the minute." Pulling up to the club and valet parking, Joules added, "But, I do know this, for all that has happened over the last week, Bennett is a good man. He has asked us to trust and support him. It is no less than he has done for us. I think we owe him that. So, please put a smile on your face, and let's just get through this night. Hopefully, we can begin to unravel this mess tomorrow. But, until then, be that shining star I know you can be and go in there and blow them away." Taylor gave Joules a long look before nodding. It was going to be a long night.

Searcy Country Club
Searcy, Arkansas
Ten Minutes Later

The cocktail party was almost over by the time Taylor and Joules arrived. Before entering the ballroom, Taylor had made Joules promise not to leave her side. Yet, almost immediately after agreeing to be her constant companion, Joules' cell phone went off. Begging for forgiveness, Joules said, "I am so sorry, Taylor, but I have to take this call. It can't be helped. Just wait here. I am going to step outside for just a second. Don't go in without me."

As Joules walked out a side door to take her call in private, Taylor weighed her options. She knew she could never face the crowd alone, so she decided to duck into the ladies' room to hide until Joules returned. She was quite relieved when she entered and saw she was alone. The room was usually one of the coolest places in the club, and tonight was no exception. The cool air felt refreshing.

Taylor checked her makeup and hair and washed her hands, anything to waste time as she waited for Joules. After about five minutes, she sent Joules a text telling her where she was and asking her to join her when she finished her call. That way, she would not have to go in alone.

Just then, Johnna Wright walked into the bathroom. "Taylor, thank goodness. I thought I saw you come in here. I've been watching for you for the last half hour. Edna's about to have a fit." Walking over to Taylor, Johnna hugged her and whispered, "Hey, how are you holding up?"

Taylor gave her a slight smile and said, "I am hanging in there. Joules said you have done a bang-up job with the gala. It looks like the Art League has found its next president."

Johnna gave her a look and said, "We'll see." After a second, she added, "I have to ask this because Edna is freaking out. Do you have any idea where Bennett or Poppy are? The gala starts in less than ten minutes, and no one can find them."

Forcing her smile to stay in place, Taylor said, "I'm not privy to Mrs. Thompson's schedule, but Bennett should be here any moment. " Taking a deep breath and letting it out slowly, Taylor said very calmly, "I think you should ask Joules about this. She might know something."

At that moment, Joules opened the door to the lounge and said, "Hey, sorry about that, TJ. I am ready now if you are?"

Taylor looked at Joules and said, "Johnna was wondering if you might know when Bennett and, um…..Poppy are going to arrive?" It took all she had to ask the question calmly and without emotion. As she spoke, she realized she was having trouble catching her breath. Trying to calm down and breathe, she added, "I thought you might know."

Joules looked from Johnna to Taylor and back again, and then said, "They are here and about to walk into the ballroom. We need to go."

Johnna gave a large sigh and said, "Praise the Lord. Let's get out there before Edna comes looking for us."

Taylor and Johnna followed Joules out of the bathroom and ran right into Bennett.

"There you are. I am glad I found you before I walked in."

Taylor looked up and started to say something to Bennett when she saw Poppy right behind him. In that instant, it was as if the world went silent. The others continued to talk, but Taylor was unaware of anything but the woman in front of her. She could not help herself. Taylor just stood there looking at Poppy, unable to move or speak.

Dressed in a long, strapless emerald green gown, Poppy was stunning. Taylor had not remembered her being so beautiful or so tiny, yet she was. Even in heels, she barely came up to Bennett's shoulder. Taylor was a few inches taller. Poppy was petite and reminded Taylor of a china doll. Her skin was pale and translucent, and her long red hair hung loose with soft curls falling down her back. The green in the dress brought out her green eyes. Taylor was mesmerized by how ethereal she looked.

The only thing disrupting her perfect features was the scowl on her face when she spied Taylor.

When Taylor saw it, her first thought was, *Seriously, I am the one who has something to frown on about her. Not you.* Of course, being Taylor, she said nothing. She just stood staring. In fact, Taylor was so engulfed by Poppy's presence that she did not notice the man standing behind her until he called her name.

"TJ? Is that you?" the man said.

Taylor looked to her left and felt the little air she had managed to draw into her lungs rush out. The man calling her name was none other than Greer Stone, and he was standing next to Poppy.

Looking from Greer to Poppy, and back to Greer's face, Taylor had no idea what he was doing there or why he was holding Poppy's hand. Panic began to rise in her throat.

Dressed in a black tuxedo, Greer was looking at her with a confused look on his face. With wide eyes, he asked, "TJ? What are you doing here?"

Before Taylor could respond, Bennett looked at Taylor and asked, "Do you know him?"

At the same time, Poppy looked at Greer and asked, "How do you know her?"

Suddenly, everyone started talking at once, but Taylor did not hear a word being said as her chest began to tighten.

At that exact moment, Edna Stone walked up and said, "Well, it is about time you all got here. Better late than never, I suppose. I am glad you have all met my nephew, Dr. Greer Stone. He was responsible for recommending Mrs. Thompson for this year's auction as he was quite familiar with her work. He is a renowned cardiovascular surgeon from Alabama. And, given the situation of late, he has graciously agreed to be Mrs. Thompson's escort for the evening."

Gesturing towards Taylor, she continued, "Greer, this is Taylor Carrington." Looking at Bennett, she added, "The current wife of the next Vice-President from the great state of Arkansas."

At that moment, Taylor saw Greer blanch. Edna kept talking, but Taylor heard none of it. In her head, it all clicked. His last name was Stone. The art in his houseboat. The reason it seemed so familiar was that several of the pieces were by Poppy. Breathing suddenly became impossible, and a roar erupted in her ears. Gasping for air, Taylor tried to keep herself upright.

"TJ, is that true?" Greer asked, confusion and hurt clouding his face.

Before Taylor could answer, Bennett looked from Taylor to Greer and asked, "Taylor, what is going on here?"

Everyone looked at Taylor and waited for an answer. Only she didn't have one. Not one that she was willing to give anyway. She opened her mouth to say something, but nothing came out. Instead, the pain in her chest intensified. Grabbing it, she groaned heavily and collapsed to the floor as everything went black.

Chapter 15

Carrington Office
Searcy, Arkansas
November 24, 2023

Harvey Cox had finished scribbling his notes and put down his pen. He took off his glasses and rubbed his eyes. Then, giving Taylor a frank look said, "This is crazy. This story is like some crazy romance novel. This is not real life. There are so many twists and turns. Greer knows Poppy and comes as her date. What are the chances? If I did not know this actually happened, I would think you were making it all up."

Nodding her head, Taylor replied, "Oh, trust me. I understand. I lived it and still have trouble believing it all happened. I will tell you that when Greer walked in with her, it was a life-changing moment. Until that moment, I did not get the whole six degrees of separation thing. Now, I am a believer. There is a consequence to every action, some good, some bad. And that we are all connected in the universe. What we put out affects others as much as us.

These are concepts I work hard to teach Rosie, even as young as she is. Every decision she makes will have ripple effects, even to people she doesn't even know. I did not know Poppy Thompson from Adam but the decisions she and Bennett made long before I was in the picture greatly affected the trajectory of my life. It ended up having a very positive impact, even though, at this point in the story, I did not yet know that. I had no idea that Greer knew her or had supported her art career."

Picking his pen back up, Harvey said, "Okay, let's keep going. What happened next?"

Searcy Country Club
Searcy, Arkansas
March 2012

Taylor could hear people talking, but it felt like they were a long way away from her. It was very dark where she was, and no matter how hard she tried, she could not open her eyes. It was so peaceful where she was. She did not want to leave it, yet she somehow sensed she had to.

Very slowly, she forced her eyes open, and the first thing she saw was Greer's face. He was leaning over her, frowning. Still, she was again struck by how beautiful he was. She felt the fingers of attraction clawing at her even as she was still in pain. She opened her mouth to speak, and another pain squeezed her chest, causing her to moan once again, "Oh." She closed her eyes again and tried to reach back for the sweet oblivion of the darkness.

"TJ, open your eyes. It's Greer. You're fine. You are just having another panic attack. Remember, like the last time. Just stay with me. You're doing great."

Slowly, Taylor reopened her eyes and tried to focus on what Greer was saying. After a few moments, she said, "Just another panic attack. Are you sure?"

"Yes, Dr. Payne is also here. She is going to check you out to make sure. I am going to talk to my aunt, but I will be right back. Don't worry. You are okay." Greer excused himself and went in search of Edna.

Taylor's regular doctor examined her for the next several moments and concluded that Greer had been correct. Taylor was probably just having another panic attack. The doctor gave her a shot to calm her nerves and offered to write her prescriptions for anxiety medications. Taylor explained that she already had prescriptions at home but had just not filled them because she did not believe she needed them. The doctor suggested that Taylor consider filling them as a precautionary measure. She also made sure that Taylor had a ride home to rest. Confident that Taylor would be okay, Dr. Payne excused herself and returned to the gala. Thankfully, Greer came back into the room a few minutes later.

"Well, you were right," Taylor told him hesitantly. "It was just another panic attack."

"Yeah, I know. I talked to Dr. Payne before I came back in." While he was being kind, Taylor could feel that things between them had turned cold.

Looking up at him, Taylor asked, "Where is everybody else?"

"Well, if you mean your husband," Taylor did not miss the sarcasm in his voice, "he carried you in here. But then, Poppy got upset about something, and he took off. He ran after her, but only after I promised to take care of you. There is a lot going on here, isn't there?"

Taylor sat up enough to see where she was. She was lying on a couch in the library. The irony of her being brought into this room was not lost on Taylor, even as her chest continued to spasm. She nodded and said, "More than you can imagine." Even though Greer was being nice, Taylor could tell he had become distant and was treating her much differently than he had the night before. He seemed angry. He definitely had a right to be. Not only had she run out on him this morning, but she had lied to him about so many things.

Wanting to keep things light, she asked, "What about Joules and Johnna and all the others?"

"Joules is outside getting the car ready. She is dying to get in here, but I asked for a few more minutes with you before she takes you home." Giving a little sad laugh, he added, "My poor, old Aunt Edna nearly had a stroke when you collapsed. We all did. I'll say this for you. You definitely know how to make an entrance."

"What about the gala? I hope my fainting didn't affect the auction. The hospital counts on the money raised each year to keep many good programs going."

"No worries. No one in the main ballroom ever even knew something happened. It has gone on as planned, and from the looks of the bids, it is going very well."

"Well, at least that is good." Sighing, Taylor added, "I guess you have figured everything out by now? I mean about my being…married to Bennett. And, about him and Poppy?"

"No, not really. My aunt clued me in on some of it. I figured out most of the rest of it, but I am struggling with why you lied to me."

Giving her a hurt look, Greer added, "You're married. Why did you let me think you were divorced? I realize now that you never said you were single, but you let me think that. I sat there and told you all about my marriage and about Christine, and you never once said a word about being married. Then, when you said you had not been with anyone in almost two years, I assumed you had been single that long. You let me assume that. Why?"

Sighing deeply, Taylor said, "You're right. I am still married, but it is only a technicality. I was telling the truth when I said I hadn't been with anyone for that long." Trying to make him understand, she continued, "My marriage has been dying slowly for a long time now. I just refused to deal with it. And then, I had to, and I didn't know how. So, I just lost it. I ran away to the beach to think and stumbled across your path. The bottom line is that my marriage is over. We are getting a divorce as soon as possible. Bennett is in love with Poppy and wants to be with her."

"If all that is true, why didn't you just tell me? I was honest with you about the mistakes I made in my marriage. Did you think I would judge you for the ones in yours?"

"Last night was amazing. I felt something real for the first time in a really long time. I thought we connected and that it meant something. I woke up feeling great. I went out to get some food to make breakfast, but when I came back, you were gone. You ran out without so much as a note. I realized then that it hadn't meant as much to you as it had me."

Taylor hung her head and was silent for a moment. When she looked back up at Greer, she looked earnestly into his eyes and tried to make him understand. "I felt very connected to you, too. I would have never been with you if I hadn't. I know that now. I'm sorry for running out. That was wrong. I didn't know how to do this, and I panicked. I have never cheated before, and guilt and shame threatened to overwhelm me. Plus, I was very hung over. I just had to get out of there. Please forgive me."

Greer was silent for a moment and then said, "I don't know. I will have to think about it. In the meantime, we need to get you home. Joules has the car ready." Greer helped Taylor out to the car. They used the same side door that Joules had gone out of earlier and Taylor was able to get in the car without being seen. Once safely in the car, Taylor looked up at Greer and asked, "So, will I ever see you again?"

Greer gave a half smile and said, "I don't know, Darling. Do you want to?" There was that darlin' again. Hearing him say that melted her heart.

She smiled shyly and replied, "Yes, once this mess I am in the middle of is cleaned up and done with, I would love to see you again."

Greer smiled and said, "Well then, I guess the ball is in your court. Until then, please, TJ, get your prescriptions filled and take care of yourself." With that, Greer lightly grazed her lips with his before shutting the car door and walking away.

As they drove away, Joules looked at Taylor and said, "How are you feeling? You scared the bejesus out of all of us back there."

"I know. I am sorry. I am feeling much better. That shot that Dr. Payne gave me is starting to work." Taylor relaxed her head on the headrest and closed her eyes as Joules drove.

"Well, good, because I need to ask you something. You know how you asked me to find you a place to get lost for the next few weeks and work with kids?

Taylor opened her eyes and looked at Joules, "Yes, did you have any luck?"

Nodding, Joules said, "I did. I made some calls and think I have found a great place for you. I have booked the plane to take you to Miami in the morning to volunteer at a children's aid relief station for intercity kids from the Dade County area. But maybe you shouldn't go. I am worried that it will be too stressful for you. I talked with Dr. Payne. She says you are basically okay but need a break from all the stress you've been under lately. What do you think? Should you go or stay and rest?"

Taylor didn't even have to hesitate a second. She knew that she needed to stay busy and that working with children again would work the same magic on her now as it had after her family died. She would be much more stressed staying here and worrying about running into Bennett and Poppy. "Go! I definitely need to go! I have to get out of here before I lose my mind. Thank you so much, Joules, you are a lifesaver."

Chapter 16

Carrington Office
Searcy, Arkansas
November 24, 2023

"So, after everything that happened, you just decided to skip town and go to Miami?" asked Harvey. "Wasn't that a bit over the top?"

Considering her response carefully, Taylor said, "I can see why you would think that. But at that moment, I only wanted to hide under the bed and never come out. I remembered what it was like to be very depressed after my parents and brother died. I worked hard on myself in therapy and with self-help techniques to learn how to better deal with my life. I did not want to end up like I did before.

"Also, Bennett had made it clear that he wanted a divorce. Truthfully, by then, I did too. It felt wrong to stay in his family home. Getting out of town and out of the spotlight was the best plan.

By this point, Bennett had dropped back from seeking a vice-presidential spot on the ticket to working hard for a cabinet appointment. At that moment, it was very doable. He was going to be hitting the campaign trail hard for Anderson. I did not want anyone from the campaign suggesting we go out stumping together. He would have hated that as much as I would have.

So, Miami gave me the fresh start I needed. It got me far enough away from Arkansas that no one recognized me. Best of all, it put me on the path of my future, though I did not know it then."

Miami, Florida
March 2012

By early evening, Taylor arrived in Miami, picked up her car, found her apartment, and unpacked. One of the first things Taylor did was take a short drive to the local market and stock up on several staples and a salad for dinner.

Once back home, she fixed herself a large glass of iced tea and allowed herself to relax and enjoy her dinner. Afterward, she dressed for bed and then, once tucked in, picked up her cell phone and called Bennett. She had avoided calling him all day. She supposed that the more things changed in her life, the more they stayed the same.

He answered on the second ring, "Hello, Taylor. How was your trip? Are you all settled?"

Taylor was struck by how normal Bennett sounded. It was the first time he had sounded like the old Bennett in a very long time. "The trip was fine. Thanks. I called because Joules said you wanted to talk."

"Yeah, I did. Umm..Joules said the two of you talked about leaving everything as it is for now and then quietly dissolving the marriage a few weeks after the election."

"Yes, that is fine. But aren't you worried that someone will find out?"

"No, not really. I have some close friends who owe me favors. I think I can keep it quiet on my end. I want to ensure that you are on board with this plan. If not, I will drop out of Anderson's campaign now. I have given that a tremendous amount of thought, but Poppy is completely against it. So are Joules and Edna. What do you think?"

"You should not drop out unless you have to. There is no other person who is more qualified or more committed. It is your dream to serve at a higher level. If you can, you should stay and see what happens."

The phone was silent for a moment, and then Bennett said, "Why are you being so nice to me now?"

"Well, as the last week proved, a lot can happen quickly, and angry, bitter women say and do stupid things. So I am working hard at not being one."

"Wow. That's impressive considering last Friday, I thought you hated me."

Taylor let out a long sigh and said, "I don't hate you, Bennett. Believe me, I tried, but I couldn't. You are right. We are very old friends, and that was all we should have ever been. Maybe if the accident hadn't happened, things would have worked out differently. You know what I mean, you with Poppy and me with someone else. I don't know with whom but someone. But their deaths, or more specifically, Tatum's death, changed everything. I realized that while I was at the beach. We ended up together mainly because of a poor attempt to hang onto him. We clung to each other out of grief."

After a moment, Bennett said, "I think you are right. I think that sums our marriage up perfectly. I still miss him every day, but the pain has lessened and is not as gut-wrenching as it was. There was a long time when I could not even think of him without wanting to hit something. Now, when I think of him, I miss him, but it is not as bad. I guess it's true that time heals old wounds."

"I agree," said Taylor. "The pain became bearable, but it was too late by then. We were stuck in a marriage more of friendship than anything else. I think that is why we never could have children. Nature knew it was wrong to put the burden of holding a marriage together on a baby's shoulders. If we had a child, you would have never allowed yourself to love her again. And you do love her, don't you?" asked Taylor. There was no need to say who the "her" was. They both knew she was talking about Poppy.

"Yes, I do, with my whole heart. I don't say that to hurt you, but it's true. I think I always have. We had one magical summer together after I graduated from law school. Things ended badly. I never told you about her because it was just too painful. The last few months before she broke up with me were crazy. Your family and Tatum had just passed. The long distance thing did not work for us. She was in New York. I was in Searcy. I was studying like mad trying to pass the bar exam. I had my first big case and was working like seventy hours a week. There were times, I literally thought, I was losing my mind.

"I want you to know that I was never with her after you and I started dating. She was already married by then. Not once during our marriage was I ever tempted to stray until I saw her again. Finding out that she was a widow was a game changer for me. Instantly I knew. I knew we were going to be together again. The chemistry and history were too strong.

"We had no contact until February of this year when I went to see her at Edna Stone's insistence. I did not want to go. The hurt and pain of being rejected and dumped coupled with the knowledge that she replaced me so quickly was still too raw. I had no idea about Ben. I would have handled things completely differently if I had known. I honestly thought that Thompson was his father.

"I have to be honest with you about something. You know how people who cheat always say it just happened. Well, I am not going to do that. I am going to own up to my own selfishness. The minute I found out she was free, I knew we were going to be together. I don't say that to hurt you."

"You were right when you said I should have fought harder for her. I didn't, and now I've hurt all of you. I hate that. I meant what I said the other day. I do love you, but more like a sister, not a wife."

"Again, I am so, so sorry. I am so disgusted with myself. It has been a hell of a hard pill to swallow that I am not the person I thought I was. I wanted to be that good, faithful husband. I was for so long. But when it comes to her, I have no control. She is my everything, and if it destroys everything I have built to be with her, it will be worth it. She is that important to me. Her and Ben."

"You may not believe this, but other than that day, we have not been together at all since Ben was conceived. We just got carried away in the library. We both feel horrible about how all of this is playing out. I should have been upfront with you about my feelings the minute I realized I was still in love with her."

Though she appreciated Bennett's willingness to be vulnerable and take responsibility for his part in this, the conversation was just too much. Taking a deep breath she said calmly, "I don't want you to take this the wrong way, but I have no desire to discuss your relationship with Poppy."

"I respect that," said Bennett.

"I am trying to be glad that you have found someone to love. Regarding bad choices, I've made a few of my own lately. We all do, but we can't beat ourselves up too much. The best any of us can do is to own up to our mistakes, figure out why we did what we did, and then work like everything to never do it again."

For a second after Taylor stopped talking, Bennett didn't say a word. When he did, he said, "You're right, and I appreciate you saying that. I am not used to you being so deep and serious. Want to tell me how you got to this point? We don't have to go into all of it now, but when you are ready, I have much to share. Now, about some of those choices you've been making? Anything I could help with?" Bennett was back to being Bennett, the big brother who wanted to take over and fix everyone's problems.

Taylor hated that he knew her so well that he could hear her struggles in her voice. Not wanting to go into the last few days' events, she said, "No, thanks. Anyway, back to the original reason I called. I plan to stay here until the election is over unless you need me for something before then. I had considered getting a teaching job in the fall, but I may stay here and help at the relief station. Can you cover up my being gone?"

"I can if you are sure that is how you want to do this."

"It is."

"Okay, fine, I will get Joules to start putting together a cover story for your absence. I'll call you later this week to check on you. If you need anything, call."

"Okay, sounds good. Take care, and I will talk to you soon."

After they hung up, Taylor lay back in bed, pretty pleased with herself. She was finally taking the first steps towards being an independent woman. She was starting a new life in a new city and had just laid the groundwork to help her untangle her marriage.

Of course, she had a lot of help, but at least she was doing this on her own. She was proud of herself. Whether it was right or not, Taylor went to sleep that night thinking about Greer and wondering if he was thinking about her. He said the ball was in her court. She was committed to not pursuing him in person until she was truly single, but that did not stop her from thinking about him all night.

Over the next couple of weeks, Taylor settled into her life. She got up every morning and went for a run. The complex she lived in had a fantastic gym and running track that she used almost daily. She would come back, have a light lunch, and then drive across Miami to the children's aid relief station located north of the city near Lake Worth. She would spend several hours each weekday tutoring students in reading and math. And she loved every minute of it.

Most nights, she and Joules would touch base and have a short visit. While they talked, Taylor noticed that Joules was always careful not to say anything personal about Bennett. Poppy and Ben were never discussed. That was fine by Taylor. She had enough to worry about rebuilding her life in a new city. For the most part, everything in Taylor's life was calming down. She was working hard to develop a routine and a sense of normalcy.

However, one nagging little issue still plagued her that needed addressing. She had promised Joules she would go and be tested after her night with Greer. Almost every night, Joules would bring it up. Taylor forced herself to find a clinic and get tested. Once it was over and Taylor had been cleared, she vowed never to put herself in that position again. With that little detail dealt with, Taylor was now free to begin her life anew.

On the weekends, she tried to rest. Taylor wasn't sure if it was the heat or the humidity, but many days she found that she was so tired by the end of the day she could barely keep her eyes open. She would grab a salad from the fresh market on the way home each night because she was too exhausted to cook. Most nights, she fell asleep watching television or reading by nine. Her life was very simple, but she was enjoying it.

Joules flew down for a visit the fourth weekend she was there, a rare occurrence during a campaign. And one that Joules would have never allowed herself if Bennett had not insisted someone had to go to Miami to check on Taylor.

Joules noted several changes in her friend. The first was that she was much more independent. In the past, Taylor would have been up, fussing around, trying to wait on her and being the perfect hostess. Now, Taylor was much more relaxed and comfortable in her own skin. She had a new air of confidence that Joules had never seen.

They explored the city. They went to museums and fancy restaurants. They even took in a show. It was quite good, but Taylor only saw half of it as she fell asleep about halfway through it. Joules teased her about her need to sleep and joked that she was becoming narcoleptic. Privately, Joules worried that Taylor was still doing too much. She had never seen Taylor so lethargic. Whenever she had a chance, she would lie down and be out for a nap in two seconds flat. When Joules asked Taylor about this, Taylor blamed it on the heat, and Joules could not deny it was blistering hot. Joules left three days later feeling good about where Taylor was in her life. Joules realized that Taylor's decision to come to Miami had been the right one.

Chapter 17

Miami, Florida
June 2012

By the middle of June, school was out, and Taylor volunteered almost every weekday at the center. On the Monday before the last weekend in June, the site's director asked to see her before she left for the day. The director's name was Lucinda, a tall Hispanic woman with dark hair and eyes.

Taylor knocked on her door just before leaving and said, "You wanted to see me?"

"Yes, I did. I don't know if you have noticed the flyers around the building about this weekend being the medical mission weekend. We have doctors that come in once a month and do routine health screening and free medical care for our families."

"Yes, I have seen the flyers," replied Taylor. "The children talked about the last one for days afterward."

"Well, I mentioned it now because we always have a huge number of children at the center on those days and could use an extra hand. How would you feel about skipping one day this week and coming then instead? We could really use your help."

"I think that would be fine," replied Taylor. "What would you want me to do?"

"Just play with children and watch them while their mothers see the doctors. Mothers can be uncomfortable taking their children with them during their exams."

"Well then, of course. Count me in. I will take Tuesday off to run my errands and be here all day on Saturday."

CHAPTER 17

The rest of the week flew by for Taylor. She spent Tuesday cleaning her apartment and doing some shopping. She noticed that even though she was running almost daily, she had gained some weight. She had to buy a couple of pairs of new shorts and some long flowing skirts as hers were getting too tight. For years, she and Joules had joked about how their emotions affected how much they weighed. She tended to gain when she was happy and lose in times of stress and unpleasantness. Joules was the complete opposite. While she was not overjoyed about gaining weight, she felt it was a sign of how happy and content she was in her new life, so she was okay with the changes in her body.

As planned, she worked at the center from Wednesday through Friday. On Friday night, Bennett called to check-in. She found it funny that she no longer dreaded his calls. Each week, he'd call and update her on her investments and to check in. Much of the conversations were the same as they had been having for years without the need to pretend they were a loving couple when they weren't.

Occasionally, he would mention Poppy or his son, but it was always in passing. Taylor gathered from their weekly chats that he was spending a lot of time with them, getting to know his son. She was happy for them, but she sometimes got a little lonely and wished she had someone special to share her life with.

In those times, she would always think about Greer. She had not heard from him since the night of the gala but had thought of him more than she probably should. If she were honest with herself, she fell asleep most nights wondering where Greer was and what he was doing and hoping he was thinking about her as much as she was thinking about him. She also wondered if she would have the courage to contact him once her divorce was finalized. More importantly, she wondered if he was still interested in being contacted.

The center was a madhouse when Taylor arrived on Saturday morning around eight. Lucinda had assigned her to the arts and crafts area. For four hours, she made friendship necklaces and colored pictures with three times as many children as usual. The children seemed to enjoy the crafts, and she could tell the parents really appreciated the help.

Around noon, Lucinda stuck her head in and told Taylor that a hospitality room had been set up in one of the classrooms if she was hungry. Lately, Taylor was always hungry, so Lucinda covered for her while she went to get some lunch. Taylor was filling her plate with an assortment of fresh vegetables and a sandwich when she heard another volunteer walk into the room. Looking up, her heart almost stopped. Greer stood in front of her in a white doctor's coat over worn-out khaki shorts and a tee shirt. And he looked as delicious as always. They just stood staring at each other for a few moments.

Then Greer said, "TJ, is that you? Woman, you show up in the most random places. I swear, I do think you are stalking me."

At his references to what he had said to her that night in the bar, Taylor could not help but laugh. Smiling, she replied, "Well, maybe you are actually stalking me. I was here first."

"Okay, you got me. Busted." Greer gave her one of his killer smiles, and she felt it all the way to her toes. "But, seriously, what are you doing here? I thought you would be back in Arkansas."

At the mention of Arkansas, an uncomfortable silence filled the room. After a moment, she said, "I don't have time to explain all of it, but the gist is that I needed to get out of town for a while and wanted to come somewhere where I could make a difference. I asked Joules to find that place. This is what she came up with. What about you? How did you get involved with the medical mission here?"

"Well, my Aunt Edna was one of the first sponsors of this relief station. I started helping out here one weekend a month back in medical school. I liked it and have continued to come whenever possible."

The first thing Taylor thought was *Edna Stone, again! That woman is always in my business. I am going to kill Joules. What was she thinking of bringing me to a relief station sponsored by her?* But what she said was, "Well, that is very nice. I am sure your aunt is very proud of you."

"I think so," said Greer. "She is a tough old bird, but she cares in her own way. Working for better medical care for those who don't have it is very important to her. Anyway, enough about Aunt Edna, how are you? You look great. Any more attacks?"

Shaking her head, Taylor said, "No, I never did get around to filling those prescriptions, but I still have them. However, I have been fine since I have been here."

Smiling and looking at her with hungry eyes, Greer said, "I need to grab a bite and get back, but what do you say to us having dinner tonight? Just as friends. We could have a glass of wine and talk. What do you say?"

Her first instinct was to say no. Even though she was dying to be with him, she was still married.

Instead of refusing him, she said, "I would love to have dinner with you, minus the wine. I still can't bring myself to drink alcohol after …you know … that night." She hesitated for a moment and added, "But I am still married. I wanted you to know that upfront. We are still planning on divorcing once the election is over, but until then, I am still legally wed. So, if you want to take back your offer, I completely understand. I can only go as friends."

Giving her a long look, Greer said, "I appreciate your honesty. But, the offer was just for dinner, nothing else. I will be finished here around four. Can you get away by then? We could have an early dinner. How does that sound?"

He was looking at her expectantly, and Taylor could only manage a nod and an "Okay, see you then."

At that point, Greer gave Taylor a large smile, grabbed several sandwiches and a bottle of water, and said, "See you later," and walked out.

Taylor's heart was racing so fast that it was all she could do to stay focused the rest of the day. She could not concentrate on the crafts she was supposed to be helping the children make. She spent more time cleaning up the messes she was making than anything else. Just knowing Greer was in the building filled her with excitement. Her body was literally humming being in such close proximity to him.

Around four o'clock, Greer appeared in the arts and crafts area looking more like a sexy surfer than a doctor since he traded in his white doctor's coat for a beat-up baseball cap. All the children had already left for the day, and Taylor was cleaning up the room.

Giving her a sweet, crooked smile, Greer asked, "Hey, you about done?"

Oh God, she loved the way he said darlin'. It made her heart melt.

"Yes," she said, "Just let me get my purse, and we can go."

"We'll have to take your car. I rode with two other doctors, and they have already gone. I told them I would catch another flight home tomorrow."

"I don't want to put you out. If you need to go, we can have dinner the next time you are in town." She schooled her face, trying to make sure it did not reflect the disappointment she would feel if he decided to back out now.

Greer put his hands on her shoulders and said, "No, it's fine. I want to stay. I don't want to wait for another time. It's no big deal. I have already changed my ticket. What do you say we get out of here and take a walk through South Beach?"

Smiling up at him shyly, Taylor said, "I think that is a wonderful idea."

For the next three hours, Taylor and Greer enjoyed walking around and looking at the Art Deco buildings. As they walked, Greer took Taylor's hand. She almost jumped out of her skin when he did that, but she didn't draw her hand back. She thought to herself, a little hand-holding could not be that wrong.

Around seven, they wandered into a little street café that served Cuban food. They talked all afternoon about everything and nothing at the same time. Once they sat down at the table, the conversation became much more serious. When the waiter came to take their drink orders, Greer ordered a bottle of white wine, but Taylor declined the alcohol and asked for a glass of sparkling water.

This made Greer suspicious, and he said, "Can I ask you something?"

"Sure," replied Taylor.

"Are you drinking water for any particular reason?"

Taylor thought that was an odd question and asked, "No particular reason. Other than what I told you earlier. Last time, I drank way too much and have not quite gotten over it. Why?"

"Oh, I don't know. Call me crazy, but in the movies, whenever a woman drinks water, it is because she's" Greer hesitated, "pregnant."

"Well, I can assure you that I am not." Laughing at such a ridiculous idea, Taylor said, "Remember I told you that is impossible. I am just parched and want some water."

"Stranger things have happened, you know."

"Not that didn't involve a miracle."

"Yeah, but we didn't use anything. We were both clean, and you said it was fine. But I just wanted you to know I would be there for you if something happened."

"First of all, I appreciate that. Second, there is a lot about that night that I still don't remember. That last bit of information would have been helpful about two months ago. I could have avoided a very awkward moment at the doctor's office.

That was my first and last trip to be tested for STDs. And, lastly, I am not now or will I ever be pregnant. So you don't have to worry about this anymore. It's all good."

Nodding, Greer said, "No baby, got it. It sounds like there is a story there."

"Yes, there is one that I am happy to share, but maybe not today. But soon, I promise."

Greer reached over, took her hand, looked into her eyes, and said, "I want to know everything you are comfortable sharing. I hope you feel this thing between us too. We rushed the beginning. I want to see where this might go. I am willing to go as slowly as you want. Just always be honest with me. Whatever you tell me, I won't judge you. But, I want to know your truth. I want to know what brought you to that rat hole of a bar that night. And I want to know what made you run the next day. I won't hurt you. We'll go at whatever pace you want." Rubbing his hand up and down her arm, he added, "I won't lie. I still have a powerful hunger for you. Seeing you today was like a rocket going off in my gut. I haven't been able to think about anything else but being with you since. I want to…" As he said this, he leaned into her as his lips were just inches from hers. His words were little more than whispers.

Taylor wanted nothing more than to close the distance between them and kiss him with all of the fiery passion that was threatening to erupt from her at any moment. But, she had promised herself that she would not break her marriage vows again. She realized she was married in name only, and Bennett was likely already in an intimate relationship with Poppy, but two wrongs did not make a right.

Pulling back slightly to give herself room to breathe, she cut Greer off mid-sentence. "I can't do this. I really want to. I can't believe how much I want to. But it is just not who I am. I am still married and will be until after the election."

Greer let out a low groan and then dropped his hand, which had worked its way up to Taylor's neck and said, "Okay, I get it. I am momentarily in the friend zone. But tell me the truth, you feel this, right?" He asked as he took her hands in his. "I have never felt anything like this before. Tell me you feel it, too. It can't just be me. If it is, I will walk away right now."

Shaking her head, Taylor replied, "No, I feel it too."

At that, Greer leaned forward and gave Taylor a quick kiss on the forehead before pulling back.

Giving her his most sexy smile, he said, "Okay, buddy, let's eat. If I can't feed one hunger, I guess I will just have to gorge myself on Ropa Vieja with Arraz y Frijoles Negros."

"Um, that sounds horrible. What is that?"

"Beef steak cooked with onions, bell peppers, and a bunch of spices served with rice and beans. I promise you will love it."

At that moment, the waiter brought the drinks and took their dinner orders. Greer ordered for them, and it was incredible.

After dinner, they went to a patio bar where a salsa band played Latin music. Greer ordered a beer and got Taylor water. The band played for about an hour. When the music ended, Greer and Taylor ordered another round and sat enjoying the breeze off the ocean. After a few minutes, Greer reached across the table, picked up Taylor's hand, and asked, "Can I ask you another question? I hate to pry, but I just got to know something."

Smiling at him, Taylor replied, "Yes, of course. Ask away."

"Is your marriage really over? I know you said it was, but you are waiting a long time to end something you say is already over. So what is the deal between you and what's his name again, that male Barbie doll-looking husband of yours?"

"Male Barbie doll husband? You mean you think Bennett looks like a Ken doll?"

"Yeah, Bennett, that was his name. And yeah, I do. With all that blond hair and prep boy good looks, don't you?"

At this, Taylor could not help but laugh as she said, "No, I have never thought he looked like a Ken doll, and he would die if he heard you say that."

"Oh, well, he does. So what's the deal? I know you said something about an election, but is that really why it is taking so long, or is it something else?"

"Yes, that is what it is. I can understand why you would question it, but the simple truth is Bennett is being vetted for a cabinet secretary position. A divorce now would kill any chances he has of getting it."

"Why do you care if he loses? Obviously, the guy is a loser. After what he did to Poppy and now to you."

"I appreciate the sentiment, but Bennett is not a loser. Just because we aren't a couple anymore doesn't mean I don't care about him or want what is best for him. He has worked hard to get to where he is politically and will do a wonderful job. It would be a shame if he lost his dream of serving his country because we made a mistake years ago. As far as what he did to Poppy, I will tell you that he would never have abandoned a child he knew about. She kept his son from him for years. What she did to him was much worse. I am not privy to what happened with them, but I know Bennett well enough to know there is blame on both sides."

"Wow! I have never heard a woman defend her ex before. Are you sure it is over? You called it a mistake. Is that why it fell apart?"

"So, we are getting into all of this, huh? It's a really long story. Are you sure you want to hear it?"

Nodding, Greer said, "More than you can imagine."

Sighing, Taylor said, "Well, okay then, but we will be here a while."

Over the next two hours, Taylor told him the whole sad story. She left nothing out. She began when she and Bennett were kids and explained how they had grown up like brother and sister. With tears in her eyes, she recounted how her brother and parents were killed and how Bennett jumped in and saved her from drowning in a vat of grief and depression.

From there, she explained how they had meandered into a marriage of convenience. She quietly told him about their fruitless efforts to conceive and their long, painful ordeal with one doctor after another. In agonizing detail, she explained how the loss of each baby had driven them further and further apart when it should have been drawing them closer together.

Finally, she detailed the last few months' events, including the roles his infamous Aunt Edna and Poppy, the Absent Artist, as she had begun to think of her, had played in it all. She concluded by explaining that her main reason for agreeing to help Bennett was because he had always been there for her.

By the time she finished her story, she realized that she had bared her soul, and Greer had never let go of her hand once during her spill. It was as if he could not stand being so near and not able to touch her.

They sat looking at each other, exhausted as much from the activities and heat of the day as from the emotional drain of the tale. Greer sat silently, thinking for several minutes.

The silence made Taylor nervous. "Okay," she said, "say something."

He took the hand he was holding, lifted it to his lips, kissed it slowly, and said, "I was just thinking how amazing you are. You have suffered so much heartache and pain, yet you are not bitter or angry. Your husband cheated on you, and yet you still defend him. If you were mine, I would never give you up for anything. And the fact that he did shows he is a fool."

"Yes, a fool in love with another woman. But it is okay because I am not in love with him. I never was. That was our problem. So, now you know my whole sordid tale. Next time, I want to hear all about yours."

"I've told you some of it already, but I am willing to tell you anything you want to know, but not here. Let's get out of here and walk on the beach."

Chapter 18

Taylor's Apartment
Miami, Florida
June 2012

It was nearly midnight. Taylor could not keep her eyes open. Yawning, she said, "That sounds lovely, but I am about to drop. I think I will need to take a rain check."

"Oh, I am so sorry. I was having such a good time I lost track of time. I don't have a hotel yet, but I have stayed at a hotel just down the street before. If you don't mind dropping me there, I will see if they have a room."

Taylor was silent for a minute and said, "I have a couch you are welcome to use. And, by the couch, I really mean the couch. I know that is backtracking from where we have already come, but given the circumstances, that is all I can offer you. But it's yours if you want it."

"Are you sure? I don't want to put you out or make you uncomfortable."

Smiling, she said, "I'm positive."

"Well, if you are sure, I would love to sleep on your couch."

Greer paid the check, and they drove back to Taylor's apartment. Once there, she showed him the bathroom and ensured he had clean sheets and towels. Then she said, "If you need anything else, just holler. It is a small apartment. I will hear you."

At that, she started to turn away, but Greer reached out, engulfed her in his arms, and said, "The only thing I need at the moment is this." And he kissed her with all the passion and desire that he had kissed her with weeks before. Only this time, he made sure to keep his hands where they were locked on her back. He made no move to take the embrace to the next level. Taylor was not sure if she was relieved or disappointed about that.

After several moments, he broke the kiss and said, "I've wondered all day whether or not you would taste as sweet as I remembered. And guess what, Darling? You do." Skimming his hands down her back, he gripped her tightly and allowed his hands to reacquaint him with her body. Walking her backwards towards the couch, Greer slowly lowered Taylor down until they were both lying down. For the next hour, they made out like teenagers. There was a lot of kissing and touching, hugging and squeezing, tickling and teasing. Knowing Taylor was adamant about not breaking her marriage vows again, Greer worked hard to keep everything mostly acceptable. A few times, things went way north of what was appropriate. During those times, things threatened to escalate, but each time Greer would bring things back to neutral.

He could sense that Taylor was starting to feel guilty. He could see it in her eyes. Placing his forehead on hers, he said, "I don't want you to start making yourself feel bad about anything we have done here tonight. I promised not to take you again until you can be with me, and I won't. But, I refuse to let you or me feel bad about enjoying each other. We have done nothing wrong."

Greer knew what he said was true, but that he was about to reach his limit of control, he added, "Now, I am going to turn you loose. You are to get up and go to your bedroom as fast as you can. Because if you stay here much longer, I will be tempted to break my word and ask for more than you are ready to give. That won't do either one of us any good. Do you understand me?" Unable to speak, Taylor simply nodded.

At that, Greer once again melded his lips to hers in an embrace that almost seared her. After several moments, he abruptly ended the kiss. Taylor all but jumped up and ran from the room. Once in her room with the door closed, she heard him yell, "Sleep tight, Darling. And as you do, dream of me, the way I dream of you, every night."

"Okay." It was the only response Taylor was capable of uttering at that moment.

She quickly got undressed and got into the bed. She lay there thinking about the man in the next room and how much she wished she could go to him. She'd spent years of her life avoiding being intimate and thinking the world made too big a deal out of sex and intimacy. Now, it was all she could think about. She so badly wanted to go to him. She wanted to wrap her arms around him and kiss him until it hurt.

As she lay there, images of all the naughty things she remembered them doing last March rolled through her head. She had never thought she would get to do any of those things again with him. Many of the things they had tried had always sounded dirty and wrong. But, at that moment, Taylor was dying to do them all over again.

How had Greer come into her life and completely changed her in such a short time? She had no idea. She just knew that she could hardly wait to be free so that she could be with him again, and again, and again. She fell asleep thinking about everything she would do to him when that day came.

The next morning, Greer was making breakfast when Taylor wandered into the kitchen. "I didn't get to do this for you last time. I hope you don't mind that I made myself at home in your kitchen. There is coffee in the pot, and as soon as the eggs are done, we can eat."

Taylor was impressed. He had already set two places at her dinette. She poured herself a cup of coffee and took it to the table. Once the eggs were done, they fixed plates and ate.

Giving him a sweet smile, Taylor said, "This looks delicious. Thank you."

"You're welcome. I enjoy cooking, and breakfast is my specialty. Does it taste okay?"

Taylor salted and peppered her eggs and took a bite. At first, they tasted fine, but the longer she chewed, the more repulsed she became. It was as if they were rotten or something. A wave of nausea overcame her, and it was all she could do not to throw up right there at the table.

Forcing herself to keep chewing and swallowing, she croaked, "They are great." Then, wiping her mouth, she said as gracefully as possible, "Um, please excuse me; I will be right back." At that point,
Taylor all but ran to the bathroom and was sick. It took several minutes to get her stomach under control and return to the table.

"Are you okay?" Greer stood when she came back in the room, a look of concern on his face. "Are you sick? Is it the food?"

"No, the food was great. I may have caught a bug from one of the kids yesterday. A casualty of being around children. The first year I taught, I was sick the whole year. It's nothing." Putting her plate in the sink and walking over to the couch, she said, "I think I will lie down for a moment if you don't mind."

Greer walked over to where she was and put his hand on her forehead to see if she had a temperature. "You don't feel warm. Lie down while I clean up the kitchen. My flight is in three hours. If you are not up to taking me to the airport, I will call a cab."

"Let me see how I feel in a few minutes."

Closing her eyes, Taylor intended to rest her eyes for a few minutes until it was time to get up and take Greer to the airport. However, when she woke several hours later, the apartment was dark, and Greer was gone. He had left a note saying how much he had enjoyed their time together and hoped she felt better soon. He said that he had put his number in her phone and then called himself so he would have hers. He promised to call her later that night to check on her.

At eight-thirty on the dot, the phone rang, and it was Greer. Taylor was feeling much better, and they talked for almost an hour. Just before he hung up, he again said, "Sleep tight, Darling. And as you do, dream of me the way I dream of you."

"That is so sweet. I loved that last night. Of course, it carries way more power when you follow that with your mind-blowing kisses."

"You think my kisses are mind-blowing? Good to know. I will make sure to blow your mind again as often as possible. Maybe you would have let me kiss you like I did that night on the houseboat."

Taylor, who was drinking a soda, spit most of it out in shock. "You did not just say that? Are you trying to kill me?"

"What? Does thinking about us doing that do it for you? I hope so because it sure does for me."

For a moment, Taylor was too stunned to respond. Never in her life had she had such an explicit conversation. Her first instinct was to deny what his words did to her. But, the new Taylor, who was determined to become her own person, replied, "Well, it goes without saying you definitely have incredible skills."

"Uhhh, I like where this conversation is going," replied Greer. "Tell me more about how much you love my skills," he said in his sexy, southern drawl.

"Oh, you have got some skills, Dr. Delicious." At that, Taylor lost it. She burst out laughing.

"Dr. Delicious? What the hell? And why are you laughing? I take my skills very seriously. You could bruise my delicate male ego."

Still giggling, Taylor replied, "Oh yeah, right. I am not laughing at you. I am just not very good at sexy talk. And besides, it is not like you don't know you are an incredible kisser."

"Incredible kisser? Wow, where were these compliments last night when I could have done something with them?"

"Trust me, you did enough with them. You sent me to my room, remember? If I had given you these compliments last night, we would have gotten carried away, and neither of us wants that."

"You're right. But I have to be frank here. November is a long way off. I can't promise that I can wait that long. You may have to hurry the old Ken doll up a little."

"Would you stop with the Ken doll? He is really a great guy. But, as far as hurrying up the process, I gave him my word. I won't be the reason he loses out on a national appointment. However, he said that he might resign and step back. If he does, that would certainly speed things up. If not, it will actually be closer to January. The election has to finish and then he would have to be confirmed before we could file for divorce."

"First, I can call him a Ken doll if you can call me, what was it, Dr. Delicious? Secondly, we are not waiting until January to be together."

"I call you that because you are so delicious to look at and to taste."

"You are trying to distract me so I will forget about how far away January is. But you make a good point. Speaking of tasting, I can still taste you on my tongue. I want to do much more than that as soon as possible. Any idea when he might make a decision about dropping out?"

"I don't know. I know Poppy doesn't want him to drop out, either. She is afraid that he will resent her later if he does. As long as he is still in, we have to remain married, and you and I must put whatever this is between us on hold. But I like talking to you and spending time with you. This was the best weekend I have had in years."

"Me too. Just so you know, I am serious about this, seeing where this can go. You are an amazing woman; I want to know you inside out. I am determined to see this through. But I have to be honest, I would prefer it if the physical side of the relationship were not delayed any longer than absolutely necessary."

"Duly noted, Dr. Delicious. I will let you know the minute my situation changes. Until then, when are you scheduled to return for another medical mission?"

"Not for another four weeks."

Taylor groaned as if in pain. "Wow, that is a long time."

"Yep," replied Greer, irritation evident in his voice.

"That is way too long," replied Taylor. "Do you think you could maybe fly down before then? Or I could come there?"

There was a long pause, and he said, "I don't want you to take this the wrong way because there is nothing I would like more than to spend more time with you."

"Oh, I didn't mean to push you or anything, I just….."

"Whoa, slow down. You are jumping to the wrong conclusions here. I like you. I mean, I really like you. I want us to be together and spend as much time with you as possible. But the more we are together, the more likely we won't be able to stop. I don't want you to regret being with me for any reason. I especially don't want to make love to you, and you walk away feeling ashamed or bad about yourself.

"When we are together again, and make no mistake, we will be together again; I want you to wake up the next morning as happy about it as you were when you laid down with me."

Taylor was silent for a moment, and she said, "Yes, I know exactly what you mean. And thank you for respecting me enough to protect me even from myself. Because you are right. The more we are together, the harder it will be to hold back. So, how about this? Let's plan to see each other again four weeks from now. Hopefully, by then, I can better understand how the election business will go and have a firmer timetable for the divorce."

"That sounds like a grand plan." At that moment, Greer got a text from the hospital. "Hey, I have an emergency, so I have to run. Have a great night, and I'll call you tomorrow."

"Okay, tomorrow. Bye," Taylor hung up, feeling happier and lighter than she had in years. As she lay down that night to go to sleep, she remembered what Joules had said about getting your trigger tripped. She laughed because she realized that Greer so tripped her trigger, and he could do it from seven hundred miles away.

Chapter 19

Taylor's Apartment
Miami, Florida
July 2012

As promised, Greer called Taylor every night around the same time, even on the nights he was on call at the hospital. They would talk about their day, what they were eating for dinner, and what they were watching on television. It was always mundane and inconsequential, but those conversations made Taylor's day.

After a few weeks, she realized she was living for them. Hearing his voice was the high point of her day. A couple of times a week, if they had about an hour to talk, they would Skype. Taylor loved being able to see Greer as she talked to him. Several times, they put the same movie on and pretended they were in the same room watching it together. They called these times their movie date nights. The only thing Taylor didn't like about them was there was no good night kiss at the end.

A few times, Greer had halfway jokingly suggested they try sexting. He reasoned that if you were not in the same room, it couldn't be considered adultery. Taylor had laughed along with him. But she told him that if he was looking for a girl to get naked with on the computer, she was not it. He would always say that was okay; he had found the girl he wanted, just as she was. Taylor hoped that was true because she realized she was falling in love with Greer more with every phone call.

On the Thursday before Greer was to come back for his next medical mission, Taylor and Greer stayed up late talking about his plans to fly in after work on Friday and for them to have dinner. He was going to stay with her.

They made plans to go to the beach and to eat at a new restaurant that Angela, the secretary at the relief station, had told her about. Taylor was almost giddy as they talked the night before he was to come again. After about an hour, she yawned big and said, "Look, Dr. Delicious, I have to get off here and go to bed, or I won't have the energy to play with you tomorrow night."

Being Greer, he responded by saying, "Oh, so we are going to play? I may skip work and come early!"

"You know exactly what I meant. We have to try to be good." In truth, she was not convinced she could resist him if he made a serious play for intimacy. For a woman who had never before understood what the big deal was about sex, she had suddenly developed a very healthy sexual appetite. Some days, all she seemed to think about was Greer and being with him again. She could literally feel her hormones screaming for a release.

Greer's joking tone turned serious, "I know. I will do my best Darling, but it's been a while, a really long while. Like March if you have forgotten. I think this is the longest I have gone without sex since high school. I don't know how much longer we can keep this up. I just wanted you to know that before I come, unless you want me to get a room elsewhere."

Taylor thought about what he said, but she knew that she would die knowing he was in the same town and not there with her. So she said, "No, I want you here. We'll figure something out."

"Well, unless that something includes you naked and in my bed, I'm not sure it is going to work. Have you talked to Bennett? Any chance he might be dropping out soon? Like today?"

"In fact, I talked to Bennett just a few hours ago for our weekly check-in calls."

"So what did the Ken doll have to say? Any news on a court date?"

"Greer, I have asked you to stop calling him that. As far as a court day, he told me that things were going well with the campaign, so there is little hope that he will drop out any time soon."

Growling in frustration, Greer barked, "Did he give you an end date?"

"Yes, he said that we could file a few weeks after the election. Then the divorce would be final in late January."

"Late January? Are you freaking kidding me? Taylor, baby, you are killing me here."

"It's not that long." Taylor was trying to keep her voice calm. She could hear Greer getting more worked up by the minute.

"Not that long?" barked Greer. Yelling, he added, "Are you seriously saying that to me right now? Let me ask you something. Do you think he and Poppy are not sleeping together?" At this point, Greer was literally bellowing.

"I don't know, and I don't care. What they do is not my business." Taylor was keeping all traces of anger out of her voice, trying to defuse the situation.

"Not your business? Why is it okay for them and not us?"

"Greer. Please. I don't want to fight with you about this. I want to be with you as much as you want to be with me. One thing I have learned in this whole mess is that two mistakes don't make a third one okay. I tried that once, but it didn't work out well. I have to do what is right for me."

Letting out another loud growl, Greer tried to rein in his temper. "I know you do, and I am trying to support that. But come on, this situation is so hard. I hate that you still talk to him every week. How would you feel if I called Christine up every week to shoot the breeze?"

"First of all, he is not calling me up to shoot the breeze. He handles all my business investments. We have to talk about issues. Plus, he is my friend, and I care about him."

"Well, I think the whole thing is weird. You should get a new business manager. He can't do it after your divorce. Wouldn't it be better to start letting another person take over now? Sort of begin cutting ties?"

"What are you talking about? Of course, he will do it then. I would never trust anyone else to take care of my interest."

There was a long pause, and then Greer snapped, "Well, what about me? Will you trust me to look after your interest, or will your Ken doll still be the one you trust after we are...." Greer never finished his sentence. He just stopped talking, and silence filled the phone.

"After we are what?" asked Taylor quietly.

"Never mind. I don't want to talk about this anymore. It always makes me mad."

"I'm sorry you are mad. You just don't understand how it is between Bennett and me."

Once again, Greer exploded," You are right. I don't understand!" Greer's voice began rising again. Taylor could tell he was angry and frustrated. She had never heard him like this. "I don't want to hear about Bennett and you. I want it to be you and me. But that doesn't seem to be happening. So you are right, Darling. There is a lot about this whole deal I don't understand. And you know what, I am getting sick of it."

Taylor sat stunned for a moment and then said, "If this is how you feel, maybe you should get a hotel tomorrow night." Taylor was amazed at how calm she sounded when she was about half a second off from crying her eyes out.

"Fine, I will!" Greer barked back at her, and then silence reigned for a couple of minutes until Greer could hear sniffles on the other end.

Taylor tried her best to hold the tears back, but lately, she cried at everything from greeting cards to cat food commercials. Having Greer raise his voice at her rattled her nerves. This was their first fight, and it was a doozy. She could never remember ever having a fight like this with Bennett in all the years they had been married. She and Greer had only been dating for less than a month and we're already fighting. Was that a bad sign or a good one? She didn't know.

Frequently, Taylor wanted to pick up the phone, call Bennett, and ask for a quick divorce. Knowing how much he had done for her over the years stopped her every time.

Tears were silently falling down her cheeks. She sniffed a few times, and Greer could hear her. Feeling terrible, Greer said, "Darling, don't cry. I didn't mean any of that. I'm going to stay with you. It's going to be okay. We will figure this out. I don't want to fight. This is too important. You are too important. Please say something."

Now, it was Taylor's turn to be silent. After a moment, she said, "Are you sure because I want to be with you so much. I want to be with you in every way possible, but it is complicated. Please give me a little more time. I know we can work this out."

"Of course we can. It will be fine. Okay, it's late, and we both have a long day tomorrow. Dry your tears and go to bed. I will see you tomorrow night at six when I land. I will meet you at baggage claim. It's going to be okay. I promise. And, Taylor.."

"Yes?

"I," he hesitated for a moment and then said, "I ... I will see you tomorrow."

"Yeah, me too."

For a second, Taylor had been sure he was going to say that he loved her. But, then, he didn't. She didn't know why she didn't say it. They were just three little words. I love you. How hard was that to say? And yet, neither one had been able to.

She had said them for years to Bennett and not meant it to the depth and level she now did for Greer. Without a doubt, she was deeply, madly in love with him. However, his harsh reaction earlier on the phone had scared her. She knew he was being driven by emotional and physical frustration. However, there was nothing she could do about it, and there probably wouldn't be for a long time.

Given that it was the second week of July, Taylor was quite concerned that she and Greer would not make it until January without breaking her marriage vows once again. They had already pushed the envelope more than she was comfortable with the last time he was in town. She didn't want to do that, but she was only human. She didn't know what they were going to do. She spent several hours worrying about that until she finally fell asleep around three in the morning.

Chapter 20

Carrington Office
Searcy, Arkansas
November 24, 2023

"Sorry to stop you again, but I am confused. So, at that point, even though you two have been… intimate, you were determined not to be again? Why?" asked Harvey.

"Because tigers don't change their stripes. My whole life, I have been a good girl. I did what was expected of me, and I followed the rules. Always, except for that one night in Gulf Shores. The guilt I felt from that was unbelievable. I was raised to believe my marriage vows meant something. My parents did not have the best marriage, but they stayed together. They taught Tatum and me to live up to our commitments.

One thing I did learn during that period is that it is a lot easier to do the right thing when you are not tempted by the wrong thing. Meaning that, until I met Greer, no man ever interested me enough even to consider cheating. After meeting him, resisting him took a tremendous amount of self-control. If I had been in the same city with him for days on end, I would have crumbled like a cookie. Not an admission I am proud of," replied Taylor.

Nodding, Harvey said, "We all have our Achilles heels. No one gets out of this world without being addicted to something. A vice is a vice. Society decides which are acceptable and which are not. My father was a workaholic. He lived to work. Missed family dinners, school programs, and family vacations. He made a lot of money and was very successful. Society considered him a success even though his wife left him; he has no relationship with any of his children or grandchildren and will die a miserable old man. Stop beating yourself up. Sometimes, trying to do the right thing is as good as it gets."

"Thanks for saying that. For all my good intentions, my life was about to go completely off the rails," said Taylor.

CHAPTER 20

Taylor's Apartment
Miami, Florida
July 2012

The next morning, Taylor overslept. She jumped out of bed and rushed around in a panic to get dressed and pick up the apartment before she left for the center. At a quarter of eight, she pulled out of her complex, heading for the relief station, but her mind was still on last night's dilemma. After a restless night, she was no closer to a solution than the night before.

Perhaps it was because her thoughts were so scattered that she did not see the car that came flying out of nowhere until it slammed into her. She felt as if she was in slow motion. She tried to swerve to miss the car, but it was too late. She had been wearing her seat belt, and the airbag deployed. Taylor's head was knocked against the side window, and then her last thought before her world went black was, *Oh my God, I am going to die just like Momma, Daddy, and Tatum.*

Two Hours later
Carrington United States Senate Office
Washington D.C.
July 2012

Bennett was in his office in Washington working on a speech he was supposed to give to a farmer's organization when his phone rang.

"Hello."

"Senator Carrington? Senator Bennett Carrington?"

"Yes, who is this?"

"This is Dr. Shawn Cole. I am an OB-GYN at St Mary's in Miami. Your wife, Taylor Carrington, was brought here a little while ago after a car accident."

Bennett, frantic, asked, "Is she okay? Can I talk to her?"

The doctor sounded very clinical and matter of fact as she said, "Not yet, we have her heavily sedated. She is currently stable, and she has regained consciousness. She sustained head trauma but no broken bones. She was very fortunate. We expect that both she and the baby will make a full recovery."

"Wait a minute. I think you have the wrong person. There is no way my wife is pregnant."

"Are you sure? We are talking about Taylor Stroupe Carrington, 33, birth date of November 10. Long brown hair, thin, about five-seven."

"That's Taylor, but there must be some mistake. There is no way Taylor is going to have a baby." Bennett sounded as shocked and confused as he felt.

"Well, I assure you she is. Obviously, the two of you need to talk. She is fifteen weeks. The baby's heartbeat is strong, and it looks to be very healthy."

For a second, Bennett sat silently stunned.

After a moment, the doctor said, "Hello? Senator Carrington, are you there?"

"Um, yes, I am here. I will be there as quickly as I can. Tell Taylor I am on my way and will see her shortly. And doctor, thank you for calling me."

Instantly, Bennett began clearing his desk and preparing to leave. As he walked out of his office, he yelled, "Joules, come here. You are not going to believe this!"

St Mary's Hospital
Miami, Florida
July 2012

When Bennett arrived at the hospital two hours later, he met with Denice, the nurse assigned to Taylor, who had briefed him on her condition. Taylor was very sedated. Evidently, each time Denice came in to check her vitals, Taylor awakened in a hazy daze and asked if she were dead. It had broken Bennett's heart to hear that.

She must have been so afraid, and she had been so alone. He knew he had let her and Tatum down. He had made his best friend a promise many years before to protect her no matter what. He had not kept the promise very well lately. He wanted to do better.

He had been sitting by her bedside watching her sleep and was trying to figure out how he could do a better job of protecting Taylor, and still live up to his commitments to Poppy and Ben, when he heard a buzzing coming from Taylor's purse. Reaching inside her purse, he took out the phone and answered it. He didn't recognize the name. The screen name read Greer.

"Hello?"

"Who is this? I was calling for Taylor. Why is she not answering this phone?"

"This is Bennett Carrington, her husband. Who is this?"

"It's Greer. What's wrong? Why are you on Taylor's phone? I want to talk to Taylor right now."

"Greer Who?" replied Bennett. After a moment, he said, "Look, it doesn't matter. Taylor can't talk right now. She is still asleep. She was in an accident, but she is going to be okay. I'll tell her you called."

"No, wait! Don't hang up! Tell me what hospital, and I will be right there."

"I don't think that is such a good idea. She is still out of it and may not feel up to visitors."

"I don't care what you think, you Ken doll. Tell me where she is now, or so help me…"

Bennett was shocked by the anger and passion in this Greer person's voice. Suddenly, he realized that this guy, whoever he was, cared deeply about Taylor and could possibly be the father of her baby. So, he asked, "It's you, isn't it? You are the father of the baby Taylor is carrying?"

Shocked, Greer was momentarily silenced. After a moment, he snapped back and said, "I have no idea what you are talking about, but if Taylor is pregnant, then yes, I am the father. Now tell me where the hell she is right now." Bennett didn't hesitate for a second. He knew exactly how he would have felt if he and Poppy were in the same situation. He would have killed someone that tried to keep her from him. So he said, "St. Mary's Room 214."

Greer said, "On my way." And the line went dead.

This is going to be fun thought Bennett as he put her phone away and sat down to wait for the arrival of the now-infamous Greer.

Taylor could hear someone talking, but they sounded very far away. She opened her eyes and tried to sit up, but every muscle and bone in her body ached. The room was really dark. In the background, Taylor could hear the faint sounds of a television playing. She supposed that was the person she heard talking. With a start, she realized she was in a hospital bed, but her brain wasn't working quite right. She kept having images of a car crash and an ambulance ride, and then images of being in the ER floated through her mind. She supposed she was now in a room. But she had no idea what hospital she was in or if anyone was with her.

Then suddenly, in the dark, a voice that she instantly recognized said, "Hey, Sleepy Head. It's good to see you awake. You have been out pretty much since I got here."

"Bennett? Is that you?"

At that moment, Bennett moved closer to the bed, ran his hand along her face, and pushed her hair out of her eyes. She had an ugly bruise forming along the top of her left temple. It hurt Bennett to see it.

"You gave me quite a scare. When they called to say you had been in an accident, my heart stopped."

"Yeah, I still can't believe I am alive."

Smiling down at her, he said, "Well, you are. Every time the nurse checks your vitals, you ask her if you are alive. You've done it so many times, she now just says, "You lived, Mrs. Carrington. Don't worry. You are still alive."

Taylor tried to laugh, but it hurt too much. "That is funny. It wasn't so funny when I saw that car flying at me. I really did think I was going to die. I wondered if that was what they thought just before they were hit." There was no need to say who the "they" were. Bennett instantly knew she was talking about her parents and Tatum.

"Well, I don't know about that, but I do know I am awfully glad you didn't die for a million reasons, not the least of which is I would never get to know who the daddy is of the baby you are carrying." Mimicking a Dezi Arnaz voice, he said, "Lucy, you got some splainin' to do."

"What?" Taylor looked at him so confused, and then she closed her eyes and said, "I thought that was just a dream. Something I was remembering from before. But I had an ultrasound, didn't I? I am pregnant, aren't I? I thought I was flashing back to another time." Putting her hands on her stomach, she looked at Bennett and asked, "Is it true? I am going to have a baby?"

Bennett nodded, smiling down at her with tears in his eyes, he said, "Yes, Sweet Girl. You are."

Instantly, a look of pure adulterated fear crossed her face, "How many weeks am I? What if…" If she had been more alert, she would not have had to ask. She would have known the answer to that question immediately. However, her mind was a little fuzzy.

She let the question hang in the air, but Bennett did not need her to finish it to know what she would say. He quickly said, "Nothing is going to happen. You are going to get your storybook ending this time. I promise. You are fifteen weeks, and the doctor said the baby's heartbeat was strong and healthy."

Taylor didn't say anything for a moment. Then, with tears of joy running down her face, she said, "Crazy, huh? All those years of trying, tests, and doctors, and nothing. And I go crazy one night, and bam, I am pregnant."

"Well, it is not that far-fetched. The doctors never could give us definitive reasons why you had trouble carrying. My question is, how did you not know? Fifteen weeks is a long time. You must have gotten pregnant back in March. Right?"

"Oh, yeah. It was the night I got so mad at you on the phone. I was determined to show you. I guess I did that in spades, huh? I am not sorry about the baby, but I am sorry about cheating."

"No, I am sorry I ever put any of us into this position. This would have never happened if I had handled things better on the front end. Well, I now know what bad choices you made. So, what's the story? Do I need to beat somebody up here or what?"

"No, you definitely don't need to beat anyone up. We are working it out, but at the moment, it is complicated."

"Isn't it always with us?"

Again, Taylor almost laughed, but the pain in her head stopped her.

"So, are you in love with this Greer guy or what?" asked Bennett.

"How did you know his name? Yes, I am. And I am pretty sure he is in love with me. We just haven't gotten around to saying it yet, but we will. Oh my gosh! What time is it?"

"It's almost seven-thirty."

"Oh no! I was supposed to pick Greer up at the airport at six. He will be frantic. Could you hand me my phone? I need to call him and tell him where I am."

"No need. I sort of already did. He called a little bit ago. I answered your phone, and we talked."

"Oh no. Is he on his way? Is he mad?"

"Well, he wasn't happy that I had your phone. I can tell you that much. Also, he called me a Ken doll. What did that mean? I didn't know if I was supposed to be offended or flattered."

Holding a hand to her head, Taylor rolled her eyes and gave a short laugh as she said, "Neither, and please don't make me laugh. So, he is on his way here now?"

Bennett nodded, "Yes, and you should know that I figured he had to be your baby daddy since I knew I wasn't. Why else would he be calling demanding to talk to you like a jealous boyfriend? And uh…"

"Uh oh, Bennett, what did you do?"

"I told him about the baby. I am sorry. I assumed he knew. I mean, come on, fifteen weeks is a long time to be pregnant and not know it." Giving her a sheepish look, he said, "I hope that was okay. If it is his baby, he has the right to know. I would have given anything if Poppy had told me." Bennett had such a sad look as he said that even Taylor couldn't even get mad at him.

Sighing, she said, "Well, it will have to be okay, won't it? I would have told him myself if I had known. We need to be prepared for when he gets here. He will be fit to be tied. Just stay back and let me deal with him. His bark is much worse than his bite."

"Good to know because he sounded like he was spoiling for a fight on the phone. Just who is this guy, and how did you meet him anyway?"

Before Taylor could answer, a doctor in green scrubs and a white coat and her nurse, Denice, knocked and walked in. Shaking Bennett's hand and then Taylor's, she said, "I am Dr. Cole. I believe I spoke with you earlier on the phone. I am glad you were able to get here so quickly."

Walking over to Taylor, she adjusted the cover and prepared to examine her.

Realizing where the situation was headed, Bennett began to feel very uncomfortable. If the situation were different, he would have no problem remaining in the room. But, as it was, he felt awkward and out of place. He also knew that Poppy would not like it one bit. So, he cleared his throat and said, "If you ladies will excuse me."

"Oh, there is no need for you to leave. The daddy is welcome to stay," the doctor replied as she took Taylor's blood pressure.

Bennett looked from the doctor to Taylor and back to the doctor but said nothing. Taylor looked at the doctor and said, "Mr. Carrington is not the father."

All the air left the room, and it went deadly silent for a moment as Taylor's words hung in the air. Then, looking back at Bennett, Taylor said, "I am fine. Why don't you go down and get a cup of coffee? I am sure we will be done in a minute."

Chapter 21

St Mary's Hospital
Miami, Florida
July 2012

Bennett left the room and took Taylor's advice. He walked down to the coffee station and was fixing himself a cup of coffee when a tall, dark, muscular man walked up carrying pink roses and a suitcase. He looked rushed and angry. The minute Bennett saw him, he remembered him. The guy had been the doctor who came to the gala back in March as Poppy's date, her friend from Gulf Shores. Bennett hadn't liked the guy then. He didn't like the looks of him any better now. For the life of him, Bennett could not understand how Poppy's friend was also the father of Taylor's child.

Suddenly, Bennett remembered that the guy and Taylor had recognized each other that night. Bennett remembered being shocked that they were acquainted but honestly had not thought about it again afterwards. Everything happened so quickly after Taylor collapsed that he had not thought of this man since. Now, he was standing at the nurses' station demanding to know where Room 214 was and to see the patient's chart. When the nurse explained that the doctor had the chart and was with the patient, Greer took off toward the room.

Afraid that the guy would barge in and embarrass Taylor, Bennett all but yelled, "Greer, stop!" across the corridor.

The nurses loudly yelled, "Shh! Be quiet! This is a hospital," but it got Greer's attention.

He stopped just short of the room, and Bennett was able to catch up with him before he stormed in on Taylor. Bennett wasn't positive Taylor wouldn't want Greer there, but he wasn't sure she would, so it was better to err on the side of caution.

Greer was not happy about being curtailed, especially by Bennett. Giving him a hateful look, Greer snapped, "What do you want? I want to see Taylor. The nurse said the doctor was with her. I wanted to hear what he has to say."

"Hey man, I get that, but slow down and think for a minute. Taylor is pretty modest, as I am sure you know. I don't think she would feel comfortable with you barging in right in the middle of an exam."

"I'm a doctor. What does it matter?"

"Yes, but you are not her doctor. You're her… whatever you are. Think about how vulnerable she is feeling right now. I think she has enough to deal with without you adding to that."

Greer hated to admit it, but Bennett had a point. Nodding, he said, "Okay, fine. I will wait until the doctor comes out and talk to him."

"Her. You will talk to her. The doctor is a lady."

"Okay, fine, I will talk to her. In the meantime, I have a question for you. What are you doing here? Why aren't you playing the golden boy politician or Ken doll or something?"

Bennett was taken aback by the anger and hostility he could feel rolling off Greer. What the hell had he ever done to tick this guy off? Giving him a look, Bennett said, "Obviously you don't like me very much, and I have no idea why. But I am here because I care about Taylor, and the hospital called me. Last time I checked, I am still her husband."

"Yes, you are. And why is that?" When Bennett didn't immediately answer, Greer charged ahead, saying, "I will tell you why I don't like you. You have hurt Taylor, and you continue to hurt her no matter how much you claim to care about her. You had an affair behind her back in front of the whole club. Not to mention, you also have a son you never told her about. Then you ask her for a divorce while you go off and play house with your mistress and son, but you never get around to actually getting a divorce. As far as I am concerned, Taylor could do with a little less of your caring."

"First of all, leave Poppy and my son out of this. They have nothing to do with Taylor. Furthermore, Poppy is not my mistress. You have no idea what you are talking about. Lastly, keep your voice down. Do you want someone to hear you?"

"I could care less if someone hears me. I have nothing against Poppy. She is a talented artist and a wonderful mom. The only thing I can't figure out is how she got mixed up with you. I want you and your sorry lying self out of my business. And make no mistake, Taylor and that baby are my business. So why don't you go back to DC and run your little campaign and take care of your family, and I will take care of mine." At that point, Greer poked Bennett hard in the chest.

While Greer talked, Bennett could feel himself getting madder and madder. He hadn't liked the guy to begin with. But add his hateful tone and words with a sharp poke in the chest, and Bennett lost it. He reared back and hit Greer square in the mouth.

Greer's head hit the wall behind him with a thud, and blood ran down his chin. For a second, he stood stunned. Then, he reacted. Lunging for Bennett, he yelled, "You son of a ……" as he dropped the suitcase and flowers scattered across the floor. From there, punches flew, and nurses screamed.

A nurse at the nursing station yelled, "Call security!"

Before security could arrive, two orderlies separated the two men. Both men were bleeding, and several pieces of medical equipment and chairs in the hallway had been turned over. Dr. Cole ran out of Taylor's room, "What in the world is going on out here?" Seeing the two men both bruised and bleeding, she shook her head. Frowning at Greer, she said, "Well, I guess you're the daddy? I knew this was going to be complicated when I found out you weren't," she said, pointing at Bennett.

One of the orderlies holding Greer back said, "Security has been called."

Giving Bennett and Greer her most fierce doctor look, she said, "If you two can't control yourselves and act right, I will have you both thrown out of here. I don't care if you will be the next, whatever. There is a lovely lady in that room who does not need this kind of stress. So what is it going to be? Can you act like you have brains in your heads? If so, I will have them cancel security, and we can act like this never happened. Or, security can hold you until the cops get here. I am good either way, but my guess is that my patient won't be."

Bennett and Greer looked at each other and then back at the doctor.

Greer threw his hands in the air as if to surrender and walked a few steps away. Seeing that Greer was backing down, Bennett said, "Fine, we will control ourselves. I am sorry this happened. Please call security and tell them it was a misunderstanding. The last thing either one of us wants is to upset Taylor."

At that point, both men and the orderlies began to straighten the chairs and equipment. Greer reached down and gathered up what was left of the roses he had brought for Taylor.

With the crisis averted, the doctor said to the orderly, "Call security and cancel them. Then, nodding to Greer, she said, "Taylor tells me that you are a doctor and will probably want a full run down on her stats. She has permitted me to discuss her case with you. So, if you will come with me, I will be happy to show you her scans from earlier and discuss her situation."

Looking at Bennett, she said, "Clean yourself up and say goodnight to your wife. I am sure that once I am done with this one," pointing to Greer, "she will want to spend some time with him. It would probably be best if you were gone by then." At that, the doctor turned and walked towards a conferencing area with Greer.

Bennett visited the men's room, cleaned himself up the best he could, and then went to see Taylor. Walking through the door a few minutes later, Taylor saw that Bennett's shirt was torn and his face cut. Horrified, she cried, "What have you two been doing? I was worried it might be you two when I heard the commotion outside."

Touching his chin, she said, "Did Greer start this? I knew he was high-strung, but I never thought he was a fighter. Oh, Bennett, I am so sorry. No one got arrested, did they? I know this is the last thing you need right now."

"Which part? The fighting in the hallway, the wife pregnant by another man part, or the getting the crap kicked out of me by the other man part?"

"All of it, I guess. I really am sorry about all of this."

"Well, don't be. As your boyfriend, or whatever he is, pointed out, all of this is my fault. I know that. I am so sorry. And for the record, Greer didn't start the fight; I did. He kept poking me, and I snapped. I am sorry, Taylor, for everything."

"You did? Really? I am shocked. But it doesn't matter. What is done is done. You had best say good night before he comes back."

"Yes, I agree. One fight a day is my limit." Giving her a quick kiss on the forehead, he said, "I am going to get a room at the hotel across the street. The doctor said earlier that you could probably go home on Sunday. I am going to stay until you are released. If you want to fly home with me, you can. If you want to stay here, I will respect that too, but I don't think you should be alone. You need to think about how you want to handle all of this. Joules is about to die to talk to you, so please call her later. If you need me, call me on my cell. I will check on you tomorrow. Love you." While talking, he picked up Taylor's hand and squeezed it.

Taylor replied, "I love you too," as he said goodbye with another kiss on the forehead.

Of course, Greer chose that moment to walk into the room. He didn't say anything but just looked from Taylor to Bennett. Scowling at Bennett, Greer all but growled, "I thought you were leaving."

Taylor frowned at him and said, "Greer, chill. This is not what it looks like. He is leaving."

"Just for the night, "Bennett added. "I'll be back tomorrow." Walking to the door, he turned back and added, "Remember, call me on my cell if you need me. I will be right here."

"Thank you, I appreciate it," said Taylor.

With that, Bennett walked out, and Taylor turned and looked at Greer.

Chapter 22

St. Mary's Hospital
Miami, Florida
July 2012

For a second, Greer and Taylor just looked at each other frowning, and then Taylor couldn't help herself; she started smiling ear to ear.

The smile lit up her whole face and turned into a bubbly laugh as she said, "I don't want you to think I am not still super upset with you about how you acted towards Bennett because I am, but I can't stop smiling. I am just so happy."

"Hey, Ken doll hit me first."

But Taylor's joy was infectious, and Greer could not help but share in it. His frown slowly gave way to his own smile, which rivaled Taylor's. In a singsong voice, he said, "I was right. We are going to have a baby. The doctor said you had no idea you were pregnant. How could you not know?"

"I really had no idea. I have never been regular, and given my past medical history, I truly didn't think it was possible. This baby is a miracle baby."

Giving him a serious look, Taylor continued, "You are happy about this, right? I mean, if you're not, I can do this alone."

"Of course, I am happy about this. And don't be ridiculous; we are doing this together. At that moment, Greer handed the smashed roses to Taylor and said, "These looked better before they got thrown against the wall." He then leaned in and gave her a long kiss.

After the kiss, Taylor took a moment to admire the wonderful aroma of the roses before she said, "Thank you." Holding the broken stems and crushed flowers, she added, "At least they still smell nice." After pulling out the four or five flowers that survived the hallway fight, Taylor handed them back to Greer and asked, "Could you put these in some water, please?"

Nodding, Greer took the flowers and put them in a glass of water as he replied, "I bought them at the airport as an 'I am sorry that I am an idiot' gift. I suppose now they are a 'we are having a baby' gift."

Lying back against the pillow, Taylor sighed and said, "Can you believe it? I can hardly wrap my head around it. It's still so wild. Just a few months ago, I was so sad and alone. I had to accept the fact that I would probably never have a child. Now I have you, and we are going to have a baby. I am thrilled but a little worried, too. You know?"

Kissing her again deeply, he said, "I know you are, but this time will be different. It wasn't right before. And, you told me yourself, the doctors never gave you a reason why you couldn't get pregnant naturally or carry to term. Maybe it was just nature's way of waiting until the time was right."

Laying her hands on her stomach, Taylor said, "As crazy as that sounds, I think you might be right. This time feels different. Before, I always sort of knew things would end the way they did. This one, I know, will end differently."

"Of course, it will," replied Greer, taking Taylor's hand. Kissing them softly, he added, "Our little guy has my powerful, manly genes."

"Our little guy? Sure it is a boy are you?"

"Boy or girl, I don't care. I am just happy that it is healthy"

"Me too. It's as if this was fated to happen. After all those years of heartache, and one time with you, bam, I am further along than ever before. That must be some mighty powerful stuff."

Shrugging his shoulders, he replied, "What can I say? It's true. I am a stud, a very happy stud."

Taylor could not help but giggle. He could be so irritating but also sweet and silly. Looking at him with love in her eyes, she asked, "Really? Are you really happy?"

"More than you will ever know. When Bennett answered your phone and told me you had been in a wreck, I almost died." Laying his hand on her stomach, he added. "You two are my whole world. I don't know what I would do if something happened to you."

Reaching down and lightly grazing her lips with his, he added, "I met Dr. Cole earlier. She said that everything looks great."

"Yeah, I told her about the problems I had in the past. She sees no reason I should have any issues now, but she wants me to use a high-risk doctor just in case."

"She told me that, too. I have a buddy in Gulf Shores who will be perfect. He is an outstanding high-risk OB. I will call him in the morning and get you an appointment next week."

"Gulf Shores?"

"Well, yeah, you are not staying here. TJ. You are going home with me so I can take care of you and the little guy."

"Oh, I am, am I?" Taylor was trying to act like she was offended that he was making plans and issuing orders. But, honestly, she didn't care. She was too happy to care because she was getting everything she had ever wanted.

"Yes, you are. The sooner you realize that, the better."

Teasing him, she said, "Really? Well, we will have to see about that."

Not realizing she was joking, Greer pulled back and said very seriously, "Damn it, TJ, I love you and this baby. You are mine, and I will never let either of you go."

Seeing his intense reaction, Taylor's eyes widened, and she tried to hide her amused expression. She knew she had pushed him too far. She reached for him and said, "Oh honey, I am sorry. I was just teasing you. Of course, we love you too, and if you ask nicely, we will consider it."

Suddenly, it dawned on Greer that Taylor had just been teasing him. Reaching over and touching her face, he said, "Oh, you think this is funny?" Reaching into his pocket with his left hand, he pulled out a small velvet box.

Taylor gasped. She had not been expecting this. With her eyes wide, she stared at him, all her laughter gone but saying nothing.

"I had planned to do this at a much more romantic moment, but since you and the little guy are so set on being asked nicely, I guess I will have to do this now." Opening the ring box to reveal a two-carat diamond solitaire, he looked into her eyes and said, "Taylor Stroupe Carrington, will you marry me?"

Without a moment's hesitation, Taylor squealed, "Yes! I would love to marry you just as soon as I can get divorced!" This made both of them laugh.

A little later, Taylor called Joules to share her good news about the baby and being engaged. Joules was thrilled for her, but Taylor could hear some hesitation in her friend's voice. Whatever concerns Joules might have, she was a good enough friend not to mention them. The two talked for only a few minutes as Joules had a huge project she was working on for Bennett and had to beg off. Promising to talk more the next day, Taylor hung up feeling more alive and hopeful than she had in years.

Taylor and Greer spent the rest of the evening making plans and discussing possible baby names. They were cocooned in their own world of happiness and possibilities. After years of heartache and tragedies, Taylor fell asleep believing that fate had smiled on her at last and nothing but sunny days lay ahead. Neither Greer nor Taylor realized that all their hopes and dreams were about to be threatened.

Chapter 23

St. Mary's Hospital
Miami, Florida
July 2012

The next morning, an early call woke both Taylor and Greer. Greer, who had slept in the fold-out chair beside Taylor's bed, answered it. "Hello," he said in a sleepy voice.

"Is this Taylor Carrington's room?"

"Who is this?" replied Greer.

"This is Lisa Shanks from the Arkansas Gazette. We are trying to verify a story that the wife of Senator Bennett Carrington is a patient at St. Mary's. Our source says that she was brought to the hospital after a car crash. Is this true?"

"How did you get this number?" Greer demanded.

"So, are you confirming the story? Also, our sources say Mrs. Carrington is pregnant and that Senator Carrington is not the father. Do you have any information about this? Are you the father of her child? If so, what is your name?"

Greer yelled, "You people are unbelievable. Leave us alone!" and then slammed down the phone.

With fear in her eyes, Taylor asked, "Oh my word, Greer, who was that?"

"It was a reporter from the Arkansas Gazette asking questions about your accident and the baby. I think we had better get Bennett over here immediately."

Once Bennett got to the hospital, Greer explained what happened. Bennett immediately called Joules, who began researching how the story got out and ways to curtail it, but their efforts were in vain. By lunch, the story had hit the Internet.

Evidently, someone in the lobby the day before had overheard Bennett and Greer's argument and ensuing fight. They had contacted the paper in Little Rock and sold the story. Greer and Bennett tried to shield Taylor from as much of what was happening as possible. Joules and her team released a statement that Taylor had been in an accident and that she was recovering, hoping that would keep the hounds at bay.

Plus, Joules called in every favor she had at television stations in Little Rock and Memphis, trying to keep the story contained. The plan seemed to be working until all hell broke loose around two o'clock.

That was when a reporter found Ben's birth certificate. Since Bennett was not listed as Ben's father, he was not able to link Bennett to Poppy Hunter Thompson and her child. But, that did not stop him from showing pictures of Bennett and Ben and making comparisons. By the time the news came on at six, every news station in Little Rock had run pictures of Bennett, Taylor, Poppy, and Ben. Since they didn't have a complete story to print, they used innuendo and half-truths to paint a vivid picture.

Since they knew nothing of Greer, they made it appear that Bennett and Poppy had been having a long-term affair for many years. They also included personal details about the problems Taylor and Bennett had experienced with infertility. They made it appear that Taylor, who was pregnant again, had been alone and miserable in Florida while Bennett had been living with his mistress and love child. Of course, that was not really true, but no one cared as it made great copy. Bennett was on the phone constantly with Joules. They were doing all they could to stop the story's momentum, but it had gone viral.

The worst part was that Taylor could see Bennett panicking because he could not get Poppy on the phone. She knew his first desire was to jump on a plane and rush home to be with Poppy and Ben. She also knew that Bennett would not do that because he had committed to stay with her until she was released.

No matter how many times she and Greer encouraged him to leave, he refused. It all stemmed from the promise he had made Tatum years before. After several tries to convince him that it was okay to leave her, Taylor gave up and accepted that Bennett was not leaving the hospital until she did. So, the three of them sat all day, waiting and worrying as they tried to stop a runaway train.

By the next morning, both local and national reporters were camped out across the street from St. Mary's. They were already running footage of Bennett coming and going from the hospital. Since they were thankfully not allowed in the hospital, they were not able to get footage of Greer or Taylor. However, once Taylor was released, a decision about where Taylor should go brought the tensions of the last twenty-four hours to a head.

Bennett felt that Taylor should go home with him until the story blew over. He thought that if she went with Greer to Gulf Shores, that would just add a new twist to the story and give it longer legs. Greer argued that she didn't need to be in the middle of all the stress. Bennett agreed but said the reporters would follow her regardless of where she went. At least by being in Arkansas, she could be protected at the family home. Security could be brought in to keep the reporters at bay. The same could not be said for the houseboat. After several hours of wrangling, the ultimate decision was Taylor's.

She had been a politician's wife long enough to know that running away from reporters didn't make them disappear. At some point, she and Bennett would have to face them. Also, she knew that the press was unfairly beating up Bennett. She could no longer leave him and run off to Gulf Shores. In all fairness, he was not able to run off to New York and leave her after her family died.

Having made her decision, Taylor said, "I think it would be best if I flew back to Arkansas with Bennett for a few days."

Greer was not happy and tried to interrupt her, "No way. I am not letting you do that. You are coming home with me. We settled this Friday night. We are getting married. You are my future wife and the mother of my child. Over my dead body are you going back with him."

"You're getting married?" Bennett was stunned. He had been too distracted even to notice the huge diamond ring Taylor was now holding up for him to see.

In the excitement of the last two days, Taylor had not gotten around to telling him the good news. "Yes, we are. Of course, you and I must get divorced first, but we love each other and want to be together."

Placing a protective arm around her shoulder, Greer interrupted Taylor again and said, "We would like that to be sooner than later."

Giving him a stern look, Taylor said, "Greer, please, you are not making this any easier with your attitude. Bennett is trying to do what is best for everyone."

"No, Bennett is doing what is best for Bennett. We could stop this charade right now. We could walk out those doors and tell the reporters everything. But he is not going to do that, is he?" snapped Greer.

"No, he isn't because if he did, several people he loves would be even more hurt, including me. Do you really think telling the truth now will make anything better? No, it will just make things much worse, especially for Ben. He is just a child," replied Taylor.

Smiling at Greer, she added, "If we lay low for a few weeks, this will die down. Somebody else will do something stupid, and the press can run after that story. Then, I can come to you. Until then, you have to trust me. And you have to trust Bennett and Joules. A lot of people are working very hard to fix this. Running off and doing something half-cocked will hurt everyone in the end."

No one said a word for several minutes. Greer walked away and stared out the window at the line of reporters across the street. After a moment, Bennett said, "She is right, you know."

Turning around and looking at Taylor, Greer said, "TJ, are you sure about this? What about the baby? Who will take care of you?"

"The baby will be fine. I will contact Dr. Payne the minute I get back. And I will take care of myself. I think I have been doing a pretty good job of that the last few months, don't you?"

Greer nodded, then, after a moment, walked over to Taylor and put his arms around her. "I will let you do this, but if you need me at any time, just call. I will be on the next plane."

"I know you will, and I love you for it. Thank you for trusting me. This is the only way to deal with this. We will be together again before you know it."

"Guys, I hate to break this up, but since this has been decided, I need to get back to Searcy as soon as possible. I don't think we should walk out together, though. Greer, you should let us go first and then follow after we leave the hospital."

Greer nodded, giving Taylor a long kiss goodbye. Then, she and Bennett donned baseball caps and sunglasses before leaving the room. Greer stayed behind and watched as they safely waded through the reporters and drove away from the hospital before quietly leaving himself.

Once airborne, Bennett looked at Taylor and said, "There is something I need you to understand about Poppy and me."

"Look, Bennett, whatever it is, you don't have to say it. I know you love her. I love Greer. It is fine."

"I know you do. Otherwise, I would be in Alabama kicking his ass. But this is important, and I might never get the chance to tell you this ever again."

Sighing deeply, Taylor said, "Okay, what is it that is so important for me to hear?"

Looking out of the airplane's window at the clouds below like he was searching for a place to start, he said, "You may not know this, but Poppy and I first got together when she and her grandmother lived over our garage. Her Gran worked for my dad."

"Yes, I knew that," replied Taylor, unsure why Bennett thought this was new information.

"What you may not know is that she was still in high school. I was in my last year of law school and twenty-five. She was an eighteen-year-old virgin. I had no business messing with her. A fact my dad and your brother repeatedly tried to beat into me. But it did not matter. A heart wants what a heart wants, and I wanted her. Luckily, she wanted me too. We started officially dating the summer after she graduated. We had some, I'll call them, moments before, but we did not become a full-fledged couple until summer."

"I don't remember that. Of course, I was in Scotland doing my student teaching. But, I can imagine that the relationship was not well received."

"It wasn't. For the most part, we kept it very secret. Poppy used to say she was my dirty little secret. I hated that because it was true. I did try to keep her secret. When we first got together, it was magical. We had the house to ourselves. Looking back, I realized we were just two kids playing house. But at the time, I thought we were going to last forever. Even before it came time for her to go to New York for school, our relationship had become strained and was marred by jealousy and mistrust. I loved her so much that I could not think straight around her. There was a crazy, out-of-control aspect to those weeks with her that drove me mad. Being with her was like being on a roller coaster. Because of her age and background, it was such a battle when we first got together. We fought so hard to be together. I have never felt so out of control or emotionally unsettled as I did during that time.

"It only got worse when she and I split up. I just wanted the craziness to stop for five minutes. When I found out that she had moved on and was married and expecting a child, I was devastated. I never wanted to feel that deeply about anyone ever again. I never wanted anyone to have that much of a hold on my heart, either. Then, we got together. It was so different. You understood my world. On paper, we clicked. Our worlds fit. You never demanded too much from me.

Our relationship was simple. God forgive me, but after the emotional vortex I had endured with her, I just was not up for all that again. Not if I wanted to have the political career I wanted. You made it easy. I could be with you and still give almost everything to my career."

"I don't think I even consciously realized all this until I saw her in New York in February. The second I saw her, all the old feelings came rushing back. I did not want to hurt you. I feel like I have failed Tatum and you. I did not keep my promise to take care of you no matter what. Please say you will forgive me."

When Bennett stopped talking, Taylor just looked at him. She appreciated his willingness to share that with her. It helped heal some of the wounds their marriage had created. Taking his hands in hers, she said, "Thank you for sharing that. It makes so much sense now why we got together and why you were so different with me than you were with her. I can't believe I am going to say this, but I think everything has worked out like it was supposed to. We only have a few more months. I know we can work together to keep this circus going until then. Now, if you don't mind, this pregnant lady could use a nap. I think I will try to get one while I can."

Chapter 24

Carrington House
Searcy, Arkansas
July 2012

Taylor and Bennett landed in Searcy late that afternoon. Since they kept their small-engine plane in a private hangar, there were no reporters when they landed. They could deplane and load their gear into Bennett's SUV without being seen.

Once in the car, Bennett tried Poppy's number again. He also had Joules trying to locate her, but so far, she had had no luck.

"Still no answer?" asked Taylor. She could tell Bennett was extremely concerned.

Shaking his head, he said, "No, it went straight to voicemail. I stopped leaving those a dozen messages ago. What is it with you women? Why do you never answer the damn phone?"

Giving him a sympathetic smile, she said, "Well, I was trying to run away from my problems."

"I am worried that is exactly what she is trying to do. But it won't work this time. She has run away from me for the last time. I mean it. She will absolutely never run away from me again."

Taylor wasn't sure she even liked Poppy, but she cared about Bennett so she said, "I understand. You need to go and find her, but we still have to face those reporters first."

"Yes, we do." Taking her hand, he said, "Thank you for doing this for me. I will never forget it."

"You are welcome." Hugging him, Taylor smiled.

"Joules said there will be security waiting to help us through the gates at the house. It's going to be much worse than it was in Miami. She says about six news crews are set up outside our house. She is there waiting for us. Remember not to look at them or react in any way to anything they say. Can you do that?"

"I've got it," replied Taylor.

"Okay, let's go, and remember I am right beside you the whole way."

It only took less than ten minutes from the airport to their driveway. Just as Joules had predicted, the place was crawling with reporters and camera crews. It only took a few minutes for them to get inside the gate and safely inside the house. Security was there as promised. But it was the longest two minutes of Taylor's life. The moment the black SUV pulled up to the gates of the Carrington estate, reporters rushed forward with microphones in hand and cameras rolling.

"Senator Carrington, is it true?"

"Are you and Mrs. Carrington separated?"

"Are you getting divorced?"

"How do you know Poppy Thompson, and what is the nature of your relationship with her?"

"Are you still on the shortlist for a possible cabinet position?"

Questions flew at the car's passengers from every direction. The lack of response from the couple inside the car did nothing to deter the horde of journalists who continued their verbal assault. Rapidly firing question after question at the couple in the car, the various new crews jockeyed for the best camera angle.

The two security guards finally forced the crowd back long enough for Bennett to pull through the gates and drive up the winding drive to the house. Bennett and Taylor did not say a word until they were inside the garage, with the large wooden door closed firmly behind them. It had only taken a few moments to clear the gates and drive up the drive, but it felt like an eternity.

Turning off the car, Bennett looked over at Taylor and, with his voice full of anguish and shame, said, "I'm sorry for all of it. I never meant for any of this to happen. The last thing I ever wanted to do was hurt you."

Nodding her head in agreement, Taylor, feeling overwhelmed and stunned, looked over at Bennett and answered, "I know. Me either. But what the hell are we going to do now?"

Giving Taylor a shocked look at her use of profanity before burying his face in his hands, he said, "I have no idea." For a man who always had an answer for everything, this time Bennett had nothing.

Taylor sighed deeply and said, "Me either, but one thing I do know, it will get a lot worse before it gets better." She had never felt so violated or attacked in her life. It seemed like a lifetime ago that she and Bennett had been the darlings of the news. Now, they were being treated like they were criminals.

As soon as Bennett and Taylor got out of the car, Joules ran into the garage and engulfed Taylor in a huge hug. "Lord, it is good to see you."

While hugging Taylor, Bennett caught Joules' eye and asked, "Any word from Poppy?"

Joules stepped back and nodded her head yes. "But you are not going to like it. Let's go inside, and I will tell you about it."

Once inside and seated at the kitchen counter, Joules said, "Poppy has packed up and gone with Ben to Tennessee."

Bennett slammed his fist on the counter, "Damn it! I was worried she would do something like that. When did she leave, and why didn't you stop her? And why Tennessee?"

"I couldn't. She was already gone by the time I got out there. They left after the story broke about Taylor being pregnant. I did what I could. I found them a safe house to hide out in. My friend from college is a real estate agent. She has a lot of rental properties. She put them up in one. I know it is not ideal, but at least you can get to her faster. Plus, she is staying there and not running to New York. It is a start."

A look of sadness and anger crossed Bennett's face, "A small one. She could have trusted me. She could have trusted me to fix this. You don't think…" he hesitated for a moment. Then, he continued, "Surely she didn't believe that I was the father of Taylor's baby? I know that was how the news made it look, but surely she realized that was not true. After all we have been through, how could she think that?"

At this point, Taylor looked from Joules to Bennett and said, "You two have a lot to discuss. I think I will go in and lie down for a while." She then went upstairs to her room. She had felt like she was eavesdropping on something that had nothing to do with her.

Once the door upstairs closed, Joules looked at Bennett and said, "I don't know what Poppy believes, but she is safe. Do what you need to here. You can go after her when that is done."

Joules pointed to the street where the reporters were still camped out like vultures circling for the kill. "What are you going to do about all of that?"

Bennett gave her a stern look and said, "I have a plan, but you are not going to like it. But, it is the only way. Call a press conference for nine o'clock tomorrow morning at my office. Did you make those calls I asked you earlier?"

"Yes, it is all set."

Bennett gave Joules a weary smile and said, "I am grateful. You have been an amazing friend to both of us. He would have been so proud of you."

There was no need to say who the "he" was. They both knew who Bennett was talking about.

Joules was quiet for a moment and then said, "I hope so. Do you ever wonder if this would have happened if he had lived?"

"Every day."

"Me too." Wiping a tear that was slowly making its way down her cheek, Joules said, "Enough of this. We have too much work to do to be sitting around talking about things we can't change. Let's get busy."

Bennett nodded, and the two of them worked the rest of the afternoon, working out the little details to make sure the news conference the next day went off without a hitch.

For the next several hours, Bennett and Joules strategized and made plans for the next day. By the time Taylor woke up from her nap and came down to fix something for dinner, Joules was gone.

Feeling famished, Taylor heated a can of tomato soup and made grilled cheese sandwiches. When it was ready, Bennett joined her for dinner in the kitchen. It was the first time they had sat together at their kitchen table for a meal in over seven months.

It should have felt awkward, but it didn't. They were what they were: two old friends sharing a meal. They kept the conversation light, sticking to topics like the work she had been doing in Miami and a book she had recently read. It was as if each one just needed a few moments of normalcy after the craziness of the last few days.

When they were done eating, Bennett said, "Thank you for this. I want you to know that even after everything that has happened, I still care about you."

Patting him on the arm, Taylor wanted to let Bennett know how much she appreciated all he had done for her over the years. "I would have never survived those first few years without you, so thank you for being there for me."

"Yes, you would have. I know that now. I am so sorry for letting you down and not being the man you needed me to be. It just wasn't meant to be."

"You are right. It wasn't meant to be. I realized something at the beach during all of those hours of soul-searching. Life is short. We have to reach out and grab every bit of happiness we can, when we can. Poppy and Ben make you happy. You should be with them. Greer makes me unbelievably happy, and I want to be with him. It really shouldn't matter what other people or the press think about it. We have to live our own lives and be true to ourselves. So let's stop apologizing and stop beating ourselves up. What is done is done. We must move forward and trust that everything will work itself out."

"Wow. I never saw that coming, but I am relieved you feel this way. You are right. I have been beating myself up emotionally for everything for months now about all of this. But I shouldn't be surprised that you would say something like that. Your willingness to forgive and your caring nature were just a few things I have always loved about you. And I do love you very much."

"I know. You love me, but you are not in love with me anymore than I am with you. But it's okay. We have both found the people we are supposed to be with. You have a son now. In a few months, Lord willing, I will have a child of my own. Things are working out. It is just going to take some time and patience. We can get through this. We have gotten through much worse."

"Well, about that. I have something to tell you. I, too, have been doing some deep thinking and have made a major decision. Tomorrow morning at nine o'clock,

I am resigning as Senator and withdrawing my name from consideration for a cabinet position."

"Bennett, no!"

"Yes. It is time. Nothing is more important to me than Poppy, Ben, and you. Staying in the race is hurting all the people that I love the most in the world. I don't think I can live with myself if I go on hurting any of you one more day."

"But this is your dream."

"It was my dream. My only dream now is seeing you happy with Greer and Poppy and me back together raising our son. I don't want to miss one more day with him or Poppy. And I want you to be happy, too."

Sitting back and studying him for a moment, Taylor added, "Oh my. What does Joules say about all this?"

"Joules totally agrees with me. She knows what it is like to lose the love of your life. I promise you, she would trade every campaign and anything else she could for just one more day with the man she loved."

"Who was that man? Did you know him? She mentioned him to me the other day but would not tell me who it was. I pray it is not Dennis Harrison. That man is not good enough for her."

Shaking his head, Bennett said, "It is not Dennis. I know who it was, but that is not my story to tell. She would have told you if she wanted you to know about it."

"I guess you are right," Taylor talked as she gathered plates and bowls and took them to the sink. "She told you, but she won't tell me. Strange. I would not have thought there was anything we couldn't tell each other."

"She didn't tell me. I knew about it for other reasons. It happened a long time ago."

"And you can't tell me?"

"No, I can't, and please don't ask me to. She'll tell you when she is ready."

"You're right, but I find it all very strange. Especially after all that has happened in the last few months. What bigger secrets could there be?"

Bennett was silent for a moment and then stood up and walked to the counter. "Well, I am going to say goodnight," he said, "I have a speech I need to work on for the morning. I enjoyed tonight. Make sure you get some rest. I will stay in the guest room tonight if that is okay."

"Of course, it is okay. This is your house."

Continuing to stand by the counter, he said, "I can hardly wait to bring Ben here. He's driven by it but never been inside. I can't wait for you to meet him. He is an amazing kid."

"I would love to meet your son, but I am unsure how his momma will feel about that," replied Taylor.

"I know. Poppy is such a sweet and giving person. She is truly beautiful inside and out until it comes to you."

"I agree with you there. She is stunning. All that glorious red hair and alabaster skin. And, tiny. I didn't remember her being so tiny. Maybe because anytime I have ever been around her, she was always frowning at me. She scares me because she comes across as being very fierce. She has never liked me. I wondered what I did to her that made her hate me so much. Now, I know that it was all about you."

"Yes, she is very intimidated by you. I told you the truth before about us not sleeping together. We haven't since we were together eleven years ago. She was hung up on not being the other woman."

As Taylor loaded the dishwasher, she said, "Well, the joke was on her then because she never was. I was the other woman," said Taylor. "She was always the only woman for you from the beginning. The irony is that we would have never become a couple if she had not run off. You go to her, and you make her understand that. If you do, who knows, maybe she and I will become friends. You two will get married, and she will become the sister I never had."

Bennett had no response to that. He just nodded as Taylor walked over and hugged him good night before heading off to bed. For a long time after she left, Bennett stood rooted in the same spot by the counter in the kitchen, unable to quite believe this would be his last night as a United States Senator. He spent his whole life working to get to where he was, and in one ten line announcement, he was going to demolish his life's work.

Chapter 25

Carrington House
Searcy, Arkansas
July 2012

Taylor and Bennett were both up early the next morning. Taylor had not slept well. She tried calling Greer several times but had not been able to talk to him. She guessed he was probably at the hospital. Today, of all days, she would have liked to have had him there with her. But she knew that was not practical.

She tried him once more as she clipped her pearls around her neck. She would forever think of him anytime she wore them. The only other jewelry Taylor wore was her new engagement ring. She had not taken it off since Greer had given it to her.

Once she was dressed in a light beige suit with a soft pink blouse, Taylor came downstairs. There, she was met by both Bennett and Joules. They were each dressed in suits and looked very somber. No one was saying much as they loaded into a blacked-out Suburban that Joules had brought to take them to the office.

A few reporters were still outside the gates, but the numbers had been significantly reduced. Most had relocated to Bennett's office, where they were waiting to pounce.

Just before the three of them got to the office, Bennett said, "Taylor, when this is over, I want you to do exactly what Joules tells you. We have planned it out to the last second to give you the best chance of getting away without anyone knowing where you are going. Promise me that you will do exactly what we say."

Taylor had gotten used to making her own decisions of late and was not exactly comfortable surrendering control. In the end, she sighed and said, "Fine. I will do whatever you ask."

Turning to Joules, Bennett asked, "Is everything we discussed ready to go?"

Nodding, Joules replied, "Yes, everything is just as you requested. I think you will be pleased."

Just then, they pulled into the parking lot of the firm. Reporters rushed at the car from all directions. The security guards at the house were now at the firm's back door. They held the crowd of reporters back long enough for all of them to exit the car. Once inside, Bennett escorted Taylor to his office door. He and Joules left her there while they went to make sure everything was ready for the press conference.

As she walked into Bennett's office, Taylor was shocked to see Greer sitting at a library table waiting for them. He looked as delicious as always, dressed in a dark suit with a blue tie. "What are you doing here?" she asked.

Walking over and giving her a quick peek on the lips, Greer said, "Bennett called me last night and told me he was going to do this. He also asked me if I could be here to support you. He sent the plane for me at five, and here I am. How are you holding up?"

Smiling, she said, "I am better now. I hate this for Bennett. This is really a sad day for our state."

"Don't worry so much about that. There will be other races. People have short attention spans. He can bounce back. In the meantime, you know he is doing the right thing for all involved. It is time for this to be over. I want you with me." Putting his hand on her stomach, he said, "How's our little guy? Everything still rocking along in there?"

Nodding, she said, "Yes, I am fine. I want this to hurry up and be over with."

"Well, hang on just a little longer, Darling. I think they are almost ready for us."

At that moment, Bennett and Joules came back to the office. Bennett closed the door and said, "We are about to go out there. I am just going to read a short speech, and I am not taking questions. All I ask of you, Taylor, is that you stand behind me and support me. Greer, why don't you stand off to the side of Taylor so that you aren't in any of the television shots? I don't want someone to see this later and make the connection that you were here. Okay? They will try to ask questions but ignore them. Do you both understand?"

Greer and Taylor both nodded yes. Then, they all followed Joules out to the lobby area of the firm where they had set up for the press conference. Like the day before, reporters assaulted them with questions the second they entered the room.

Bennett and Joules moved to the front by the podium. Taylor stayed a little to the back. Greer stood just to the right of Taylor.

Stepping up to the microphone, Joules said, "Senator Carrington will be making a short statement. After which, he will not be taking questions."

Then, Bennett stepped up and read his statement thanking everyone for the support and explaining the need to withdraw from the race due to family issues. He did not go into any detail about what those were. As soon as he was done, they all quickly exited the room.

Several reporters shouted questions about a possible separation or divorce as they went. Others focused on Taylor and the baby she was carrying. None of the questions were addressed. Now that it was almost over, the questions did not have the emotional impact they had the day before. They were simply questions and no longer had the power to hurt any of them.

From the back door of Bennett's office, they were all hustled back into the black Suburban and driven to the airport. Once inside the hangar, Bennett hugged Taylor and shook Greer's hand. "I hate to do this after you have been so wonderful to help me, but I have to get out of here and go get my family. You two are going home on the firm's plane."

Looking at Taylor, he said, "I plan to file divorce papers the second I get back. I will call you, and we can work out a settlement. You can have anything and everything you want, except for the house. I can't give you that because, as you know, it is entailed. But the rest is yours if you want it. I'll call you, and we can work it out next week. But for now, I know you are in good hands."

"We'll figure it out. For now, just go get her. That is all that matters," replied Taylor. At that, she hugged him one last time, and he got in Joules's car hoping to throw the reporters off when he left shortly.

Joules hugged Taylor and promised to call her soon. Taylor and Greer boarded the firm's plane and prepared to take off. As they buckled their seat belts, the pilot called, "Are you ready, Mrs. Carrington, to go home?"

Taylor had realized that for the first time in a very long time, she finally knew where home was. She hadn't really had one since her parents and brother had died. Now, she did. It was with Greer.

With a huge smile, Taylor confidently responded, "Yes, thank you." Turning to Greer, she whispered, "Wow, I just realized something. I have not felt like I had a real home of my own since my parents died. Being with you has given me my sense of home back. As long as I am with you, I will always be home. You will be forevermore my home."

Wrapping her in a massive hug, Greer said, "You and this baby are the only home I will ever need again, though I guess you are going to tell me we can't raise a child on a houseboat."

Laughing, Taylor said, "Well, it might be a little difficult when he or she is learning to walk. So, yeah, we will have to work on getting us a house, but let's keep the boat. It holds some pretty terrific memories I still can't completely remember."

With a bark of laughter, Greer says before devouring her lips in an embrace, "Oh darling, don't you worry. If I have my way, we will have a million more new black silk memories that you will never forget."

Chapter 26

Carrington House
Searcy, Arkansas
November 24, 2023

It took all morning and part of the afternoon for Taylor to finish recounting her and Greer's story to Harvey Cox, the reporter writing the article on Bennett. Taylor was exhausted. The reporter looked a little overwhelmed by the tale himself. A feeling Taylor greatly understood. Reliving it all had left her feeling the same way.

Harvey recorded her as she spoke and made notes for hours. Greer had texted nearly two hours before that he and Rosie were back at Edna's, and the car was packed and ready to leave as soon as she finished.

"So let me get this straight," asked Harvey, "When you left after Bennett resigned, you returned to Gulf Shores, but you still had no idea about Mrs. Carrington's true identity? The other Mrs. Carrington, the former Mrs. Thompson?" The reporter actually blushed and appeared embarrassed at having to clarify which Mrs. Carrington he was talking about. Again, Taylor got it. Oh, what a tangled web they had weaved!

Shaking her head in the affirmative, Taylor said, "That is correct. I did not find out about all of that until after Rosie was born."

"Rosie, your daughter?"

"Correct. I returned to Gulf Shores with Greer. True to his word, Bennett filed for divorce the next week. It took a little over thirty days for the paperwork to be completed. Our marriage of eleven years was over in just over a month. Greer and I flew to Vegas and married in a wedding chapel on the strip. When he first suggested it, I thought he was joking, but the idea grew on me over time. After all, it was the quickest, cheapest way to do it. We had both been married before and had big weddings, and look how those turned out. We just wanted to be married and together. That was in August. Rosie was born in late December."

"When did you learn about your connection to Poppy Thompson Carrington?"

"After Rosie was born. But, look, I am not comfortable talking about that. If you want to know more about that, you need to ask Poppy."

Smiling at her like she was hiding something he was determined to figure out, Harvey said, "Oh, I most definitely intend to."

Feeling like she had shared everything she cared to share, Taylor said, "I think I have told you all there is to tell. If you don't mind, I am exhausted and have a long car ride home to Gulf Shores tonight. If it is okay with you, I would like to end the interview here."

Having been a reporter long enough to know when he had gotten all he could from a source, Harvey smiled and thanked her for her time. "Thank you, Mrs. Stone, for taking the time to talk with me. Would it be okay if I took your number and called you with any follow-up questions I might have?"

Not really wanting to give him her number but unable to think of a reasonable reason not to, Taylor gave him her number. Then she went in search of Bennett, Poppy, and their family to say her goodbyes. Bennett and Poppy had left to run a few errands, so Taylor hugged and kissed Ben and the girls and then texted Greer she was ready to go. Ben promised to give her regards to his parents.

In a few minutes, Greer pulled up in front of the home Taylor had called home for many years. She quickly got in the car and gave Greer a quick kiss as she buckled herself in for the long car ride. As they pulled out of the drive, she could not help but take one last look at the house. Having spent the better part of the day recounting everything that had happened eleven years before had left her exhausted and emotionally raw. But one thing she knew for sure. She was as happy to leave that old life behind today as she was eleven years ago. She said a quick prayer that they were making the right decision to air their dirty laundry. Bennett would make a fabulous governor. Only time would tell if doing this would be worth all it was going to cost them.

Part Three - Ben's Story

Carrington House
Searcy, Arkansas
November 24, 2023

Ben and Ella were in the backyard with Lizzy and Lola. Ben was pushing them on the swings of their playset. Truthfully, the girls had outgrown the structure but still enjoyed swinging, especially when they had their big brother to push them. Ella sat in an Adirondack chair watching.

Harvey Cox came outside looking for Poppy. Walking up to Ben, he stuck out his hand and said, "You must be Ben. I am Harvey Cox. I am writing an article on your family."

Ben shook the reporter's hand and said, "Nice to meet you. Dad said you were here talking with Aunt Taylor. She just left if you were looking for her."

"No, I think I have everything I need from her now. I would like to speak with your mom. Do you know where she is?" replied the reporter.

"She and Dad had to run to Des Arc to Guess and Company. I think they plan to run by Dale's and hit the Black Friday deals. Ella and I offered to stay with the girls while they were gone. I don't think they thought you would finish with Aunt Taylor so quickly. I can call them if you need me to. They should be back shortly."

Nodding, the reporter asked, "That is not necessary. I can wait. Any chance you and I could visit for a few minutes until they get back?"

Ben had known this was coming. His dad had prepared him that he would need to answer a few questions. Ben did not like talking to reporters. He sometimes thought he had PTSD from having to deal with them as a child. But, he promised his dad he would speak with Harvey. Now seemed as good a time as any.

Looking over at Ella, he asked, "You're good to watch the girls while Mr. Cox and I talk?"

"Please call me Harvey. I know that calling me Mr. Cox means your parents raised you right, but it makes me feel old."

Nodding, Ben amended, "While Harvey and I talk?"

Standing up and hugging Ben, Ella said, "Of course."

By this point, Lizzy and Lola had abandoned the swings and were currently racing each other around the yard, laughing, screeching, and being very loud.

Yelling, "Girls, chill!" Ben gave Ella a look. "You sure? They can be a handful."

Giving him a smirk, Ella replied, "Six younger siblings remember? I got this. We will be fine."

Giving her a quick peck on the lips, Ben said, "Okay, well, if you're sure, let's give it a go, sir." Looking back at Ella as he and the reporter headed back into the house, Ben said, "We won't be long. Have one of the girls come and get me if you need me."

"We'll be fine. No worries," Ella called back.

Harvey followed Ben into the house. Ben entered the kitchen, where he grabbed a couple of bottles of water. He handed one to Harvey before heading back to his dad's office.

Settling into the library chairs on each side of the fireplace, Harvey took a long sip of his water. Swallowing, he sat down his water bottle and picked up his handheld recorder. Showing it to Ben, he asked, "You good for me to record this?"

Nodding, Ben replied, "Sure, man, but I must tell you that I am not sure how much I can tell you. This whole deal is my mom's and Aunt Taylor's deal. Most people would probably think we were one screwed-up family, and in some ways, I guess we are. But I feel fortunate to be in this family. My parents have always worked hard to protect me and ensure I knew I was loved and wanted."

"You are very lucky. A lot of kids don't get that."

Nodding, Ben agreed, "Yes, I am blessed. So what exactly is it that you want to know?"

The reporter was fascinated by the well-mannered young man's accent. It was a combination of New York Bronx meets Southern gentleman. His voice carried a certain roughness that had been softened with the infusion of a Southern drawl. It was an interesting mix.

As a man who made his living asking people questions and getting to hear many different accents, he wondered which side of his voice would be more dominant if he were angry or a little drunk. In his experience, it was in those moments that one's actual voice came out. He considered asking Ben if they could exchange the water for something stronger to see if he could get his true self to emerge. Deciding against that, he decided to get him talking and see if he could bring out his natural voice that way.

"Tell me about growing up in New York. It had to be very different from your life here in Arkansas," said Harvey.

"You have no idea," replied Ben. "I lived in New York until I was almost eleven. Then, we moved here. It was like moving to another world, not just another state. I was not prepared for how different my life was about to become. Before we moved here, I had visited once. But, during that visit, we mainly stayed home and just hung out together. Once we moved here, and I started attending school, my life changed in a million ways. Ways I could never have predicted."

"Before we get into that, tell me what your life was like in New York."

"New York. Well, it was the typical life of a big-city kid. We lived in a brownstone apartment in Red Hook. It belonged to my dad. I mean, the guy I thought was my dad until I found out about Bennett, my real dad. His name was Thomas Thompson. He was an artist who married my mom because she was pregnant with me."

"I have heard of him. He made a big splash in the abstract art world in the late 1990s. He died really young, didn't he?"

"Wow. I am shocked. Most people have never heard of him. How did you find out about him?"

"I took an art appreciation class at UALR, and he was one of the artists we studied. My professor knew him and really thought a lot of him."

"Yes, he was an amazing artist. Many of his pieces still hang in several museums. I also have several pieces my mom has stored for me. Whenever I settle down, I will get them."

"Lucky you. They are worth a mint."

"Yeah, but it is not about the money. Not anymore. Thanks to both of my dads, I am pretty set financially, but I don't like talking about it."

"Understood." Shifting gears, Harvey asked, "Do you have any memories of Thompson? You had to be very young when he passed."

"I was six when we lost him. I have wonderful memories of him. He always smelled of turpentine and had paint stains on his fingers. He had a huge roar of a laugh. I remember loving being with him and Uncle Jack. They were always together. All of us lived together in that tiny apartment. We must have been cramped, but I don't remember it that way. I remember lots of laughter and family dinners. Or at least until Dad got sick."

"He died of a long-term illness, right?"

"Yes, he fought it for years. I don't remember knowing he was sick or anything until the end. I remember when they brought in a hospital bed. It seemed like it went fast after that. Mom and Uncle Jack took turns taking care of him. He died three days before his fortieth birthday."

"That must have been a really sad time for you."

"Yes, it was. I remember Mom spending hours comforting Uncle Jack. He took Dad's death really hard. Mom did, too, but it was different."

"So the three of you continued to live together in the apartment for the next few years?"

"Yes, Uncle Jack, Mom and I continued as a small family until Uncle Jack met Uncle Jorge. They fell in love and had a massive wedding in Boston. I got to be a ring bearer. I thought I was so cool. All dressed up in my first tux.

"After that, Uncle Jack moved in with Uncle Jorge. The apartment was always Mom's. Dad, Tommy left it to her. From then on, it was just the two of us until my real dad, Bennett, showed up."

"Did you always know your dad was gay and not truly your dad?"

"Gay, yes. It is no big deal when you are raised with all the love I was given. It was just my normal. As far as the fact that a gay man might not be my dad never occurred to me. I was too young to question it all. It was not until later that I realized he wasn't my biological dad. But, make no mistake, Tommy Thompson was a great dad. So was Uncle Jack. Again, I have been blessed to have so many people who have loved and cared for me. In fact, part of the reason I went to California for school was that Uncle Jack and Uncle Jorge lived nearby. They moved there in 2011. I love running over for a family meal or doing my laundry. How lucky am I to have that."

"Okay, so tell me a little about your life after your dad passed.."

"Well, I was your typical eleven-year-old boy. Other than video games. Mom absolutely forbade them. I used to sneak to my friends' houses to play with them."

"Weren't you a chess champion at a very early age? That is hardly typical."

"Well, it was for me. I went to a private school, and all my friends played chess. We also started learning foreign languages. I studied French and Spanish. I also took cello lessons. The one thing I refused to do was take art lessons. Art was so much of my life; I could not stand being surrounded by it at school."

"Chess, cello, and foreign languages? That is all not typical for a young man."

"Was for me."

"So, of all your interests, what was your favorite?"

"That is easy, baseball."

"Baseball? How did you get into that?"

"Well, when I was ten, my buddy Joseph and his dad, Mr. Brad, moved into the apartment next to us. His mom had lost her mind and took off with a rocker. Mr. Brad spent hours playing catch out front of our complex. He was trying to make up for the mom leaving. Well, one day, as I was coming home from a cello lesson, I discovered my throwing arm."

"Joseph's dad overthrew him. I was coming up the sidewalk. I dodged the ball as it whizzed past my head. Trying to be helpful, I reached down, picked up the ball, and threw it back to Mr. McNeil. In that minute, my life changed. Mr. McNeil coached Joseph's baseball team. He was so impressed with my arm that he invited me to join his team. It took some convincing, but eventually, my mom let me join the team. Almost overnight, I lost interest in everything but baseball."

"Okay," said Harvey as he continued to make notes and record the interview, "so baseball becomes your focus. Did that continue once you moved to Searcy?"

"Oh yes, it only got more intense. I played on traveling teams and then pitched for the Lions. We won three state championships. We did have an awesome coach. Coach Davis and I are still close. I greatly respect him. I also played in college until I almost blew out my rotator cuff in my junior year. I was lucky. I did not have to have surgery, but my playing days are over. That was a hard pill to swallow. Crazy thing, my dad had the same issue in college. Sometimes it feels like we are so connected on so many levels even though I didn't even know he existed the first half of my life."

"Well, before we dive too deeply into your high school and college years, let's go back to when you met your dad."

"Okay, what do you want to know?"

"What do you remember about the first time you met him?"

"Hum, let's see. The first time I met Dad was actually at a baseball game. I saw him talking with my mom by the stands. I could tell that Mom was acting weird, even from the dugout. Even though it took some convincing to get her to let me play baseball, she was my biggest fan once I started playing. Normally, she would be the loudest mom in the stands. I got a double, and she did not even notice. Once I got on base, I looked up and saw her arguing with a guy in a suit. Since everyone else was dressed in jeans and sports gear, the guy stood out."

"Did you meet him that day?"

"Yes, I did. After the game, my mom introduced him to me. She said he was an old friend from Arkansas. Honestly, I had forgotten my mom was even from Arkansas."

"What was that first meeting like?"

"Well, truthfully, what I remember most is that we all went for pizza afterward with the whole team. My dad slipped me a twenty to play video games. I think he just wanted to spend time with my mom."

"When we left, I expected to go home with Joe and his dad. I was shocked when this big town car pulled up. My dad pulled my mom off to the side. The next thing I knew we were driving uptown to see the view from his hotel suite. When we got there, Dad took us out on one of the balconies to look at the city. It was so beautiful. Dad pointed out various constellations and asked me about baseball and school."

"Did he tell you he was your dad during that first visit?"

"Oh no. I did not find that out until much later."

"Well, what happened after that?"

"Well, we ended up watching a movie about baseball. I fell asleep on the couch. The next thing I remembered was waking up there the next morning. I got up and went looking for my mom. She was asleep in the second bedroom in the suite. My dad was already up and talking on the phone. When he saw me, he ended the call, handed me the room service menu, and told me to order anything I wanted."

Giving an eleven-year-old boy free rein to order anything he wants to eat is a ridiculously bad idea. I think I ordered everything on the breakfast menu except the English muffins. Even then, I hated English muffins. Dad and I were working through our breakfast smorgasbord when Mom entered the living area.

Dad told us he had to return to work for a few days but would be back on Saturday for Mom. I think she had to come back to Arkansas for something. I did not care because I was staying at Joe's all weekend.

"Did you see him when he came to take your mom to Arkansas?"

"Maybe for like a minute. But, honestly, I was so excited to have two days to play video games; that was about all I was focused on."

"So when did you see him next?" asked Harvey, trying to ensure he kept the relationship timeline accurate.

"When my mom came back, she was different. She told me we were going to North Carolina for several weeks. She switched me to homeschooling. I started seeing my dad on weekends. He would fly over to see us. He had rented a house for all of us on Caswell Beach. We spent the next several months there. Anyway, the first night we were there, Mom and Dad sat me down and told me that Bennett was my biological dad. They also told me he was a senator, and we had to keep it all quiet."

"How did you feel learning Bennett was your dad?"

"Well, I was fine with that. I had already lost two dads, one to illness and one to love. Uncle Jack was still in my life, but not like he had been when I was younger. However, I was pissed as hell that I had to move and leave my school, Joe, and baseball. I think I made my mother's life a living hell during those months.

Imagine a kid thinking his life is over because he has to move to the beach. I would love it now. But then, I was pretty awful. I must remember to apologize to my mom when I see her later."

"Did they tell you he was a senator or that he was being considered as a possible cabinet secretary after the presidential election?"

"They talked about him being a senator and that we had to keep everything secret. I don't remember them mentioning the other part about the election. I remember wondering why he lived in DC if he was from Arkansas."

"Did they tell you that he was married?"

"No, they definitely did not."

"Why do you think they left that part out?"

"Probably because I was just a kid and would not have been able to understand it, much less process it. Honestly, I had enough to process finding out I had a new dad and having to move."

"You said you all three spent a lot of time together. Do you know if your dad and mom had become a couple by then?"

"You know, I don't think so. Until after my dad's divorce from Taylor, I never saw my parents kiss. Lord, after that, I could not get them to stop kissing. That is how I ended up with two little sisters I never saw coming."

"So you were all together, but you don't think your parents were romantically involved?"

"Correct. Looking back, I can see that the feelings they had for each other were obvious, but no, I don't think they were together, together, if you know what I mean. Ewww. This is so gross. I mean, those are my parents, dude. Can we talk about something else?"

"Sure," said Harvey, nodding. He got it. No one ever wanted to think about their parents and sex in the same sentence. Changing directions, he asked, "How did your life change after the press discovered what was happening in July 2012?"

"Well, Mom and I came to Searcy for a visit. We were staying in a condo in River Oaks. I remember we had gone out for snow cones after my first-ever golf lesson at the Country Club. There was an award winning golf pro who gave lessons, Bruce Baxley. He and dad had been friends for years. Dad arranged for me to have a lesson from him. I remember it was a lot of fun but so hot. I had to carry my bag and not being accustomed to the heat, I thought I was going to die.

When we came back to the condo, a news crew drove up in a van. A reporter jumped out and started asking Mom and me a ton of questions about my dad, mom, and Aunt Taylor. At the time, I had no idea who Taylor was. Mom hustled me into the house as quickly as possible."

"What did you say to the reporters?"

"I was so stunned by it all that I don't think I said anything. Dad and Mom had made it pretty clear that I was not to talk about who my dad was. Once back in the house, we closed the blinds and sequestered ourselves there for the rest of the day. The news crew camped out on the street all day. Mom told me not to turn on any lights as it started getting dark. I was sitting in my room playing my cello. I remember my mom coming into my room and telling me to get my stuff and to quietly go to the car. I remember being scared when we had to drive through the horde of reporters, all yelling questions at us as we drove away. The whole experience left me terrified."

"As we drove through the night, I remember asking Mom where we were going. She said we were going someplace where no one would find us. I also remember asking her who Taylor was. When she said my dad's wife, I understood why we had to keep everything quiet. It was such a shock. By this point, my dad had become my hero. In an instant, I lost all respect for him. I realized why he had kept us hidden."

"You and your dad have a great relationship now. What happened to change how you felt about him?"

"Time. Maturity and learning all the facts. I realize now that my parents were dealing with a lot. To my dad's credit, even though my mom kept me hidden from him for years, he never blamed her for that or tried to use that against her. I don't know if I would be so forgiving if someone kept my child from me."

"Okay, so let's get back to your story. You and your mom are driving through the night. Where did you go, and what happened next?"

"At some point, Mom must have talked to Joules, Dad's right-hand person. Joules is a miracle worker. She can find a needle in a haystack in the dark. Somehow, Joules arranged a house for us in a little town in Tennessee that no one had ever heard of called Bolivar. The little town is about an hour east of Memphis. By the time we rolled into town at one in the morning, Joules had arranged a house with a fully stocked kitchen for us. How she did it, I have no idea. She rented it under her name, so no one knew where we were. We unloaded the car and basically fell into bed. The next morning, Mom made us pancakes. I remember because we were watching one of those women's talk shows when, across the bottom of the screen, an announcement said that Senator Carrington had withdrawn his work on the Anderson campaign and was resigning his Senate seat effective immediately.

"As she read it, Mom blanched and ran to find her phone. She went into the bedroom and closed the door. She stayed there for what felt like forever. When she came out, her eyes were red, and I knew she had been crying. She told me that my dad was on his way."

"She spent the next hour showering and doing her hair and make-up. I was a little shocked. Mom has always been into the natural look. It was weird because I knew she was making herself beautiful for him. But let's not talk about that. Eww.

"Anyway, when Dad got there, he immediately went and gave Mom one of those long, gross kisses that I would soon come to hate. Then, he dropped down on one knee and proposed. And the rest is history. We moved into his house in Searcy. My parents had a small wedding at the First Presbyterian Church. This time, I was promoted from ring bearer to best man, but I still looked very cool in my tux."

"I am sure you did," replied Harvey. "How long was it until your sisters were born?"

"Well, I think my folks wanted me to have time to get used to having two parents and being a normal family. Maybe they just wanted some time together before having more children. Either way, they waited until I was in the ninth grade to have Lizzy. That was fun. Having a mom as beautiful as mine and then having not one but two babies while you are in high school. Talk about taking a ribbing. My buddies did not hold back. But I can't blame them. I would have done the same thing. Giving each other hell is how teenage boys show love."

"So, back to how life was different after you moved here, can you tell me more about that?"

"Sure, the major difference was in a small town like Searcy, everyone knows everyone. If you go out to eat, everyone stops to visit. Driving down the road, everyone waves, even when they don't know you. That was a huge change from being in New York, where no one speaks and everyone minds their own business. Another big change was church. I am not saying my mom was not religious or spiritual, but we did not attend church in New York. In fact, I did not know anyone who did. When we moved here, suddenly we went to church all the time. Most of my friends' activities involved church. At first, it was a little overwhelming. But I got used to it. I made a lot of really good friends through my church youth group. That is something I would have missed if we had stayed in New York."

"Anything you really missed about New York once you were here?"

"The food. We often got Indian or authentic Chinese delivery. Here, that does not exist. If you want food, you have to go and get it. I miss that. I was surprised by how much I missed the cello. In high school, I joined the orchestra. I also continued to compete in chess tournaments. There were only a few a year, but I enjoyed them. To keep my skills sharp, Dad would play with me. Unfortunately, chess is one of the things Dad is not that great at. Don't tell him I told you that. I would sometimes just let him win because I felt sorry for him. I mean, just how many times can a guy lose before he refuses to play ever again."

"Anything else?" asked Harvey.

"No, not really. I had my life there, and I have my life here. They feel like they belong to two totally different people. That is how I feel about myself now. I have loved living and going to school in Cali. I can't imagine leaving. Yet, I graduate in May. Ella and I have a lot of decisions to make between now and then."

"Will you come back here after you graduate?"

"I don't know. That was the plan. Finish grad school and come home and go to law school. But things have changed. I will have to wait and see."

"How does Ella feel about all of this?

Ben paused for a moment. He had been very forthcoming and honest up until this point. However, Ella was off limits, so he said, "You know I am uncomfortable talking about Ella. She has nothing to do with my dad or what happened years ago. I see no reason to bring her into any of this."

Nodding, Harvey said, "Understood, but just for clarification, what is your relationship? Dating, engaged, friends?"

Ben thought for a moment and said, "We are engaged."

"Congratulations. When's the big day?"

"Soon. We have not set a date, but it will be very soon." With that, Ben leaned forward and stretched. "Unless you have something else specific you need to know, I would really like to get back to Ella and the girls. I am sure they have worn her out by now."

Reaching out to shake his hand once again, Harvey said, "I think I have all I need for the moment. I might need to follow up later, but I will get your email address from your dad if I do.

Thank you for your time. It has been nice talking and getting to know you. Best of luck with your wedding and whatever the future holds."

Firmly taking the reporter's hand, Ben replied, "Thank you, sir. I hope you can write an article that will show the people of Arkansas how great my dad is. There is no finer man in the state, and he will make a fabulous governor." Ben left his dad's office and searched for his fiancee and sisters.

Part Four - How It All Started

Carrington Kitchen
Searcy, Arkansas
November 27, 2023

The Monday after Thanksgiving, Poppy arranged to meet with Harvey Cox, the reporter doing the article on Bennett. The original plan had been for Harvey to interview all the main players, Bennett, Taylor, Ben, and her on the previous Friday. However, by the time Harvey finished with Taylor and Ben, it was too late to start on another one on Friday. Harvey and Bennett spent all day Saturday talking in Bennett's home office. Sunday was family day as everyone wanted to spend as much time with Ben and Ella before they left early Monday morning.

Unlike the questions Harvey asked Taylor and Ben, Bennett's interview focused on his plans for Arkansas if elected. Much of the discussion focused on various bills and initiatives he had pushed as a United States Senator. Harvey felt the article would be better if the relationship aspects were covered by the women most affected, and Bennett did the political side of things. Poppy could not help but think that Bennett got off a little easier than everyone else. Talking politics was in his wheelhouse. No stress there. No, she and Taylor were baring their souls and airing all of the dirty laundry to a stranger. It was petty, but it irritated Poppy just the same.

Of course, she did not say any of this to Bennett. If she had, he would have immediately told her they would shut the whole thing down, and his chances of being governor would go down the drain. So, she pulled up her big girl panties and prepared to do battle with the demons that had haunted her. If she was going to do this, and she was going to do it, she would do it right. Whole hog, as they say in Arkansas. She was holding nothing back. When she was done, every dirty, little secret would be out there for all the world to know. Her main concern was for her children. But, given the fact that Ben had already followed in their footsteps, apples and trees and all that, and gotten a girl pregnant out of wedlock, he had lost the right to be horrified by his parents' story.

As far as the girls went, they were still too young to understand it all. Once they were old enough to process it all, she hoped they would be proud of her for being brave enough to put her truth out in the world.

At twelve on the dot, Harvey rang the bell, and Poppy welcomed him with the offer of a cup of coffee. He declined but asked if she had any water. Harvey followed Poppy into her warm and spacious kitchen. Suspecting she might be more relaxed and forthcoming in her kitchen than Bennett's office, Harvey suggested they do the interview at the large granite island in the middle of the room. Handing him the water, Poppy agreed, and they both sat down to talk.

Looking him straight in the eye, Poppy asked, "So, where would you like me to begin?"

"How about at the beginning."

Poppy nodded, thinking that Harvey had no idea what he had just asked for but remembered her promise earlier to be completely honest about everything. Poppy said, "Well, get your recorder ready. I hope you have new batteries because this will take a while." With that, she took them back to where it all started.

Chapter 2

Carrington House
Apartment Garage
Searcy, Arkansas
July 1999

It was so stinking hot. Poppy did not think she had ever been so miserable. Her clothes were soaking wet, and sweat oozed from every pore on her body. It felt like even her red hair, which was currently in a ponytail, was sweating. It was a typical July day in Searcy, Arkansas, 98 degrees with 100% humidity.

It's not the best day to be moving into a new house. But that was exactly what Poppy found herself doing. She had spent all day carrying boxes to the second-story apartment over the garage of the Carrington mansion, her new home. To say that Poppy was unhappy about the move would be a major understatement.

For the first eighteen years of her life, Poppy had lived on a farm just outside of Pangburn, Arkansas, a sweet little town no one outside of White County had ever heard of. She had lived with her grandparents, Papa and Gran, on their farm and attended the local school with less than a thousand students. She loved her school. Her art teacher, Mrs. Roe, made every day wonderful. She introduced Poppy to watercolors in middle school. Now, a few years later, Poppy's sketches and paintings had greatly improved.

As a senior, Poppy was not happy about having to go to a new school where she knew no one. Gran had promised that Searcy had a great art department, and she would love it. Poppy was not so sure. On her fifth trip up the two flights of stairs loaded with boxes, she was ready to throw away what was still in the truck. But she knew she could not.

As much as she hated to admit it, much of what she had been hauling up the stairs had actually been her art supplies. Most of their possessions had been sold at auction when they sold the farm. After Papa died last fall, the farm proved too much for Gran. She decided to sell and move to town. A decision that was made without consulting Poppy, she might add. Poppy understood the need to sell the farm, but why did they have to move to Searcy? Why could they not find a small house in Pangburn?

This was a conversation that Poppy had repeatedly had with Gran to no avail since she had first told Poppy about the plan to move. Gran had arranged to work for Mr. Carrington, a local lawyer whose wife had died many years before. She said he was lonely and needed someone to help with the housework and cook as his long-time housekeeper had retired. Poppy felt terrible for the guy that he had lost his wife. After all, losing people was something Poppy knew well. Her own mother had died in childbirth, and she had never known her father. She had been raised by her grandparents. Now, she not only lost her Papa, but also her home and school. So, from Poppy's perspective, she lost much more than Mr. Carrington.

Why should she have to move and uproot her life just because he wanted a housekeeper who lived onsite? She could not understand why her grandmother could not work for the guy during the day and then come home to Pangburn at night. It wasn't that far.

But, no matter how much she begged, her grandmother would not relent. They were moving to Searcy and into the garage apartment that came free with the job. That was the one part of the deal that Poppy could not combat. Free was free. Money was tight even after selling the farm and most of their possessions. But, no matter how tight things were, Gran always found the money for art lessons and supplies. So, Poppy begrudgingly continued hauling boxes until the truck Gran borrowed was empty.

While Gran returned the truck to the guy she borrowed it from, Poppy fixed herself a tall glass of water and planted herself on the plastic chair she found on the balcony outside her room.

In truth, as much as she hated moving, she was secretly in love with her new room. The garage apartment was two stories. The first story had a small living room, kitchen, Gran's bedroom, and bath. The second story was an open loft space with incredible windows, a bath, and a balcony that ran the length of her room. It was all hers. Gran had given her permission to make it into her own private art studio/bedroom.

Sitting in the late afternoon heat, enjoying her cool drink, Poppy heard splashing down below. From her vantage point, she saw a guy and two girls running around in swimsuits, pushing each other into the water. The girls looked younger than the guys but still older than her. A second guy was swimming in the pool, but she could not see him.

Oh, how she would give anything to strip off her sweaty clothes, don her swimsuit, and join them. She was young, not stupid. She might be living in a house with a pool, but she was just "the help," same as Gran. She would not be welcome at their little pool party.

Not being able to join the swimmers did not keep her from spying on them. One of the guys was tall with dark hair. He kept running up and grabbing the girls and throwing them in the water. The girls shrieked and carried on as if they were being killed, but Poppy could tell they loved it. The girls were screaming, "Tatum! Stop it!" But he ignored them and tossed them in one after the other.

The other guy did not join in. Instead, he steadily swam laps up and down the pool. He kept his head under the water so Poppy could not see him. After several minutes, the Tatum guy seemed to halt the fun and began packing up. He put on a tee shirt and flip-flops and gathered up his keys.

Poppy heard him tell the girls to get out as they had to go. The guy swimming laps stopped and stood in the shallow end with his back to her. Poppy still was not able to see him properly. From what she could see, he was built. As the girls packed up and put on cover-ups, the guy, still in the water, pushed himself up on the side of the pool. He still had his back to her, but something about this guy interested her.

She had never had a boyfriend. Papa and Gran would have never allowed it. Not after the way her mother had gotten pregnant at 20 without being married. Knowing Gran as she did, she knew she had to have been so embarrassed. If she was, to her credit, she had never held Poppy accountable for her mother's sins.

Poppy continued to watch as the girls and the Tatum guy left in one of the two red Jeeps parked in the drive. Once they left, her mystery guy, as she had begun to think of him, slipped back into the pool and swam for about thirty more minutes.

Poppy watched each stroke and honestly felt herself getting hotter with each one. No boy had ever commanded her interest the way this one did. Just when she thought she could not take watching him anymore, he pulled himself out of the pool and walked into the main house through the sliding glass door. To Poppy's dismay, he never turned to face her, so other than seeing that he was built like the Adonis statue she had learned about in art, she had no idea what he looked like up close. But it somehow did not matter. He had captivated her attention on a cellular level.

Once he went inside, Poppy lost all interest in being out in the evening heat. She returned to her room and began to arrange her art supplies and personal items. Gran returned home with burgers and fries, a rare treat as she did not believe in eating out if it could be helped. Poppy suspected it was a bribe to try and make up for forcing the move. A fact that was confirmed when she looked in the bag and found a fried apple pie for dessert. Though she would have loathed to admit it, maybe living in town might have some advantages. Eating juicy burgers, fries, fried pies, and watching a gorgeous, half-naked guy swimming laps was not all bad. No, life in town might just be okay after all .

After a shower, Poppy put on a tee shirt and shorts. Without turning on the light, she quietly wandered out to her balcony to check and see if her mystery swimmer had returned. Much to her delight, he had.

She watched from the balcony for a few minutes. He was diving off the board and then swimming to the opposite end. He did this several times. The lights in the pool were on, as well as the lights around the perimeter of the pool. For the first time, Poppy could see the mystery swimmer clearly. He took her breath away.

Just as she had suspected, his face was as perfect as the rest of him. As gorgeous as he was, it was not the face that had enraptured Poppy. He was completely nude. She had never seen a naked man in the flesh before.

From an artist's point of view, he was perfect. He was art come to life. She had spent hours studying the works of masters and was enamored with the statue of David and the works of Bernini. Suddenly, she knew she had to draw him. As quietly as possible, she raced inside and grabbed her sketchbook. She spent the next half hour drawing her mystery man.

By the time he finished swimming and went inside, Poppy was exhausted. The move had worn her out physically, and concentrating on sketching him zapped her mentally. Poppy quickly fell into a deep, satisfied sleep and dreamed of her naked mystery, Adonis. Her last thought as she drifted off to sleep was that Searcy was turning out to be much better than she had anticipated.

Chapter 3

Carrington House
Searcy, Arkansas
July 1999

The next day and the days that followed, Poppy enjoyed a simple but very enjoyable pattern. She spent her mornings drawing and painting, taking advantage of the beautiful morning light in her room. Afternoons were spent helping Gran prepare dinner for the Carringtons. The need to know more about her mystery swimmer had driven Poppy to volunteer to help Gran with the Carrington's laundry and housework. It gave her a reason to wander through the house, including his personal space. His name was Bennett, and he was Mr. Carrington's only child. She discovered that the sliding glass door by the pool opened into his room.

Talking to her grandmother, she discovered he was about to leave to do his final year of law school at the University of Arkansas. She was able to piece together that Bennett was twenty-four. Twenty-four and eighteen seemed far apart in age and world experience, given that she was still in high school.

She comforted herself with the thought that she should have already been out of school and in college. She was born prematurely and had spent several months in the hospital as a newborn. When it came time to send her to school, her grandparents did not let her start kindergarten until she was six. Poppy guessed it was partly to hold onto the only grand baby they would ever have and because her birthday was in June. She would have been among the youngest in the class if she had gone at five. Whatever their reason, Poppy realized that if they had sent her on at five, she would be out of school and in college.

The difference between a law student and a college student sounded better than the difference between a law student and a high school student. Poppy did not know why she was even thinking about all of this. It was not like Bennett was ever going to be interested in her. She doubted he even knew her name or that she existed.

Instead, she focused on her art. Each night after Gran would go to bed, Poppy would sit on her balcony and wait for Bennett to appear. Then, she would spend the next half hour sketching him.

Poppy worried she was becoming obsessed with him. She thought about him all day and most nights as he had taken up a starring role in her dreams. He was practically all she thought about. She had drawn him in the nude no less than ten times but did not feel like her sketches were doing him justice. It got so bad that she considered using the digital camera that Gran gave her for her birthday to take pictures of him so she could draw him more accurately, but she did not have the nerve.

She made sure only to draw him from the neck down. If Gran found them, she could say she was sketching from an art book. Even though it was unlikely Gran would ever see any of them, Poppy had become quite good at keeping her drawings hidden.

Three Weeks Later
August 1999

School was slated to start the next week, so Poppy and Gran went by the high school and got her registered. While there, the counselor told them about a few classes that Poppy could enroll in for free at the local community college in town, ASU Searcy. She registered for a college-level drawing class and a pottery class.

The following week, school started, and Poppy was not at all excited about it. If not for the art classes, she would have been miserable. Every day that first week, she rushed home, raced through her dinner prep with Gran, and then spent her nights sketching Bennett. All of that came to a screeching halt when he returned to Fayetteville on the Friday of her first week. After that, she had to rely on her memory and previous drawings to perfect her sketches and paintings of her Adonis. She greatly regretted not taking pictures when she had the chance and promised herself she would never make that mistake again.

For the most part, school was just something to be endured with one notable exception. As it so happened, Gran had been right about one thing. The art department at Searcy High School was top-notch. Under the tutelage of Mr. Hickey, the art teacher, Poppy could pour everything into her art. The quality of her work and attention to detail showed marked improvement thanks to her classes at both SHS and ASU Searcy. Her college drawing class was focused on the human form. She was able to use what she learned in that to greatly improve her Adonis series.

Over the next few months, Poppy developed a sixth sense to detect whenever Bennett was home from school. During holidays and school breaks, she kept her eyes peeled for any glimpse of him. Whenever their paths crossed, he was polite and friendly, but she could tell he just saw her as the housekeeper's kid. She could not blame him, but being invisible to someone who dominated so much of her thoughts was hard.

Sometimes, his friends Tatum and Taylor would drop by for dinner. Once, Poppy had to help serve dinner when they came for some big event. Taylor was not ugly to her. But, Poppy felt like she was dismissive of her and saw her as nothing more important than a plate or a fork. Something to be used and then forgotten. It was as if Poppy only existed to serve them. She hated how that made her feel. After that dinner, Poppy begged Gran to let her just help in the kitchen when Taylor was there. She wanted to avoid seeing her if at all possible.

While her dislike of Taylor grew, so did her interest in Bennett. As the weeks passed, the pictures she drew felt stilted. They lacked definition. She had to find a way to get some photos of him. Over Thanksgiving break, she saw an opportunity.

Bennett would go for a run every morning. He would start off in a tee shirt and running shorts but would return in just the shorts. His shirt would be hanging around his neck and sweat would be glistening on his chest. He was glorious. Poppy had never felt more like a stalker, hiding in the hedges with her camera, taking pictures of him. With those pictures, she completed a project she had been working on since before the July holiday.

Poppy's ASU art classes ended in early December. Her college professor praised her for her class drawing and encouraged her to apply to art schools as she had a natural gift. Poppy had no idea how to do that, and the only person she knew to ask was Mr. Hickey. Two weeks before Christmas break, Poppy got up the nerve to show her drawings from her ASU human form class and those of Bennett, minus his head to her teacher. Mr Hickey was convinced she had talent. He made some calls and got her several applications to various art schools. He helped her take photos of her portfolio of work with a focus on her drawings of Bennett. Lastly, he wrote her a glowing referral letter. Her college professor did as well.

She did not tell Gran that she was applying to the various schools. She did not want Gran to see her portfolio submissions. She did not relish trying to explain how a girl who had never so much kissed a boy had such intimate knowledge of a man's body. To her teacher's credit, neither teacher ever questioned it. She assumed they thought she used a school model, as if any of those people could hold a candle to Bennett.

A second reason she did not mention it to her grandmother was her chances of being accepted were slim. Even if she did get in by some miracle, she had no idea where they would find the money for tuition. Mr. Hickey had said money had a way of taking care of itself. That had not been Poppy's experience, but she hoped he knew something she did not. From where she was standing, she had no idea how she could ever afford college. Any college. Without a scholarship, Poppy did not see it happening for her.

It had not happened for her mom, and she had been valedictorian of her class. She knew that her mom had been working and trying to save money for college when she had gotten pregnant with her. Well, they all knew how well that had worked out. Her mom died at twenty without ever having taken a single college course.

Poppy comforted herself with the thought that with the two college classes she took the first semester and the two she was planning to take in the spring, she would have twelve undergrad hours of art under her belt when she left high school. It was a start. Just as a backup, at the last minute, her college professor convinced her to apply to Arkansas State University Jonesboro. He promised that if she did not get accepted to any of the big art schools, he would try to help her get a partial scholarship at ASU.

She had to have at least one reference letter from an academic teacher. That one gave Poppy pause. Grades and school had so not been on her radar this year. She considered calling and asking one of her former teachers to write her letter of recommendation. But, in the end, she decided to go with her English teacher, Mrs. Dacus, who was always kind to her. She agreed and wrote Poppy an outstanding reference letter. Poppy realized that she was lucky to be at Searcy. Without the help of her teachers, she would have never gotten through the process. On the day she was to mail everything off, she got a nice surprise. Mr. Hickey had contacted Mrs. Roe, her previous art teacher. She drove to Searcy and hand-delivered her reference letter. It was wonderful to see her old teacher and catch up. She was relieved she did not have to show Mrs. Roe her portfolio. The photos were already sealed, and the actual pieces were safely hidden at home. It was silly, but she would have been embarrassed. Mrs Roe still saw her as a kid. Those drawings were anything but. It would have been too weird.

Chapter 4

Carrington Kitchen
Searcy, Arkansas
November 27, 2023

"So you're telling me you lived here on the property, and yet you and Mr. Carrington, Bennett, never personally interacted that first year?" asked Harvey Cox. He had been listening and taking notes as Poppy told him about how she and Bennett met.

"Not exactly. We saw each other in passing but did not actually meet until Christmas break. Bennett came home a few days before the big Carrington Christmas party. That is when things began to change," replied Poppy.

"Tell me all about that first meeting," replied Harvey.

"Well...."

Carrington House
Searcy, Arkansas
Christmas 1999

The Christmas season began with a bang, even before Thanksgiving. Mr. Carrington was set to host his annual Sleigh Ride Soiree holiday party for his big-wig friends. Decorators began transforming the house into a wonderland starting on the first of November.

Poppy had never known anyone who did not do their own decorating. A tree, some lights, a Santa, a snowman or two, and you called it done. But that's not how the Carrington's did Christmas.

Lights, greenery, bows, and extra stuff like pine cones and bells adorned the gates, windows, and doors. There was even a decorated tree outside by the pool.

Inside was a true winter wonderland. A twelve-foot tree covered in gold and silver stood proudly in the entryway. Ten-foot trees adorned every room. Each had a different theme, and the rooms were decked out with various pieces of decor that coordinated with it.

When they first moved in, Poppy had been shocked by the number of teapots on display in the butler's pantry and kitchen. Her grandmother told her that the late Mrs. Carrington had collected two things: teapots and Santa Clauses. Poppy had been excited to see if the Santa collection measured up to the teapots. To say she was amazed by the sheer number and types of Santa Clauses the late Mrs. Carrington had collected would be an understatement. Hundreds of them were scattered throughout the house in various sizes. It took the decorators until the middle of December to complete everything.

The party was always held on or near the closest Saturday to the seventeenth of December.

Over two hundred guests were invited, including the current and former governor, all of the members of the White County Bar Association, most members of the Arkansas legislators, state and local businessmen and women, and a slew of bankers, doctors, farmers, lobbyists, leaders from both political parties, and all of their significant others. Anybody who was somebody was invited. It was one of the main social events of the year in Searcy.

This year, Gran told her that President Clinton and the first lady had promised to attend. Poppy had been sworn to secrecy for security purposes. If they could come, Gran had said the Secret Service would be coming a couple of days before to ensure the house was secure. It was all very overwhelming for Poppy. She was excited to see all of those important people in person, but at the same time, it terrified her.

Gran had already prepared her for her role the night of the party. A caterer had been hired and was in charge of everything food and drink-wise. She and Gran had been assigned specific roles for the night. Gran would stay in the kitchen and be the chef's second pair of hands. Poppy knew her grandmother was not thrilled to have someone else in her kitchen, but it was out of her control. Poppy had been assigned to door duty. She was to open the door, greet the guests, and direct them to where coats and purses were stored.

The upside to having to do this was that Gran took her shopping for a new party dress. Gran had been told everyone had to wear black. Poppy bought a black satin slip dress. Gran even splurged and got her a pair of strappy black heels.

On the day school got out for Christmas break, Poppy mailed her last application to art school and came home pleasantly surprised. Bennett was back.

As she came up the drive on her bike, he was helping some men unload a huge sleigh in the front yard. It was a beautiful sleigh with red velvet seats. It was a full-size sleigh that had once graced the album cover of a country music band. A local man bought it and rented it out for parties.

As she came up the drive, she saw something lying on the grass. Getting off her bike and picking it up, she realized it was a man's wallet. She flipped it open and saw it belonged to Bennett. She knew the men were busy and didn't want to disturb them. She quickly put her bike away and hurried back to the front yard. By this time, the sleigh was settled, and the other men were loading up and leaving.

"Hey," called Poppy as she approached Bennett and handed him the wallet. "I think this is yours. I found it a minute ago on the grass."

Taking the wallet, Bennett smiled. "Thank you so much. I felt it fall out, but my hands were full of sleigh." Laughing, he added, "That is not something you say often."

Laughing softly as she nodded, Poppy replied, "No, I guess not."

Reaching out a hand, he said, "I'm Bennett. You are Mrs. Margaret's granddaughter, right? I have seen you, but we have never been properly introduced."

Shaking his hand, Poppy replied, "Yeah, I know. Gran has mentioned you a time or two. I am Poppy Hunter. Nice to meet you…properly."

Poppy wondered what he would think if he knew she knew his body intimately and had drawn and painted him nude many, many times. He had a starring role each night in her dreams and fantasies. Nope, he did not know that. He also did not know she had basically stalked him whenever he was home. She had gone so far as to sniff his sheets after he slept on them. Worse, more than once while helping Gran with laundry, she had offered to put his clean sheets on his bed so she could kiss his pillow. Craziness, she knew. But, she had not been able to resist. She had a mad, out-of-control crush on him, and it was taking all her energy not to show it. No, he knew none of that. Next to art, he was her reason for breathing. To him, she was just a kid of the help.

"Are you excited about the party tomorrow? It will be a big shindig," asked Bennett, looking at her, smiling with his perfect teeth, tousled blonde hair, and his perfect body.

For a second, Poppy could not answer; all she could think about was that she so regretted she had not been able to include his face in her drawing. It was just wrong that that gorgeous face had not been drawn. She was making a mental note to start a new sketch tonight from her photos.

"Earth to Poppy," said Bennett when she just stood there looking at him.

Shaking her head embarrassed, Poppy stammered, "I am here. I am here. I just got distracted for a moment. What did you ask me again?" Poppy was sure he thought she was a complete fool standing there with her tongue hanging out, ogling him.

"I asked if you were going to the party?"

She nodded yes and replied, "Oh yes, I am working the door. Gran got me this great dress and heels to wear. I have never felt so sexy in my entire life." Oh my God, thought Poppy, why did I say that?

Giving her a surprised look, Bennett chuckled softly before reaching out to push a red curl back behind her ear that had come loose. Giving her a smile, he said, "Well, that is great. I can't wait to see that sexy dress. I bet you will be the Belle of the Ball. I look forward to seeing it. See ya later." Then, he turned and went inside the house.

Poppy stood there a moment longer, nodding and wondering what just happened.

The next day was pure craziness with caterers, florists, and half a dozen other people rushing in and out. To her knowledge, the Secret Service did not show up, so that meant a no-go on the President showing up. The party planner, Mrs. Liz Blaine, brought a huge tent and set up about twenty tables around a massive dance floor. Everyone did exactly what she said. Her word was law. Poppy was more than a little afraid of the lady. She had already seen her get angry with two delivery guys who were not paying attention to what they were doing. Poppy did not want to tick her off.

Poppy spent her day putting out tablecloths, setting out centerpieces, and helping with the overall party setup. All day, she kept wondering who would want to sit down and eat a meal or dance out in the thirty-degree weather expected that night. When the party place delivered the portable heaters, Poppy got it. Rich people and their toys. She had never even heard of an outdoor heater. This party opened her eyes to just how different her life was from theirs. She might reside on the property of the Carringtons, but she lived in a totally different world.

Chapter 5

Carrington House
The Next Day

Poppy was dressed and met with the caterer for final instructions at 6:45 the next evening. She thought she looked nice. She had actually washed, dried, and styled her long red hair using the hot rollers Gran had given her the year before. Usually, it was too much trouble. But tonight, she wanted to be beautiful. She had added a little more makeup than usual, done her eyes, and added blush. She liked how she looked.

Being height-challenged as she preferred to think of herself, Poppy would look you in the face and tell you she was five feet tall every day of the week. The truth was, she was a little under that at four-eleven. Tonight, in her four-inch heels, she felt tall. Tall and beautiful.

She had gone without a bra for the first time since sixth grade. She was boob enriched as she was height challenged. She hated them. They were always in the way, and she usually wore a bra that would tape them down and keep them under wraps. Nothing was worse than walking through the halls at school and having perverted teenage boys gawking at her chest or, worse, making jokes about them. And she had heard them all, motorboating, milk jugs, future Hooters' girl. So, normally, she kept them under lock and key. But tonight, she could not, as she had no bra to wear with her dress. She should have thought of that at the store, but she had been so excited about the dress that it slipped her mind. Now, she found herself going braless because the spaghetti straps of the dress would not allow her to wear one of her regular harnesses. She comforted herself with the thought that no one would even pay attention to her to notice if she wore a bra. The rich and important guests coming would be so focused on seeing and being seen that they would not even notice her.

Honestly, she did not care what anyone but Bennett thought. She wanted him to believe she was the Belle of the Ball. It was silly. He probably would not even see her. It was his family's party, after all. He would be busy entertaining his guests, not hanging out at the door with her taking coats.

The first guests arrived precisely at seven o'clock. After that, a steady stream of guests came and went all night. Two and half hours in, Poppy thought her feet would fall off, and her face would crack from all the smiling. She had said, "Welcome to the Carrington House. Thank you for coming. May I take your coat/ purse/ gift?" so many times, she was sure she would be hoarse the next day. Poppy was not a big talker. She was sure she had said more in the few hours than in the last year. The party was set to go another two hours. Poppy was unsure she would make it when Mrs. Blaine came up with a young girl with gorgeous black hair and royal blue eyes.

"Poppy, you have done wonderfully so far. I am very impressed. It is time for a break. Jenni is going to relieve you so you can get something to eat. Also, at the end of the party, do you mind staying and helping pack up all the toys in the sleigh?"

Poppy's first thought was *no way. I am going to be doing good to survive another two hours.* But, being Poppy, she said, "Of course, Mrs. Blaine. The party is for a good cause. I would love to help."

Even though her body was crying out for a rest, her mind knew it was the right thing to do. After all, it wasn't just a party for the sake of having a party to hobnob with the power players. It was also a toy drive for the underprivileged.

The large sleigh placed in front of the house was now filled to the brim with toys that would be given to various groups around the community for needy children. How could Poppy say no to helping with that? It was the only part of this party she liked so far.

Having been given a thirty-minute break, Poppy headed to the food tent. She was starving. The party planner had said that as she lived on the property and dressed appropriately, she could grab a plate and eat at one of the empty tables in the back of the tent. The food was amazing. The chef that had been brought in knew what he was doing with prime rib. Poppy had never had it before and fell instantly in love.

Sitting at a table in the back, she audibly moaned as she ate. Years later, Bennett would tell her he thought he fell in love with her watching her eat. Seeing the pleasure she got out of eating red meat was the most erotic thing he had ever seen. But that was not said that night.

No, that night, Bennett stood in the shadows watching the tiny, redhead nymph eating prime rib like it was better than sex. And Bennett knew nothing was better than sex. At first, he did not recognize her as the young girl he had spoken with the day before. He had seen her around and thought she was cute. Because she was so tiny, he had thought she was much younger. Yesterday, after meeting her, he asked his dad about her. His father told him she was a senior and was a very talented artist. He shared that she had been taking classes at the local community college. How his dad knew so much about her was a mystery to Bennett. Regardless, he was grateful for the intel. Of course, Bennett made sure not to let his interest in the girl be too obvious. His father would not like the idea he was sniffing around the help. Not that Bennett thought of her that way, but he knew his father would.

So armed with what he knew about her, Bennett approached her table and said, "If I were half the artist you are, I would draw you just as you are, enjoying your meal."

Poppy, who had a mouth full of prime rib at the time, nearly spit it out. Instead, she forced herself to swallow and got choked. Coughing and sputtering, Bennett reached out to help her just as she managed to get the lodged piece of meat down. Sputtering, Poppy reached for her water and took a big gulp. Once she could breathe again, she said, "No, I am okay. Just got shocked for a moment." So much for making a good impression. She was not sure how beautiful one could be coughing up a lung.

Ever the gentleman, Bennett said, "Are you sure you are alright? Can I get you anything?"

Shaking her head, Poppy said, "No, I am fine. You just startled me. You can't just sneak up on a person like that. I am not looking for a death by prime rib tonight. I don't care how amazing it is. And it is amazing if you have not tried it." She was rambling. She was so nervous.

Laughing, Bennett replied, "Sorry about that. You are right. Death by prime rib is a terrible way to go. And yes, I did have some earlier. It was fantastic, as you know." The conversation felt stilted and strange. After meeting her yesterday and seeing her again tonight, he wanted to get to know her better. So he said, "Let's start over."

"Start over?" asked Poppy, still holding a prime rib sandwich.

"Yes, I will start. You look lovely this evening. You were right about the dress. You look fantastic. Have you enjoyed the party?"

"Enjoyed the party, um?" Poppy was not sure how to answer that. The party had been a lot of work for her. She wondered if he got that. After a moment, she replied, "I have been a little busy. But I have seen many people I have only heard about on the news. Not that any of them remember me."

"Oh, I think you are very wrong about that," replied Bennett quickly. "You are impossible to forget in that dress with all that red hair. You really are a knockout. Did you know that?"

Poppy could feel herself blushing from head to toe, a curse all redheads must bare. Shaking her head, Poppy looked into Bennett's eyes and replied, "No, no one has ever said that to me. But, I am glad the first one who did was you."

Wow, what was happening? Suddenly, Bennett felt like a lightning bolt had hit him. No one had ever looked at him the way she was looking at him. In her eyes, Bennett could see her innocence, passion, and desire, all directed at him. When he approached her at the table, he knew she was off limits. For God's sake, she was not even out of high school. But she was so incredibly gorgeous sitting alone eating he had not been able to stop himself. Seeing her desire for him in her eyes was almost his undoing. If he were not the man he was, he would take her by the hand to somewhere more private and sample all she was offering. He looked at her, then asked, "I know you are a senior, but how old are you?"

Without breaking eye contact, Poppy whispered, "Eighteen. Why?"

Bennett did not respond to her question aloud. In his head, he thought *because I need to know if you are about to land my stupid ass in jail.* Of course, he did not say that. Instead, he said, "No Carrington Sleigh Ride Soiree is complete without a trip around the dance floor. I have spent all night glad handing people for future support. I could use a little break from that. What do you say? Care to dance with me?"

Words were no longer an option. Dropping her prime rib sandwich on her plate and hastily wiping her hands on a napkin, Poppy stood and took his hand. Bennett led them out to the dance floor. The song was a slow jazz number that Poppy had never heard before.

It took Poppy a few minutes to relax into Bennett's arms. She had never danced with a boy before but had seen it on television. She just relaxed into him and followed his lead. Years later, she would consider that a metaphor for her life. Just relaxing into him and following his lead. Tonight, though, she was beyond conscious thought or words. She could feel his heart beating as they moved together. He smelled so good, all woodsy and clean. Poppy was so under his spell that she had to literally stop herself from reaching up and licking his neck where her head was currently nuzzled. The song ended, as did the bubble she had been in for the last few minutes.

Mrs. Blaine tapped her on the shoulder and gave her a stern look. "Poppy, dear, we need you back at your station. Your break is over."

Poppy had never been so embarrassed in her life. She felt like a little kid who had just been sent to the principal's office for being naughty.

With her head down, Poppy mumbled thanks to Bennett for the dance and quickly scurried off the dance floor and back to the front door. That was where she stayed for the rest of the party. Most of the guests were gone by midnight. The catering staff had already cleaned up food and were loading their vans when Mrs. Blaine reappeared.

"Poppy, if you can, we still need to pack all of the gifts we received tonight in Mr. Carrington's vehicle. Are you still good to help us with that?"

Nodding yes, Poppy asked, "Can I run upstairs and grab my tennis shoes? My feet are killing me."

Mrs. Blaine gave Poppy her first genuine smile of the night. Chuckling, she said, "Of course. Go now and be back in five. I will have you some help."

As Poppy hobbled back to their apartment, she thought perhaps the party lady was not so scary after all.

Poppy quickly changed her shoes. Her feet rejoiced as she mourned the extra height the heels had given her. Racing back to the sleigh, Poppy realized she had forgotten her jacket. Not wanting to upset the caterer, Poppy decided she could brave the cold and get through it.

When she got to the front of the house, Bennett's red Jeep was parked in front of the sleigh. He had already put down all his seats and was loading his car with the bikes and larger toys first.

Poppy had been so busy inside she had not had a chance to see how many toys had been donated. It was actually shocking. Several hundred toys had been collected.

Turning to Bennett as he finished putting a bike in the back, Poppy asked, "What should I do first?"

"I'd start by putting on a coat. Aren't you freezing?"

"Not yet. I forgot it and did not want Mrs. Blaine to be mad if I took too long getting back."

Shaking his head, Bennett immediately removed his coat jacket and handed it to her.

"No, I can't," replied Poppy, shaking her head.

"You will freeze otherwise. Put it on. We have a ton of toys to load before they come for the sleigh. The guy should be here any minute. They don't like to leave it out if rain is in the forecast."

Poppy knew that rain was predicted to begin around six the next morning. Seeing she had no other option, she put on his jacket that hung on her like a curtain. But it was warm, and it smelled like him and his sheets. For the next half hour, they worked together, loading the toys. They had just finished when the sleigh folks showed up.

To Poppy, it was crazy. It was the middle of the night but when rich people wanted something; money spoke. It was after one in the morning, but you would have thought it was one in the afternoon for all the people cleaning up and running in and out of the house. Poppy knew the next day would be more of the same as they broke down the tent, dance floor, and tables. She was not looking forward to that and was so tired that she wanted to lie down and sleep.

She was just about to return Bennett his jacket when he asked, "I need to run these toys over to a warehouse where they are going to sort them beginning early in the morning. Any chance you would want to come and help me?"

It was as if someone had reignited her; Poppy was suddenly wide awake and full of energy at the thought of getting in Bennett's Jeep and going anywhere with him. Turning to the caterer, standing on the front steps looking like a movie director directing a complex movie, Poppy called out, "Mrs. Blaine, will you tell Gran that I am going to help deliver the toys and will be back shortly." The caterer gave her a look that said she did not think that was a great idea. But to her credit, she said nothing. Just nodded and gave Poppy a thumbs up.

Once they were in the car, Poppy asked, "Now, where exactly are we going?" She was so excited she could feel every nerve ending in her body. She felt like she was buzzing,

Turning to look at her as he drove, Bennett said, "My dad owns the warehouse where the toys are stored. Tomorrow, a group of community volunteers will come to organize the toys and distribute them. As late as it is, I would much rather bring the toys over now than have to get up at the crack of dawn and do it. I appreciate your help. It will make it go so much quicker."

Poppy just nodded. She had no idea what to say. She had never been in a car with a boy. And Bennett was so much more than a boy. He was a man. A man she could not stop picturing naked. After all, she had drawn him enough to be able to do it very accurately.

Trying to make conversation, Bennett asked, "Why so quiet? What are you thinking about so deeply over there? I can almost see the wheels in your head spinning."

She wondered what he would say if she told him the truth about what she was thinking. She'd bet he would be the one shocked and left speechless. Turning to him and giving her a sweet smile, she said, "I think it is really great your family does this toy drive for the kids. I was shocked at how many toys were collected. I can't believe you got them all in the car."

Laughing, Bennett replied, "Years of practice. If you get the big items loaded first, you can fit most of the smaller items around them. Just know that my dad gets a lot of political mileage from that party. It is not all for charity."

"What do you mean?" asked Poppy.

"You may not know this, but I will graduate from law school in May. My dad is already laying the groundwork for my future political career."

"You want to go into politics?"

"I want to make a difference in the world. My parents have been grooming me for it my whole life. Did you know I spent part of my junior year in DC as a page? I only came home when it was time to start baseball. The only thing I love more than politics is baseball. I was a good player, but not great."

"What position did you play?" asked Poppy.

"Pitcher. We won the state championship three years in a row. I also played at U of A for two years, but my arm gave out. Plus, I knew I did not have a career ahead of me in baseball, so I put down my glove and focused solely on school."

"Do you miss it?"

Giving her a look, Bennett replied, "You know you are the first person ever to ask me that. Most people just say how much the team misses me, or how I need to come back. But, yeah, parts of it I do miss. I miss being part of a team and having a common goal. I miss the feeling I got every time I struck a batter out. Or the feeling of jubilation when you win a big game, and all of your buddies swarm the field and celebrate together. Knowing I will never have that again. I miss all of that. What I don't miss is the pain. Blowing out your rotator cuff and having surgery is no joke. I don't recommend it."

"Duly noted. I will be very careful about what I blow." As soon as the words were out of her mouth, Poppy wanted to suck them back in. Had she really just said that?

Bennett audibly gasped and said, "Wow. Okay, on that note, we are here."

He pulled into a dark warehouse. Bennett clicked the overhead remote, and an oversized garage door went up. They drove into the space and lowered the door behind them. "Stay in the car while I turn up the heat. I will be right back."

Poppy waited in the car. Bennett was gone just a few minutes. When he returned, Poppy got out. He opened the back door, and they started unloading. There was a long table on which they set the toys.

"Just put the toys anywhere. Tomorrow, they will sort them."

At first, it was freezing in the warehouse, but it got really warm very quickly.

"Wow. That heat really works," remarked Poppy as she took another toy to the table.

"Yeah, we have to keep the doors open during the day. It has to put out a lot of heat to warm the place with open doors. With the doors closed like tonight, it gets hot quickly."

"No kidding. I am almost sweating." Poppy went to remove Bennett's jacket to keep it from getting sweat on it. The jacket sleeve caught on her spaghetti strap. Not realizing this, Poppy gave the sleeve a yank, which snapped her spaghetti strap. And Poppy yelled, "Oh shit!"

Bennett snapped his head around to see what had caused her to yell out. What he saw stunned him. Poppy stood before him, trying to get her dress back on, but part of her dress was still caught in the sleeve. Her left breast was exposed for all the world to see. It was the most beautiful breast he had ever seen, and honestly, he had seen his fair share. But seeing her standing there with all her red hair around her shoulders in all her glory shot an arrow into his gut.

Poppy was working like a mad woman to get the dress pulled up. Her motions were getting jerky and out of control, and the dress appeared to be ripping even more with each try. Suddenly, Bennett was jarred out of his stupor. Dropping the toy in his hands, he quickly untangled the jacket from the dress without looking at her any more than he had to. He did not want to embarrass her further. He could hear her starting to cry. With deft hands, he got the jacket free and got it back on her. Pulling the front together and buttoning it, he said, "It's okay. You are all good now." He softly kissed her hair and added, "Please don't cry. It is not a big deal."

With tears running down her face, Poppy looked at him and said, "Not a big deal? Not a big deal? What you must think of me? One minute I am helping you; the next, I am flashing you my tits."

Letting out a bark of laughter, Bennett replied, "Flashing your tits at me? Listen, Poppy, I have had my fair share of tit flashing, and that was not one of them. That was just a … wardrobe malfunction. Yes, that was what that was."

Drawing her close and hugging her in hopes of reassuring her, Bennett realized the error of his thinking once she was entirely in his arms. He had a small taste of what she felt like in his arms earlier when they were dancing. Of course, that was before he got an eyeful of her gorgeous body. Now, he had to fight heaven and earth to keep his hands from roaming all over. From unbuttoning his jacket, ripping the other strap, and feasting on her incredible breasts, the only thing stopping him was a mantra running through the back of his mind, "*She is still in high school. She is still in high school. She is still in high school.*"

Pushing her back, he rested his forehead on hers and asked, "Better? All good?"

Poppy nodded, and she pulled back and looked deeply into his eyes. "Thank you. You are so kind."

Shaking his head and thinking that if she knew what he was thinking, she would not think him to be so kind. Pulling back from her, he turned to leave when Poppy reached out and caught his arm.

Giving him a shy look, she asked, "Can I ask you a favor?"

"A favor? Sure. What do you need?" asked Bennett earnestly, trying to act like he was not so completely affected by her. He knew what he needed but was damn sure it was not what she was going to say.

Swallowing her fear, Poppy said in a small voice, "Would you kiss me? I have never been kissed, and the only way to wipe out the horrible memory of standing here naked in front of you would be to replace it with something warm and good."

Dropping his forehead back down on hers, he closed his eyes. She had no idea what she was asking. He was hanging on by a thread. But if one kiss would help, he could man up and do it.

Reaching down and cupping her face, he looked deeply into her eyes and saw the same all-consuming desire for him that he had seen earlier in the evening. Someday, he would have to teach her not to be so open and vulnerable with her feelings. Other men would take what she was unknowingly offering. He would have to teach her how to protect herself. But all of that was for another night. Tonight was about helping her get over her embarrassment. Tipping her head back, he said, "One kiss, Poppy. Just one or this will go places you are not ready to go. Nod if you understand."

Poppy was beyond words, but she nodded her head.

Slowly and softly, Bennett lowered his lips to hers. At first, it was a very chaste and innocent kiss. It reminded him of kisses he had shared with girls playing kissing games. But before he could pull away, Poppy wrapped her arms around him. Pressing her breasts into his chest, she opened her mouth, taking them both down a rabbit hole of lust, passion, and desire. Without thinking, Bennett pressed himself into her, letting her feel his desire for her. As she adjusted her body to bring him closer, a warning bell went off in Bennett's head, and he practically shoved her across the room. "Shit Carrington. Get a hold of yourself. She is in high school."

"Who are you talking to?" asked Poppy, still dazed by the kiss.

"Myself. That was way out of line. I didn't mean for that to happen. I said one kiss. Not one volcano."

Not knowing what she was supposed to say, Poppy stood motionless and said nothing. Bennett ran to the back of the building and turned off the heat, leaving Poppy with a shocked expression on her face. Next, Bennett raced around to the back of the car and quickly got the last of the toys out. Dumping them quickly, he motioned for Poppy to get into the empty Jeep.

As soon as they were both in, Bennett raised the garage door, and they were off. Neither said a word until they were halfway home when Bennett said, "Can I ask you something?"

"Yes," replied Poppy in a small voice. She could feel a change in him since the kiss, and Poppy did not know why.

"That was your first kiss, wasn't it?" asked Bennett incredulously.

Nodding, Poppy replied, "Yes, I knew I did it wrong. Is that why you pushed me away and stopped it so suddenly? I am sorry I messed it up."

Giving out a sharp bark of laughter, Bennett quickly replied, "No, Red, you did not do it wrong. You couldn't have done it more perfectly. I pushed you away because you are in high school. I don't care that you are eighteen and legal. You are still too young to be messing with a guy my age. If you were my sister, I would kick my own butt for how I handled things tonight. You deserved better."

"Well, you don't have to worry about any big brothers coming for you. I am an only child. But, if I thought your butt needed kicking, I would do it myself. For the record, you handled it great. My first kiss was everything I ever imagined it would be."

Grinning, Bennett said, "I am glad. I hope it wipes the memory of your wardrobe malfunction from your mind forever." Bennett knew it would never leave his mind. In fact, he was pretty sure it would have a starring role in his nightly activities for weeks to come. Pervert that he was.

"Oh my, speak of that awful moment no more. It is gone. Banished from my mind," she replied.

"Good, but I have to ask, though, you are so gorgeous. No boyfriends? No kisses? What's wrong with the boys at Searcy High School? I would have been all over you," said Bennett honestly.

"You would have?" Poppy smiled hugely at that. "My grandparents were really conservative, and it would have been such an ordeal if a guy had ever asked me out. Truthfully, I never found a guy that I thought was worth the effort it would take to date."

Poppy said, "Only one guy ever really got my heart racing, seeing him in the nude."

"Really, was it strange having naked people model for you?"

"The first time in class. Yes. So weird. But surprisingly, not for the models. They get paid really well, and it seems like no big deal to them."

"Wow! I did not realize those classes even existed. I am totally regretting not taking more art classes in college."

"Well, they are not easy classes. The human form class was tough."

"So why are you taking college classes when you are still in high school?"

"Oh, my previous high school art teacher suggested it. My college professor and high school teacher have been complementary and said I have talent. I guess we will see."

"That is so cool that you are so talented." Reaching out and patting her knee, he added, "I am glad you are over being upset about what happened earlier. It was not a big deal."

"Yes, I am over it. But, honestly, I think it was Karma."

"Karma? What are you talking about?"

"Well, I have seen you naked many times. I guess it was only fair you saw me naked."

"What?" Bennett nearly had a wreck. Pulling the car off to the side of the road, he said, "Explain."

So Poppy did. She told him about watching him swim nude last summer and how that had inspired her to draw him. Leaving out the part about taking his photo at Thanksgiving, she told him how he inspired her "Adonis Series." She told him about using it as the main part of her portfolio.

"So you're telling me that people all across the country are going to have naked drawings of me?"

"Yes, and paintings. I painted you in watercolor. I took photos of all my pieces and submitted them with my applications."

He could feel his temper rising, feeling exposed and much like she must have felt earlier. "Are you crazy? You can't just go around drawing and painting people in the buff without their permission. What if someone recognizes me? I told you I have a political career ahead of me. I can't have those pictures floating around out there. We have to get them back immediately."

"Calm down. No one is ever going to know it is you."

"How can you be so sure of that"

"Because I cut your head off."

Seeing the confusion in his eyes, she pointed to his head and said, "That head. I left it off of all the pictures. I only concentrated on your body."

"Did you draw…" he gestured to his crotch.

"Yes, it would be pretty hard not to, given I drew the rest of your body."

Quickly spinning around and restarting the car, he said, "I must see these. You said you only sent photos. Where are the originals? "Gone was the easy-going guy from earlier who thought it was so cool she was talented. Now he was freaking out, much like she had been on the inside earlier.

"Hidden in my room."

"Great, let's go."

Once back home, the workers were gone. All the lights were out. Bennett dragged her to the backstairs by her room as Poppy tried to slow him down.

"Look, I know, Gran. She may be in her bed, but she is not asleep. Not with me out with some guy she hardly knows."

"She will be awake until I get home. You go and wait in your room. I will go up the regular way. I will grab my portfolio and meet you in your room shortly."

"You know where it is?" Bennett asked questions.

"Of course. Who do you think changes your sheets?" she asked as if he should know the answer to that question. He did not, but he would never look at his sheets the same way again.

Bennett thought about it for a minute, then nodded and quietly headed to his room.

Poppy did just as she promised. The minute she had walked in the door, Gran had called her. "Poppy, is that you? Everything all right?"

"Yes, Gran. It is just me. Good night." Poppy had barely reached her room and pulled out her portfolio when Gran's snores began roaring through the apartment.

Positive her grandmother was asleep, Poppy slipped down the back stairs. She grabbed her coat as she went.

Bennett was pacing around his room when he heard the soft knock. Opening the door quietly, he motioned for her to come in.

"Okay, Michelangelo, let's see what you have done to my future," said Bennett, reaching for the leather satchel with the artwork.

One by one, he went through them. Holding up the largest one, he asked, "This is really me? It is amazing. I would have never known. How could you draw me so correctly without me sitting for you? I see how you were able to do the ones from class."

"Well, hum… I hum…" Poppy was unsure how to tell him about photographing him without sounding like a stalker, which was basically what she had been.

"Come on, Hunter. What is it you are not telling me?"

"Well, I took photos of you when you returned from running with your shirt off over the Thanksgiving break."

Bennett was silent for a moment; then, he let out a huge peel of laughter. "You little perv. If you had wanted a picture of my chest, you didn't have to hide and take one. I would have posed for you."

"Yeah, right, like I was ever going to ask that." Poppy began gathering her artwork and putting it back in her satchel. "Look, it's late. I need to go." When Poppy began unbuttoning the suit jacket, Bennett immediately reached to stop her.

"Just keep it. I don't need to see all that again."

Poppy laughed. She had put her coat on under the jacket before she came downstairs.

She slipped off the jacket, but her coat kept her fully covered.

"Oh, thank God," Bennett muttered. There was just so much a red-blooded male could take in one night.

As she started out the door, Bennett asked, "You are sure no more pictures are floating around somewhere out there that have my face?"

Poppy nodded. As she passed in front of him, Bennett could not let her go without giving her a final warning. "Poppy, that kiss tonight was incredible, and you are an awesome girl. There is obviously something between us, but it can't happen. I am way too old for you. If anyone found out about tonight or the artwork, it would wreck my future before it even began. I have to ask you not to tell anyone about this."

Poppy nodded. "I promise. I won't tell anyone."

"Good." Bennett gave her a huge smile, and then, because he could not stop himself, he reached down and gave her a soft goodnight kiss.

Poppy was so stunned that she snapped back and just looked at him before asking, "What was that for?"

"That was because I could not help myself. Now go back to your room before I decide to throw all my good judgment out the window along with my future career."

Poppy gave him a military salute and headed for the door.

"Oh, and Poppy, " Bennett called out. "Have a great Christmas. I leave tomorrow for the lake. I will spend a few days with Dad there and then head to Aspen with the Stroupe family for skiing. I won't see you again until at least spring break. Good luck with your art applications. I will be thinking good thoughts for you."

Poppy nodded and then made her way back to her room. Bennett watched until he saw her light go on. Then he released a breath he had been holding. Poppy had no idea what she did to him. He had played it all cool around her, but that had just been an act. He had not planned to go to the lake house until Christmas Eve. However, he did not trust himself around her. He was completely under her spell. He felt something with her that he had never felt with anyone else. What kind of messed up business was that? A high school kid? The universe seemed to have it in for him.

He felt it in her kiss and saw it in her eyes. Whatever it was, it was real. He just needed to remove himself from the situation long enough to figure out how to deal with whatever it was. Right now, though, any more alone time with her and all bets for his future would be off. Nope, if he could not trust himself to do the right thing, he had to remove himself from the situation. Problem solved. Heading to bed, Bennett made a mental note to be up and gone by the time Poppy woke the next day.

Chapter 6

Carrington House
Searcy, Arkansas
November 27, 2023

Harvey Cox was scribbling notes as fast as his fingers would go. Poppy excused herself to take a phone call from one of the girls' schools. Coming back into the room, he asked, "Everything okay? Are we still good to keep going?"

Poppy smiled at him and said, "Yes, it was nothing—just a question about the upcoming PTO Bingo night. I am ready to keep going if you are. Ask away."

"Just want to ensure I have this right; you and Bennett officially met just before Christmas 1999. You shared a dance and kiss, but for the most part, it was still very innocent."

"Yes, I would agree with that."

"That party sounded pretty amazing. Do you still hold it?"

"We do. I don't go all out with the decorating or the expanded guest list, but we still do a massive toy drive party. If Bennett goes back into politics, that is something else that will change. The party will return to being more of a vehicle for power brokers to see and be seen. I hate that, but it goes with the territory I suppose."

"It sounds like you are not excited about your husband's upcoming run for governor. Why is that?"

"Don't get me wrong. Bennett will be an amazing governor. It just brings so much change into our lives."

"Starting with this article."

Poppy sighed. "Yes, but that is just the beginning. Our lives are about to become public property. No more secrets. No more privacy. Everything about our lives is about to be hung out for all the world to see and judge."

"That is why it is so important I get this article right."

"Agreed. That is why I am so committed to being honest with you about everything. If we are going to put it out there, let's put it all out there. No more hiding."

"Well, that's great to know. To that end, I do have to know. When did things heat up between the two of you? Guessing by your son's age, things picked up quickly. Did you see him over spring break?"

"No, well, yes, but only briefly. And we talked a lot on the phone."

"Okay, tell me about that."

Carrington House
Searcy, Arkansas
January – March 2000

Poppy had been practically living for Spring Break. She had a crush on Bennett before the kiss. She was madly consumed with him now.

Bennett had not been home since the night of the Christmas party, but that had not stopped her from hoping and praying he might show up each weekend. He never did.

Though she did not see him, she did have the opportunity to spend quite a bit of time talking to him on the phone. In late January, Gran was supposed to put together a large spread for Mr. Carrington to take to Fayetteville for a Razorback basketball tailgate. She was not sure how much food to prepare. Since her hands were full with making bread, she asked Poppy to call Mr. Carrington and ask. Gran gave her two numbers to try. The first number just went to voicemail. She left a message, and then tried the second.

Bennett picked up on the second ring, "Hello?"

The minute Poppy heard his voice, she faltered. She fumbled with what to say. Finding her voice she said, "Umm, Bennett, this is Poppy. Poppy Hunter. I met you at the Christmas party."

Bennett nearly dropped the phone when she said her name. He had not been able to stop thinking about her since their kiss. Swallowing deeply, he replied, "Yes, I know who you are. What can I do for you?" He wondered how she got his number. A question she quickly answered for him.

"Gran gave me your number. I am trying to get in touch with your dad. She needs to know how much food to prepare for the Razorback tailgate party that he is hosting tonight. Mr. Stroupe is flying up later today with it. Would you mind asking him how many people she should plan for?"

"Not at all," replied Bennett smoothly. "He is not with me at the moment, but I will have him call her as soon as I see him. It should be in about twenty minutes."

"That sounds great," said Poppy. "Okay, well I um…" Poppy was about to say goodbye and hang up when Bennett stopped her.

"Hey wait, don't hang up. How are you? How have you been?" Bennett was not sure how appropriate it was to continue the conversation. He just knew he was not ready to end the call. He thought about her several times and here she was calling out of the blue. He wanted to keep it going as long as possible.

"I am good. You? How are your classes going?"

"Good. Your art? Working on anything special?" Bennett did not add, like are you still painting me naked? But, he did wonder.

"My art classes are going well. I am taking another watercolor class. I think that may be my favorite type of painting so far." Trying to think of something clever to say, she added, "So are you going to the game tonight?" Poppy immediately castrated herself. Of course he was going. She'd called about the tailgate. He must think I am stupid asking such a question, she thought.

"I am," he replied. "Are you going to watch me on television? Dad has floor seats. If the camera flashes on me, I will wave. It will be just for you." Bennett said the words before he could stop himself. A natural flirt, he responded as if she were a college girl who knew the score. Not some high school kid. He was losing it.

"We never miss a game. Are you kidding me? Gran is a huge Razorback Hog fan. We watch every game-football and basketball. I will be watching for you," she replied shyly.

"Great, what time do you go to bed? I will give you a call and make sure you saw me," replied Bennett. It was just the thing he would have said to any co-ed. But, she was not. She was a kid. Ignoring that fact, he said, "Is that okay, if I call you later?"

Poppy nearly died on the phone. Of course it was okay if he called her. As long as he did it after ten and on her cellphone. "Sure if you call me on my cell after ten that is fine. Gran is always asleep by then. Do you need the number?"

"Are you on your cell now? If so, I have the number."

"Oh, yeah, duh," replied Poppy, feeling stupid again. She had no idea how to talk to boys, much less men.

"Great, oh Dad just drove up. I have to go. I will have Dad call Mrs. Margaret. Talk to you tonight."

With that, Bennett hung up. Poppy was literally dancing on air. All day, she could not stop smiling. Gran asked her about it. She put it off to the Razorbacks winning. She didn't say it was because Bennett had waved at her on national television, not once but twice. It didn't matter that no other person on the planet knew that. She did and could not wait for the call coming later that night.

At ten fifteen, her cell phone rang. It was Bennett. They talked about the game, school, and life. They talked for over an hour. Poppy was sure they would run out of things to talk about, but they never did. At the end of the call, Bennett said he might call again the next night if that was okay. Poppy almost peed her pants as she said it was fine if he wanted to talk. Trying to be cool when you weren't was never easy.

After that first call, it became a tradition between the two of them. They talked every night. Bennett was sure to keep the talk clean. Nothing inappropriate or off color was said. She was in high school after all. He just enjoyed her company. Both of them seemed to understand that they could not be open about these nightly conversations and had to keep it just between them. It quickly became the highlight of each other's day. If a call had to be missed, the next day, they talked twice as long. They never made plans for anything in the future. They just talked. Bennett told Poppy things he had never shared with anyone else. Poppy shared as much of herself as she could. Bennett was often amazed at how mature and together Poppy was even compared to the girls he knew at school. Maybe it was because of all of the heartache she had already faced in her young life. Bennett was not sure but when they were talking, it was just a guy and girl talking. He would often forget she was so young. She was an old soul.

For Poppy's part, she just managed to keep her feelings for Bennett unspoken, even though she was sure he must sense her raging crush on him. She had no idea how he felt about her. She worried he saw her as some kind of little sister or something. If he did, she was sure it would kill her. Some days, Poppy worried she would go insane from obsessing and thinking about Bennett all day.

Thankfully her sanity was saved when she saw his red Jeep pull in the Friday of Spring Break around six in the evening. He did not mention that he was coming home the night before. She knew he was asked on a trip to the Bahamas, but he said he did not want to go. The last she heard he was still trying to decide what to do for the week.

The minute Poppy had gotten home that day, she raced through her dinner chores, so she would be free all night in case Bennett called from wherever he went.

Now, knowing he was in the house and unable to see him drove Poppy mad. She searched for a reason to go back over to the main house. Dying to see him, Poppy pulled her wild red curls into a high ponytail and threw on a pair of black pants and a white top. The expected uniform when the family was served. Gran usually served dinner when it was just Mr. Carrington or his son. Helping with the serving was the only reason Poppy could come up with for being in the house. Gran was busy finishing dinner when she came in the backdoor.

"What's up, Buttercup?" called Gran as she took a pan of cornbread out of the oven. Reaching over to kiss her granddaughter on the cheek, she looked Poppy's outfit up and down and said, "You are all dressed up for a Friday night."

"I thought I would come over and give you a hand. You work so hard. Since I am off next week and have the whole week to rest, I wanted to give you an early night. I will serve the food and clean up. After the plates are fixed, you can head up and take a nice long bath."

Gran gave her a stern look and said, "Who are you, and what have you done with my granddaughter?"

Poppy laughed and said, "So funny. I know I should help more. This is me trying to do that."

Poppy felt more than a bit of guilt at lying to her grandmother. The truth was, if Bennett were not home, she would not have even thought to offer to help. That realization bothered her deeply. Promising to be attentive and a better granddaughter beginning immediately, Poppy smiled broadly and said, "So what can I do to help?"

Pointing to the kitchen door, Gran said, "Go and let Mr. Carrington know that dinner is ready when he is." Poppy was only too happy to do that chore.

Poppy found Mr. Carrington and Bennett in the office. They were seated on each side of the fireplace, enjoying a pre-dinner drink. The door was open. Standing in the doorway, Poppy called out, "Mr. Carrington, Gran asked that I let you know that dinner is ready when you are."

At the sound of her voice, Bennett's head snapped up. He drank her in as if he were a man dying of thirst. He ate her alive with his eyes. Poppy could feel it from where she stood. Poppy returned the look as she feasted on the sight of him. All the bent-up passion and desire building since December flooded out in silent energy between the two. If Bennett's dad was aware of the passionate charge in the air, he gave no indication of it. Instead, he stood and began making his way to the dining room. Bennett joined him. Poppy followed behind, taking slow, deep breaths.

Over the next hour, Poppy served dinner. She and Bennett did their best not to look at each other but whenever they did, both felt the electric charge zing through the room. Once dinner was over, Bennett and his dad returned to his office. This time, Mr. Carrington shut the door.

Poppy spent the next hour clearing the table and washing up. She finished putting away the last clean dishes when Bennett entered the kitchen.

"Whoa, what are you doing here?"

"I was just finishing putting away the dishes."

"I did not know you were doing so much for us. Other than the sheets." Bennett felt like a fool mentioning the sheets. Those damn sheets. He would never get in his bed again without thinking about her hands being all over them. He could almost swear he could smell her on his pillow at night. Thoughts of her had been driving him crazy ever since he saw her standing in the middle of that warehouse with her beautiful black dress ripped and hanging down.

Poppy was talking, and Bennett realized she had been doing so for a while. He was so caught up in thinking about that night, he did not hear a word she said. Shaking his head to clear it, he said, "I am sorry. What are you saying?"

Poppy laughed nervously, "It is not important. I explained that I don't usually serve or wash up, but I wanted to give Gran a break. She works so hard." Poppy felt that stab of guilt again.

"That's really nice of you. I don't know what we would do without her. Dad would be lost without her."

They stood staring at each other for a long moment. The tension was palpable.

Wanting to break the uncomfortable silence filling the room, Poppy asked, "So, was there something you needed when you came here?"

"Yes, I wanted to fix some popcorn and a soda. I am about to watch a movie." Knowing it was a terrible idea but unable to stop his mouth from issuing the invitation, Bennett asked, "You wouldn't want to join me, would you? On my way into town, I picked up some new releases at the video store." He rattled off the titles, but Poppy could have cared less. He could have said he had a DVD of paint drying, and she would have said she wanted to watch it.

"Sure, I would love to. Let me run upstairs and change, and I will be right back. Where should I meet you?"

He gave her a weird look and said, "The DVD player is in my room. Is that a problem? I promise to be a complete gentleman."

Poppy shook her head and said, "No, that is not a problem." She added, "See you in a minute."

"Great," replied Bennett, "I will get the popcorn ready. Diet okay?"

"Sure," replied Poppy as she headed out the back door and raced to change. She'd drink arsenic if it meant she could spend time with him.

When Poppy knocked on Bennett's sliding door ten minutes later, he had changed into a tee shirt and jogging shorts. Poppy had put on a tee shirt and a pair of knit pants.

"Hope you don't mind sitting on the bed; it is the only seating I have," said Bennett.

"No problem," replied Poppy.

Both of them started out sitting at the edge of the bed, but their interest in the movie soon waned when their interest switched to little touches and shared looks.

After playing this game for ten minutes Poppy said, "Oh, screw it," and reached out and took Bennett's face in her hands and kissed him for all she was worth.

Unlike the kiss they shared at Christmas, this one did not start soft or gentle. It began wild, and with each second, it grew wilder and hotter. One minute, they were at the foot of the bed, sharing popcorn and pretending to watch the movie, and the next, they were lying across Bennett's bed, kissing each other with abandon.

Bennett and Poppy spent the next hour exploring each other's bodies. As their tongues fought a duel for control, they could not stop touching, squeezing, and giving over to the desires that had been haunting both of them for the last three months.

To Bennett's credit, he did everything he could to stay away from her. She was obviously his kryptonite. He had distanced himself from her. He had stayed away. He even tried to move on with other girls. But, not one of them did what this redheaded vixen did for him.

Several times, he tried to slow them down. He would attempt to pull back or end the kissing, and each time, Poppy would lean into him, touching him more intimately, kissing him more deeply. He was lost to deny her. The whole time, the voice in his head kept saying, "Stop. You have gone too far."

Bennett was unable to heed his own advice. Poppy was driving this lust train, and he was just along for the ride. He knew he should call a halt to it all. And he would, just a few minutes more, he thought. She fit him so perfectly with her tiny little body.

Bennett needed to find the strength to pull back. Ultimately, the only thing that saved him from making a huge mistake was a loud knock on his sliding door.

"Bennett, dude, are you in there? Open up. I've got to talk to you."

Bennett and Poppy sprung apart as if they had been scalded. It took a moment for each to realize what was happening. Then Bennett rolled off the bed and whispered, "It's Tatum. Get yourself together." He gestured to her clothes and hair, either missing or in great disarray. Her ponytail holder had been lost a while back. Her red hair was curling all over her head in wild abandon.

"Come on, buddy. I know you are in there. I can hear the movie," said Tatum, getting annoyed.

Frowning at the door, Bennett got himself sorted and then, after a minute, looked back to make sure Poppy was as presentable as possible. All her clothes were back on and in the right place, but she looked like a woman doing exactly what she had been doing. Tatum was not stupid. Bennett knew his friend would take one look, and the dirty little secret he had been hiding since Christmas would be out. Bennett Carrington had fallen for a high school girl.

"You ready?" Bennett asked just before he opened the door. Poppy nodded. Pulling back the curtain and sliding open the door just enough for his head to slip out, Bennett said, "Hey, what's up?"

"I want to come in. That is what. Dude, do you have company? I am so sorry. I will come back later."

"No, it is just me. I just need a minute. Go around to the front. I will let you in there."

Tatum gave him a strange look. He always snuck into Bennett's room this way. If Bennett asked him to go to the front, he was hiding something. Not surprising. He had been acting weird since Christmas. As far as Tatum knew, he had not hooked up with a single girl since then. Tatum watched Bennett turn down super hot girls, saying he was not feeling it, and had outright rejected several sure-thing setups. Tatum had worried his buddy had lost his mojo. Now, he thought, maybe he just left it at home. Nodding, Tatum said, "Sure thing, bro. See you in a minute."

Bennett waited until he saw Tatum head around the side of the house to say, "I am so sorry about that."

"That's okay; you didn't know your friend would show up."

"Yeah, well, I better go. I don't want him ringing the doorbell and waking up Dad. He is a bear when his sleep is disturbed."

"Okay," said Poppy as she moved towards the door. "I am going." At the last second, she paused next to him and asked him, "When will I see you again?"

Running a hand through his hair, Bennett said, "I don't know. I am not sure this is a good idea. You and me. In fact, I know it is a really bad idea."

Wrapping her arms around his neck, Poppy said, "Sometimes bad ideas become good if they have enough time to grow." With that, she gave him a goodnight kiss he would not soon forget.

Breaking the kiss, Poppy headed to the door. Grabbing her hand, Bennett stopped her and said, "Okay, bad idea. I will think of something. Maybe we can go out on the lake tomorrow on the boat or something? Maybe grab some food at Janssen's?"

Smiling at him, Poppy said, "I would like that."

"Great, I am here all week. I have no plans. Be ready around nine. Does that sound like something you would like?"

"It sounds wonderful." Reaching over to give her a final peck, he added, "Now, go before all hell breaks loose."

Poppy quickly and quietly made her way back to her room. She did not know that Tatum had been watching from around the corner the entire time.

Interesting thought Tatum. *His boy was in deeper trouble than he had ever imagined.*

Next Morning...

On Saturdays, Gran liked to hit all the local garage sales. She usually left the house around six and returned at noon. Poppy knew she would have a large window to get ready and to write her a note explaining her absence.

She got up at seven, took a shower, and spent a ridiculous amount of time doing her hair, given she would be out in the wind all day on a boat. She dressed in her cutest jeans, a tee shirt, and a sweatshirt tied around her waist. She added the barest makeup and lip gloss and called it good.

She was up half the night coming up with an excuse for Gran strong enough to cover her being gone all day. Lying to Gran was getting easier by the day.

In the note, she said she was going to the library to get a jump on her research for her upcoming term paper. She hoped Gran would buy it. Gran knew she was stressing about doing two college classes and writing a term paper. Hopefully Gran would buy it.

With the note written and placed on the kitchen table where Gran could easily find it, Poppy threw some sunscreen and a hat into an over-sized tote and headed down the backstairs.

Her excitement died a quiet death when she got to Bennett's door and saw a note addressed to her. In it, he explained that his plans had changed. He had to leave town for a few days. He was going to the Bahamas for spring break with Tatum, his sister, and her friend. Poppy burned with anger and hurt when she read the note. She had no idea what happened in the last twelve hours to cause Bennett to make a 180. Poppy stood there holding the note, feeling like her world was crumbling. A giant, gaping hole was now where her heart used to be.

Chapter 7

Carrington House
Searcy, Arkansas
November 27, 2023

"Wow. The guy stood you up after such a heated night? I must say, you are way more understanding than my wife. She would have never spoken to me again if I had done that to her."

"I very nearly didn't. But as you can see," Poppy held up her left hand, "I came around. Not before much more water roared under our bridge, mind you. But, even then, I knew I loved Bennett and that loving him would cost me. That day cut deep, but in a way, it helped prepare me for much more painful days to come."

"Before we dive into that, did you ever find out why Bennett left again so abruptly without a goodbye?"

"Yes, it was because of conversations he had with Tatum and his dad after I left that night."

"Tell me about those."

"Tatum saw me leave Bennett's room and confronted him about it. Supposedly, Bennett had acted strange all semester."

"What do you mean by strange?"

Poppy gave him a look and then said, "I guess he was not chasing tail the way he had in the past. He was more subdued and studied more than dating or hooking up with random girls."

Harvey made notes on his paper and said, "So Bennett was acting strange, and now Tatum knew why. Bennett had a thing for you. How did Tatum feel about that?"

"How do you think he felt? His friend was poised for a great political career. He was a twenty-five-year-old man messing around with a high school girl. It did not matter that I was over eighteen. To Tatum, I represented Bennett's downfall. He was trying to protect his friend from making a career-ending move by keeping us apart. He was sure it would have ended poorly if Bennett had stayed in town that week. So, he got Bennett to go to the Bahamas with him and his crew."

"A crew that included Taylor Stroupe?"

Poppy nodded but said nothing.

"How did you feel about that?" asked Harvey.

"I was pretty ticked off about it. I had seen the picture of Taylor and Bennett on his dresser. He was her prom date her senior year. I hated that picture. It represented everything she got that I was never going to have."

"Did you ever discuss that with Bennett?"

"Eventually. But not then. I was too upset at the time."

"Okay, well, before we go down the Taylor rabbit hole, let's backtrack for a minute. You said Bennett's dad also talked to him that night. What did they talk about?"

"Yeah, his dad heard Bennett and Tatum arguing. He got up to see what was going on. He overheard enough that he got the jist of what Tatum was upset about."

"How did Mr. Carrington react to the news that you and his son were becoming a couple?"

"Just as Bennett had expected. He was convinced that being with me would ruin his son's future." Snorting, Poppy said, "Turns out he was right. I mean, not when or how he thought, but ultimately, he was right. I did cost Bennett his career. Not just me, but I was a huge part of it. He told Bennett to stay away from me. He may have even referred to me as the help. Knowing what I know, Bennett did what he felt he had to. At the time, it almost broke me."

"So, what happened next? How long before you saw Bennett again?"

"Umm, it was the week after I graduated high school."

"Tell me what that was like."

"That was wild and wonderful and awful all at the same time."

"Sounds interesting. Tell me more."

Carrington House
Searcy, Arkansas
June 2000

The second week of May, Poppy graduated from Searcy High School. The only family Poppy had in the stands was Gran. So many students had ten or twelve people there cheering them on. Poppy wondered if they knew how lucky they were.

Much to her surprise, in the week leading up to graduation, Poppy was accepted to all three art schools to which she applied. Two of the schools offered her a scholarship. The Art Institute, her first choice, offered free tuition only. The one in Cincinnati offered her a full ride. Poppy wanted to go to New York, but she would need funds.

The college counselor, who contacted her with her scholarship offer, told Poppy about the hardship scholarship she qualified for. She encouraged Poppy to apply. Hopefully, if she got it, she would be able to go to New York. Poppy had until July 1 to submit her confirmation and accept her scholarship.

As a backup, Poppy got a waitress job at Colton's, a local steak restaurant, the week she graduated. She signed up for every hour she could get and saved every dime.

She did not tell Gran about her plans. As far as Gran knew, she would stay in Searcy, attend ASU, and work at Colton's. It was ironic as the only thing Poppy was positive about was that she was definitely not doing that. After having her heart broken over spring break, she wanted to get as far away from Searcy, the Carrington house, and Bennett as possible.

Poppy knew that Bennett graduated from law school the same weekend she graduated from high school. She saw some kind of twisted symmetry in that. Having no idea that Poppy and Bennett had any history, Gran was notorious for dropping little nuggets about what was happening in his life, which was how Poppy had found out about his graduation. To Poppy's relief, Bennett did not move home after school. And, according to Gran, Mr. Carrington was not set to be at the house until the end of the summer. Gran set her vacation to correspond with Mr. Carrington being gone. She had plans to go to her sister's in Memphis for two weeks. With work, Poppy couldn't join.

On Poppy's nineteenth birthday, Gran made her a huge breakfast and gave her a large easel that Poppy had wanted for years. After breakfast, Gran packed her car and left for Tennessee. While Gran hated leaving Poppy alone, especially on her birthday, Poppy was super excited. It would be the first time she would be all on her own and she couldn't wait.

Poppy worked a double shift that night and got home a little after eleven. Tips had been good all night. After counting them, Poppy hid her money in her sock drawer and considered taking a shower before going to bed. However, the idea of a dip in the pool spoke to her. She was the only one on the property. No one would know. After all, she spent all last summer watching other people enjoying that pool. Why should she be the only one missing out?

Poppy decided to go skinny dipping. Before she could change her mind, Poppy raced down the backstairs and through the hedge, promising herself that she would dive in, swim around a few minutes, and then get out with no one being the wiser. Without turning on any of the pool lights, Poppy used the full moon's light to guide her. Once in the pool area, she quickly removed her flip-flops, Colton's tee shirt, and denim shorts. The last item to remove was her bra. With that gone, Poppy decided to dive head first off the diving board into the deep.

A fabulous swimmer, she swam the whole length of the pool underwater, only surfacing once she reached the steps of the shadow end. She pulled herself up the ladder and began making her way back to the board, totally forgetting her promise to dive in, swim, and get out. Poppy felt more alive than she had in months. She had just dived into the pool for the fourth time when she heard something above her. Surfacing in the shallow end, she was stunned to see Bennett standing between her and the ladder.

"What the hell are you doing here?" demanded Poppy. Bennett was not supposed to be there. If she had known he was home, she would have stayed in her room and avoided him at all costs.

Walking slowly towards her with his hands on his hips, Bennett said, "Don't be like that, Red. I have missed you."

Putting her hands up to stop him, she kept her body under the water and said, "Red? Don't call me that, and don't come any closer. I'm not dressed."

"A fact of which I am well aware," said Bennett, creeping ever closer. "I've been watching you since I heard the first big splash. I must say you have fabulous form. Your diving isn't bad either."

Rolling her eyes at him and slowly swimming backward, Poppy could not stop herself from blushing. As he came closer, she said, "No, I mean it. Stop. I'll scream."

"Chill, Red, you know I would never hurt you." Bennett stopped and kept his position still. He did not want to scare her but he had to talk to her. He had been waiting to do it for months.

"I have been waiting for this day for so long. Thank you for having your birthday on the same day my dad always takes his vacation. That was very helpful."

"What are you talking about? How did you even know today was my birthday?"

Holding his ground, he tread water and said, "I have my ways. The hardest part was staying gone as long as I did. You are one tough woman to stay away from. Please tell me you missed me as much as I missed you. Did you think of me at all? I am not sure what kind of witchy voodoo magic you have, but not a single day has passed since March that I have not thought of you and planned for this moment."

"I have no idea what you are even talking about. Why are you even here? You know what, don't answer that. All you do is get me going and full of hope, make a bunch of promises, and disappear. So why don't you do that now? Turn around and disappear back to wherever you have been since March."

"You knew where I was and why I had to go."

"Let me guess, I was in high school and was going to ruin your life."

"Yeah, something like that. But great news, Poppy, I don't know if you heard, but rumor has it you are all graduated, and as of today, you are nineteen. Can't get much more legal than that." As he said that, Bennett began swimming towards Poppy.

Poppy continued to back up until her back was against the edge of the pool. With nowhere to go, she planted her feet on the underwater edge and held on the sides with her hands. When Bennett reached her, he put his arms on each side of her head and held on to the side. Without touching, he pressed his body in close.

He was so close Poppy could not breathe. Forcing herself to look into Bennett's eyes, she said, "Whether or not I am legal has nothing to do with you. Whatever you and I had is over."

Bennett let her finish. Then, he pushed her wet curls behind her ear. Allowing his finger to drift down over her cheek and to the crease in her chest, he said, "Poppy, what we have is far from over. I know it and you know it. Tell me you feel this."

Without missing a beat, Poppy replied, "Yeah, I felt it before, and it left me alone, sad, and feeling like a fool."

Poppy could tell her words cut him. Part of her was glad. He had cut her with his actions. It was only fair that he should suffer as she had. The other part of her wanted to pull him close and see if he was right and if what they had started before was still there.

Looking deeply into her eyes, he said, "I am deeply sorry I hurt you. For what it is worth, I was right there with you. You were never far from my mind. I just knew that I had to be the strong one for us both. You were too young. I wanted you to finish school and graduate without the threat of scandal. And, I'll admit the choice I made was selfish. I wanted both my career and you. The only way I could think of how to do that was to go away until now. So, what do you say? Are you ready to give us a second chance, or will you hold on to all that hurt and keep us from seeing if this thing between us can be something?"

When he finished talking, all that could be heard were the cicadas croaking around them. She took several seconds to think and then, having made up her mind that they had both suffered enough, Poppy slowly let go of the sides of the pool and allowed her body to float into him. Using one arm to hold them steady and the other to haul her in close, Bennett tucked Poppy's tiny perfect body into his. Reaching to place soft kisses on his neck, she whispered, "Please don't ever leave me like that again." Capturing her lips in a deep kiss, he responded, "I promise I won't."

Chapter 8

Carrington House
Searcy, Arkansas
Summer 2000

The following two weeks flew by. Poppy and Bennett got to know each other's minds, as well as each other's bodies. It was an idyllic two weeks. They swam, cooked, laughed, and worked. They had so much fun playing house, and Poppy watched more Razorback baseball than she ever thought was possible. Often after dinner, they would ride over to Bald Knob to get strawberry shortcake from The Bulldog. It was Bennett's favorite dessert.

That first night together, Bennett had asked Poppy about birth control. She told him that she had been on the pill since she was fifteen for her periods. The relief he felt from hearing that was evident on his face. He told her that he would wear a condom if she wanted him but that he was clean. He had not been with anyone since before Christmas. Plus, he told her he had never been with anyone without a condom. The conversation embarrassed Poppy even though she knew it was necessary. She was innocent but not stupid. One could not do adult things if one could not have adult conversations. In the end, Bennett let it be her decision. Wanting to please him, Poppy said it did not matter to her. She was unsure whether that was true or not, but she could tell it was what Bennett wanted to hear. In the end, they skipped the condom.

Gran would call each night and check to make sure everything was okay. Each one knew things would have to change when Gran came home, so there was this unspoken sense of urgency to spend as much time together as possible. It was during this time that Poppy told Bennett about the Art Institute and her tuition-only scholarship. He understood why she was working so hard to save her money.

While Poppy waitressed, Bennett officially joined his dad's law practice along with Tatum. Both were working while they studied for the bar exam. Bennett never mentioned to his dad or Tatum that he and Poppy were together. Bennett knew that the less people who knew about them, the better.

The nights were just for them. Most nights, Poppy would work the day/night shift, which meant she went in at ten in the morning and was done by seven. She and Bennett enjoyed cooking together in the kitchen of the main house. After dinner each night, they would spend hours lounging around in the pool.

Growing up in Searcy, summers meant golf and tennis tournaments every weekend. One week would be golf and the next tennis. There were always bands and big dinners on the Friday and Saturday nights of these tournaments. Bennett had grown up participating in all of it. It was a regular part of his summer. His partner in those events was always Tatum. They played together in the two-man golf and doubles tennis events. Bennett was the stronger golfer. Tatum was a stronger tennis player. But this summer was different.

Bennett was less into the whole country club scene this summer than in previous years. If he knew Poppy was working until seven, he would play golf or tennis after work. He worried how he would get out of the first tennis event of the summer when Tatum surprised him by saying he had plans and that Bennett would have to get another partner. It was the perfect out for him. Bennett was able to skip it without anyone asking too many questions. It was not the playing that would have been the issue. It was the huge party afterwards. He would not have felt right going without Poppy, but he could not imagine taking her either.

Bennett had a hard time seeing Poppy at a country club dance. It was not her scene. She confided in him about being an introvert, hating large crowds, and having to make small talk with people she did not know. Large crowds and making small talk summed up every country club party he had ever attended. So, instead, Bennett skipped the club altogether and never felt like he missed a thing. He knew he could not escape that all summer but would cross that bridge when the time came.

The Friday before Gran was to come home, she called and said her sister was very sick. Poppy knew her aunt had been ill but thought she was improving. Turns out, her great aunt had cancer and had not wanted to worry anyone. Once Gran got there and realized how bad it was, she decided to stay for a few more weeks since Mr. Carrington was not expected back home until August. She ensured Poppy was okay with her staying in Tennessee until at least the end of July. Poppy was sad her great aunt was so sick, but she was grateful for the private time with Bennett.

Knowing they had more time together took the pressure off to spend every minute together. Over the summer, Bennett found himself falling back into old habits. He would play golf until dark and then eat dinner at the club. The first time he did that, Poppy fell asleep in his bed waiting for him to come home. Same for the second, third, and fourth time he did it. The fifth time, he came home to Poppy asleep in her bed. A bed she had not slept in since that first night he was home. He knocked on her back door, and when she did not answer, he slinked down the back steps, unsure if they had just had their first fight.

The next day, he tried to say goodbye, but she still did not answer. Later that day, he showed up at Colton's during lunch and paid well to ensure he was seated in her section.

"Hey," said Bennett, giving her a huge smile. He reached up to give her a quick peck on the lips, but Poppy turned her head at the last second. "Okay," he muttered. "So you are still mad," said Bennett.

"I am not mad. I am fine," replied Poppy. Handing him a menu, she asked, "What can I get you today, sir?"

"Sir? Can you get my sweet girlfriend back? I seem to have lost her."

"Your girlfriend? Hum? Maybe you lost her at the country club. I hear that is where all the important people hang out every night. Maybe you left her there." Poppy gave him a fake smile, saying, "I will bring you some tea. I will be back after you have had time to look over the menu and decide what you want."

Bennett didn't know if she meant the food or her. He knew when he was still out past midnight with his old buddies watching a late baseball game and drinking beer that he was not making good choices. He did not realize just how bad those choices would be.

A few minutes later, a new waitress showed up at his table with his tea, letting him know that Poppy had taken a break, and she would be taking care of him. Bennett considered demanding that Poppy come out and talk to him, but he decided that would not be a good idea. Instead, he ordered and ate his lunch alone. Later, he picked up some flowers and came home early, canceling the golf game he had set up the day before. With rain in the forecast, his friends never questioned it.

Bennett took the back steps to Poppy's room, two at a time. He looked through the window and saw her in her room, cleaning closets. She was like a madwoman. He had never seen her like that. She was a closet-cleaning maniac.

When he knocked on her back door, Poppy answered. Rain poured down. Standing under an umbrella with the flowers in his hand, Bennett reached out to kiss her. She pulled back and did not move to allow him into her room. Instead, she looked at the flowers and said, "It was so nice of God to send the rain so I could be graced with your presence before eight."

"OK, you are still mad. I get that." Handing the flowers toward her, he waited for her to take them. When she did not move, he said, "Come on, Poppy. I know you got your feelings hurt that I was a little late getting home last night."

She interrupted him and said, "I did not get my feelings hurt. I just got tired of being taken for granted." With that, she slammed the screen door and returned to her closet to continue cleaning.

Growling in frustration, Bennett grabbed the spare key over the door and let himself in. He was unsure why he never thought of the key before. Barging in, Bennett said. "Damn it, Poppy. Stop being a brat. I was only a little late." He shook the water off him and dropped the flowers on her dresser.

Sticking her head out of her closet, she said, "Did I say you could come in?"

Walking over to her closet, Bennett squatted down on her level and said, "Come on, Red. Don't be like this." Reaching to touch her face, he added, "I have missed you. I don't want to fight." Leaning into her, he said, "Can we just kiss and make up?" When she made no move towards him, he said, "You know what they say, there is no sex like make up sex."

Poppy gave him a look and said nothing. Then, she got up and walked over to the flowers. Picking them up and dropping them in the garbage can, she opened the door and said, "Go home, Bennett."

Bennett stood and just looked at her. He could not believe she was not letting this go. "Red, is this really about one night? What do you want from me? You want me to say I am sorry. I am sorry. I am so sorry I stayed out late one night."

Holding her body stiff, Poppy said, "I don't believe you are sorry. I don't think you believe you did anything wrong. That is the issue. And, for the record. I am not being a brat. It was not one time; it was five. And, worse, you are acting like a jerk. If you want to spend time with your friends, that's fine. I want you to do exactly what you want to do. But respect me. Respect my time. Call me and let me know when to expect you. Don't leave me waiting like my time is less valuable than yours. Don't show up looking for easy sex whenever you get around to me. I am better than that, and I won't be that. Not even for you. Now, leave and think about what it is you want." With that, Poppy returned to her closet and started banging and clanging again. Once Bennett left, she threw all the crap she had just gone through in her closet into a pile and cried her eyes out. She crawled into her bed and cried herself to sleep.

The next morning, she found a note outside her door.

Dear Red,

I am so sorry. You are right; I have been a jerk. I should have called. I messed up. Please forgive me. I promise not to disrespect you again. Your time is just as valuable as mine. Please say we can start over. I will be home early. Meet me for dinner, and let me spend the night making it up to you for treating you like you did not matter. You do matter. I am sorry. So, so, so sorry!

Love,
Your Jerk of a Boyfriend,
Bennett

That night, Bennett and Poppy made up. Turns out Bennett was right. Make-up sex was the best. Even though they worked it out, Bennett could feel a distance from Poppy he had not felt before. The rest of the summer, Bennett called when he would be late. His guy friends gave him nine kinds of hell over it, but Bennett sloughed it off. They would demand to know who he was hog tied to, but he refused to tell them. He never really let himself question why he worked so hard to keep her secret. Some things are just better not too closely examined.

On the fourth of July, the country club did a massive fireworks display. Poppy went to see it the year before. She expected that she and Bennett would go to see it this year. Nearly everyone in town did, whether they were a club member or not. When Poppy asked Bennett about it, he looked like he had seen a ghost.

"You want to go to the club's fireworks?" asked Bennett as if that was a normal question.

Poppy gave him a funny look and said, "Well, yes, of course. Everybody in town is talking about it. You don't?"

Bennett looked lost in a maze and could not find his way out. "I don't know. I thought we could do the fourth here."

Poppy gave him a funny look and said, "Here, with no fireworks and no people?"

"No, here, just us," replied Bennett. "I thought you did not like crowds. I thought you would prefer to stay here and celebrate with you and me."

Poppy gave him another look and said, "Okay Carrington. What's up? We both went to the club last year. It is the best fireworks show in the city. Is it me? Are you embarrassed to be seen with me? We don't ever go out. I get it. I am young. That gives you pause. But, if you avoid going in public with me because you are embarrassed by me, that is something we need to talk about."

Bennett said nothing for a few minutes, then sat down, ran his hands through his hair, and said, "Look, I am not embarrassed by you. Hell, I am in love with you. You are the best thing about every day. I just… I know that when my dad and Tatum find out about us, they will do everything in their power to break us up. They already did it last year. I have kept it a secret to protect us from that."

Poppy realized he was telling the truth. That was when he told her about the conversations with his dad and friend the night before he disappeared.

Nodding understandingly, Poppy asked, "So what? We are never going to be seen in public? Is that how this is going to work? I get it. I am leaving in three more weeks. I guess I can see that you thought you could keep it hidden until I left. But then what? In a year or two? When were you going to come clean with them?"

Putting his head in his hands, Bennett sat on this bed and said, "I don't know. I have not thought this through." Reaching out to pull her to him, Bennett said, "But if you want to go public, I am all in. That means Gran will know because I promise you Dad will tell her. I had to all but promise to name my first son after him to get him to back off from telling her at Christmas."

"Aren't you like the fourth or something?"

"Yeah?"

"Don't you rich folks reuse names four or five times anyway?"

It took Bennett a moment to realize she was making a joke. "Ha! Ha! You are so funny. We will see how funny you think this is when your grandmother calls you and wants to know who has been warming your bed all summer."

"First of all, my grandmother would never ask that. Second of all, we need a plan. What exactly am I to you? Just a bit of fun until the summer is over?" Poppy tried not to let the hurt show in her face. She had worried that might be the case from day one. But, every night, Bennett told her he loved her. He repeatedly told her that on calls and in random conversations throughout the day. In Poppy's world, those words meant something. She wanted to think they did in his as well.

Going to her and wrapping her in a hug and then raining kisses down her face and neck, he said, "You are my everything. You're my girlfriend. I love you. But you are so young. You have so many experiences ahead of you, and I don't want to steal those. At the same time, I want all of you. I have to figure out where you fit in my world."

Pulling back from him, Poppy repeated his words, "Where I fit in your world? I seemed to fit pretty well last night."

Pulling her back to him, Bennett said, "My other world. My work and social world. Everyone is much older than you. They are going to see you as the innocent kid you are and me as some predator who has taken advantage of you."

"That is not the case."

"I know that, and you know that, but we don't make sense to the world. I am trying to keep what we have safe so the world does not destroy us before we even have a chance."

"What does that even mean? Maybe I am too young because your words make no sense."

"You know my future career has been planned for me for years. I can assure you that my falling in love with a kid right out of high school was not part of that plan. I am trying to figure out how to navigate us and merge you into that life plan my dad has stomped into me since I can remember. I want you. I want a life with you. I realize you are too young to hear that. We have only been together for a summer. We have years to grow into each other. You have to trust me as we do it. In the meantime, you will go to New York. Study art and become the amazing artist I know you will be. Then, you will return to Searcy. We will get married and have two point five kids. I will run for Senator and then President, with a few other appointments sprinkled in. It will all work out. Doesn't that sound like a perfect life? We just have to get over the hump of you being so young."

Poppy leaned back and looked at him. She thought about everything he said and replied, "You seem to have this all figured out. Huh?"

Nodding, Bennett said, "I do." He pulled her back to him and continued to kiss her all over. He had learned the best way to stop an argument was to engage her in something other than talking.

"One question. I still need the money for art school. What happens if I end up here at ASU Searcy, still working at Colton's? Will I be good enough for your friends and family, then?"

"You are good enough for them now. You are just too young for their taste. Besides, of course, you are going to New York. Your tuition is covered. I will rent an apartment for you. The money you are saving should be enough to cover anything else. What it doesn't cover, I will. Problem solved.."

"No. You are not paying for my rent. Are you crazy? You just got out of law school. You can't afford that."

"Actually, I can. I have a trust fund from my mom. I know you. If I don't do it, you will find some dinky little hovel that I will hate staying in. And I will be staying there a lot."

"Oh, you will, will you?"

"Yes, I plan to fly up to see you as often as possible. Like every other week. Can't let those artsy college boys have a shot with my woman."

Laughing at the ridiculous idea that any boy could ever hold a candle to Bennett, Poppy said, "Well, in that case, I guess you had better make sure you get your butt to New York as often as possible."

With that, Bennett scooped her up in his arms and carried her to his room as his kisses smothered her giggles. All discussion of the fireworks was forgotten. Ultimately, Poppy and Bennett went to a fireworks display uptown at a local college.

Chapter 9

Carrington House
Searcy, Arkansas
August 2000

Over the next two weeks, Poppy and Bennett continued the routine they had followed all summer. True to his word, Bennett contacted a real estate agent in New York and rented a furnished apartment for Poppy near the school. He also set up a checking account for her. At first, she refused to use it. He argued that she would need it for the apartment they would share when he was in New York. She did not like it, but it was hard to argue with Bennett. He made a strong case that it would be easier if she had a local account in which he could put money if she needed it than trying to send her money in an emergency. In the end, she went uptown to the big, local bank on the town square and signed the check card and necessary forms. She got a debit card and promised it would only be for emergencies.

She officially accepted her scholarship and began making plans for the fall. The college called and let her know that she had been awarded the hardship scholarship. She was very excited. Now, she had the funds for school. She offered to pay half the rent, but Bennett refused. He said she would need the money for other things, and that now she would not have to worry about getting a job in New York.

Bennett arranged to take off the week before she left for orientation. They would pack her things and then drive up in his Jeep. Poppy was getting excited about it all.

The only drawback was that she had not told Gran any of this. The original plan had been for Gran to come home the last week of July, and Poppy would tell her then. However, with Poppy's great aunt back in the hospital, she never got the chance. Gran felt like she couldn't leave her sister. Instead, it was decided that Gran would remain in Tennessee for the foreseeable future.

Realizing she had to tell her grandmother about her college plans, Poppy gathered her courage and called her early the morning before she and Bennett were to leave for New York. Over the phone, Poppy shared about her scholarship and that housing and incidentals had been covered. She did not mention Bennett in any way other than to say that he had a business trip planned to New York and had offered her a ride. If Gran was suspicious of that, she did not say.

Gran was too shocked by Poppy's news and overwhelmed with caring for her sister to ask too many questions. Of course, she was happy that Poppy would be able to study what she loved. Before Poppy hung up, she asked Gran for the code to the safety deposit box in Gran's closet. It had Poppy's social security card and a few other documents she needed. Gran gave her the code.

As Poppy was getting the things she needed from the box, something caught her eye. It was an older diary. Unable to resist, she opened it. Stunned, she realized it had belonged to her mom. She should have been packing, but instead, she spent the whole day devouring her mother's words. What she discovered would shape her life from that moment on.

Poppy assumed the diary was a graduation gift since the first entry was a few days after her mom graduated high school. The first few entries were pretty sweet and simple. Only when her mom started her new job at Mr. Carrington's law firm did the entries get interesting.

From reading the diary, Poppy learned about who her father might be. She also got a front-row seat to her parent's relationship. Even though her mom did not name any names, Poppy discovered he was a married man with children. He had promised to leave his wife, who was battling some form of cancer, as soon as she was in remission. Her mom clearly loved her dad and completely believed him when he said he would leave his family for her.

In her last entry, her mom described a huge fight between she and Poppy's dad regarding the timeline around when he would leave his wife. He promised it would be before Poppy was born. Her mom wrote that he proposed and promised they would marry by August. The next day, her mom had a car crash that put her in labor. She never made it out of the hospital.

Reading this, and thinking about what might have been if her mom had lived sent Poppy's stomach rolling. Every page answered questions Poppy had for years. It also created new questions left unanswered. At least from her mother's perspective, her mom and dad were madly in love. Poppy wanted to believe that was true.

She did not know or understand why her father made no move to get to know her or support her after her mother's death.

Several times, when her emotions got the best of her, she ran to the bathroom and was violently ill. Poppy felt overwhelmed and stressed out by all she had learned. She planned to have a long conversation with her grandmother very soon about all of it. But, at the moment, Gran was doing all she could to care for her sister. That conversation would have to wait.

She could, however, talk to Bennett about it. She could hardly wait to tell him what she read. She made them grilled cheese and soup for dinner and sat down to wait for him.

It was nearly nine before Bennett got home that night. His secretary Katie had called and said there had been an emergency, and he would be late. The secretary assured her that Bennett was fine.

When he walked in the door, Poppy took one look at Bennett and knew something terrible had happened. His eyes were swollen, and she could tell he had been crying.

Running to him and wrapping him in her arms, she asked, "What is it? You look terrible. Katie said you had an emergency. What happened?"

Grabbing her and holding her close, Bennett erupted in a torrent of tears. He cried for several minutes and then said, "It was Tatum. He and his parents were killed today in a car wreck in Fayetteville."

Poppy was stunned by the news. Bennett continued to hold her and sob. After a few minutes, when Bennett seemed to be getting himself under control, Poppy asked, "Do you know what happened?"

"A truck crossed the center line. They were killed instantly." As soon as he said the words, his tears fell harder.

Poppy held him close for several minutes and asked, "Do you want to talk about it?"

He just shook his head no.

Trying to be supportive, Poppy asked, "Are you hungry? Can I get you something to eat?"

Again shaking his head, he said, "No, all I want to do is go to bed."

Together, they walked to his room and got ready for bed. Once they were under the cover, Bennett took her in his arms and said, "I am so sad. He has been my best friend since I was in preschool. I cannot imagine doing life without him."

As he said this, tears filled his eyes. Poppy offered him the only comfort she could. She gave him her body to lose himself in for a little while. Later, just before they drifted off to sleep, Bennett said, "I need to tell you. My dad is coming back from the lake in the morning. You will need to take everything back to your room."

Poppy hated bringing it up, but they were supposed to leave for New York the next day. She needed to know if the plans had changed. "I hate to ask this, but remember, we were supposed to leave for New York tomorrow. I understand if you need to push that back, but I must be there in less than a week."

Bennett closed his eyes and shook his head before looking at her. "Oh babe, I totally forgot about that with all that happened today. I don't see any way I will be able to drive us. If you have everything together, ship it tomorrow so it will be there. I will get us tickets and will fly there after the funeral."

As soon as he said that, his eyes began to water. Hating to stress him any more, Poppy said, "We will figure it out tomorrow. I love you. Try to get some sleep."

The next day was a blur for Poppy. With the return of Mr. Carrington, Poppy returned to her apartment with all of her things. Following Bennett's request, she boxed up everything she planned to bring in the car for school and shipped it all to the new apartment.

She was glad she had the debit card from Bennett. It was not cheap and would have stressed her to think she had spent so much on shipping things. As it was, knowing she had him backing her up made the process easier.

Bennett and his dad spent the day huddled up in the firm's conference room with the firm's other lawyers. It was after ten when Poppy heard the light knock on her outside door. She opened the door to find a completely drained Bennett. She had never seen him like he was. He looked like he had been to hell and back.

Coming in, he loosened his tie and let out a long, low sigh as he sat on her bed. "I've got some bad news that you will not like. But before you throw a fit, I want you to know. There is not one thing I can do about it."

Poppy gave him a confused look and said, "I am not a fit thrower, so I think we will be good. But you are scaring me. What is so bad that you think I will?"

"I can't take you to school. I have to go to Scotland. No one has told Taylor yet. The decision was made to send someone to tell her in person."

"She doesn't know her parents or brother are..." Poppy left the part unsaid.

Bennett just shook his head before pulling her close and burying his head in her stomach. "I know you are mad, but I don't have a choice. My dad decided I should go and break the news to her. Then, I am to help her pack up and bring her home. I think it will take me at least a week to do that. I leave first thing in the morning."

Poppy stood there with him wrapped around her, processing what he said. She would have to figure out a way to New York by herself. Thank God she already sent her things ahead. She knew it was wrong to think about how this would affect her with all that Bennett had on him, but she couldn't help it.

After a few minutes, she said, "I guess I need to call the bus station and see how much a ticket to New York is."

Bennett looked up at her like she was insane. "Don't be stupid. I had Katie book you a ticket for New York tomorrow. We will fly to Atlanta together out of Little Rock. You will go to New York, and I will go to Scotland. Hopefully, I will get everything done and be able to come to you in two or three weeks."

"Do you think it will take that long?"

"Yes, once I get her home, Taylor will have to plan funerals and all of that. She doesn't have anyone else. I already let my dad know that that will be my main focus over the next few weeks."

Looking up at her, Bennett said, "This is our last night together for a while. Let's make sure not to waste another second."

"I guess you have a point. If I don't get to see you for a few weeks, let's make it memorable. I will need something to hold onto."

"I couldn't agree more," said Bennett. With that, he began to kiss his way up her chest and neck.

The next morning, Bennett and Poppy caught an early flight to Atlanta. It was Poppy's first time on a plane, and she held Bennett's hand so tightly that she was worried he would complain. He never did.

Saying goodbye in the Atlanta airport was harder than she expected. She wanted to let the tears loose and cry, but she forced herself not to. She had chosen art school. She had chosen to leave. She knew she would have to say goodbye at some point. But thinking about it was one thing, actually doing it was another.

Carrington Kitchen
Searcy, Arkansas
November 27, 2023

"That week sounds like it was a lot. You went from expecting to drive with Bennett to New York to get settled and learn the city together to shipping your things and flying there alone. In addition, it must have been tough to see Bennett deal with his friends and his parents' tragic deaths. That was a lot to place on him so young, especially going to Scotland to break the news to Taylor," said Harvey Cox as he put down the pen he had been making notes with and gave Poppy a sincere look.

"Yes, it was. Thinking about those days brings back such sadness. Watching Bennett mourning the loss of his best friend was so hard. I am not going to lie. There were so many times I wanted to throw the fit he suggested I might. I never did, though. He had more than he could carry emotionally. I did not want to be the one to add to that," replied Poppy. "Plus, I was still processing what I learned about my father. It was all too much. I did not get to discuss that situation with anyone for weeks. I needed to come to terms with the fact that my dad had been married and had never made any effort to see me or support me, even though he had claimed to love my mom. Also during that time, my great-aunt continued to decline, so I was not able to see Gran or discuss it all with her. I never did bring it up to Bennett. I knew he had too much else on his mind.

"When we did talk, it was always hurried and very surface. He would always ask about the apartment and my classes. He would ask how I was doing and if I was okay. I realized that my answer was supposed to be 'fine' even if I wasn't. Another answer, and he would have felt the need to try and fix it. He had enough he was trying to fix dealing with Taylor.

It took over two weeks to get her home and help her get her family properly buried. I felt bad for her. I really did. She was only a few years older than me. I was an orphan my whole life. I understood the rules of the road regarding life without parents. Thank goodness I had Gran and Papa growing up to help me. Taylor had it all thrust upon her at twenty-two with no one but Bennett and his dad to help her. So, I tried to kill the ugly, green monster when she would rear her ugly head. But, being in New York alone was hard when I knew Bennett and Taylor spent every day and night together in Searcy. I was happy to be in school, and learning, but I missed Bennett like mad." Poppy got up and went to the counter to make herself a cup of coffee. Pointing to the coffee maker, she asked, "Would you like a cup?"

Harvey shook his head and said, "I am really more of a soda guy. Any chance I could get a soda?"

As Poppy fixed his drink, Harvey asked, "What was it like in New York once you got there? Did you love it? Was art school everything you expected it to be?"

She handed him the drink and said, "The short answer, yes, no, and it depended on the day."

Picking his pen back up, Harvey said, "If that is the short answer, I can't wait to hear the long version."

Sitting back at the kitchen counter, Poppy took a deep breath and said, "Well, here it goes."

Chapter 10

Poppy's Apartment
New York City, New York
September–November 2000

Poppy had been in school for eight weeks. She loved everything about her art classes. Watercolors continued to be her favorite course, but she also loved her abstract class. It was taught by a very up-and-coming artist, Thomas Thompson. He already had several successful shows, and Poppy felt so lucky to be able to learn under him.

The hardest part of the first few weeks had been learning how to navigate the city. Having not grown up using a subway system, it took some getting used to. Poppy lived alone and didn't know anyone else in the city. This gave her so much time to pour into her craft. Every night, she would come home from class and repeatedly practice what she learned. She was ahead on all her required readings and was so focused on school that there had been little time for anything except for the weekly calls with Bennett. During the first few weeks, the calls felt like check-in calls rather than conversations between lovers.

Bennett called her the day he cleaned out Tatum's office, and she could hear the sorrow and heartache in his voice. She hated that she was not there to hold him and comfort him. Finally, life for Bennett began a return to normalcy after the funerals even though Poppy could tell that Bennett was really missing his friend. However, slowly but surely, it felt like things between them were beginning to return to how they had been before the accident.

Their conversations focused more on them and their respective days. It also got way steamier. It had been several weeks since they had been together physically and that was taking a toll on each of them. Bennett promised to come up for a visit the last weekend of September and Poppy was living for that visit. She could not wait to see him and show him all the pieces she was working on. She also wanted to show him the little Indian restaurant she had fallen in love with around the corner from their apartment.

The Friday Bennett was to fly up to New York, he called her on her cellphone, "Babe, please don't be mad."

Poppy had been with Bennett long enough to know that conversations that started that way never ended well. "Do not tell me you are not coming." Poppy could sense what he was going to say before the words came out.

For a second, Bennett said nothing. When he did speak, he said, "I am so sorry, but I am not coming. Something has come up with Taylor, and I can't leave her. She needs me."

"She needs you? She needs you?" Poppy's voice got louder with time as she said it. "Trust me, Bennett Carrington, the fourth, I need you. I need you badly. Please get your butt on that plane, now."

Sighing loudly and sounding defeated, Bennett said, "I know, Babe. No one needed this weekend more than me. Trust me. I am halfway to carpal tunnel syndrome without you. But Babe, it is bad here. I did not realize how bad it was until earlier today. A pipe burst at the Stroupe house. I called a plumber to go fix it."

Poppy interrupted him and said, "Great, if the pipe is fixed, problem solved."

Sighing again, this time exasperatedly, Bennett said, "If you stop interrupting me, I will tell you. Anyway, I sent over a plumber. You are right. He fixed the pipe but called me afterward to say he was worried about Taylor. He said something was not right. She was acting weird. He kept telling me I had to go over and check on things. So, as I was headed out of town to Little Rock, I swung by Taylor's house. Babe, you would not believe what it was like. The whole place was a mess. Pizza boxes were everywhere. Soda cans and empty fast food bags. I don't think she had even unpacked her suitcase from Scotland. And it gets worse. Taylor has always been the cleanest, sharpest-dressed person I have known. I don't think until today I have ever seen her with a hair out of place. Red, she was so nasty. I don't think she has showered or washed her hair in weeks. I am really worried about her."

"Fine," said Poppy. "Make her take a shower and call her friend, who is always around, to come be with her. But don't cancel our weekend. Please. I need you too. If you don't come, I may stop taking showers and washing my hair if that is what it takes to get your attention."

Bennett did not say anything for a moment. When he did, his tone was abrupt and frustrated. "Poppy. That is not even funny. This poor girl has been through so much. How can you make jokes about her situation when you, of all people, know what it is like to be left orphaned and alone? At least you still have your Gran. Taylor has no one but me."

Poppy wanted to snap back that she had been all alone for months, too. Gran was busy in Tennessee, she knew no one in New York, and he was always busy with Taylor. But, she had been chastised enough for one call. Instead, she said, "Okay, so this weekend is out? No chance you might fly up tomorrow if she is doing better?"

"I think I need to be around here. I have called and gotten her a doctor's appointment. I think she is depressed and may need some meds to help with that. I plan to hang around all weekend and see her get back on track."

Poppy did not like it but knew when to walk away from a fight she could not win. Bennett's mind was made up, and he was staying with Taylor no matter what she said. So, instead, she went in another direction. "Okay, so when can you come?"

Bennett thought for a minute and said, "Honestly, the next few weeks, I will be slammed. I have my final prep for the bar exam. I need to stay home and study. I am really behind with all that has happened in the last few weeks. Maybe I can come like the last week of October, after I take the exam."

Poppy was silent for a moment and then said, "Another month. You want to go another month before you see me?" Once again, Poppy's voice rose, and she practically yelled.

"Stop screaming at me. Of course, I don't want to go another month without seeing you, but I don't see how it can be helped."

"What if I fly down and see you?" Poppy hated how needy she sounded. But that was where she was. She had been so lonely the last few weeks, and she missed Bennett. A lot. She missed waking up next to him. She missed little kisses throughout the day. She missed how he smelled when he got out of the shower. She was learning that loneliness was most deeply felt in the little, everyday things you took for granted when you were in the thick of them. But, oh my, how you yearned for them when they were gone.

Bennett hemmed, hawed, and then said, "I don't think that is such a great idea. I really need to focus on studying. And, besides, with your grandmother gone, how would I explain your presence to Dad?"

"How are you explaining this apartment to dear old daddy?" Poppy had progressed from needy to smart ass. This time, she did not care.

"Look, I know you are mad. There is nothing I can do about that right now. I need to get back to Taylor. It is almost time to leave for the doctor's office. I will book tickets for the end of October. I love you. I will try to call you tomorrow night. Maybe then you will be in a better frame of mind to talk."

"Bennett Carrington, don't you dare try to turn this around on me and act like I am just some spoiled brat not getting their way." Once again, Poppy was basically yelling.

"Then stop acting like one. Not everything is about you," snapped Bennett. "Look. I don't want to argue with you. I just called to let you know what was going on. I will call you tomorrow. I love you." Bennett waited for Poppy to say she loved him, too. They never hung up without saying those words to each other. This time, Poppy did not respond. So Bennett said again, "I love you."

Again, he waited. And still nothing. Then he pleaded, taking the anger and frustration out of his voice, "Poppy baby, please don't be like this. I love you. I promise. I will book the tickets for October. I will come there, and we will celebrate the bar being over New York style. What do you say? We good?"

"No, " replied Poppy flatly.

"No, we are not good?" Bennett asked, surprised. He expected her to give in and agree with him. It was what she had always done. Maybe it was that she was finally growing up and learning to live in a big city alone or that he had avoided addressing her daddy questions about the apartment. But Poppy was tired of Bennett hiding their relationship. He acted like if anyone knew they were together, the world would end.

"No, don't book the tickets. If you can go another month without seeing me, you can go a little longer. I think maybe we need a break. Maybe this long-distance thing is just not going to work for us."

Now, it was Bennett's turn to raise his voice. "Damn it, Poppy. You are overreacting. Just calm down. God, you make me crazy. I love you, and you love me. This is not something to break up over."

"I make you crazy? Try being someone's dirty little secret. The way you act every time you think someone is going to find out about us is ridiculous. It's a miracle I am not the one needing antidepressants."

"Come on, Poppy, stop overreacting. It is not like that. How many times do I have to tell you? This is just temporary. I want to tell the whole world we are together but now is not the time. Just be patient. You know…" whatever Bennett was going to say was cut off by Taylor telling him it was time to go to the doctor. "Look, I have to go. I will call you tonight. I love you."

Poppy said in a very sad, small voice, "I love you, Bennett. Goodbye." She hung up and cried herself to sleep.

The following week, Poppy decided to give herself a break from Bennett. She declined all of his calls and did not respond to any of the voicemail messages he left. He sent her several flower arrangements, which Poppy dropped off at the senior citizen's hall on her way to class.

She left Searcy convinced she could not survive without Bennett. He seemed to be doing just fine without her. She had to try and see if she could forge ahead without him. She would have liked to have said she was doing just fine without talking to Bennett, but that would have been a lie. She was dying inside, but she was determined to cut ties and move forward without him until he was ready to claim her publicly. All the sneaking around and hiding was over. Having made that decision, Poppy realized she could not stay in the apartment Bennett had rented. She had to find a new place to live if she meant to move on.

Luckily, Poppy quickly found a room to rent with another art student. She moved in the following week. Bennett continued to call several times a day and leave messages. Poppy forced herself to stop listening to them. She had to be strong. She yearned to talk to him so badly that she had to get a new phone to keep from becoming weak and answering. She mailed the cell phone Bennett had given her for graduation back. If Bennett came to New York at the end of October, Poppy never knew it.

Bennett was the center of Poppy's world for months, and now he was just gone. Most days, Poppy felt like someone had shoved a hand down her throat and ripped her heart out. She felt hollow and empty. Her art kept her going.

Once she moved out of Bennett's apartment, she stopped accessing the account he set up for her as well. The money she got from her hardship scholarship thankfully covered her expenses.

The week before Thanksgiving, Poppy came down with a raging stomach bug. She was violently ill for several days. She missed three days of classes and knew that with final pieces due the first week of December, she could not afford to miss anymore. She dragged herself out of bed and into her abstract art class. She had only been in the class for a few minutes when she collapsed.

Several hours later, Poppy came to hooked up to IVs and monitors beeping in the emergency room. Not sure where she was, she looked around the room and saw her teacher, Mr. Thompson, sitting in the chair beside her bed. She was thankful to not be alone.

"Welcome back, Ms. Hunter. You sure gave me the scare of my life. I know my lessons are stimulating, but I have never caused a student to collapse from one," he said.

"Mr. Thompson? What are you doing here? Where am I? What happened?" asked Poppy, breathless and confused.

Mr. Thompson got up and walked around to the side of the bed. Taking her hand, he said, "You upstaged me in class today. You fainted dead away during my explanation of Max Ernst's sgraffito painting technique. We tried everything to get you to come too, but when you did not, we called an ambulance. I must say, young lady, it was quite the afternoon."

Closing her eyes, Poppy said, "I am so sorry, Mr. Thompson. I hate that I disrupted your class. I have been sick for several days and did not want to miss any more classes. I pushed myself to go to class today. I should have stayed home."

Nodding, Thompson said, "Well, given the near level of heart attack you gave me today, I think it is time you called me Tommy."

"Oh, I don't know if I can do that, Mr. Thompson," said Poppy. "It doesn't feel right calling my teacher by their first name."

"Darling, over the last two hours, I have seen you naked like three times, so I think you can call me by my first name."

The shock and embarrassment that rolled over Poppy's face was laughable. "Oh my, for a student who earned a scholarship for her nudes, you seem very shy about being seen in the buff yourself," quipped Thompson. Then he added, "If it makes you feel any better, I am playing for the other team, so it did nothing for me."

Even as bad as she felt, Poppy could not stop the laugh that rippled from her. "Okay, since you put it that way, Tommy, it is."

"Is there anyone I need to call for you and let them know where you are," asked Tommy.

Shaking her head, Poppy said, "Sadly, no. The only person I could call is my Gran, but she is taking care of my great aunt, who is dying of cancer. I don't want to bother her unless I have to. I am sure I am just dehydrated and will be fine after I get enough fluids."

Nodding, Tommy said, "Okay, if you are sure."

Just then, there was a knock at the door, and an older doctor and nurse came in. "Well, young lady," said the doctor, "how are you feeling? It is good to see you awake."

In a weak voice, Poppy said, "Yes, I am feeling better, embarrassed, but better."

"That is good. I am Dr. Lonnie Burk," said the doctor as she listened to her breathing. "Nothing to be embarrassed about. Lots of pregnant women get dehydrated."

Poppy almost fell off the bed. "I am not pregnant."

Giving her a surprised look, the doctor said, "Oh, I assure you, young lady, you are. Your HCG levels say otherwise. It is standard procedure to do a pregnancy test before we treat a patient, especially one who can't answer questions. Your test came back positive. When was your last period?"

Poppy was so shocked at the news she forgot to be embarrassed talking about her periods in front of her teacher. "The birth control I take keeps me from having periods. I did miss a few pills back in August, but I stopped the packet. I had a mini-period and started a new pack."

"Hum," said the doctor. "Most likely, the bleeding was from implantation." Turning to the nurse, she said, "Amy, could you please bring the ultrasound machine in? We need to determine just how far along this little peanut is."

It only took a few minutes, and the nurse returned with the machine. When Poppy saw her baby pop up on the screen, she burst into tears. She was not the only one. Tommy grabbed her hand as a steady stream of tears fell from his face.

The doctor took several measurements and determined that Poppy was almost eighteen weeks pregnant. She also found out she was having a boy. It was a lot to take in.

With worried eyes, she asked the doctor, "Given that I had no idea I was pregnant, is the baby okay? I am not a drinker or anything, but I have been on birth control the whole time. Did that hurt the baby?"

The doctor patted her and said, "From what I can see, the baby looks great. The heartbeat is strong. He is measuring right on time. All the organs look good. I would obviously stop the birth control. I am leaving instructions for you to follow up with your OBGYN. Given how far along you are, I would make an appointment as soon as possible. Be sure you tell them about the birth control and any other drugs you have taken while pregnant."

"I will. Thank you so much," said Poppy.

With that, the doctor headed to the door. Before leaving the room, she said, "Congratulations, you two. I hope this is a happy surprise for you both."

Neither Poppy nor Tommy corrected the doctor. The second she was out of the room, they erupted in laughter at the absurdity of her gay teacher being the father of her child.

Within a few hours, Poppy was discharged and Tommy offered to help her get home. On the way, Tommy asked about the father. At first, Poppy was hesitant to talk about it, but Tommy was so open and kind that the whole story soon flooded out.

Poppy told him that Bennett was older and always tried to hide their relationship. She told him about how the summer they had together and how it had all come to a crashing halt when his friend was killed.

Based on the dates from the ultrasound, Poppy realized that she must have gotten pregnant the night that Tatum died. She was sick several times that day as she read her mom's diary. Then, with all that happened that night and the following days, she forgot to take her birth control pills. She had abandoned her pack and started with a new packet the following month after her next period.

On the way to Poppy's apartment, which she shared with five other girls, Tommy suggested she come back to his house to rest as it would be quieter. He was happy to look after her. After declining several times, Tommy made it clear he did not intend to take no for an answer. He had the cab turn around and go back to his place.

What started as a one-night thing turned into a week-long sleepover. Tommy had a second bedroom and told Poppy to stay in it as long as she needed to, at least until she went home for Thanksgiving. Truthfully, it was so much more peaceful at Tommy's. By the end of the week, Poppy was feeling better. She had seen a doctor at one of the free clinics offered by the school and started prenatal vitamins. She was coming to terms with how her life was about to change forever.

Poppy had promised her grandmother she would come to Memphis for Thanksgiving and Gran sent her a bus ticket. Poppy was not sure how she was going to tell her grandmother about being pregnant and unmarried, just like her mother. She knew it would destroy her. Since she was barely showing, Poppy decided to wait to tell Gran until she talked to Bennett. She planned to do so Thanksgiving in Memphis and then take a bus to Searcy. She tried calling Bennett. She wanted to tell him she was coming early Saturday morning. But, every time she called the house, Mr. Carrington answered. She would hang up without saying a word.

When she returned the cell phone, she had purposely not kept his cell number. Having it would have made it so easy to call him in a weak moment. Instead, she made a clean break. Now, when she actually needed that number, she did not have it. She did call his office and ask Katie to speak to Bennett. He was in meetings all day, but she promised to have him call her. In a moment of bravery, Poppy asked Katie about Bennett's Thanksgiving plans. She told her Mr. Carrington was going on another cruise, but Bennett planned to stay home.

Feeling confident about her plan, Poppy boarded a bus out of New York and spent all day reading baby books. She rolled into Memphis late Wednesday night. Gran met her at the station downtown and Poppy's heart broke. She had never seen her grandmother looking so haggard. She immediately decided she would not mention the baby. In her mind, she had begun to fantasize about what would happen when she told Bennett about the baby. In her fantasy, he would immediately demand they marry. She would finish the semester, then move back to Searcy and live happily ever after raising their perfect little boy. In this fantasy, she did not allow thoughts about what this would do to his career to intrude into her future.

Around midnight, Poppy's phone rang. She was already asleep but roused herself enough to answer.

"Hello?" she answered.

"Poppy?" said Bennett.

"Yes, Bennett?"

"Oh baby, I have missed you so much. When Katie said you had called, I was almost afraid to believe her. Where have you been? I have been trying to find you for months. You just disappeared. Why would you do that?"

Poppy took a deep breath and said, "Let's not get into all that right now. Just know I did what I thought I needed to do at the time."

"Do you know what the hell you have put me through? First, you won't answer your phone. Then, you send the phone back and move out of the apartment. I even went to New York a week ago and hung out at your school, but I never saw you. Where the hell have you been? Why would you do this to me?" Bennett sounded so out of control and unBennett like that Poppy could hardly make sense of everything he was saying.

"Okay, so much for not getting into it right now. I really did not want to do this over the phone, but here we go. I was sick recently and missed some classes. But since we are doing this, what took you so long to come to New York if you were so worried? Like you said, you knew where to find me."

"I was tied up with the bar exam and was assigned my first big case. I have been working my butt off trying to get to the point I could take off several days and come and find you. When I finally got away, I guess that was when you were out sick. Are you okay now? Why did you not call me? I would have come immediately."

"I am fine. Just dehydrated after a stomach flu. But really, you would have come immediately? If you wanted to talk to me, why did you not call Gran? She knew where I was. You could have called her anytime and got my new number."

"You know why I could not do that. I would have had to explain why I was looking for you."

"Oh, great, back to being Bennett's dirty little secret."

"Poppy, baby, please don't start that again. It is so good to hear your voice. God, I miss you. I miss talking to you. Kissing you. Holding you. I even miss fighting with you. Tell me where you are. I will fly to New York to see you."

"I am in Memphis with Gran for Thanksgiving."

"Oh, that makes sense. How are your grandmother and your aunt?"

"Sadly, she is not good. She could go any day. I promised Gran to come here for the holiday."

"How long will you be there? Could you get away if I come over and get a room?"

"Well, I thought I would come to Searcy on Saturday. Thought it would be okay since Katie said your dad was gone."

"Oh baby, that is perfect. We will have the house to ourselves just like the old days. Tell me where to pick you up. I will drive over and get you."

"No, I have already got a bus ticket. Gran is expecting to drop me off at the bus station. If I changed my plans, she would want to know why."

"Okay, I get that, but knowing you are so close and I can't be with you is killing me."

"You've missed me. I mean, you have really missed me?"

"Missed you, Baby, I have burned for you. I love you. When you just cut me off, I lost my mind. Dad even called me in and told me to get my shit together. It has been a rough couple of months. Please tell me you still love me the way I love you."

"Oh, Bennett, of course, I still love you. I never stopped loving you. I just felt hurt. I was just tired of feeling like your piece on the side. I needed to protect myself. You promised never to leave me again, but it felt like that was all you did. I felt like I was losing you bit by bit to Taylor."

"Taylor, no baby, Taylor has nothing to do with us. I promised her brother I would take care of her if anything ever happened. That is all I have been trying to do. Honor my commitment to him."

"What are you talking about?"

"The day before Tatum died, he told me he knew you and I were back together."

"I bet he loved that," said Poppy sarcastically.

"Actually, he said he could tell I was happier than I had been in years. He just wanted me to be careful. He understood how damaging our relationship could be to my future but he got how much I loved you. As for Taylor, one of the last things he said to me was to make sure to take care of his sister no matter what happens in the future. That is all I am trying to do. She had really suffered. You are so good-hearted; if you knew her, you would love her."

Poppy seriously doubted that but did not say it. Instead, she said, "So, Gran and I are going out for lunch tomorrow before we go to the hospital. What are you doing for Thanksgiving?"

Bennett was quiet for a moment and then said, "I am scared to tell you. I am worried you will take it the wrong way."

"Hum, why do I think I am not going to like this?"

"Well, this is Taylor's first holiday all alone. I decided to stay in town and do Thanksgiving with her."

"Of course you did," said Poppy, rolling her eyes.

"Poppy baby, please don't make more of this than it is. It is just me being there for a friend who has been through more than anyone should ever go through. She is like a sister to me."

"Okay, I will let it go. But, admit it, it has been a lot to take. If the situation was reversed, and I would always be with some other guy, you would have hated it."

"Not going to deny that any thought of you with another guy makes me see red. I have been half out of mind thinking of you hooking up with all those artsy college guys. Please tell me you haven't been with anyone else."

"Are you kidding me? I have been too busy missing you to see, much less talk to another guy. What about you? Have you… been with anyone else?" Poppy was not sure she even wanted the answer to that question. It would destroy her if he said he had been with someone else. But she had to know.

"Hell no. All I have done is work my butt off trying to get to you. You are it for me. Don't ever doubt it."

It was ridiculous how happy his words made her feel. She was so happy, she almost told him about the baby. But that was not a conversation she wanted to do over the phone. Instead, she said, "Not going to lie. Even though I was not tempted to be with anyone else, some days, I think my hormones are screaming your name."

"You think I don't get that? Just the belief that I would find you and fix this is all that has kept me going. Please tell me you thought of me every time you touched yourself because you have had a starring role in all my naughty fantasies. Speaking of naughty things, tell me what you are wearing."

Chuckling, Poppy, who was wearing sweatpants and a tee shirt, said, "Oh, you know, I am just laying here naked."

Bennett shouted an expletive and said, "Red, are you trying to kill me?"

"Nope, just trying to get you going."

"Done. Just hearing your voice did that. But now, let's get back to you being naked. Tell me more."

Chapter 11

**Poppy's Aunt Brenda's House
Memphis, Tennessee
November 2000**

For the next two hours, they took turns revving each other up. It was so sexy and fun, and for the first time in months, both felt a sense of hope and peace that this love could be saved.

The next day, Poppy and Gran actually ate at the hospital to be near her aunt. She had planned to spend all day Thursday and Friday with Gran, but her aunt needed her grandmother. So Poppy told Gran she needed to return to New York to study.

**Carrington House
Searcy, Arkansas**

Of course, instead of going to New York, Poppy headed to Searcy to surprise Bennett. She moved her bus from Saturday morning to the first bus out on Friday. Her bus would get in around eight that next morning. The bus left at approximately five in the morning, and Poppy pulled into Searcy right on time. She hitched a ride to the Carrington house with a kid she knew from art class who was on the same bus from Memphis.

As soon as she got to the house, she went to the back to the sliding glass door to Bennett's room. She still had her key. She unlocked the door and slipped in quietly in case he was still asleep.

The first thing she noticed was the bed was unmade and empty. She could see where two heads had indented the pillows. Obviously, two people had slept in that bed the night before.

The next thing she saw was clothes. Women's clothes on the floor. The dress, heels, and underwear were all dropped as if they had been removed haphazardly.

Slipping around the corner to the bathroom, Poppy was stunned. Through the glass of the shower, she saw Taylor Stroupe. She did not know where Bennett was, but she had seen enough. Like a sister, my ass, thought Poppy as she slipped out of the bedroom, with Taylor never being the wiser. She was storming down the driveway when she took a moment and decided maybe there was a reasonable explanation. Taking a deep breath, Poppy turned around and walked towards the front door. She was about to ring the bell when she saw Bennett walk across the entryway wrapped in a towel. She could hear him whistling, something he always did each morning after they were together. That was all Poppy needed to see. Almost collapsing, she forced herself to put one foot in front of the other and walked the entire way to the bus stop.

New York, New York, Memphis, Tennessee, Gulf Shores, Alabama November-December 2000

Bennett started calling early Friday morning. Poppy blocked his call and promised never to be so gullible again. Once she was back in New York, Poppy told Tommy everything. She left nothing out. She even told him she was so scared to tell her Gran since she was following in her mother's footsteps. She was knocked up by a man who was not going to stand by her.

She told him how Bennett had cheated on her the night after telling her she was the only one. Truthfully, she would have never believed Bennett could be so deceptive if she had not seen it with her own eyes.

She replayed the events of that morning in her head over and over again. She had really believed he loved her. How could she have been so wrong? She should have trusted her instincts. She knew Taylor and Bennett were too close.

As bad as everything was, it only got worse on the Monday after Thanksgiving when her great-aunt passed. Gran offered to send her another bus ticket, but Tommy would have none of it.

Instead, he booked two tickets to Memphis. He held her hand and stayed by her side through the funeral and dinner afterward. Poppy knew Gran was dying to ask what the deal was with her and Tommy, but to her credit, she did not. Right before Poppy and Tommy left Memphis, Gran took her aside and told her to be careful. She said that Tommy was too old for her.

Given that Tommy was only a few years older than Bennett, she conceded that Bennett might have been right about the age thing. Of course, Poppy assured her grandmother they were just friends. Poppy could tell she did not believe her.

On the trip back to New York, Tommy made her a deal she could not pass up.

They were sitting in the gate area of the Atlanta airport. In front of them was a family with a young boy. The dad was playing chase with the toddler. Tommy couldn't look away.

After several minutes, Tommy took her hand and said, "Poppy, my girl, I am going to tell you something that only my doctor and I know. I have a fatal disease. I am okay now and hopefully will have several good years ahead of me. But, ultimately, it is going to kill me. I have always wanted to be a dad. I had thought when my art career took off I would hire a surrogate to carry a child for me. But this illness is genetic. I refuse to pass it on and bring a baby into this world that will be orphaned before he is grown. But, if you let me, I can be a dad to your son.

"We will have a marriage in name only. We will figure it out if you find someone you want to be with. As long as you always let me be his father, I will ensure you that you will be taken care of. You may not know this, but I am very well off financially. My paintings are selling well; and hopefully, they will continue to appreciate in value. You are too talented to drop out of school to take some minimum-wage job.

"Marry me. I have insurance that you are going to need. You can live with me. We will raise this baby together for as long as I have."

Poppy was so shocked by the offer. She couldn't believe it. She asked Tommy to give her time to think about it and Tommy agreed as long as Poppy agreed to go ahead and move in with him to save money in case she decided against it. Over three weeks, they fell into a companionable routine. Poppy took her first finals and completed her class pieces. She had just finished her last class when her cell phone rang. It was Gran.

"Hello, sweetheart. How are you? Classes all done?" asked Gran. Her grandmother sounded better than she had in months.

"Yes, I just submitted my last project. I am so tired. How are you? Did you meet with Aunt Brenda's lawyer?"

"I did. You will never believe it. I knew Brenda's husband left her well cared for, but I had no idea how well."

"That was good, I guess," said Poppy. "What happens to all that money now?" Aunt Brenda did not have any children.

Gran said, "You won't believe this, but she left it all to me. Her investments, life insurance, all of it. She had a house in Collierville and a condo in Gulf Shores. I feel so guilty that she had to suffer and die for me to get it. I would trade it all to have her back and healthy. But, I am glad she is out of pain."

"So what are you saying?" asked Poppy, unsure she was following her grandmother.

"I am saying my days as a maid and cook are over. I have already let Mr. Carrington know that I won't be back. I have listed her house in Collierville. I plan to move to her condo at the beach. I will have to pay her medical bills, but even after that, if I am frugal, I can live on the money for the rest of my life. You know how much I love the beach. This is a dream come true. I can't wait. In fact, I am planning to move by Christmas. I can't wait for you to come and see it. And even better, I will be able to help you out with money when you need it. I don't want you working when you need to be studying."

"Oh Gran. You don't have to worry about that. In fact, I have been meaning to call you and tell you that I am getting married." Poppy did not decide to take Tommy up on his offer until she heard her grandmother talking about moving to Gulf Shores. She knew that if Gran thought she was pregnant and alone in the big, bad city, she would leave the beach and move to the city to help her raise her son. She could not do that to her. She had already raised her mom and her. It was her time to rest.

"What in the world are you talking about?" demanded Gran.

Poppy could tell her grandmother was dumbfounded. Poppy knew she needed to sell this to Gran, or she would be on the next plane to New York. "Tommy is the best man I have ever known. He is kind, considerate, and cares about me. He will never hurt me. He has asked me to marry him, and I said."

"What about art school?" asked Gran.

"Tommy wants me to continue; he insisted on it."

Gran was quiet for a moment, then she asked, "Do you love him?"

If she had asked if Poppy was in love with him, she would have broken and told her the whole story. But she didn't, and the truth was she did love Tommy and their friendship.

"Yes, Gran, I love him."

Poppy and Tommy married over Christmas in Gulf Shores at Gran's. They returned to New York in January and started preparing for the baby they had already fallen in love with.

Chapter 12

Carrington Kitchen
Searcy, Arkansas
November 27, 2023

"Well, there you go. That is the story of how I ended up married to Tommy. It's a doozy, isn't it," said Poppy with a self-deprecating laugh.

"It is beyond a doozy. And you were just nineteen. You were still nineteen when you delivered, right? Just a baby having a baby," replied Harvey Cox, who had already begun to pack up his things. "This is a good place to take a break in your story. You said earlier that you need to pick up your girls after school. Would it be okay if I came back tomorrow and we picked it up then?"

Nodding, Poppy walked Harvey to the front door and said, "Yes, that is fine. It takes a long time to retell a love affair over twenty years in the making. Sometimes I can't believe it has been so long."

Waving as he headed to his car, Harvey said, "If the next twenty are as crazy as the first year, this is going to be quite the article."

Closing the door, Poppy thought to herself, "You have no idea."

Carrington House
Searcy, Arkansas
November 28, 2023

The next day, as Poppy waited for Harvey to arrive, she sat outside on the heated patio. It still amazed Poppy that rich people did things like heat their patios. She now had made a nice following as an artist and was financially set in her own right, but she would never think of herself as a "rich person." In her mind, she would always be the maid's granddaughter. One of her fears about sharing this story was that it would also be how the public would see her. She would forever be the help's granddaughter who trapped the rich guy.

Poppy was still thinking about this when Harvey Cox showed up with a steaming cup of coffee from Midnight Oil for her and a large soda from Sonic for him. When he came in, he handed Poppy hers and said, "Two creams and two sweeteners? Right?"

Taking the cup, Poppy said, "Perfect. How did you remember that?"

"It is my job to notice things like that," he said with a smile. "So, where do you want to do this today?"

Walking into the living room, Poppy sat on one sofa and gestured for Harvey to sit on the one across from her. "I thought we would start in here today."

Setting up his recorder and getting out his notepad and pen, Harvey settled in and got ready to get to work. "Okay, when you left off yesterday, you told me about how you ended up married to Tommy Thompson and were preparing to have your son."

"Yes, what do you want to know next?"

"Well, when did you see Bennett again?"

"Oh, not until the winter of 2011. He came to see me to ask me to do a fundraiser for the Searcy hospital like the one I did for a hospital in Gulf Shores," replied Poppy.

"What was your life like between the time you married Tommy and saw Bennett again?" asked Harvey.

"Oh wow, it was hectic. Ben was born on April Fool's Day, 2001. Thanks to Tommy and Jack, I was able to finish school and even get my master's degree. I took a position teaching at the Art Institute."

"Let me interrupt you, just a second. Ben mentioned Jack as well. What was his full name, and how did he come into your life?" asked Harvey.

"Jack Masters was the love of Tommy's life. Well, him and Ben," replied Poppy.

"Do you know that your voice always softens when you talk about Tommy? You were married for over seven years. Were the two of you ever a real couple?"

Poppy could not hold back the bark of laughter that erupted from her at the question. "Lord, no. It was never like that between us. But I don't know what I would have done without him. He changed the trajectory of my life. He was like my brother. My very gay brother. He met Jack a few months after we got married. They met at one of Tommy's gallery shows. He came home with him and never left. The delivery room was a little crowded the day Ben was born, as all three of us did it together. I would never have made it without them."

"Okay, I got it. Sounds like you had a wonderful support team in them. That had to be a hard time for you. Did you ever have a moment where you thought you should contact Bennett and tell him he had a son?"

"Of course, I was lonely and missing Bennett. The worst was when Gran told me that Bennett and Taylor had married. I found out a few weeks before Ben was born. Truthfully, if I had not known they were married, I would have broken and called him the day Ben was born and begged him to come to us. But they had. Plus, I had promised Tommy he would be Ben's dad. I had to honor that promise. In the end, Ben got two great dads.

"Our life in New York settled into a comfortable routine. Tommy's health began to decline in 2005. He continued to paint and had his last show in the spring of that year. Jack quit his job to take care of Tommy and Ben full time. By this time, Tommy's paintings were selling for a ridiculous amount of money and I continued to teach at the Institute. By early 2007, Tommy was put on hospice. He passed away in Jack's arms in February of that year. I finally understood how Bennett must have felt when Tatum died. It took me a long time to come to peace with being unable to pick up the phone and call him. I can still hear his voice in my head. He was such a loving, giving, kind man. I miss him every day of my life. Poor Jack; if not for Ben, I think he would have had a nervous breakdown. That was why I was so happy when he met Jorge. The light came back in his eyes. I selfishly hated that he moved to Napa, but honestly, I am so happy they found each other. It made sending Ben to school out there so much easier."

"When did Jack marry and move?" asked Harvey.

"Umm, let's see. It was the summer of 2011."

"So you and Ben were alone for the first time beginning then?"

"Yes, it was an adjustment. I had never had to think about childcare. Of course, Ben was ten by then and did not think he needed a sitter. I am sure you can imagine how that went," said Poppy with a look.

Harvey, who had two teenage boys, replied, "Absolutely. Let's talk about your art for a minute. When did you begin the *Growing Up New York* series?"

"I started it during my master's program and continued adding pieces through Christmas 2011. Jack's idea was to make sure the icons of New York were incorporated into each picture after 9-11. Once the towers were gone, we knew we wanted to do something authentic that showcased our beautiful city. Personally, I wanted to document Ben's life.

"Down deep in the most secret part of my heart, I never stopped mourning not being able to share Ben's life with Bennett. It was my way of doing that. Somehow, I knew someday he would see the pictures and be able to share in art what he missed in life."

"Wow. That is amazing. So, you worked on the pieces for over a decade. How many pieces did you complete in all?"

"There are thirty paintings in the collection," said Poppy proudly.

"Where are they now?" asked Harvey.

"The whole collection is a part of a permanent exhibit at the Emerson Childhood Museum in New York. The museum is a celebration of childhood. I still own the originals, but they pay a yearly stipend for the right to show them."

"How did you get into doing art fundraisers for hospitals?" asked Harvey.

"That came about after Gran had her heart attack. Thank goodness for Greer Stone. He is a miracle worker. He was Gran's surgeon. She would not have made it if that hospital had not been there. At the time, the hospital was struggling financially. As a thank you to Dr. Stone and the hospital, I offered to do a fundraiser. I arranged to do a traveling exhibit of the pieces and to sell signed, numbered, and framed prints of the work. I also donated two original pieces to be raffled."

"So that was how Edna Stone found out about you?" asked Harvey.

"Yes, she started emailing and calling me about doing the same thing in Searcy. I was totally against it. In fact, I told her I was never stepping foot back in Searcy. That just goes to show you to never say never," said Poppy with a laugh.

"So if you said no, how did you end up doing the show in March 2012?"

"Because Bennett came to see me," replied Poppy.

"Really," said Harvey. "That sounds interesting."

"Oh, it was," replied Poppy.

The Art Institute
New York, New York
February 2012

Poppy was finishing up her Human Form drawing class when Bennett slipped into the class. At first, she did not see him. He stood in the back of the room, leaning casually against the back of the classroom, watching her.

Walking around the room talking with students, Poppy said, "Great work, Sabrina. I can see real improvement in your shading." Moving to another student, she said, "Pat, this is your best work yet; Catherine, Daryn, and Julee, you have really improved since last week. Melissa I love the shading." Looking over to the next student she said, "Donna you ...." Whatever she was going to say next was lost as her eyes landed on Bennett, and all rational thoughts fled.

Quickly recovering herself, Poppy instructed the students that they had done enough for the day and to pack up. The students only took a few minutes to collect their things and quickly exit the room. The whole time, Poppy ignored Bennett until everyone was gone.

When it was just the two of them, Poppy looked at him and said, "Senator, what the hell are you doing interrupting my class?"

Bennett gave her a look and said, "Look, I am not any happier about this than you are. But, I owe Edna Stone a favor."

Whatever Poppy expected Bennett to say, it wasn't that. "Edna Stone? The lady who keeps calling me trying to get me to come to Searcy to do a fundraiser?"

"Yes, one and the same. She has been a huge contributor to my campaigns over the years. She has called my office several times asking me to approach you about the fundraiser given our past."

Poppy blanched, "How in the world would she know about that?"

Bennett frowned at her and said, "Not that past. The fact your Gran was our housekeeper. She mistakenly thought you might change your mind if I approached you. I tried to tell her I had no influence over you, but she insisted. She said you have done some amazing series about growing up in New York.

Edna says it is fabulous. So, here I am. Asking you again, will you please come to Searcy to do for our hospital what you did for the one her nephew works at?"

For several seconds, Poppy said nothing. She just looked at Bennett. Words would not come. He was so close she could smell his cologne. It was all she could do to keep herself from launching herself into his arms and begging him to take her right there on the floor of her classroom. All rational, reasonable thought was gone.

When she said nothing, Bennett added, frowning even more, "If the answer is no, just tell me now. I will get out of your hair. I can then tell Edna I tried."

"Do you want me to come and do it?" Poppy had no idea why she asked that question. What difference would it make if he did? She knew she could never go back. That part of her life was over. She had tried to tell Mrs. Stone that.

"I think the better question would be how would your husband feel about you doing it?" replied Bennett.

The mention of Tommy was so unexpected that Poppy almost gasped. She lowered her head and took a deep breath. Then, looking back up at Bennett, Poppy said, "Tommy passed away in 2007. But if he were here, he would want me to do whatever I wanted to do."

At her words, heat flared in Bennett's eyes. Poppy had seen it too many times before to miss it. Without breaking eye contact, he said, "Well, then, what do you want to do?"

Poppy was not sure they were even talking about a fundraiser anymore. Quietly, she said, "I don't know. What do you think I should do? Should I come back to Searcy or not?"

They just looked at each other; Bennett seemed to pull back mentally. He smiled and said, "I think it would do wonders for our hospital and community. I hope you will seriously consider it."

She knew she could not go back. She knew she could not exhibit her art there without all her secrets being blown wide open. Her mind was made up; she was never going back. But, her heart was not so sure. Before she could stop herself, she said, "I will do it on one condition. You go to the Emerson Museum and look at the originals. If you still want me to do it, I will."

Poppy did not for a moment think that once Bennett saw the pictures of his son, he would want her to show them to the world. But, she stupidly hoped that he might realize he had a son by seeing them. Ben had lost two dads. He needed his real one. Seeing the pictures could spark something between the two of them.

"I don't think that is necessary. I am sure your work is terrific."

"I will only come if you go and look at it, and tell me you want me to show it in Searcy after you see it."

Nodding, Bennett said, "Of course." He reached in to hug her goodbye.

The minute his arms went around her, Poppy felt like she had come home after a long trip to a sad and dreary place.

Instinctively, Bennett pulled her closer and held her tightly. They stayed like that for a few minutes. Neither one wanted to pull away. Bennett's lips grazed her neck, and it was just before working their way up to her lips when his phone buzzed.

Instantly, they both jumped apart. He pointed to the phone and said, "I have to take this. It was great to see you. I hope you will come and do the show. I will go to the gallery right now and see it. I will let you know." Bennett left the classroom, and Poppy collapsed in the nearest chair.

Chapter 13

Carrington House
Searcy, Arkansas
November 28, 2023

"Sounds like all the old feelings just came roaring back the minute you saw him after all those years?" asked Harvey Cox.

"The feelings never went anywhere. They were always there. They were just buried under a lot of hurt and pain. Eleven years dulls the pain of being cheated on and lied to. It shouldn't, but trust me, it does," replied Poppy.

"So what happened next? Did Bennett go and see the paintings? Did he realize he had a son?"

"No. Bennett, being Bennett, had a work thing come up as he left my classroom. The call he got was from the Anderson campaign. They told him he was being vetted for the vice-presidential spot, and they had to meet with him that day. So instead of going to Emerson as promised, he called one of his staffers, Kelly, to go and look at the paintings."

"If he did not go that day, when did he see them?" asked Harvey.

"The day of the incident at the club. That was the first time he saw them. That was how he found out. Twenty minutes before the luncheon started, he found me making final preparations on the exhibit and hauled me into that library room."

"You are telling me he had no idea until then?"

"Correct. The staffer he sent told him the exhibit was great and to give his approval. The next day, I got a text from him saying he was good with the exhibit. He told me he would be tied up with a new political opportunity for a few weeks and would like to talk soon. He also said he would be in DC for several weeks and gave me his office number if I needed anything.

"How did he get your cell number?" asked Harvey.

"From Edna Stone," replied Poppy.

"Makes sense," replied Harvey. "What happened next?"

"What happened next is that I got mad. I mean, I got really, really mad. At this point, I am still thinking he has seen the paintings. I had expected some reaction from him. I don't know exactly what, but something. I would have expected him to demand some answers, and demand to know his son. I knew I was opening Pandora's box when I sent him to see the paintings. I guess part of me wanted that from him. Some kind of a fight to prove that he cared. That he was the kind of man I always thought he was before he cheated on me. But I got that super casual message giving me the exhibit's go-ahead. I was so angry that I picked up the phone and called Edna Stone. I thought, if he did not care enough about his child to ask any questions, what did I care about what this might do to his 'new political opportunity'? Of course, after I booked it, I had hours of worry and regret that I was doing the wrong thing by going."

"I can see that. Question, how did Greer Stone end up your date?"

"Oh, that. After I was totally committed and had already had the work crated and sent to Arkansas, I found out about the gala. I tried to get out of attending. Being in a room with Bennett and his wife with our son's pictures everywhere sounded horrible. I don't know if you have met Edna Stone, but she is a force of nature. She would not take no for an answer. When I told her I did not have anyone I could bring as a plus one, she said she would take care of it. A week later, I got a text from Greer saying he would be my date.

"You know, in all the years I was alone, I was too busy raising my son, caring for my dying friend, and building my career to worry too much about dating. Before Bennett showed up in my classroom, I was ready to start dating again. I had even considered Greer and wondered if he and I might be a good match. Gran was still in Gulf Shores. I had thought the next time I was in town, I might try and see if there was anything there. One look into Bennett's eyes, one minute back in his arms, I was done for. Loving Bennett is like a lifelong disease that can go into remission, but you never can get totally over."

"Ouch! A disease, huh?" asked Harvey. "I hope my wife never refers to our love like that."

"Okay, that was a little extreme. But, you get what I am saying," said Poppy.

"I do, "replied Harvey. "so, let's get back to the story. When exactly did Bennett first see the pictures? How did he react?"

"How did he react? Aw, he exploded," replied Poppy.

"Oh, this is getting good. I can't imagine Bennett Carrington ever losing his cool."

"Oh, he did, and then some. You have to understand. Bennett figured it out before he saw the pictures or at least the possibility of it. The night before the luncheon, he overheard the staffer he sent to see the exhibit in New York talking about it. They worked late in DC. Bennett was scheduled to fly to Searcy later that week for the gala. Many of the staffers were coming with him. They talked about what to wear, and someone asked about the art. I guess Kelly gave a brief explanation, but one part caught Bennett's ear. She loved the piece that showed Ben at his first birthday party in a shirt that said, "I am my Mom's Best April Fool's Gift."

"After work that night, Bennett asked her to stay. He wondered if she was sure about the birthday picture. Kelly assured him she was. It stood out to her because it was so funny. At that point, Bennett pulled some strings by the next day and had a copy of Ben's birth certificate.

"Ben had been three weeks early, but Bennett did not know that. He looked at the dates, and it clicked. I don't think he totally accepted that Ben was his, though, until he saw the pictures.

"I found out later that February, after we broke up, Bennett, Taylor, and Mr. Carrington were having dinner at the club. Out of the blue, Mr. Carrington told Bennett that he talked to my grandmother. She shared that I had gotten married and was having a baby in June.

"Obviously, that was not true. It was just what I told Gran to keep her from being upset. Mr. Carrington told Bennett that because he had been really down after we broke up. He wanted Bennett to snap out of it and move on with someone more appropriate. That was exactly what he did. Based on the dates, he knew the baby was not his. That night, when he took Taylor home, he supposedly proposed. They married less than a month later."

"Wow. There is a lot to unpack there. You brought up two different issues. Before we go deeper into Bennett's reaction to the news, you mentioned Bennett's relationship with Taylor."

Poppy, who had been very forthcoming, got very quiet. "You know, I am not comfortable talking about my husband's first marriage. I only mentioned it so you would understand why Bennett had never questioned if he was Ben's dad."

"I respect that," said Harvey. "Actually, she said something similar about your marriage to Bennett. Okay, let's backtrack. So, Bennett overhears a conversation the night before the luncheon, giving him pause. He pulls Ben's birth certificate. He sees the dates. What does he do then?" asked Harvey.

"He came charging into the Searcy Country Club like his hair was on fire."

Searcy Country Club
Searcy, Arkansas
March 2012

Poppy wanted to get to the club early to make sure everything was ready. But, she overslept and got to the club late. She was worried because the chairperson had said Mrs. Stone liked everyone on time. She slipped in the back and was making sure everything was ready. She was just about to head into the main room to meet up with Edna Stone and the other ladies putting this event together when Bennett stormed in and grabbed her by the arm.

"How could you? How could you keep my son from me?" Bennett was practically yelling.

"Shhh, someone is going to hear you," Poppy admonished.

"I could give two shits." Dragging her a short distance to the library room, Bennett followed Poppy in and shut the door.

Grabbing her by both arms, he pulled her to him and growled, "He is my son. Admit it. You have kept him from me all these years. Admit it."

Tears threatened to fall as Poppy said, "Yes, he is yours. But.."

"No buts. How could you do this? How could you keep him from me? How? I loved you so much. I would have moved heaven and earth for both of you." The look of devastation in Bennett's eyes was almost her undoing. All those years ago, she had thought she was doing the right thing. Now, she was not so sure. He was squeezing her arms so hard it was starting to hurt.

Trembling, she said, "Bennett, please, you are hurting me."

Bennett loosened his grip but did not let go of her. "Why? Why would you do this to me?"

Shaking her head, trying to gather her thoughts, she said, "I know this does not make any sense, but you have to remember I was only nineteen. I was alone in a big city. You lied to me and cheated on me. I did not think I could trust you. I did not want my son to be another one of your dirty little secrets. I knew how much your future career meant to you. If word got out that you had knocked up your maid's granddaughter, your future would've been dead. I knew you would try to marry me and do the right thing. But over time, you would resent us. I could not go through that. So, I cut ties and moved on, making the best of a bad situation."

"Moved on is right. You call me out of nowhere on the night before Thanksgiving, disappear without so much as a word goodbye, and then you are married by Christmas. Talk about moving at the speed of light."

"You are a liar and a cheat. I do not owe you a damn thing. Not then. Not now."

"I don't know what the hell you are talking about, but I do know you owe me a hell of a lot. I am going to start collecting right now."

With that, Bennett swept her up in the most punishing, angry embrace of her life. It carried all the pent-up passion, anger, sorrow, and heat building up for over ten years. It was a brutal, punishing kiss that left her starving for more. In an instant, Bennett reached down and ripped the buttons off the front of her dress and tore her bra with it. Burying his face in her still-perfect bosom, he lost himself in her as she lost herself in the sensations he was generating in her. Pushing her back onto the closest table, Bennett bent her back. Without pause, he was just about to reach under her dress and touch her more intimately when he heard his wife call his name.

"Taylor?" called Bennett as Poppy shoved him hard in the chest, and the two of them collapsed in a sea of red hair as half of the women of Searcy looked on.

Carrington House
Searcy, Arkansas
November 28, 2023

"That sounds like it was a very traumatic day. What did you do once the ladies left the room?" asked Harvey.

"I did what I always do when I get scared. I ran. Before he chased out after Taylor and the others, Bennett emphatically warned me to go to the hotel and wait for him. I was not in the mood to listen. I got in my little rental car and drove as fast as possible to Little Rock. Then, thanks to Joules, I took the next flight to New York," replied Poppy.

"Was Bennett mad that you left?" asked Harvey.

"Blindingly mad. He left me several blistering voice messages before I even landed. He was mad about it all, my leaving, not telling him about Ben, the fact he still wanted me, you name it. He was furious about everything. Ben was staying at a friend's house as I was not expected back for several days. I got home early Tuesday morning. I was so tired I went to bed and slept all day.

I only let Ben know I was back on Wednesday afternoon when I showed up for his baseball game after school. I needed a little time to think. Joules had already called me to make sure I got home safely. She told me the crazy scheme that had been cooked up for all of us to attend the gala in Searcy. I told her that was not going to happen. She begged me to reconsider, as it would destroy the fundraiser for the hospital. At that point, I could have cared less. That fundraiser was the least of my concerns. I remember telling her that Bennett could do what Bennett wanted to do. It had nothing to do with me. Brave words from a woman who was running scared."

Harvey looked at Poppy and said, "What did Bennett do next?"

"He showed up Wednesday afternoon at Ben's ball game. How he even knew Ben played ball or how to find us is beyond me. I guess that is something I should ask him someday. Anyway, I was sitting in the stands yelling like a crazy person when I looked up and saw Bennett off to the side. I nearly had a heart attack. At that point, Ben knew nothing about Bennett. I could not have him show up and announce himself as Ben's dad. I understood why Bennett was upset. Fine, he had every right to be mad at me. But, when it came to Ben, all bets were off.

"Ben had already had enough trauma in his life, losing his father and Jack moving to Cali. Bennett was going to follow my timetable with Ben or else," replied Poppy.

"It got pretty heated. We were both yelling. Bennett demanded that I tell him why I had preferred a sham marriage to a gay man than to marriage with him. Until Bennett knew Tommy was gay, he assumed my marriage had been real. I yelled back "because it was the only choice I had."

"That fired him up, and he yelled, "Like hell it was!" At one point, Ben's coach came over to see if everything was okay. I could see Ben. He was worried that his mom and a stranger were getting into it. To defuse an escalating situation, I got Bennett to promise to sit down and watch the rest of the game without calling attention to us. He promised not to tell Ben who he was until I gave him the okay to do so if I agreed to return to Searcy for the gala. I unhappily agreed.

"After the game, I introduced Bennett to Ben. I will never forget the look on Bennett's face when his son stuck out his hand and introduced himself properly, as Jack had taught him to do with adults.

"It was a game tradition for all the kids and parents to go for pizza afterward. I had not intended to invite Bennett. It did not matter. He invited himself. I was relieved that he introduced himself as Bennett without mentioning him being a senator.

"Even though I was a nervous wreck, for the most part, the night went fine without issue until it was time to leave.

"Ben's best friend's dad was the coach. He had been divorced for about two years and made it clear he was interested in being more than friends with me. Before Bennett came to my classroom, I was open to it. Now, I knew it was hopeless, but I needed a buffer between me and Bennett. If McNeil could offer that, I would not be above using it.

"McNeil sat next to me in the booth at the pizza place. He got me a drink and offered to pick up the ticket. Bennett never broke a sweat. He calmly paid the bill and took McNeil's seat when he went to the bathroom. As we got ready to leave, McNeil walked out with us. He hailed a cab and held the door for Ben and me to go with him. Before we could get in, a long black town car pulled up. Bennett let him know we were going with him. I assumed we would head to our apartment.

"Instead, Bennett told Ben he had an amazing penthouse hotel room with an incredible view. Ben begged to see it. The next thing I knew, we were all on the balcony looking at the stars. Then, Bennett encouraged Ben to order a dessert from room service, and they stayed up watching a movie. It was a school night, but every time I tried to make a move to leave, Bennett would beg for a little more time. I agreed because, honestly, I loved seeing them together.

"Ben fell asleep on the couch. I ended up sleeping in the guest room," said Poppy.

"What was the relationship like between you and Bennett? You said he was very mad, and it got heated at the game. How did he treat you once Ben went to sleep?" asked Harvey.

"I need to make something clear. Bennett has always treated me well. He would never physically hurt me. If anything, it was the opposite. He was so sweet, so kind, so Bennett. It was tough to resist him. But, remember, at this time, he was still very married. He told me that his marriage was over and that it had been for a while. He kept saying that he was coming for me as soon as he was free. It was so much like what my own father had said to my mom before her death that it spooked me. I tried to stay in the moment and not let my heart get away from me.

"The worst part was he shared with me that he was in the vetting process for vice-president. By this point, he had decided to forgo the vice-presidential spot for a possible cabinet position. He was going to spend the next few months stumping for Anderson. He could not afford a scandal. He explained that we had to keep Ben a secret to have any chance for an opportunity.

"It was exactly what I had tried so hard to avoid with the decisions I made years before. That fact alone helped cool Bennett's anger. It was hard to be mad at me when we were right back where we were from day one."

"You were right. Even with all you did to keep Ben from being put in that position, it still happened," replied Harvey. "What happened next?"

"Well, this is where it starts to get sticky. McNeil agreed to keep Ben for a long weekend. True to my promise, I flew back to Searcy with Bennett on his plane."

Chapter 14

Capital Hotel
Little Rock, Arkansas
March 2012

The flight from New York to Little Rock was filled with hungry looks and unfulfilled desires. Poppy brought a book to read and a headset to listen to classical music, but neither was used.

Bennett and Poppy were the only passengers other than the pilots. Once airborne, Bennett softly took her hand and held it the way he had the first time they had flown together all those years ago when she had left for art school. It was too loud for conversation, so neither tried. Instead, they spent the whole time innocently touching each other's hands, arms, and faces. The looks they shared said more than a thousand page book. Poppy nearly came out of her seat belt when Bennett reached out, took her hand, lifted it to his lips, and licked her wrist before kissing it softly.

When they landed, Bennett and Poppy loaded up in his SUV and drove to the Capital Hotel. Poppy knew it was a terrible idea for Bennett to follow her to her hotel room. God forgive her, she was too far gone to do anything other than follow his lead. Bennett had held several lunch meetings and attended functions there for years. He knew he couldn't just walk in the front door unnoticed. Instead, he had Joules check in early and then meet them in the parking lot with the key. The look Joules gave him could have taken two years off his life, but if Bennett saw it, he did not respond to it.

Once they slipped inside Poppy's hotel suit without being seen, they fell into each other in a passionate embrace. Picking her up, Bennett carried her into the bedroom. Laying her on the bed without breaking the kiss, he reached for her zipper. It was then that Poppy pulled back.

"We can't do this," said Poppy breathlessly.

Leaning toward her to recapture her lips, Bennett responded, "Oh yes, we can, and we are going to, several times."

Rolling away from him and jumping off the other side of the bed, Poppy said, "I don't mean we can't, I mean we aren't. I am not going to be your piece on the side. You are still married, in case you have forgotten."

Groaning loudly, Bennett said, "Not this again. I told you. I am getting a divorce. It is you. It has always been you. We belong together. We are going to be together."

Poppy said, shaking her head, "That may be true, but we are not going to have sex. Not today. Not any day until you are free. It almost destroyed me when you cheated on me. I won't do that to Taylor."

"Hate to break it to you, but she is convinced we already have," replied Bennett, sitting on the bed and putting his head in his hands." And for the record, I have never cheated on you. Never. I don't know why you keep saying that."

"Because I saw you," replied Poppy, almost crying, thinking back on that day.

Bennett took a deep breath and said, "Okay, since this," he pointed between himself and her and the bed, "isn't happening, let's get a drink and go over what it is you think you saw when you say I cheated on you."

Thinking it over, Poppy nodded.

"Also, I know that it is two in the afternoon. However, if I have to spend my time with you in a hotel talking instead of doing what I want to be doing, then I will do it lying next to you in bed."

Looking at her dress and heels, he added, "Change into something comfortable, and by that, I mean a whole lot fewer clothes. I promise to be good, but it has been a long time since I laid beside you in a soft bed. I am not waiting another minute to do that. I am going to fix us a drink. Wine okay?"

Poppy nodded and then went into the bathroom to change. She changed into an over-sized tee shirt. She took off her bra but left on her panties. When she came out, Bennett was standing in his boxers with two glasses of wine in his hands. He handed one to her and kept the other.

"Did you forget about the part where I said no sex? I mean it, Bennett," declared Poppy as if she were repeating this as much for her sake as for his.

Frowning, Bennett replied, "If I had forgotten, you would already be naked, on your back, three seconds from screaming my name in ecstasy. So chill. We are just going to talk."

Seeing her tee shirt, he said, "I know it is wrong to ask, but it has been so long. Please take off the tee shirt and let me see them. I have missed them so much."

Poppy did not need to ask whom or, rather, what he was talking about. She hesitated for a moment, and then, seeing the almost begging look in his eyes, she shrugged and pulled off her tee shirt, giving him a full view of her luscious breasts.

He audibly gasped. He came towards to touch her.

Poppy scooted out of reach. "Oh no, you don't. No touching."

Bennett frowned and then nodded. Moving to the side of the bed, he threw back the covers on the bed and said, "Get in. Let's talk."

Once they were both comfortable, Bennett hauled her in and snuggled her. At first, Poppy tried to argue, but Bennett kissed her softly and said, "I just want to hold you. No funny business. I promise. Now tell me why you think I cheated."

"Because you did. I saw you," replied Poppy.

"You saw me when and with whom?" asked Bennett.

Poppy recounted the story of how that long ago Thanksgiving holiday when she had seen Taylor in his shower, the indentations on the pillows in his bed, and him in a towel in the kitchen, whistling.

When she finished, Bennett sat up in the bed, looked at her hard, and said, "Now, would you like me to tell you what really happened that morning?"

"What do you mean really happened?" replied Poppy. "All of that really happened."

"Yes, but not the way you think," said Bennett. "First of all, you are right. I did lay down with her the night before, but just as friends. It was her first Thanksgiving without her family. She drank too much and was crying. I was comforting her. We were looking at old yearbooks and photo albums. I stayed with her until she fell asleep, in her clothes. I slept upstairs in the guest room. I took a shower there. I was so excited about seeing you that I decided to drive to Memphis and talk you into coming back to Searcy early. Just thinking about you got me excited. I was wrapped in a towel because I needed to get some clothes out of the laundry. If you had just stopped and talked to me, our whole lives would have been different."

Poppy looked at him for a moment and said, "Oh my God. So you didn't cheat on me?" The look of shock on her face was genuine.

"No, Red, I would never have cheated on you. You were my whole world. When you left, it nearly destroyed me."

"Oh, Bennett, I am so sorry," said Poppy as she wrapped her arms around him and held him close. "Things would have been so different if I had known. I am sorry I did not talk to you."

Bennett held her without saying anything, then said, "You were not the only one who jumped to conclusions."

Looking up at him, Poppy said, "What do you mean?"

"Well, after you went MIA that Thanksgiving and stopped taking my calls, I flew to New York. I hid out at your school and planned to demand you tell me why you left. I saw you with the guy you married. You came out of the building. Before I could approach you, he hugged and kissed you. I was close enough to hear him say, "Come on, you hot momma. Let's get home. I am freezing out here."

"I hate to admit it, but I followed you. You stopped off at the grocery and picked up food. Once you returned to the apartment I figured out was his, I waited outside for you to leave all night. I saw you the next morning, leaving with him for class. He kissed you and said he would see you for dinner. I could not believe you were living with a guy so quickly. I was so angry and hurt. I went home to Searcy to lick my wounds. At first, I vowed to never speak to you again. Then, I decided to wait for you to get this guy out of your system. You were young. Maybe you felt like you needed some more life experiences before you settled on one guy. So, I decided to wait. Then, my dad told me you were married and had a baby coming in June. I literally threw up at the club after he told me. I did some quick math. I knew the baby wasn't mine. I knew it was over. It was the worst day of my life. If I had gotten up the courage to approach you and forced you to talk to me, our lives would have been different. So, see, we are both to blame."

Poppy was quiet for a moment and then said, "Well, as much as I hate to say it, I just don't think it was our time. You would not be a current US Senator if we had gotten together eleven years ago. You would have had to give up on your political dreams. I could not have been responsible for that. Also, remember, I was only a nineteen-year-old orphan kid. I did not have the life experience to deal with all that. Please forgive me for not telling you about Ben. I did what I thought was best based on what I knew then."

"I know, Baby." Taking her face in his hands, he looked deeply into her eyes and said, "I know. He is such a great kid. You have done an amazing job. Thank you. What a gift you have given me."

They kissed long and softly. When they pulled back, Bennett said, "We have to talk about when you plan to tell him I am his father. I want him to have my name. The sooner, the better."

Poppy shook her head and pulled back both mentally and physically. "We can't do that as long as you are campaigning for Anderson. As a candidate for a cabinet position, you are a fodder for the press. They would love nothing more than to run a story about your baby momma and bastard son. I won't let that happen. As long as you are married, we keep this to ourselves. We will tell him when the time is right."

Bennett pulled her back to him and then placed his forehead on hers. "I hate it, but you are right. The best thing to do is to call Anderson and take my name off all shortlists. Then, resign my post and ask Taylor for a super quick divorce."

Poppy pulled back so fast that she almost fell out of the bed, "Oh no, you won't. You have worked your whole life for this moment. I refuse to be the reason you walk away from all you have built. There has to be another way."

Bennett stood and started pacing around the room. "The only other option is to stay married until the end of the election. After I am confirmed for a cabinet post, Taylor and I can divorce quietly. You and I could then marry. No one gets fired up about divorces of cabinet members."

Considering what he said, Poppy asked, "How long would all that take?"

Bennett was quiet for a moment and then said, "Well, it is March now. The election is in November. Cabinet members will be confirmed by February. So, a year at the most. Maybe sooner."

"A year?" The words sounded hollow to Poppy. She had gone eleven years without, and now the thought of going one more was unfathomable. "Have you talked to Taylor? What does she say about all this? Will she even agree to a divorce?"

"I have told Taylor that I am in love with you and want a divorce. She is processing that. In the end, she will grant the divorce. She is not in love with me and never has been. We should have never married. It was a rebound thing to try and get over you. It did not work. I hate to say this, but I am glad we could never have children. I would have hated to put them through a divorce. But I would have. Now that I have you back, I am never giving you up. Do you understand?"

Poppy nodded. "Just promise me we will both ask questions and demand answers before jumping to conclusions."

Bennett said, "I promise. I think I have an idea of how we can navigate the next few months. What do you think about taking Ben out of school and homeschooling him for the rest of the year? I have a buddy who has a fabulous house on Caswell Beach. You two could stay there. It is only a short flight from DC. I could come down and stay on weekends. I could get to know Ben. It is a three-bedroom house. We would all have our own rooms. You could paint. The house is right on the beach. What do you think?"

Poppy gave him a look that said he was insane. She took a deep breath, let it out, and said, "I will think about it."

"Well, okay then," replied Bennett. Checking his watch, he said, we have about three hours before we have to head to Searcy. "Want to fool around?" He winked at her, and she could not help but laugh.

"As long as our underwear stays on. I am serious about not having sex until you are free."

Bennett said, "Okay, underwear stays on. For tonight. I reserve the right to re-negotiate in the future." With that, Poppy and Bennett spent the afternoon reacquainting themselves with each other, sharing stories, kisses, and laughing at the most surprising things.

Chapter 15

Carrington House
Searcy, Arkansas
November 28, 2023

"Sounds like the two of you just picked right back up where you left off," replied Harvey Cox.

"Yeah, you know how that is true of close friends? Well, it turns out it is even more true of soulmates," replied Poppy.

"Is that how you see Bennett? As your soulmate?"

"Oh, yeah. Definitely. But even though we were soulmates, it did not mean our love story was easy after this. We knew we wanted to be together, but we still had a lot of obstacles ahead of us. One was that when we were together, it was hard to remember he was still married. I am proud to say we never broke his marriage vows, but we did push it to the limit: stolen kisses, soft touches, and intimate moments that pushed our control.

"The night of the gala, we came so close to losing it. Bennett was supposed to pick up Taylor. Things got out of hand, and he had to call Joules to get her. I felt so guilty walking into that club with him. Everyone could tell we had spent the afternoon necking like hormonal teenagers.

"Greer was waiting just inside the door. I remember walking in, thinking, how is this my life? I was so dreading having to talk to Taylor. But, as you know, that did not happen. Taylor collapsed when she saw me. I felt so guilty; all I wanted to do was run back to the hotel. Shockingly to me, Bennett was concerned about Taylor, but he grabbed my arm, held me close, and insisted that I not run. It took all that I had not to, but I trusted him and didn't."

"What happened next?" asked Harvey.

"I decided to do as Bennett asked. I switched Ben to homeschooling and moved to Caswell Beach in North Carolina. Bennett rented the house from his buddy. It had three bedrooms, so there was plenty of room for all of us. The hardest part was that Ben had to leave his friends and quit his baseball team. I had to decide between keeping him there and giving him a chance to get to know his father. I chose the latter. Every weekend, Bennett would spend the weekend with us."

"You have said earlier that you two never broke his marriage vows. How hard was that once you were settled at the beach?" asked Harvey.

"So hard. When you find the person you want to spend the rest of your life with, you want that life to begin immediately. Our life was on hold, marking time. For a couple like Bennett and I, who have always had a very strong physical attraction, denying that for weeks on end, after years of being celibate was difficult. Not going to lie. There were many nights I wanted to chuck my whole "I don't want to be the other woman" mantra out the window and jump his bones. But I did not. There is more than one reason I did not, but the main one was I did not want to be that person. Only I get to decide what kind of person I will be. I did not want to be a person who cheated, and so I held to that, even when it was hard. Even when it hurt. Even when it made Bennett mad as hell. Even when it made no sense to anyone except me. And, you know what, I am proud of that decision. Maybe it is because I was so embarrassed my mom did it, but I am glad I can sit here today to say I stuck to my guns. For all the things I did wrong in my life, and oh my, there are a lot of them, I never slept with another woman's husband. It isn't much, but it is something."

"I agree with you. That is something to be proud of. I must ask; you said there were other reasons you did not cheat. Can you share those?" asked Harvey.

"Well, another reason was that Bennett was killing himself, traveling around the country, campaigning twenty hours a day. He would roll in every Saturday morning around four in the morning and get about three hours of sleep. Get up, play catch, go fishing, play chess, go swim, whatever Bennett wanted to do all day Saturday and Sunday. Then, he would fly out Sunday night around ten to be wherever he was needed the next day. On days he was not campaigning, he was in DC trying to catch up on his work there. The man worked fourteen-sixteen hour days. He was exhausted most of the time. When he had time to rest, that was what he needed," replied Poppy.

"Changing directions for the moment. What are your favorite memories of that time?" asked Harvey.

"Easy, when Bennett came to the beach, he was all in on Ben. Of all the decisions I have made, that was one of the best. Going to that little quiet beach and giving them several months to get to know each other was the best. Even if we had never gotten together, it would have been worth it, "said Poppy.

"Okay, anything else you think I should know about your time in North Carolina?" asked Harvey.

"No, actually, I think you have covered it. I love thinking back on that time. It was magical and difficult all at the same time," said Poppy with a sad smile.

"Let's move forward to July of 2012. Tell me about the day reporters showed up at your condo in River Oaks?" said Harvey.

"How did you know about that?" asked Poppy.

"Ben told me. He said that day terrified him."

"Yes, it was a hard day. But, like the rest of the story, we survived it."

River Oaks Condo
Searcy, Arkansas
July 2012

Poppy and Ben got to Searcy early that July morning for a short visit with Bennett. He was flying in from DC for a fundraiser in Little Rock and could not get to Caswell Beach. He asked Poppy if she would bring Ben to Searcy instead. He wanted to show him the town, his home, and start getting him accustomed to it as he would eventually move there once the election was over.

Bennett called Poppy about four hours before he was supposed to be there to say he had been delayed. He had to fly to Miami. Taylor had been in an accident. He did not have all the details but would call when he knew more. Poppy swallowed the giant green monster that threatened to come up and destroy the peaceful place she and Bennett had gotten to in their relationship. Instead of doubting him, she decided to trust him. Rather than focus on being sad, Poppy took Ben out to the ball fields and let him watch several games, and then they took in a late movie. The next day, Ben had his first golf lesson. By the end of the day, he was hot and sweaty and needed a snow cone. Poppy took him to Cream & Sugar. They were enjoying their cool treats and singing to the radio as they pulled into the drive of the condo that Joules had rented for them for the weekend. At first, neither saw the reporter or news crew that seemed to appear out of nowhere.

Poppy did not roll down her window, but she had to go slowly to avoid hitting anyone as she pulled into the garage. She opened the door, and the reporter followed the car into the garage. They continued to yell questions at the car. Poppy turned the music as high as she could. All you could hear inside the car were isolated words: Bennett, Taylor, Pregnant, Love Child, Mistress, Divorce. Poppy started putting the door down with the reporter and crew inside the garage. She ignored them and told Ben to do the same. When they saw the door going down, they quickly pulled back. Poppy thought they reminded her of vultures she had seen at the beach. Once all of the reporters were out, she put down the garage door and turned off the car.

She tried to call Bennett, but it went straight to voicemail. She next called Joules, who told her to stay there until Bennett returned. He was on his way. And that was what she did all day. But then, panic set in when she looked out around eight. The mob outside had grown. She really did not want Ben to wake up to that.

Making a split-second decision, she decided to pack up the car and get them as far from Searcy as possible. She hated to leave but she saw no other option.

She rolled into Memphis around eleven. Pulling in for gas, she took a minute and called Joules. She explained where she was and that she and Ben needed a safe place to hide for a few days.

Joules promised to make some calls and find her something. Not ten minutes later, Joules called back.

She had a friend from college named Julie Craft, a real estate agent who lived about forty minutes from where Poppy and Ben were. Julie promised she would have a house in Bolivar ready when Poppy and Ben arrived. True to her word, they rolled in just before one. Julie was there with the key and a stocked fridge. Poppy cried when she hugged her.

Helping her unload the car, Julie said, "You are safe now." And she was.

The next day, Poppy woke early. In the rush to leave, she had left her phone charger. She fed Ben, and then they made a quick trip to a store to get a new one. Back home, her phone, which had been dead for hours, was plugged in to charge. It took only a second, and messages started rolling in from Joules and Bennett, one after another. Before Poppy could listen to them, Ben yelled for her to come into the living room, where he was watching television. That was when Poppy saw it. Across the bottom of the screen, it read, Senator Carrington of Arkansas, a leading supporter of Presidential Candidate Larry Anderson, has resigned effective immediately as Senator amid a possible marital scandal. More details to follow.

At that moment, Poppy's cell phone rang. It was Bennett. "Why did you run? You promised you would not run? Damn it, Poppy. When are you going to trust me? What more do I have to do? The baby is not mine." All of his words came out in a rush. Poppy could hear the hurt and desperation in his voice. And something new. Defeat. All of this had defeated him. He had been running on fumes for weeks.

"Baby, I did not run. I just tried to get someplace safe, so Ben would not be scared. I know you are not the father. How could you be? It's you and me. All the way."

Hearing her calm, sweet words and total faith in him broke him. He started crying. Crying like he hadn't since Tatum died. She trusted him. She loved him. She hadn't left him. A weight was lifted off his shoulders.

Hearing him cry caused Poppy to tear up. She hated the thought of her sweet, dear Bennett thinking she had left him again. She was his forever. "We miss you. Come and get us. We are in some tiny town in West Tennessee called Bolivar," replied Poppy, crying harder each second she talked. Now that she had opened the floodgates, there was no stopping it.

Wiping the tears from his face, Bennett said, "Poppy Baby, please don't cry. It is all over now. We can be together. I will come and get you and take you home."

Worried that the reporters might still be there, she asked, "Do you think it is safe? Are the reporters gone? I do not want to expose Ben to that again," said Poppy.

"I don't know. You are probably right. Maybe we should hide out there for a few days until this settles down. I have missed you both so much."

"We've missed you. We love you. See you soon."

Carrington House
Searcy, Arkansas
November 28, 2023

"So, is that what you did?" asked Harvey Cox.

"Yes, we actually stayed there for over a week. After that, Bennett filed for divorce. He then flew Ben and me back to Caswell Beach for two weeks. We packed up the house and came to Searcy. His divorce came through the last week of August. We were married on the first day of September at our little church. It was a beautiful wedding," said Poppy.

"What a journey your love took you on," said Harvey, almost in awe.

"Yes, it did. Looking back, I sometimes wonder how I survived it all, but you do what you must," replied Poppy.

"I do have one last question. You have yet to explain how you, Bennett, Ben, Taylor, Greer, and the girls became one big family. Given how it all went down, one would have expected you to go your separate ways and never cross paths again if you could help it."

"Oh, that. I was wondering when you would ask about that," replied Poppy. "You are right. Most people would have reacted that way. But there is one piece you are still missing. One piece that would have always remained missing if it had not been for Rosie."

"Rosie, what does she have to do with it?"

"Everything."

Chapter 16

Carrington House
Searcy, Arkansas
February 2013

Bennett, Poppy, and Ben were in the middle of dinner. Ben recounted a funny story in his Next Level GT class when Bennett's cell phone rang. Glancing at the screen, Bennett could not suppress the look of surprise that flew across his face.

Since he had resigned from office and was mainly just focused on them, the number of calls that Bennett fielded each day had dropped dramatically. It was rare now for him to get a call at night, so it had to be something serious.

"Who is it?" asked Poppy.

"Taylor," replied Bennett, getting up and leaving the table to talk privately.

Poppy hated that even after several months of happy marital bliss, her first instinct at hearing Taylor's name was always jealousy. Memories of the past when Bennett seemed to get wrapped up in Taylor and forget about everything else still had a hold on her. Determined to rise above them, Poppy forced herself to concentrate on Ben's story and trust that the Taylor show days were behind them.

After a few minutes, Bennett came back into the kitchen. Poppy could tell by the look on his face that he was pretty worried. "Is everything okay?" she asked.

"That was Taylor. Baby Rosie is very sick. She has been diagnosed with aplastic anemia."

"Oh no, that is terrible. What does that mean?" asked Poppy.

Before Bennett could answer, Ben asked, "Who is Rosie?"

Bennett and Poppy looked at each other as they tried to decide how best to answer that. Finally, Poppy said, "Rosie is Taylor and Greer's daughter. She was born in late December."

"Taylor? The lady Dad was married to before you?" asked Ben, looking confused.

"Yes, Dad and I will talk about this later." Giving her son a reassuring smile, she added, "Why don't you back up and start your story over? I know Dad will enjoy hearing it."

Later that night, after they had sent Ben up to get his shower and get ready for bed, Poppy said, "Okay, since Ben is upstairs, tell me about Rosie."

Bennett shrugged, saying, "All I know is that the baby needs a blood transfusion. I am not really clear on the science of it all, but the gist is that neither Taylor nor Greer are a match. Typically, when a kid has this, the parents give blood, and it fixes the problem. In this case, since neither is a match, they are frantically searching for someone who is. Taylor thought I might still have some contact in DC who might help her get a match quicker. The best option would be a family member. Most likely, they would work, but as we know, Taylor does not have that. They have reached out to Greer's family, but no one has matched. I will call my friends at the Capitol tomorrow and see if they can help."

"Do you know if this could be fatal if she does not get the transfusion quickly?" asked Poppy.

Shaking his head, Bennett said, "I did not ask that. Taylor is pretty upset. I gathered that the faster they get the transfusion, the better. Evidently, Rosie is in a lot of pain and has been crying for days. Taylor sounded like she was at the end of her rope."

Poppy was silent for a moment and then said, "I can, or at least, I might be able to."

"You can what?" asked Bennett, unsure what his wife was saying.

"I possibly can help, or Ben might be able to," replied Poppy.

Giving her a look of confusion, Bennett asked, "How?"

"Because I mean because…" Suddenly, Poppy could not get the words to come out.

"Because of what?" demanded Bennett, getting frustrated from having trouble following what his wife was trying to say.

Taking a deep breath and letting it out, Poppy looked Bennett dead in the eye and said, "Because Jonathan Stroupe was my father."

Whatever Bennett thought his wife would say, it sure as hell was not that. He knew better than to doubt his wife. She did not say things she did not absolutely believe. Giving her a frank look, he barked, "Explain."

Over the next hour, Poppy told Bennett about finding her mother's journal the day before she was to leave for school. She explained that while she wanted to demand her grandmother tell her everything, she had held off because Gran was caring for her sister. By the time her grandmother was in a mindset to talk about her mother's secrets, Poppy had her own. After a while, it did not seem so necessary to know who her father was. She just let it all go until Gran had her heart attack.

Worried she might never know if Gran passed, Poppy waited until her grandmother was healed, gathered her courage, and broached the subject.

At first, Gran was defensive and did not want to answer. Poppy wore her down. In the end, Gran told her that her mother had an affair with her boss, Jonathan Stroupe, and confirmed what Poppy had read in the diary. They were very much in love. Gran said he was devastated after her mother's death and begged them to let him have the child. Of course, his wife, Janice Stroupe, was battling cancer and knew nothing of the affair. Knowing that he could not care for a sick wife and three children and hold down a busy career as an attorney, Gran and Papa convinced him that Poppy was better off with them. They argued his wife and children would never accept her. In the end, he relented and gave up his parental rights.

Poppy also discovered that he had given them a substantial amount of money over time to help cover the cost of raising her. Almost all the money went to keep the farm going. No matter how hard they tried, each year, they went further and further into debt. That was why when Papa died, Gran sold. She was trying to salvage something to send Poppy to school.

Ultimately, Stroupe took care of that as well. He actually funded the hardship scholarship she won. He had cared and tried to help where he could. He had orchestrated the job for Gran at the Carrington house so he could be near Poppy. The thought that she might have had a relationship with him had he lived left Poppy feeling bereft.

The last thing she shared with Bennett was that Gran told her a few days before his death that Tatum had approached Gran, saying he was going to confront his father. He wanted Poppy to be a part of the family. She begged him not to do that. Gran felt it would disrupt Poppy's life. Selfishly, Gran worried they would take Poppy away from her. Sadly, he died before he got the chance.

Once Poppy shared all of this, Bennett just stared at her. After a few minutes, Poppy said, "Say something."

"I am thinking," said Bennett. "This is a lot."

"No kidding," said Poppy. "So, if this is serious with Rosie, I should contact Taylor. Ben or I might be able to help as her closest biological relatives."

Bennett continued staring into space and then said, "Oh my God, I get it now."

"Get what?" asked Poppy, confused.

"The week before Tatum died, he came to me and told me he knew I was messing with you again. I thought he would be mad about it, but he wasn't. As you know, I ate every day you were working at Colton's. Most days, he came with me. He saw how I looked at you and realized we were a couple again. Anyway, he pulled me into his office one day and said he knew we were back together. He asked me to be careful. He realized what it would do to my future career if word got out that I was sleeping with a kid just out of high school."

"You have never told me this before. Why?" asked Poppy.

"Like I said, it was just days before his passing. Afterward, I was too focused on what came next," replied Bennett.

"What was that?" asked Poppy.

"He made me promise to take care of his sister no matter what happened. He said he thought I would make a great husband for his sister and made me promise to always be there for her no matter what happened. I thought he was trying to warn me off you and push me towards Taylor. I thought he was talking about her. I realize now he was talking about you. Oh my God, he was talking about you. He was giving me his blessing to be with you."

Taking Poppy in his arms, Bennett held her close. Somehow, suddenly, it all made sense. Bennett felt years lighter. He felt a closeness to his friend's spirit that he had not felt in months.

Still holding her close, he said, "I knew from the minute I walked into your classroom last March and found out you were widowed that I was going to have to break my promise to my best friend. I had spent the last eleven years of my life trying to make sure that Taylor was taken care of. Knowing that I would leave her to be with you bothered me only because of that. Honestly, that was the hardest part of this. I was determined to find a way to be with you, come hell or high water."

Leaning back, Poppy asked, "From the moment you found out I was a widow? You knew then we were going to be together?"

"Damn straight. Never doubted it. Seeing you was like seeing the sun come up. It was a chance for a new start. I was not going to let you go. Not without a fight. What did you think when you first saw me that day? Did you think we could work it out and have a future together?"

"Honestly, all my brain could focus on was how hot you were. It took all I had not to drag you to the front of the room, throw you across my desk, and have my wicked way with you. Remember, it had been a long sex drought at that point."

"Why did you not say something? I would have been all yours." Bennett grinned, giving her a brief kiss.

"Because you were a very married man, you belonged to someone else," replied Poppy.

Nuzzling her neck, he said, "Baby, I have been all yours from the first time you stuck your tongue down my throat."

Laughing, Poppy said, "Okay, gross. And also, so not true."

"Yes, true," replied Bennett, giving her little kisses across her face. "Want to go upstairs and let me prove it to you?"

Giving him a quick kiss before pushing back, Poppy said, "Rain check. Right now, I need to know if you think I should contact Taylor."

Instantly, the conversation turned serious again. Sighing deeply, Bennett said, "I don't think you have a choice. One question. Why did you never approach Taylor about this after discovering who your father was?"

Poppy shrugged and said, "I did not want to hurt her. She had already lost so much. Learning her father had cheated on her mom, and she had a sister seemed like it would do more harm than good. It might destroy her memories of her father. I did not want to do that. Just because I knew our father was a cheater did not mean she had to. I guess I was protecting her.

"Now, though, if this information would help her child, that changes things," said Poppy.

"I agree," replied Bennett. "It is too late to call them tonight. Why don't we fly down there tomorrow and tell her in person? Then, if she wants to see if you are a match, we will go from there."

Nodding in agreement, Poppy said, "That is a great idea. I don't want Ben to know anything about this until we see how she reacts. I think you should call Joules to see if she can go with us. She can stay with Ben while the four of us talk. Whatever Taylor decides, she will need her best friend there for moral support once it is over."

"Perfect," replied Bennett. "Why don't you go on up? I will call Joules and be up shortly."

Giving Bennett a quick goodnight kiss, she headed upstairs, knowing that after tomorrow, no matter how Taylor reacted, she would have done the right thing and offered. Just thinking about the next day filled her with terror. But, if it helped save baby Rosie, it would all be worth it.

Chapter 17

Gulf Shores Regional Hospital
Gulf Shores, Alabama
February 2013

The next day, Bennett, Poppy, Joules, and Ben flew to Gulf Shores. Taylor and Greer were shocked when they saw them all walk in. Taylor updated everyone on Rosie's condition. So far, no one in Greer's family was a match. At this point, Bennett asked Joules to take Ben to the cafeteria so the others could talk. Sensing something significant was coming, Greer found a private room. Quickly, Poppy recounted the story that her Gran had shared.

For a moment, Taylor sat shell-shocked, saying nothing. Greer, fearing that the news had made a bad situation worse, was just before demanding they both leave when Taylor launched herself at Poppy in a hug that almost knocked her over.

"Oh, thank God. Thank you for telling me. Thank you for being willing to be tested," said Taylor in a rush. Turning to Greer, she said, "Can you take her and Ben down for blood work? If they match, we could start transfusions today."

In the next hour, they received news that Poppy and Ben were both matches. They each gave blood, and baby Rosie got her first transfusion that afternoon. Taylor had not been able to stop crying since she got the news that Poppy was a match.

Poppy and Ben knew they would need to continue to give blood each week for months to build up a supply that could be available should Rosie need it.

Later that night, it was decided that Joules would stay to support Taylor. Poppy, Bennett, and Ben prepared to return to Searcy. Taylor and Greer each hugged and thanked Poppy and Ben.

As Taylor embraced her, she said, "I will never be able to thank you for what you did today. You came forward to help me when you did not have to. I am so grateful. You may have very well saved my daughter's life." At that, the tears began to fall again.

Poppy reached out and wiped Taylor's tears and said, "I was so worried you were going to be mad at me for destroying the memories you had of your father."

Shaking her head, Taylor said, "I can see why you might have worried about that, but I was under no illusion that my parent's marriage was perfect. My mom was sick for a long time. Even as a little kid, I knew they did not seem very happy with each other. I never worried they would divorce, but on some level, I sensed problems. I never saw them hold hands or kiss. I think they slept in separate rooms for the last ten years of their marriage. As a teen, I did not spend any time questioning that. As an adult, I see that was a major red flag. My dad often seemed lonely. It makes me happy to think he eventually found someone he loved. I feel like he has sent me a miracle from beyond the grave. I hate that we never got to know each other as sisters. Maybe once this is behind us, we can."

At that, Poppy teared up. "I would love that. I have waited my whole life for a family. Now our children will have cousins and aunts and uncles. Maybe we can find a holiday to celebrate each year as a family.``

"I'd love that," replied Taylor.

With that, they hugged one last time, and the new Carrington family returned to Searcy with all the old secrets shared and old hurts beginning to heal.

Carrington House
Searcy, Arkansas
November 28, 2023

"You and Taylor are sisters?" Harvey Cox practically yelled the question.

"Half sisters, but yes," replied Poppy. "Blown your mind yet?"

"Blown and more, "replied Harvey, nodding. "I just realized. That is the other reason you were so adamant about not cheating. It was your sister's husband."

"Yes, that and not wanting to make the same mistake as my mother," said Poppy.

"What is your relationship with Taylor like today?" asked Harvey.

"It is still evolving. We ended up settling on celebrating every Thanksgiving together. Some years have been easier than others. She was wonderful when the girls were born. She offered to come and help, but having her in my house when it had been her house would have been too weird."

"I can see that," replied Harvey.

"What about the guys? How do they get along?"

"Hum, they try to keep it to sports and guy topics."

"Makes sense. Do the four of you do anything other than Thanksgiving?" asked Harvey.

"They came for Ben's high school graduation. But not really. Even though we have never discussed it, I think it is harder for Greer and me to be all together than it is for Bennett and Taylor. Eleven years was a long time to be married. I know that Bennett would not have achieved all he did without her. She helped him attain his political goals. She was the wife I could never have been able to be then. She shined as a DC Senator's wife. I would have hated that, so I am grateful that he got that with her. But it's tough to be in the room with someone you know your spouse had a long-term intimate relationship with. Eww. This is not something I like to think about," replied Poppy.

"I get that. One last question, why do you think you would like being the Governor's wife if you were so sure you would not have liked being a Senator's wife?" asked Harvey.

"That is a question I have asked myself, actually. I hate that Bennett had to give up everything he had achieved for us eleven years ago to make our lives work, but he did. And, until recently, he has said he would do it all over again if he had to. I know he would, too. He would walk away from being Governor if I asked him. But, this time, it is my turn to make the change. He will be a great governor. It would be criminal to keep him from the opportunity to serve the people of Arkansas and equally wrong to deprive them of him.

As a teacher and artist, I can spotlight education and the arts. I am not Taylor, but I am not a poor man's second, either. She was there for her season. This is mine."

"Sounds like you have grown more comfortable with the idea of Bennett running," replied Harvey.

"I have. Twelve years ago, I never saw myself ever stepping foot back into this state. The thought that a little over a decade removed from that, I might end up as its first lady is mind-boggling. Maybe sharing all this with you has helped me process through how we got here. It has been a long and winding road, but we made it," said Poppy.

"I think that is all I need unless you have anything else you want to share," said Harvey as he began packing his supplies.

"No, I have shared our dirty laundry and aired our family secrets. I ask that you be kind with our love stories, Bennett and mine, as well as Taylor and Greer's. Our lives have not been perfect. We are all doing the best we can. Just remember that when you write your article."

"I promise," said Harvey. "The article should be out in two weeks. When do you think Bennett will make it known he is planning on running for office again?"

Poppy gave him a look. "I am not sure. This has caught all of us off guard. Since you work with Jameson Williams, I am sure you are much more familiar with how all of this works. Right now we are supposed to be in the preliminary stages of getting his name and our story out there. Bennett can't officially announce until this Presidential election is over. There are a lot of assumptions being made about who will win and possible appointments that will lead to a special Governor election should one of those appointments be our current Governor. All of that is still up in the air. Who knows what will happen in the next few months? In some ways knowing all our secrets will all be out there is freeing. In other ways, it is scary as hell."

"I get that, and again, remember I work for you guys. I will make sure this article makes the best of what was a complicated situation for all of you. Since you don't know when Bennett will be able to announce, what is next for the two of you?" asked Harvey.

"I asked Bennett that same question last night. He said we had to begin building a war chest to fund the campaign through small fundraisers and events. Also, we are both very involved with getting ready for the upcoming solar eclipse expected in April. We both help with Beats and Eats, a local community project that brings the whole community together several times a year. They are planning a huge event for that," replied Poppy. "What about you?" she asked. "What is next after writing this article about us?"

"Funny you should mention the solar eclipse. I have already been working on several pieces about it and will be at that event. Hopefully, I will see you both there," replied Harvey. With that he gathered his things and headed to the door.

"Yes, that would be great. There are going to be several food trucks there that day. Let's make sure to meet up."

"Sounds good. I will send you a copy of the article once it is done. Thanks again for everything." With that, Harvey Cox gave a wave and left.

Epilogue

Capitol Steps
Little Rock, Arkansas
January 7, 2026

Harvey Cox stood off to the side, behind the news crews and the reporters from all the local and surrounding areas. From his vantage point, he could plainly see the smiling faces of the Carrington clan as he had come to think of them. It was Bennett's inauguration day for Governor. He was joined on the Capitol steps by his family, Poppy, Ben, Ella, baby John, Lizzy, and Lola, along with Taylor, Greer, and Rosie. They all stood next to him as he took the oath of office.

Harvey felt a sense of pride that he had played a significant role in helping Carrington win the election. It was his article after all that had successfully relaunched Carrington back into the political arena. Just as he had told Poppy, it took him two weeks to write the article. He honored his promise to be kind to their stories. It appeared in the January 2024 edition of *Arkansas Now*, a glossy high-end magazine that profiled up-and-comers around the state. Entitled *Politically Incorrect Affairs of the Heart*, it recounted the love stories of Bennett, Poppy, Taylor, and Greer in such a way that left the reader cheering for them all. Harvey beautifully wove the family connection between Taylor and Poppy into their story. He also handled the issue of why Bennett stepped away so quickly ten years before by explaining that family always comes first. He illustrated their commitment to protecting each other in every situation. He glossed over how young Poppy was when she and Bennett first fell in love, focusing instead on how mature they handled themselves and how committed they had been to their careers. If one did not read carefully enough, one might walk away from the article thinking they separated all those years before because they were pursuing different goals.

At the end of the day, it was a marketing piece, and it did its job. Harvey would be the first to admit that he whitewashed their stories. He had purposely left out some of the more shocking parts, choosing to focus more on them as people and the depth of their love for each other.

He had no guilt about what he had written. It was all true. They were all lovely people, and he wished only good things for them. After all they had been through, they deserved it. They had found a way forward out of a situation that had threatened to destroy them all. They weathered the storm of their making and came out the other side a strong, loving family. And the rest of it, well, he supposed, those pieces could remain forever their buried dirty little secrets.

Letter to the Reader

January 1, 2024
Dear Reader,

Now that you've read the book, I wonder if you've figured out that there actually aren't any secrets in Searcy. Even when you believe you've buried them, someone knows. Usually, that someone is me. I am The Secrets Keeper. The key to surviving the dirtiest of secrets in our small town is in managing control of them. They are their own sort of currency, and the juicer, the more power and value they hold. I learned the hard way, many years ago, how to be a master player in this game. After years of holding many of the secrets shared in this book, I think it is only fitting that I let you in on the biggest secret of all. In case you have not put it all together yet, it was me who orchestrated these two love affairs.

As you know, Greer is my great nephew. What you might not know is that his mother was my favorite niece, Rachelle. When she died, I promised to be there for him. I never thought his first wife was a good fit. She was a lovely girl, but she was so needy. Plus, I could plainly see that Greer was more in love with medicine than with her. That marriage was doomed. Once it ended, I began looking for just the right woman for him.

I found her in Taylor. The only problem was Taylor was already married to Bennett. A more sad, boring marriage the world has never seen. It was a shame really. Both young people were from such nice families. They should have been perfect for each other. But, one needed to only spend a few minutes with them to sense how miserable they both were. In the South, being miserable is not a good enough reason to divorce. No, we need a little more. A long lost love child was the game changer.

I will never forget the first time I saw Poppy Thompson's Growing Up New York collection at the Emerson. I was shocked. For once, a secret had gotten past me. I had known back in the day that Bennett had been messing around with the maid's granddaughter. I, like everyone else, thought that it had run its course.

You could have knocked me over with a feather the first time I saw the pictures of the boy. I knew immediately it was Bennett's son.

I also knew very well that Poppy and Taylor were half-sisters. We all did back in the day. Even Janice, Taylor's mom, had known. Wives always know. She just had too much going on fighting for her life to make it easy on John, her husband, by bowing out. He never demanded a divorce, so she pretended it never happened. Who knows what would have happened if Poppy's mom had lived? Janice never had to face that issue. Seeing those pictures reminded me of that affair. Knowing how miserable both Bennett and Taylor were, I brought Poppy back to Searcy.

I am not going to lie. I had an agenda. I hoped that by driving Bennett back into Poppy's arms, I might drive Taylor into Greer's.

It took a lot of work to get those two couples together. I was able to help all of them find their forever person without any of them being the wiser. Taylor came pretty close to telling me to butt out of her life a time or two. But, that was mostly just because she, like her momma before her, still held me responsible for the whole homecoming/prom business. Look, I am not saying that I did not have a hand in all of that. Regardless, there must be a statute of limitations on resentment held for events that happen in high school. Certainly, we must have passed that by now. I did always feel bad for Janice though. Eventually, I tried to make it up to her posthumously by helping her daughter.

Speaking of how I helped those young people, I can't tell you how exhausting playing fairy godmother to four grown individuals who are determined to do things their own way is. Adults can be a lot like toddlers, especially the men. They like to think everything is their idea. So, I played along. I made sure processes and events occurred to keep the four of them moving ever closer to each other. I did not see Taylor getting pregnant while still married, but I couldn't be expected to account for everything. In the end, everything worked out just as I had hoped. And, I ended up with the most precious great-great niece ever. Greer's mom, Rachelle, would be so proud.

So now, dear reader, you know all of the dirty little secrets of Searcy. Or at least, all that I am ready to tell. You never know when more juicy tidbits are going to find their way into another book about our sweet little town's secret affairs.

If you get the chance, you should come for a visit. We'd love to share our town with you.

Sincerely,
Edna Stone

Book Club Questions

Book Club Discussion Questions

1. Explain how the author uses the first scene with Bennett swimming as a metaphor for the book.

2. Explain why you think the author picked the name Poppy for that character.

3. Explain why you think Poppy was so determined to have Ella fall in love with Searcy.

4. Explain how Searcy is a character in the book.

5. Explain what impact non-essential characters like Edna Stone and Havey Cox have on the story.

6. What transformation is the author going for with the main two female characters, and do you think she achieves what she is trying to do?

7. Explain how the phrase, "Physician, heal thyself" applies to Greer.

8. Bennett is often referred to as a pretty boy Ken doll. Dolls are usually considered a female toy. Explain in what way Bennett shows he is in touch with his feminine side most?

9. What are some common themes you see repeatedly used in the book?

10. This book was written with little regard to social media as the affairs were set in 2012. How much different would it be if the affairs were set in 2024?

If you would like to ZOOM or Google meet with the author during your

book club, please set up a time by going to my website. I look forward to hearing from you soon.